The
Ambitious Stepmother

By the same author

The
Ambitious Stepmother

A Countess Ashby de la Zouche Mystery

FIDELIS MORGAN

HarperCollins*Publishers*

Collins Crime
An imprint of HarperCollins*Publishers*
77–85 Fulham Palace Road, London w6 8jb

www.fireandwater.com/crime

Published by Collins Crime 2002
1 3 5 7 9 8 6 4 2

ISBN 0 00 713423 1

Typeset in PostScript Linotype Janson and Adobe Caslon
by Palimpsest Book Production Limited,
Polmont, Stirlingshire

Printed in Great Britain by
Clays Ltd, St Ives plc

Acknowledgements

Thank you Celia, Jill and Michele W. for accompanying me to Paris, Versailles, St Germain-en-Laye and Madonna; to Mme Martine Anstett at the Potager du Roi, Versailles; to Michele B. for services to Cowes; to Sian – aka Phoenicia Geeky-Fobb – for keeping me laughing; to Karin Slaughter for suggesting chitterlings and other things; to Samuel Bourdeau for looking over the French; to Anne O'Brien for a lovely book about vegetables.

And as ever to Julia Wisdom for being a fantastic editor, and everyone else at HarperCollins for their wonderful support, gorgeous covers and enthusiasm.

And to my marvellous agent Clare Alexander, without whom . . .

Usually we condemn the luxury of ancient Princes who were not content to have anything but the most rare and expensive food from all corners of the earth brought to their tables. They were so selfish they forgot the religious principle of equality between men.

Though some people have wanted to suggest that because life is short, food should be simple, it is that simplicity in our way of life which reaches for a greater pleasure in our food.

But it would be an injustice to blame people who create complexity and mixtures of seasoning to create great pleasure, for us cuisine is an art and the cook becomes an Artist. Each dish takes its own place in the Society of the table.

For a great repast one must begin one's preparations a day beforehand . . .

François Massialot
Le Cuisinier roïal et bourgeois 1691

Contents

ONE

Ragoo — a high season's dish after the French way

'Twould be hugely voguish to have an enormous looking glass on the mantel. Very French and à la mode.' With a sweep of her chubby hand, Lady Anastasia Ashby de la Zouche, Countess of Clapham, Baroness Penge, etcetera, twirled round to address Alpiew, her writing partner and erstwhile maid.

'Surely not, madam.' Alpiew was trying to keep her temper. They had acquired this money through hard and dangerous work and she wanted it spent instead on improving their living conditions. 'If we are to spend our well-earned money upon renovating the house, 'twould be better utilised in repairing the roof and the upper chambers, which are currently fit only for pigeons, rather than ornamenting this already comfortable room.'

'Nonsense!' The Countess span round in the other direction, arms extended. 'This is the showpiece. It might as well be our advertisement. It shows the world how successful we are become.'

As she swung back to face Alpiew she swayed sideways and almost knocked Godfrey, her decrepit manservant, to the floor.

In a vain attempt to break his fall Godfrey grabbed at the air and staggered forward, arms outstretched, lunging towards Alpiew.

'Hands off those, you filthy old cur!' yelped Alpiew as, with a wily jab, Godfrey's knobbly fingers came to rest upon her ample bosom. She shoved him back in the direction whence he came. Projected backwards from Alpiew's push, Godfrey landed with a loud crack on a chair, which immediately disintegrated beneath him.

'If you won't consider the upper chambers,' snapped Alpiew, 'perhaps the money would be better spent obtaining some solid furniture.'

'Nonsense, Alpiew, we have more than enough furniture!' The Countess sank down on to an easy chair, which made a strange creaking noise, causing her to edge herself slowly back to a standing position. 'A mirror on the mantel is the latest thing. Remember the saying: "One might as well be out of the world as out of fashion."'

'In that case, madam –' Alpiew surveyed the Countess's mantua, of high quality certainly but, despite recent alterations, still noticeably of an earlier era – 'let us get the roof done and buy some new dresses.'

'I don't want new dresses,' grumbled Godfrey from the floor. 'What would I look like in a dress! I'm not a sodomite, you know.'

'The plasterer will be here any moment, Godfrey. He is going to make good the fireplace so that the looking glass will "sit plumb", as the glazier called it.' The Countess moved out of the room. 'And, I thank you both, but there will be no more discussion on the subject.'

Alpiew followed her out into the hall. She looked up the staircase with a sigh. All those unused rooms upstairs could do with a new skim of plaster, and the roof with a new set of tiles, and here was her mistress deciding instead to redecorate the only decently appointed room in the house.

The Countess was already swinging a kettle on to a hook over the fire when Alpiew reached the kitchen.

'If we spent the money carefully, milady, we wouldn't have to live in the kitchen.' Alpiew surveyed the mess of papers, books,

2

beds and tables and realised that if the upstairs rooms were made habitable they could at last each have a bedroom of their own and she would not be kept awake by the midnight rumblings, snores, groans and other unthinkable noises emitting from Godfrey's bed.

'Nothing wrong with living in the kitchen.' The Countess gave the room a cursory glance. 'At least it's nice and warm.'

'I think we should spend the money on a holiday,' said Godfrey from the door. 'We could travel abroad and see all those awful disgusting French women.' He lurched over to the table and hacked a couple of slices of bread from the loaf. 'I've heard they get up to all sorts of bawdy amorous tricks. Revolting.'

'Thank you very much, Godfrey, but there's quite enough to revolt me here at home.' The Countess turned round to make a further announcement but was interrupted by a heavy thudding on the front door. 'Please answer that, Godfrey.'

'But I'm makin' me toast.'

'Godfrey!' The Countess glared. 'The door!'

With a grunt, Godfrey slouched out.

'To spend all that money on a looking glass does seem pretty extravagant, madam, when you look about and see how much we could get for just the price of one silly mirror . . .'

'I have said I'll have no more discussion on the matter, thank you, Alpiew.' The Countess sat at the table and sighed. 'If only my darling Pigalle was here, she would back me up. She knows all about the latest fashions in décor. Mirrors are the most à la mode thing in the world.'

'Well,' said Alpiew, clutching at a possible straw. 'Why don't we wait until the Duchesse de Pigalle comes back from France, then we can take her advice?'

'But, Alpiew, I have told you, she could be there for years. She has a new vocation: founding a school for impoverished young ladies. She might not be back before Christmas. And I am not keeping a stack of money here in the house, living in fear and trembling that thieves will come in and steal it, until Pigalle comes home. I would prefer to invest the money in something to enhance all our lives.'

'It's for you.' Godfrey slouched back in, tore a hunk from his bread and shoved it into his mouth.

'Well?' asked the Countess. 'Who is it?'

'A workman of some variety,' said Godfrey, spitting out white globs of chewed dough as he spoke. 'He's waiting for you out there, cap in hand.'

With a tut, the Countess trotted into the hall.

'Good morning, madam,' said the man. 'I am here to offer you an irresistible opportunity. This special is a once in a lifetime chance to have all your casement windows taken out and replaced with the latest in window design: the sliding sash.'

'I'm sorry?' said the Countess. 'Are you not here to do the plastering?'

'The sliding sash represents a breakthrough in the technology of window-glazing, being both easy to open, and easy to close ... And all this could be yours for one down payment and twenty-four monthly payments thereafter ...'

The door knocker banged again.

'Godfrey!' the Countess called back to the kitchen. 'The door.'

'Well, you're just beside it,' growled Godfrey from the kitchen. 'I'm makin' me toast.'

Smoothing down her dress, Alpiew came into the hall.

'Mr, er ... ?' said the Countess.

'Wells,' said the sash-window man.

'Mr Wells is telling me about the latest thing in windows, Alpiew,' said the Countess. 'Perhaps that might be an alternative to the looking glass. Or maybe we could do both. Tell me again about this payment method?'

Alpiew pulled open the front door.

'Good morning, madam,' said a dapper fellow dressed head to toe in velvet. 'I am here to offer you the opportunity of a lifetime. Finest velvet curtains, which draw open from the middle. A real investment for any property, and I can propose very reasonable payment terms . . .'

Alpiew slammed the door shut.

'But, Alpiew!' the Countess groaned. 'Curtains which open from the middle! That sounded like a wonderful idea. How à la mode!'

'Tell me what is the point of velvet curtains, madam, whether they pull from the middle or from the side?' Alpiew sighed. She'd seen it so many times before. 'Whenever the window is open every prigging hand in the street will reach in and steal them in a minute, and then what will you do? You'd have to go on paying for years for an empty window, while the curtains are miles away making a tidy profit for some opportunist thief who needed a bit of money to pay for his next mug of ale or wad of tobacco.' She looked at the sash-window salesman. 'Nor do we need your newfangled windows, thank you, mister.'

The door rattled a third time. 'Here we go again,' said Alpiew. 'They won't take no for an answer, these people.' Alpiew pulled the door open. 'Not today, thank you,' she yelled, ready to slam it again.

'Countess?' A lady had her delicate satin slipper wedged firmly against the door. 'Lady Ashby de la Zouche?'

Through the crack Alpiew could see that the woman was wealthy. Her clothes and the carriage that stood behind her were new and of a very high quality.

'Who should I say is calling?' said Alpiew, indicating to the Countess that she had better dismiss the salesman without delay.

'Mrs Franklyn-Green, the wife of Alderman Franklyn-Green,' said the woman. 'I have an offer to make the Countess with regard to Virginia, my daughter.'

Alpiew could see a sulky-looking girl at the woman's side, kicking at the dusty doorstep with her elegant satin slipper.

'Stepdaughter, actually.' The girl slouched from one foot to the other and scowled. 'Though why do you bother to pretend consulting me, Stepmama, dearest? I'm just the baggage you want parcelled off –'

Mrs Franklyn-Green yanked the girl's hand while still maintaining a fixed smile. 'Adolescents!' She raised her eyebrows and gave Alpiew a conspiratorial shrug. 'May we step inside and have a word with her ladyship?'

The Countess was in the front room, hastily picking up pieces of the broken chair. Once Alpiew saw her toss them into the fireplace she pulled the front door open and showed the two women into the receiving room.

The Countess waved Mrs Franklyn-Green to a sturdy easy chair while she sank gingerly into the wobbly one.

'A cup of chocolate all round,' said the Countess. But Alpiew had shut the door on her and was busy in the hall ejecting the sash-window salesman.

'I heard that you take on chaperone work?' Mrs Franklyn-Green smiled.

'Not exactly,' said the Countess. 'I did used to, but I now work for the *London Trumpet*.'

'I feel sure that you will want to take this job. I will be offering good money.'

'Really?' The Countess gave a coy smile, the best way she knew of eliciting such vulgar information as pecuniary figures without seeming too grasping.

'A small allowance to pay your way, and a large reward when you have accomplished the task in hand.'

'Large . . .' said the Countess, 'is an indefinable word.'

'One hundred guineas.'

The Countess spluttered. That *was* good money. Quite enough for her, Alpiew and Godfrey to live in luxury for a year at least.

'And what exactly does the task entail?'

Mrs Franklyn-Green glanced across the room at her stepdaughter, who was gazing idly out of the window where two men were busily adjusting the traces attaching a sleek horse to the very expensive-looking carriage.

'You must find my daughter a suitable match. A man with a title. A man who has financial means sufficient to upkeep her so that she need not drain her dear father's purse. And preferably a man to the child's taste, so that she doesn't keep bouncing back like a bad penny.'

The Countess was already seeing quite a few drawbacks to Mrs Franklyn-Green's scheme. 'This is your husband's idea?'

'Of course it isn't, you silly old frump!' Virginia turned into the room and put her hands on her hips. 'My father isn't a crackpot. This cow of his just wants me out of the way so she can flaunt herself without the encumbrance of a daughter not of her own making.'

The Countess looked at the girl and wondered where she would find a man willing to subjugate himself to a lifetime of such shrewish temper. Or how long would it take to tame the shrew. The job could take years, and even then there might not be a suitable man who'd take a shine to the child. And all for a hundred guineas . . . The Countess decided that, even for a thousand, the job was not worth it. 'Mrs Franklyn-Green . . .' She tried to rise, but the creaking of the chair made it seem unwise to try. 'Lovely as your stepdaughter is, I feel that my time is limited at present, and I could not . . .'

'That's a pity.' Mrs Franklyn-Green rose. 'Paris at this time of year, I am told, is beautiful. In the springtime, Paris . . .'

'Paris!' The Countess got up from the chair so fast that she set it wobbling on its uneven legs. 'Paris, in France?'

'France, yes. St Germain-en-Laye, in fact, just outside Paris. The royal court there.'

'The Stuart court in St Germain-en-Laye in Maytime!' The Countess went into a reverie of her youth during the exiled days of the Commonwealth. 'You want me to go to Paris with your daughter . . .'

'*Step*daughter!' bawled Virginia.

'Not only you, Countess. You must take your woman, er . . .'

'Alpiew.'

'Alpiew, yes. I will pay for a carriage to take you both

7

there, and pay too for the packet-boat voyage. I hear that a decent standard of living is had for nothing for friends of the Stuart court.'

'Ah yes.' The Countess blushed. Mrs Franklyn-Green had obviously heard that she had once been mistress of the late king, Charles II. 'I do not know King James personally, but I was close to his brother, Charles. So James is sure to know of me.'

She looked to the girl again. Having tightened the girth strap, the two men had moved out of sight, and Virginia turned back, facing into the room. As she caught eyes with the Countess she gave a wide and appealing smile.

The Countess winked by way of reply. So, the girl did possess charm, and with charm anything was possible.

'I'll do it.' The Countess rubbed her hands together, trying to remember where she had stored her baggage. 'What are the arrangements?'

'I will order the coach to be here before sunrise tomorrow morning.' With a relieved grin, Mrs Franklyn-Green rose. 'As I said, all the expenses of the journey will be prepaid by Alderman Franklyn-Green. I will give you a few guineas to see you on your way; the remainder of the fee you will pick up from me when you return to London and Virginia announces her betrothal to a suitable young man.'

'I have told you before, I am not going to France, and that is that.' Virginia turned back to face the window and stamped her foot.

The Countess winced. The girl was as up and down as a barometer.

'I want no gawping French rakes pawing me.' Virginia craned her neck round to glare at her stepmother. 'I will run away into the woods and get murdered by rogues and gypsies rather than go to France. Then you'll all be sorry.'

'There are no woods in the City of London, Virginia. And anyhow, I have told you before: St Germain-en-Laye is full of *English* people. People who had to flee the country when the last king ran off. Some of them are very well-bred and dashing,

'I am told.' Mrs Franklyn-Green faced the Countess with a hand outstretched. 'Once she is safely in France and sees the goods on offer, I am sure she will settle down.'

'The business is sealed with this handsel, Mrs Franklyn-Green.' With a sideways look to the surly child, the Countess shook on the deal. 'Tomorrow it is.'

When Virginia and her stepmother had gone, the Countess sent Godfrey to the Cues' office with a note proposing that, while in France, she and Alpiew write a special column for the *London Trumpet* about the thousands of ex-patriot Britons who, eleven years ago after the so-called Glorious Revolution, had settled in Paris and its environs.

'But Alpiew's already gone to the Cues,' he muttered.

'She is delivering this week's copy, Godfrey. I am sending you with a special and rather urgent message.'

By the time Alpiew arrived back in the Countess's German Street home, she found her mistress flustered and surrounded by packing cases.

'Pack your best clothes, Alpiew! We are bound for the land of gay balls and all-night gambling parties. It's wonderful! And all we have to do is go to France and help a pretty girl find a nice husband. What could be easier in the delightful court of St Germain?'

'France!' Alpiew shuddered. She had learned from experience that nothing involving the Countess was ever easy. 'What on earth for?'

'We have a job. We are going to chaperone a young lady.'

Alpiew collapsed against the table. 'Not that horrible little tit that was here just now?'

'Her name is Virginia, Alpiew. And she may be a little sulky, but what of that?'

'How are we to look after an insolent little madam like that, milady? If she is thus rude to her stepmother, what chance have we of controlling her?'

'That's the thing, Alpiew. Mrs Franklyn-Green told me the

important thing was getting her to France safely, and then standing back and letting nature take its course. We are to make our way to the English court, where she is expected. Once we are there, all we have to do is parade a line of eligible men in front of her and hope she snares one.' She rubbed her podgy hands together. 'And if we succeed in that we will receive a handsome reward.'

'So answer me this . . .' Alpiew ran her finger over her lips. 'If it is such an easy and pleasant task, why could not the stepmother take her there herself?'

The Countess thought for a moment. 'Perhaps her duties as the wife of an alderman . . .' She stooped to open a trunk at her feet. 'But what matter if the woman is too busy or unconcerned about her stepdaughter? The fact is that she has employed us to do it for her, and I for one am very excited at the idea.'

'But our job, madam – we are under a contract to write about *London* society.'

'I don't think there is mention of the word "London" in our deal with the *Trumpet*. And I am certain that Mr and Mrs Cue will be delighted to receive news of all the disgruntled ex-patriots, not least our ex-king, James, with whom we are to share a roof. Godfrey will be back any moment with confirmation of that.'

The Cues were, as the Countess had predicted, bewitched by the idea of printing reports about the English exiles on the other side of the English Channel. Reluctantly Alpiew prepared for the journey.

'We won't have to know the lingo, madam, I hope,' said Alpiew in a last-ditch attempt at getting out of it. 'I'm sorry, but I can't speak anything except English.'

'We are going to St Germain,' the Countess chortled. 'The *English* court. And I assure you, Alpiew, you have all the language requirements necessary.'

TWO

Poor-Man's Sauce
— or Carrier's Sauce, a
sauce made of shallot cut very
small, with salt, white pepper,
vinegar and oil of olives

'You see! It's a fact!' The Countess wafted her dimpled hand through the carriage window. '*Everything* is better in France.' She took a draught of the misty air blowing through the coach. 'The food is tastier, the balls and masquerades gayer, the society more dazzling, the fashions more gorgeous, the houses better decorated, warmer and more comfortable. I know we shall have a perfectly wonderful time.'

Alpiew, sitting opposite, gazed out over the flat grey fields of Picardy and shuddered. If she'd had her way they would still be in London, sitting in their cosy kitchen, quietly scribbling their scandal column for the *London Trumpet*.

She glanced across the carriage to the cause of this seemingly endless journey. Virginia sat grimly beside the Countess. This morning the child seemed polite enough, but Alpiew had an inborn mistrust of rich young things. Why the Countess had said yes to the girl's stepmother, Alpiew would never know.

At dawn two days previously a coach containing the sullen

stepdaughter, Virginia, had pulled up in German Street and, once laden with the Countess and Alpiew and their bags, it had sped along the lumpy road to Dover, with a night's stop-over at a dismal inn just outside Canterbury to await a boat and a fortunate wind.

For the entire journey the girl had sat in silence in a corner by the Countess. She gazed out at the ever-changing countryside and never uttered. Once on the boat, she huddled up inside the captain's cabin, casting her eyes to the floor, spurning all attempts at conversation.

Upon docking in Calais, the trio had spent a night in a comfortable French inn and early the next morning, as pre-arranged, Mrs Franklyn-Green's coachman took charge of a hired coach to speed them to the English court at St Germain-en-Laye.

'It will be like a holiday, Alpiew,' said the Countess. 'We are bound for the most civilised place in the world, with plenty of money. Who knows, perhaps we may find husbands for *ourselves*.' She shifted in her seat; her husband, though absent, was, as far as she knew, still alive. 'You did remember the money, did you not? 'Twould be a disaster to be in such a place as France, where the very term beau monde originated, and be penniless. We will need money to buy some lovely new clothes, and to gamble, and to entertain . . .'

Alpiew grinned. At least the precious money had not gone on a looking glass. She pulled the moneybag from her side-pocket and waved it before the Countess before putting it back. 'Forty-five guineas, milady.' Their joint savings from writing for the *Trumpet*, the lion's share of the money they'd made from their last big investigation, and the expenses money given them by Virginia's stepmother. 'All safe and held close to my person.'

'I cannot tell you how excited I am.' The Countess sat back and smiled. 'I wonder if King James will remember me?' She displayed a winsome, though brown-toothed smile. 'He knew all about my amour with his brother, King Charles, of course.

Though it must be said Charlie was by far the handsomer of the two, and was considerably wittier . . .'

In the corner of the coach Virginia broke her silence and let out a low moan. 'I hate France. I don't want to marry some boring old cross-biting cully that you take a shine to, especially not a French one. I want to go home.'

'Don't be silly, Virginia.' The Countess shook her finger. 'You are young. You must open your eyes to Life. As for France, you haven't even tried it yet. I think a spirited young thing like you will find life here very stimulating and, I promise you, within days you are sure to meet an abundance of highly eligible young men, rich, handsome, artistic . . .'

'That is exactly what I don't want.' The girl groaned. 'I'm tired of all the foppish men my father's hideous wife parades before me. Anyway . . .' The girl paused and gave them a sly look. 'I know something that you haven't been told.'

'And I know many things that you don't, you pert creature.'

'She's made a fool of you, just like she does everyone.' The girl smirked. 'I'd love to see your faces when you find out.'

'Find out what, exactly?'

'Wouldn't you like to know!' Virginia pursed her lips and raised her eyebrows.

Alpiew resisted the temptation to give her a clip round the ear.

'But you'll find out by and by. You'll be seeing a lot of France, I expect.'

Deciding that the girl was going through a moment of normal adolescent pique, the Countess was about to relax back into her seat when the coach lurched to a halt. Outside there were raised voices. Someone leapt up on to the coachman's perch.

Concerned, Alpiew thrust her head out, and pulled it back in pretty smartly. 'Oh criminy, madam, 'tis a hold-up.'

'The moneybag, Alpiew . . . Oh fie!'

While Alpiew tried to untie her pocket and push it under the seat, the coach door whipped open and two masked men thrust pistols through it.

Slowly the Countess, Alpiew and Virginia Franklyn-Green raised their hands.

'*Argent . . .*' said the taller of the two in a husky voice, wafting his pistol in the direction of their valises.

'We are *English* travellers,' said the Countess, hoping it might make a difference. 'We speak no French.'

One of the highwaymen spat on the road.

Alpiew tried to push the moneybag out of her pocket and into a crack in the leather seat.

The other coach door was suddenly jerked open and a third bandit reached in, grabbed Virginia by the wrist, and pulled her, whimpering, from the coach. He thrust his hand round her waist and carried her away from the road into a small copse, the muzzle of his gun thrust against her head.

The Countess lurched up to grab at the man. His companion pushed her back on to the seat. '*Argent!*' he repeated, pressing his pistol into her neck.

'Oh fie, Alpiew, what if they kill the child?' She looked the masked man in the eye, and spoke slowly. 'We . . . are . . . English.' She shook her head. 'No money.'

The masked man slapped her cheek with the back of his gloved hand, while pointing the gun at Alpiew. '*Argent! Maintenant!*'

'Leave her alone, you big bully,' shouted Alpiew, shoving him away as she rose from the seat and delved into the upholstery. 'I have money here.' She pulled out the bag of gold coins. 'Take it, but release the girl.' The short robber grabbed the bag, then roughly pulled Alpiew forward and plunged his hand into her pocket, then down her bodice.

'Get your filthy French hands off my bosom!' Alpiew struggled with him. 'I have given you all that my lady and I have. And though it is in English coin, I assure you 'tis a fortune.'

The robber grunted and threw Alpiew back against the seat.

A gunshot rang out, echoing through the woods and sending crows cawing wildly into the sky.

The Countess crossed herself, and Alpiew blanched.

The two men yelped some incomprehensible words and ran for their horses. The third man emerged from the wood, leapt up on to his horse, and the three sped away, leaving a cloud of dust in their wake.

'Pshaw, Alpiew! They have killed the girl!' Whiter than the cracked paint on her face, the Countess fumbled for the door.

'You stay, madam,' said Alpiew. 'I'll go out.'

'Are they gone away so quick?' The Countess peered up and down the long highway. 'God save us, Alpiew,' she cried. 'They have killed her. A rich alderman's daughter in our charge!' She crossed herself again, and put her hand to her mouth.

Alpiew dived from the coach, shouting up to the driver to help her.

He was bound and gagged on his perch. He gave a miserable grunt in reply.

'Untie the driver, madam, so that he might help me search.'

Alpiew stumbled across the ditch at the roadside and into the woods while the Countess clambered up on to the front of the coach and started picking at the driver's gag.

The wood was dark and damp. Clumps of toadstools grew from the tree bases. Ferns and bracken blocked Alpiew's view. 'Virginia?' she called, staggering round, scanning the ground. 'Oh lord!' she exclaimed under her breath as ahead of her she saw Virginia's mantua bunched up at the foot of a tree. An exposed stockinged leg lay still on the bed of dark brown leaves.

Alpiew crept forward, her heart thumping.

Virginia was not moving. She lay face down in the undergrowth.

'Oh no,' Alpiew muttered. 'Please, not dead.' She stooped and held her fingers against Virginia's neck. There was a pulse.

'She's alive,' cried Alpiew, carefully rolling Virginia over on to her back and inspecting the rest of her travelling mantua for patches of blood. 'I think she has swooned away from mere fright.'

Having freed the driver, the Countess made her way towards the wood.

As he leapt down behind her, the driver let forth a string of Anglo-Saxon phrases concerning the ways of the French.

'That's enough of that,' panted the Countess, staggering across the ditch. 'Let us see to the child.'

'Virginia?' Alpiew pulled the girl up and cradled her in her arms. 'You're going to be all right.'

When the coachman arrived, he and Alpiew lifted the prostrate Virginia and carried her back to the coach.

'So much for lovely France,' said Alpiew as she and the driver heaved Virginia on to the back seat of the carriage. 'And lovely French men.'

'Sorry, Alpiew,' said the Countess, kneeling on the road, fumbling about in her bag for a bottle of hartshorn. 'But even if those French rogues took our money, they at least spared our lives. I've known highwaymen in England to rob you, then kill you into the bargain, for fear of your being able to discover them to the authorities. They shoot the horses, too, in case you might come alive again and give pursuit.' She glanced up at the horses standing patiently in their traces, waiting for a command to continue. 'To be sure, these French bullies have let us off lightly.'

'And left us penniless.' Alpiew thought of all the money that they would never have a chance to enjoy, and wished now that she'd let the Countess spend it on the looking glass.

The Countess climbed into the coach and wafted the hartshorn under Virginia's nostrils.

With a flutter of eyelashes the girl came to her senses murmuring, 'Where am I?'

'In a coach bound for the court of St Germain,' said the Countess. 'You have had a nasty fright. Are you hurt?'

'I'm all right, thank you.' Virginia Franklyn-Green sat up, laid her head against the side of the coach and stared out of the window. 'I must have fainted.'

'Alpiew and I were very worried about you.' The Countess

gently stroked the girl's hair. 'They took all our money, but that doesn't matter. We must thank the lord you were spared.'

'I wish they had killed me,' said Virginia, jerking her head away from the Countess's hand. 'If they'd have killed me at least I'd have been spared the boredom of this wretched and pointless expedition.'

Alpiew reached out to upbraid the girl, but the Countess held her back.

'I mean it,' said Virginia, bursting into tears. 'I'd be better off dead.'

'Poor child! She's had a horrid shock, Alpiew.' The Countess leaned out of the carriage door to slam it shut. 'And now, my man,' she shouted, banging her hand against the roof of the coach, 'without further ado, please let us resume our journey to St Germain-en-Laye.' She brushed herself down and took her seat beside the girl. 'I am afraid, Alpiew,' she added in a low voice, 'that this little setback will make our stay in France more trying than it need be. St Germain is an expensive town, and one thing is certain: without money, we must be obliged to everyone.'

Alpiew shrugged. They were back to how they had always been, living on their wits. Only this time they also had a tiresome girl to deal with.

'Who knows,' said Alpiew with a sigh of resignation. 'Perhaps the business will be sealed in a week or two and we can go home.'

In the corner of the coach Virginia shuffled in her seat. Alpiew gave her a sideways glance, and although she couldn't be certain, she felt sure that, through her tears, the girl was smiling.

It was almost dawn when they pulled up outside the Chateau Vieux de St Germain-En-Laye. Under normal circumstances travellers on this route would have spent another night in an inn and arrived next day, but with no funds it was only possible for the driver to change horses (the hiring agreement made by

Virginia's stepmother included such necessities) and continue their journey until they arrived exhausted in the early hours.

The chateau loomed in the dark like a giant fortress. The Countess and Alpiew walked across the bridge spanning the moat and looked up at the forbidding stone and redbrick edifice, while the driver got the luggage down from the back of the coach.

Virginia was curled up inside, asleep.

Alpiew banged on the great wooden door. 'It looks more like a prison than a castle, milady.' She shuddered. The night air had quite a nip.

'For five hundred years,' said the Countess with some excitement, 'it was the home of all the kings of France. I am sure inside it will be lovely.'

Alpiew banged again. The coachman piled their bags up at the door and went back to fetch Virginia.

The girl, bleary-eyed and looking even more grumpy than before, slouched along and waited shivering at Alpiew's side.

Eventually a guard bearing a flaming link pulled the great door open and let them in.

'I wonder if they're expecting us,' said the Countess, feeling ill at ease as she realised that she had not thought to ask Mrs Franklyn-Green what procedure they should follow.

They waited silently in the cold stone hallway until an upright woman with a chamber candle came to greet them.

'I am Lady Prude,' she announced, pulling her dressing gown tighter. 'Welcome to the Court of St James at St Germain. You are refugees?'

'Not exactly. We are here to chaperone a young lady.' The Countess presented the letter that Virginia's stepmother had given her. 'But I have private reasons to come here and pay my respects to King James. I was a personal friend of His Majesty's brother, Charles . . .'

'You are Catholics?'

Alpiew shook her head, and the Countess gave her a kick.

'Of course, Lady Prude, we are of the True Faith.'

Lady Prude ran her finger up and down a list. 'We are exceedingly pressed for space here at the chateau at the moment. Yesterday we had a large group of Irish priests arrive, without a groat between them. Her Majesty Queen Mary is an angel and provides for anyone who needs succour . . .' She pursed her lips and sighed. 'But if you were a friend of His Majesty's elder brother, I am sure we can find something for you.'

She led them up a grand staircase, then across a great gallery, through a small panelled door, along a narrow corridor and up a stone spiral staircase. There she took a bunch of keys from her pocket and unlocked a door.

'I think you will find this chamber comfortable enough.' Lady Prude walked across to the great curtained four-poster bed. 'There is a lovely view over the river. You don't mind sharing the bed with your charge, Countess? And your servant can take the truckle bed at your feet.'

The Countess and Alpiew looked round the room and marvelled. It was exquisite: the panelled walls were painted in a bright cream and adorned with beautiful paintings; the bed was hung in a pleasant green silk brocade, the armchairs and stools upholstered in the same fabric and the other furniture, a small table and a bureau, was inlaid with copper and tortoiseshell, and quite unlike anything they had ever seen in England.

'I'm sure we will be very comfortable here.' The Countess fingered the damask bed-hangings and prodded the feather-filled mattress. 'Thank you so much, Lady Prude.'

'I hope you sleep well.' She pulled the door ready to close it behind her. 'We will speak properly tomorrow.' She nodded politely and clicked the door shut after her.

Virginia went to the window and stared out into the dark grey of dawn.

The Countess and Alpiew exchanged a look of delight, then, without bothering to undress, they flopped down on to their beds and fell asleep in a moment.

*   *   *

A bell was tolling somewhere very near. The Countess opened her eyes. The curtains were still drawn, but sunlight spilled in around the edges. She could hear Alpiew lightly snoring in the truckle bed.

She tiptoed to the window and pulled back the curtains.

'Lord, what an infernal cacophony.' Alpiew rolled over, then sat up squinting and peered about her. 'Where in heavens am I? Oh, madam – see the view!' Alpiew ran to the window and let out a gasp. 'I have never been in a place so splendid in all my life.' She looked out across miles of beautiful countryside, divided by a meandering river. Immediately below the window there were elegantly laid out parterres and fountains, and beyond them miles of woods.

'What matter if we have no money, Alpiew?' The Countess sank down again on her bed. 'Whenever have we lived in such comfort?' She pulled the covers up over her and flopped back on to the pillows. 'If only they'd leave off ringing that hellish bell.'

Alpiew perched on the foot of the Countess's bed and yawned. 'So the girl served a purpose after all.'

Alpiew sprang to her feet, while the Countess sat bolt upright. 'The girl!'

Virginia's side of the bed lay empty.

'Oh lor', madam, where is she? Where is Virginia?'

They leapt up and dashed out into the hall.

'I hope she has not run into those too convenient woods hoping to be murdered by gypsies,' the Countess panted.

'Where to look?' hissed Alpiew, wondering briefly at the Countess's wild imagination, as they dived down a spiral stone staircase and sprinted along an open gallery lined with portraits in oil. 'This place is vast.'

They dived down another flight of stairs and could see an inner courtyard through the windows.

'Pshaw! Where is everyone?' huffed the Countess. 'That woman last night said the place was packed with people.'

'Look –' Alpiew peered out at the courtyard – 'this building is a sort of oblong circle.'

'Very geometrically put, Alpiew. However, your observation does offer a logic to our search,' wheezed the Countess, hitching up her skirt. 'I'll head this way, you go that. We should eventually meet up again. Please God, let the girl be safe.'

Alpiew sprinted off, and the Countess lurched forward, pulling open a large door. She trotted through another long room and heaved the end door open.

The Countess found herself in a stone vestibule, thronged with people. They all turned and peered at her. She realised she must look a fright, still wearing the clothes she had slept in, with the same flaking make-up she had put on to travel, and to top it, she was feeling very flustered. Raising a chubby hand, she pushed her wig straight, and gave a cheery smile.

'I'm looking for . . .'

'Countess.' A hand clamped on her shoulder. It belonged to Lady Prude. 'I'm glad that, despite your very late arrival last night, you thought fit to rise in time for Mass. Devotion is the true way to redemption.'

The Countess shrugged and crossed herself in an effort to show willing. 'You haven't by any chance seen my charge, Miss Franklyn-Green, have you?' she whispered to Prude. 'The girl left the room a while before me. This place is so confusing, stairs up and down, winding ins and outs . . . like a labyrinth almost.'

The heady scent of incense and swirls of music wafted from the chapel as the crowd slowly pushed inside.

'She will be exploring. St Germain is a wonderful chateau,' said Lady Prude, her voice almost drowned out by a particularly impressive musical flourish. 'I find there's nothing quite like the throbbing swell of a huge organ.'

The Countess decided it was safer not to respond.

'Heavy going to the uninitiated, but you get used to it,' murmured Prude. 'Personally, I find it utterly exhilarating.'

The Countess gave her a sideways glance, wondering whether Lady Prude was still on the subject of the music.

'A typical erection of Charles the Wise,' Lady Prude continued, while the Countess gawped open-mouthed, 'the chateau is laid out on a simple irregular pentagon.' Lady Prude threw an ornate black mantilla over her greying hair. 'No doubt the young lady is already inside, otherwise she will find her way eventually. Come along.' Gripping the startled Countess by the arm, she led her in to Mass.

Alpiew slowed down as she completed the tour of the ground floor. There were doors either side of the room she stood in; one led into the courtyard, the other, she presumed, led out of the chateau.

She pulled it open and found herself in another courtyard. Whereas the inner one was laid out in an ornate flowery parterre, this was cobbled and clearly a working area.

A serving girl sat on a pile of boxes, writing notes. A carthorse, nostrils steaming, paced its hoof against the large black cobblestones. A man was unloading cases of vegetables from the wagon.

'*Assez!*' cried the girl, ticking her list. '*C'est tout. À demain, Pierre.*'

The drayman gave her a wave, leapt up on to his perch and steered the cart out into the street.

Alpiew was in home territory here in the kitchen quarters, but was stumped for words. How to ask after Virginia in French?

As if on cue, the serving girl swung across the yard to two open doors and yelled inside in a broad Irish accent: 'Come on, you lazy great lug. If it's staying here you're after, you start by getting this lot inside. Then you can get the fire stoked up.'

'Excuse me,' said Alpiew to the girl, as a tall dark man in muddy clothing strode out and started heaving the crates into the kitchen.

'Yes,' said the Irish girl, hands on hips. 'Are you lost? They're all at Mass.' She pointed back into the chateau.

'No, no,' said Alpiew. 'I'm looking for a young English girl. Fair hair, pale, with rosy cheeks . . .'

At this moment Virginia tripped out from the kitchen chewing on an apple.

'That her?'

Virginia straightened up, looking sheepish. 'I was hungry,' she blurted. 'I came down looking for food.'

'It doesn't help if the nobs come and sit in my kitchen,' said the Irish girl. 'Perhaps you'd be so kind as to take her back inside and let us get on with our work.'

Alpiew grabbed hold of Virginia's elbow and steered her into the chateau.

'What were you thinking of?'

Virginia put her hand up to her head. 'I have a headache.' She shook Alpiew off. 'I'm going to lie down. I won't be ordered about by a mere servant.' She strode off up the grand staircase. 'If you, or that stupid old harridan you work for, want me, you can look for me. No doubt I will be somewhere-abouts.'

'I have been talking to your ward, Virginia,' said a Scottish lady in a flamboyant dress and brightly beribboned cap marching along behind the Countess in the gardens. 'She tells me you are a writer.'

The Countess smiled acknowledgement.

'I am Lady Isabel Murdo-McTavish. From Scotland.'

'Lady Anastasia Ashby de la Zouche, Countess of Clapham, Baroness Penge . . .'

The sun beat down, and a refreshing breeze blew across the river, rippling the heads of beautifully laid out rows of flowers along the pebbled walks. The Countess thought she couldn't be happier.

'You see . . . I am a writer too!' interrupted Lady Murdo-McTavish. 'I lead a very lively writers' circle here at St Germain. I feel sure you would like to join.'

'I . . . I . . . er . . .' In dismay the Countess slumped against one of the lime trees that lined the walk along the terrace. The one thing she didn't want was to be inveigled into a group of amateurs. She'd experienced that before and knew they only expected you to heap praise upon their meandering scribbles. 'Of course. A writers' circle! It sounds admirable. But before

I start enjoying myself, I have some urgent business which I must attend to.' She started to walk back to the chateau.

'Splendid.' Lady Murdo-McTavish turned with her and walked along at her side, pulling a small shagreen notebook from her pocket. 'I'm sure you will find our sessions most invigorating.' She jotted down the Countess's name in her book. 'Do you keep a notebook, too? I carry mine with me everywhere I go. Unless I am going somewhere I fear my pocket would be picked, then I secrete it. Certainly, Countess, I would be lost without my little book. It has months of notes.' She thrust the book back into her pocket. 'I could get some of the pieces our members have written sent up to your chamber, if you like.'

'No need,' said the Countess, increasing her pace. 'I would prefer to save them up as a glorious treat,' she said, hoping that the day would never come.

'By the way . . .' Lady Murdo-McTavish, striding along beside her, bent closer to the Countess's ear: 'I should warn you about Prude. She's odd. Brim-full of the most absurd notions possible. Quite dangerous, in her own way.'

'I can deal with her sort,' said the Countess, peering across the parterre in the hope someone would come and rescue her.

'Wherever she goes all faults are represented by her with magnifying optics, and many innocent things are interpreted as criminal from her ill nature.'

'Thank you so much for letting me know.' The Countess prayed that Virginia or Alpiew would appear soon.

'The rules of Society and etiquette here in France are so strange you will need protection.'

'Oh, don't worry about me. I stayed here briefly when I was a mere child of sixteen. I know the French ways. I can easily cope with a wild rush of social activity and endless partying.'

'That is what I feared. You will find things are much changed, Countess. At King James's court our occupations have all the air of being very serious and Christian, for this is no place for those who do not spend, or pretend to spend, more than half the day in prayer.'

'Really?' The Countess squinted into the distance, not listening. 'How lovely.'

'The friendship we profess is always simulated; the hatred and envy we conceal is always sincere. There are all sorts of cabals and factions here at St Germain. And as you will find it *de rigueur* to join some, I would say that our writers' circle would be the least hazardous to the enjoyment of your stay here.'

'Hazardous?' The thought of sitting round a table discussing other people's tedious jottings seemed like a pretty hazardous activity to her. 'In what way?'

'You will be watched and you will be judged. Prude has probably already got a file on your past. She makes it her business to know your business. It's a wise idea not to let her know too much about yourself.'

'I see.' The Countess smiled. 'I'm used to her sort. Let her think what she will.'

She had at last spied Alpiew in the distance. 'Ah, look, there is my woman. We have some urgent business to attend upon.' She threw her arms up, waving frantically in Alpiew's direction.

'And whatever you do, don't let Prude lure you under her sanctified wing, and don't cross her, or she'll find a bed for you in the dungeons,' said Isabel Murdo-McTavish with a wave.

'Dungeons?'

'Only a jest. The dungeons have been disused for centuries. Too damp. But if she could find a way to put us down there, she would! *À bientôt*, Countess. And may all your scribbles be masterpieces.'

'Yes, indeed. I shall look forward to many hours of pleasant writerly activities very soon.' The Countess hoiked up her skirts and trotted briskly across the parterre towards Alpiew. As she arrived at Alpiew's side she had to side-step a man dressed head to toe in black, who was standing gazing out across the crowded garden through a spectacle-glass.

'My word, milady, the men here are a set of debauched

coxcombs and no question.' Alpiew was smoothing down the front of her mantua. 'I have been importuned by four of them between the bedchamber and the garden. One queer prinked-up fellow had the nerve to play upon my bosom as though it was a pair of drums.' She hitched up her bodice and gave an indignant sniff. 'I gave him a dowse in the chops, and warned him that next time he tried anything like that I'd knee him in the breeches.'

'Let us find a quiet salon, and make some inquiries about lunch.' The Countess nodded in acknowledgement to a gaggle of chattering Jesuit priests who passed nearby. 'Did you find Virginia?'

'Oh, she is everywhere, madam. I found her in the kitchens, then she went upstairs and painted her face a little. Since then she's been scampering about like a child, darting from room to room. I can hardly believe her to be the same girl that we travelled here with. She seems to have settled in with gusto.'

'*Jamais! Jamais! Jamais! Mademoiselle Smith,*' screeched a rotund little man in a voluminous grey wig, '*quand je dis anchois, j'exige anchois!*'

'*Je vous assure, Marquis –*' a pretty dark-skinned young woman was trying to calm him down – '*avec votre genis culinnaire la sauce sera formidable avec n'importe quel poisson.*'

'*Avez vous des lardoons d'ail pour le potage?*'

'*Oui, d'accord! Mais les anchois . . .*'

'*De temps en temps un poisson n'est pas un poisson.*'

'What a quaint pair, Alpiew. Look! So typically French – all that passion. They must be talking about Love.'

'Countess!' The voice of Lady Prude boomed out across the lawn. 'Could we use this moment for a little chat?'

The Countess let out a low groan.

Panting, Lady Prude arrived at their side.

'As you see, society here at St Germain is civilised and stimulating. We have the elite of British society amongst us: writers, experimental philosophers, artists, historians, experts in all branches of the humanities.'

'How lovely,' said the Countess, stifling a yawn.

'I believe you are a writer. One of your plays was performed at Drury Lane, I'm told.'

'That's right. *Love's Last Wind*,' said the Countess, hoping that this admission was not going to shackle her permanently to Lady Murdo-McTavish and her writers' circle.

A tall man with long brown hair strode past and disappeared into the chateau.

'That is Dr Stickworth. He is a very clever man, and a staunch and loyal supporter of the cause. He served bravely in the Irish campaign. On a number of occasions he risked his life for his King. I believe there is some sort of rivalry going on between him and the Duc de Charme, a renowned engineer. The Duc is working on plans for some new kind of flying fire-engine.'

'I suppose people have a lot of time on their hands.' The Countess squinted across the lime walk to a group of women sitting chatting in the sun.

'Absolutely not,' said Lady Prude. 'Everyone contributes to the successful running of our own little kingdom within a kingdom. Which brings me to the important question of your donation . . .'

'Donation?' The Countess eyed her warily.

'To our noble cause. The support of the thousands of refugees, like yourself, driven from England by the draconian laws of the Royal Usurper, that agent of the devil, William of Orange.'

'Ah yes,' said the Countess. 'Of course we planned to give an enormous sum, but, sadly, we were set upon by bandits, who took all of our gold – *all of it*. And in short we are thrown upon your generosity, Lady Prude, both as poor as nuns.'

Lady Prude's face tightened. 'You mean you have no money?'

'Well, yes . . .' The Countess did not like the change in Lady Prude's expression. 'Thanks to the highwaymen who set upon us yesterday, we are poor as church mice, God bless our souls.' She crossed herself, trying to impress the sour-faced woman.

'I'm sorry, but I will have to reconsider your accommodation.' Lady Prude whipped a notebook from her pocket and gave Alpiew a stern look. 'Can you cook?'

'Not really, I . . .'

'Never mind that. Please to follow me, woman.' She glared at the Countess. 'And as for you, Countess, please repair to your chamber, where I will meet you as soon as is convenient.'

'And what of Virginia?'

'A charming girl.' Lady Prude beamed. 'Her mother made a most generous contribution and has well provided for the child's nurture. With you as her appointed chaperone, of course. But if that is all you are – a duenna – I'm afraid you must be accommodated as such.'

'Which means . . . ?'

'You're not out on the street quite yet. For the moment we will find you somewhere in the chateau, but only until you find yourself more suitable accommodations in the town.'

The Countess and Alpiew winced.

'And as for your servant . . .' Lady Prude eyed Alpiew up and down, and sneered. 'Whoever heard of a duenna with a servant! The woman must live with the household staff.'

The Countess was left gaping as Lady Prude strode away, dragging Alpiew along behind her.

The kitchen was huge and busy. A great fire belched smoke up the chimney, and the steam from a score of huge pots hung over it plunged the entire room into a thick but aromatic fog. Silently a handful of people chopped and stirred and washed dishes, amid the clatter of iron lids and bubbling kettles.

'You will work in here. The kitchen staff have a dormitory in the stables. You will find it as comfortable as your situation merits.'

'But the Countess . . .' Alpiew stood, open-mouthed. 'What will become of my lady?'

'Your lady can look after herself. While you stay here at the chateau you will put in whatever hours Lord Wackland, the maître d'hôtel, demands, and you will be fed and given a bed. Any income you receive will be from perqs.'

'Perqs?'

'Someone will explain. But if you can neither cook nor speak French, I imagine your status as a perquisite earner will be on the low side.' She swept from the room just as the maître d'hôtel came in.

He nudged the dark young man Alpiew had watched earlier who was down on all fours prodding the fire with a long poker. 'It's your lucky day, John,' he said. 'Lady Prude has brought us a woman to replace you.'

John got up and brushed himself off, wiping the sweat from his blackened face.

'You'll be more use outside, loading the carts and chopping logs, anyway.' The maître d'hôtel gave him a crack across the legs with his cane. 'Off you go. Now, woman, are you familiar with the duties of a turnspit?'

Alpiew groaned inwardly. She knew the job well. It was a living hell.

'On your knees, woman. Let us see you clean that fireplace, and all the while you must keep the spits moving. If I see one piece of meat burned due to your negligence you will be whipped.' He cracked his cane down on a nearby table. 'Understood?' He swept out of the kitchen.

Before Alpiew could regain her composure someone was tugging at her sleeve. She turned to face the Irish girl she had seen earlier. 'Don't you worry, Alpiew,' she whispered. 'It's not so bad as it looks. Last one in is always turnspit. John only arrived here last night. Maybe someone will come as quick to relieve you. The turnover of people in this place is prodigious.'

John came back into the kitchen, laden with boxes. 'Where do I put these, Pipe?'

'Empty the asparagus on to the table, the rest stack up in the pantry, next door.'

John spilled out a boxful of white fingers of asparagus,

then carried off the rest of the boxes and put them out of the way.

'I'm Pipe,' said the Irish girl. 'I came over with Lord Whippingham, but he ran out of funds years ago, and so I was reallocated to the kitchen by that hell-cat, Prude.' Pipe sat down on a barrel and swung her legs. 'I'm lucky. I'm marketing maid, because I have a skill at finding the best prices in Town and at the farms. The perqs are good, and life is really rather better here than it was when I lived on his lordship's estate in England.' Pipe looked towards the stable building. 'Your girl's back, Alpiew. Perhaps she's looking for you this time.'

Virginia was peering into the kitchen.

'Are you looking for me?' shouted Alpiew. 'Or the Countess?'

Virginia recoiled. 'Mistress Alpiew! I seem to be lost. Could you direct me back to my room?'

Pipe moved over to the pantry door. 'Come on, handsome!' She strolled towards John and stroked his sweaty back. 'You could do with a rest. You take the pretty lady round to the front of the chateau. She'll find her way easily enough from there.'

'Thank you, Pipe.' John ran his hands through his black mane of hair. He swaggered across to Virginia. 'Far from home, young lady?'

'Now, Alpiew –' Pipe grabbed her by the hand – 'how would you like me to fetch you a nice dish of something hot before I go to serve lunch to the snobs inside?'

'In London, servants aren't separated like this. We eat and live with the best of them.'

'You're forgetting where we are. This is France, where the different classes are kept well apart, with all sorts of mad levels of importance. Do you know that over at Versailles they have bizarre rules about which seats you can sit on, and whether you may knock or scratch on a door to gain entry – even for duchesses and princesses. All of it depends on your rank. I know this is the court of an English king, but he has decided to honour his host by imitating him. You cannot believe the fuss over rank and precedence here at St Germain compared to life back home.'

Alpiew took all of this in. 'So where is my lady in all this, and where are we?'

'At the top there is the Royal Household, consisting of the King, the Queen, the Prince of Wales, and all their ministers and advisors. They live on the second floor and we never catch so much as a glimpse.'

'Are the King and Queen frightful snobs, then?'

'The King, from what I gather, is a miserable old thing. Very bitter, especially since losing all those battles in Ireland. The Queen, however, is a saint.'

'Really? But my lady will be allowed to mix with them?'

'Oh no. There is another level above her, they mix mainly with the second-floor folk, then there are the stragglers. She will be put in with them. We wait upon the stragglers. The royals have their own kitchen, their own staff. In my opinion those servants rank above the stragglers, and *we* are the lowest of the low.'

'What a place!' said Alpiew, more determined than ever to get home as soon as possible. 'And who are the stragglers, exactly?'

'They're a rum lot. People who have shown loyalty but are not of the highest rank. Lady Prude bridges the gap between the two households. The poor old stragglers don't get treated very well.'

'So why do they stay here?'

'Because it's better than plodding round Europe like a vagrant.' Pipe laughed. 'Here at least they have a roof over their heads, English-speaking companions . . . What more could you ask for, if you're an émigré?'

The Countess sat in a desolate heap upon her truckle bed in an airless attic room with only the tiniest window set high in the ceiling. There were two beds in the room and she prayed the other was for Alpiew, and not some stranger.

She rested her feet on her packing case and put her head in her hands. That it should come to this – dependent on the charity of others. She'd frequently been penniless before, but somehow that didn't matter within the impoverished cheer of her own home.

And now here she was, stuck in an attic, supposedly in charge of a surly child who was lording it in comfort downstairs, and without even her friend Alpiew for company. Poor Alpiew. She dreaded to think where she'd been hauled off to.

She heard a ripple of laughter, followed by some low chatter and another laugh. On the roof above her a wood pigeon cooed.

She stepped out of her depressing garret and strolled along the winding wooden corridor, passing innumerable doors similar to hers. Behind one of them she heard a groan. Just as she reached the stairs she heard raised voices, followed by a slap. She turned and looked back along the empty hallway. Low voices murmured behind a door beside her, a man and a woman speaking insistently.

'Try it. Go on. It's not as bad as you might think . . .' said the male voice.

The Countess smirked. So the old French ways still continued, even here in the English court.

'Save it for your ladies of the town,' said the woman. 'I'm sure your French slatterns love this sort of thing. But I do not.'

'Put it in your mouth,' the man wheedled. 'Go on. At least try it.'

'All right.' The woman sighed. 'Go on.'

A little fumbling and mumbling, then a chair slid back and there was a spitting noise and a raised female voice. 'Enough, enough! 'Tis enough to make you disgorge.'

'Some people enjoy it,' said the man. 'In fact, my dear wife, I would suggest you have the wrong kind of teeth for the job. This sort of thing is a vocation. My girls in Town make quite a good living doing nothing else.'

Good Lord! The Countess grimaced and skipped down the

steps and out of sight. Now there was a relationship with no boundaries. She made a note to be sure to find out who lived in the room at the top of the stairs.

'I have the best job here, I think.' Pipe got her basket and swung it over her shoulder. 'Some of the boys are candle-changers. I envy them a lot. Hardly any work; lots of money. Over at Versailles, they have it even better. There they change candles at set times, whether they've burned down or not. But here the Queen insists on economy, so the stumps are rather small. Still, if you have a basketful you can get a nice price for wax down at the market. Valets and footmen do very well, too. As long as their masters aren't stingy, of course.' She pointed across to a tall blond boy in a pristine livery. 'That's Roger, the Duc de Charme's valet. He has the best of both worlds: all the lavishness of Versailles, and the freedom of this place.'

Alpiew looked the valet over. He had a pouty face, with one perpetually raised eyebrow. He was busy seeing to his cuticles.

'I'm very lucky,' Pipe continued, 'because I do the market, and you can swing all sorts of things down there. I have a few tricks I've perfected, too.'

'Tricks?' Alpiew wondered whether these were the same ones she had employed in London.

'I go up to the second-hand food market, and then put in a bill for the prices at the real market.'

'Second-hand food market?' said Alpiew, appalled. 'What on earth is that?'

'Whisht! It's a French thing. Some of these grand houses round here, especially the royal households, have much more food laid out on the table at each meal than they could possibly eat. So what gets left, gets sold. I suppose there's a perq in there for someone, making sure how much food falls off the side of the table, as it were.'

'What kind of food?'

'There are tomatoes, for a start. They're only used in the

best houses for a bit of table colour, but peasants don't mind eating them, so they go quite cheap. On a good day you can get a half-eaten roast chicken, or a clutch of quails . . .'

'The aristocrats of France don't eat tomatoes?'

'They think they're poisonous! Red for danger. I thought everyone here quite mad when I first came over, but now I'm used to it. The nobles don't eat roots either. Sure, carrots and turnips are strictly peasant fodder, while asparagus and peas are all the rage. People are starting to experiment with mushrooms. And there is barely a part of any animal that doesn't get served up, from the tongue to the tail, garishly decorated with all kinds of colourful things: cocks' combs, gizzards, larks' tongues, lemons, carrots – and tomatoes, of course.'

'I hope someone comes soon so I can get moved up a place.' Alpiew wiped the sweat from her face. Her hand was black from smuts from the fire. 'Or even better, I hope my mistress comes to her senses and we can go home to England.'

Manicure finished, Roger turned, raised both eyebrows, gave Pipe an impertinent pout and marched out, swiping a carrot from the table and biting on it as he went.

'Home? You'll be lucky!' Pipe stared at Alpiew for a moment before continuing. 'Agh, sure, it's not so bad here. I've learned a lot. I can even *parlez vous*.'

'What's that?'

'I speak a bit of the old French, don't you know. You need it for the bartering. The market people are all very friendly. You'll like them.'

John slammed into the kitchen and slumped down on the table. 'I've had enough of this place.' He gave Alpiew a sly glance and sniggered. 'I'm off to sample the delights of the town.'

'I assure you, John, you are not.' Pipe leapt up from her chair. 'I am in charge here at the moment, and I tell you, you impudent spalpeen, you cannot go out without the permission of Lord Wackland.'

'Go hack, Pipe. I won't be told what to do by you or weird Wackland. I'm into Town to get fuddled.'

'Whisht, boy, but you won't get far. You've no money.'

'I think I'll get by.' John grabbed his cloak and made for the door. 'Thanks for your opinion, Pipe, but I'll see you tomorrow. Perhaps!' He stared at Alpiew, let out a guffaw and went.

'Have you played cards long, Countess?' Isabel Murdo-McTavish leant away from the gaming table to inspect her cards.

'I play in London, of course.' The Countess glanced down at her hand. She couldn't believe she was winning. She never won in her games with her friend the Duchesse de Pigalle back in London. 'But I am only a social player.'

Virginia sat hunched up in a corner, reading a book. The Countess kept an eye on her. She seemed to be slowly settling in. At least she had stopped growling and grumping so much.

Isabel threw down her cards and pushed a pile of walnut shells they were using as counters to the Countess's side of the table.

'So tell me more about Lady Prude,' said the Countess. 'She is so miserable, I presume she is a spinster?'

'*Au contraire*, Countess.' Isabel shuffled and dealt another hand. 'She married shortly after the revolution. He was an elderly chap, a loyal supporter of the King. He died five years ago but left her with the title and a high position here at court.'

'Not as high as she would like, I gather.'

'You are astute, Countess.' Isabel Murdo-McTavish slammed her cards down a second time. 'And you win again.'

'She left it late to marry,' said the Countess. 'She would have been in her forties at least.'

'Well, look at her!' Isabel laughed. 'Her miserable disposition is etched all over her face. She was lucky to find *anyone*, in my opinion. Although I believe back in London she was a rich heiress. See, you have beat me again. I suspect you are some kind of professional sharper, or else you have bewitched the cards.'

'*Vive les femmes anglaises!*' said the rotund gentleman in

the voluminous wig, whom the Countess had seen earlier shouting in the garden. Now much calmer, he stood nursing a bumper of red wine by the fireplace. '*Elles sont formidables!*'

His companion, a tall gentleman in a yellow velvet jacket and red wig, raised his glass.

The Countess gave a polite smile in their direction, while casting a sly glance at Virginia.

'The fat one's the Marquis de Béchamel,' said Isabel. 'He is chief cook to the King of France. He pops over here to try his recipes out on us, before risking the wrath of the almighty Louis.'

The Countess's stomach rumbled in anticipation.

'It's lucky you didn't take a real wager with me,' said Isabel Murdo-McTavish, dealing again, then taking a disgruntled glance at her hand. 'For I'd surely be paying out.'

Why had she not thought of that? With players as bad as this Scotswoman she could make money at this game. The Countess again ran her eyes over her cards. It was unlikely she could lose this time either. She gave the Frenchmen a coy smile. 'Tonight I'm just lucky, I think.'

'No good speaking to them,' said Isabel. 'Hardly have a word of English between them.'

'Why is the tall one here?' The Countess placed her stake. 'Is he a culinary student or something?'

'No. That is Baron Lunéville. He's a Versailles courtier. He comes here because he hates peas.'

'I'm sorry?'

'A lot of them come to St Germain to escape peas, because they hate them. At Versailles peas are the craze. More than that, I'd say pea-eating at Versailles is a frenzy.'

'Only for a few months of the year though, surely?'

'Oh, no. To please the King, who adores peas, the gardeners at the potager there have found ways to grow them practically all year round. Everyone is expected to eat buckets full to please the King. I gather many of the poor French creatures stuff them down their throats only to go into the next room and spew.' She gave a tinkling laugh. 'In my mind's eye, I see the whole chateau at Versailles spattered with bright green vomit.'

'How gruesome.' The Countess laid down her winning hand and wondered to herself if Lady Murdo-McTavish might not be slightly cracked. But the talk of putting things into mouths had reminded her of the exchange she had heard through the door that morning. 'Prude has moved me to the garret. I was wondering who my neighbours might be up there. Who lives at the top of the staircase?'

'That'll be the Whippinghams. They're an odd couple. I gather they get up to all sorts of bizarre activities. Most mysterious pair. I feel sure they'll want to snare you into their wee "games".'

'Ah!' The Countess shuffled the book of cards. 'I think I overheard something like it earlier.'

'Oh yes, of course, you're up top with us now! I'm sure you'll be thrilled to know I too live in the paupers' quarters, Countess. Maybe we can set up a desk and a pair of quills in one of the rooms and do a little writing together.'

Trapped! The Countess dropped her cards and took a deep breath.

'Oh, dear. I have seen your hand, Countess,' cried Lady Murdo-McTavish triumphantly, as a bell started tolling across the courtyard. 'And for once I think I might have won.' She laid down a knave. 'Perhaps you could advise me. I usually write fairy stories, but I want to move into an area with a bit more . . .'

'Commercial pull? Try cookery books or things about how to decorate your home. They are all the rage.'

'No. I was going to say with more literary expertise. I have an idea for a story. I wonder what you think?'

'Ah!' The Countess edged uneasily on her seat. She could hardly run from the table to avoid what was to come. 'Shouldn't you keep it to yourself if it is such a good idea?'

'Don't be silly, Countess. You are a professional. I trust you. Anyhow . . . I was born just after the civil war, and brought up in the peace that followed, and then came the second revolution and we Catholics had to flee. I came over here and there was more peace and then war and now peace again, and I want to set it all down.'

'And have you a name for this captivating tale?' The Countess chuckled.

'It's only a working title, you understand.' Isabel ducked down and spoke in a low tone to make sure she was not overheard. 'I thought *War and Peace*.'

The Countess opened her mouth to reply when the door thudded open and a flustered man, painted and powdered, teetered through the room on incredibly high-heeled shoes. Ribbons fluttered from his lacy sleeves, his potbelly slightly protruded from his bejewelled damask silk jacket, and his bracelets and earrings clinked as he wobbled through the room. The door slammed behind him.

The two Frenchmen started fanning themselves with papers they were reading, and snorted with laughter.

Virginia, still reading, was holding her nose between two fingers.

'More odiferous than a Paris perfumier!' The Countess giggled. 'And as for his heels, one could believe he was a circus performer, walking on stilts. I presume the fellow is French?'

'How did you guess?' said Isabel without surprise. 'The Duc de Charme fancies himself the portrait of elegance.'

'*That* is the Duc de Charme?' The Countess wished she had taken a closer look, for Lady Prude had described him as an engineer. The fellow looked more like a blown-up version of a little girl's doll.

'Oh, Countess!' Isabel threw down a three of clubs. 'Yet again you have me caught like a kitten up a tree. You win. I am so lucky we had not staked money on it.'

'Lady Murdo-McTavish,' said the Countess, puffing slightly, embarrassed at her easy victory, 'you flattered me earlier. Mere beginner's luck. I cannot possibly take your spoils. It seems almost unfair.' She spread her cards out, pushed the walnut shells across the table and moved over towards the French gentlemen at the fireplace.

The bell doubled its pace, calling the faithful.

'No time for chat,' said Lady Murdo-McTavish, jumping to her feet and pulling a mantilla from her side-pocket. 'That's the bell for Benediction. Come along, Countess, Virginia!'

Ignoring her, the Countess hovered near the Frenchmen. 'Lady Anastasia Ashby de la Zouche,' she said with a smile, pointing to herself. 'Countess of Clapham, Baroness Penge . . .'

The Marquis de Béchamel interrupted her: 'Me Marquis de Béchamel, *mon ami* Baron Lunéville.'

They all grinned at each other as Baron Lunéville pulled a chair for the Countess to sit.

'You have wives?' said the Countess, miming along as best she could. '*Femmes?*'

The two Frenchmen shook their heads. The Countess thought either of them would be a very suitable match for Virginia. It would be good to get an introduction in as soon as possible.

'You Lady Ashwashwoosh,' said Lunéville. 'But you 'ave 'usband, no? 'E cunt?'

'In a manner of speaking,' said the Countess. She was anxious to change the subject back to whether either of these men might be potential matches for Virginia.

'Benediction,' wailed Murdo-McTavish from the doorway. 'We shall be late.'

'I'm right behind you,' said the Countess, staying put. She summoned up what little French she could remember. 'You have grand chateau? Bowcoo de terre?'

'Please, Countess!' moaned Murdo-McTavish. 'You don't want people thinking we're Protestants –' She slammed her fingers over her mouth.

While the Countess edged over to fetch Virginia, a sprightly footman in spotless powder-blue livery entered the room. He bowed before the French lords and whispered something into Lunéville's ear.

Lunéville took a quick look towards the door, blanched, and exchanged a look with Béchamel. For a short moment the Countess saw again, momentarily standing behind the Scotswoman, the Man in Black she had noticed in the garden that morning. This time he was without his spectacle-glass. When she turned back she found that, with much bowing and scraping, the Frenchmen were suddenly taking their leave, Lunéville following the footman, Béchamel striding off in the opposite direction.

With no company but Virginia, there was nothing for it but to accompany the Scotswoman to prayers.

'Come along, child,' said the Countess. She bent down to whisper in Virginia's ear. 'Bring the book. No one will guess it isn't a prayer book.'

'Who said it wasn't?' Virginia bobbed to her feet and flounced off after Isabel Murdo-McTavish.

As they made their way to the chapel Lady Murdo-McTavish murmured to the Countess, 'You must be very careful whom you speak to and what you say in this place. Everyone is watching and anyone will report you with no qualms if it improves their own standing at court.'

'Phough!' The Countess spoke aloud. 'I have nothing to hide and nothing to be frightened of.'

'Beware!' Lady Murdo-McTavish applied her lips again to the Countess's ear. 'There are spies everywhere.'

'And pray tell me what are these spies looking for?' The Countess glanced about her at the ladies and gentlemen making their way into the chapel.

'Spies!' said Lady Murdo-McTavish. 'They're looking for spies.'

'You are telling me, Lady Murdo-McTavish . . .' The Countess shook her head, hoping it might clear her under-standing, 'that there are spies here whose job it is to search out spies?'

'*Cave*, Countess. Take care.' The Scotswoman gave her a penetrating look and clamped her mouth together. She raised her finger to her string-thin lips. 'Nothing here is what it seems.'

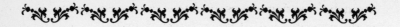

THREE

Vinaigrette — or vinegar and pepper sauce for beef

Alpiew wished she could tear off all her clothes and dive into the river below the terrace. The heat from the fire, together with the steam puffing from all the pots and the splashes of fiery fat dripping from the roasting venison, had left her rosy red and dripping with sweat. But at last the meat was almost cooked, and Wackland was busy supervising the laying out of the platters and chargers.

Pipe exchanged a sympathetic look with Alpiew, who raised her eyebrows in reply.

Béchamel fussed over the saucepans.

'*Je vous assure, Marquis, j'ai repete tout ce que vous m'avais dit au Lord Wackland.*' The young translator turned to the maître d'hôtel. 'Lord Wackland, the Marquis is worried that the seasoning will not be sufficient in the *jus lié* and the *andouille* will suffer as a result.'

The Marquis was lifting all the lids, peering inside, and sniffing the air. He walked over to the vegetable rack and pulled out a bunch of ciboulets. Mademoiselle Smith, his translator, followed him dutifully.

'*Tranchez! Dans la sauce!*'

'Please could you chop these and put them in the sauce,' said Mademoiselle Smith.

While everyone watched Wackland slamming the knife down

42

through the spring onions, Béchamel continued rooting about in the vegetable box. Without warning, he let out a piercing scream, causing Wackland to slip and nick his finger.

Béchamel was holding up a potato.

'*Oh non. Non, non, non! Pommes de terre? Dans une cuisine? Jamais, jamais, jamais!*'

Mademoiselle Smith turned to Wackland. 'The Marquis wants to know why you have a poisonous fruit in the kitchen?'

'Tell the little French faggot that in England potatoes have been popular since the days of Good Queen Bess.' Wackland gave a weary sigh and went back to chopping.

'*Les Anglais sont cochons*,' said Béchamel. He tossed the potato into the fire and strutted out of the kitchen, followed by his interpreter.

'Enough mirth for one day,' snapped Wackland, throwing the knife down so hard that it stuck in the wood of the table. No one dared speak for fear of a stinging rebuke. 'We will be serving boiled potatoes, as we always do, whatever the fat little Frenchman says. Let him make any variety of dishes, we English like potatoes.'

All hands chopped and stirred and beat in silence.

'Why do we have to put up with this fellow at all, with his tortoise in a fricasseé and potage of frogs?' Wackland announced. 'I don't see why we can't have good old simple traditional English dishes, like battered rabbit, ox-cheek broth and calves'-head jelly.'

Eventually Alpiew managed a hissed inquiry to Pipe as to why the kitchen was so woefully under-staffed.

'The experienced ones are directed up to work in the royal kitchens,' said Pipe. 'But, as you see, it's not a joyful place down here, so folk don't tend to stay around. They move off to other parts of France; Paris mainly. No one lasts more than a few weeks.'

'But you're still here?'

'I am.' Pipe tapped her nose. 'But I have my reasons.'

'Pipe, tell me something . . .' Alpiew took the moment to

stretch and move herself a few paces from the fireplace. 'Why do they have separate kitchens for the royal entourage and the other people here? Surely it would be easier to have one big kitchen?'

'Too risky, they think. They fear another outbreak of the national pastime.'

'What on earth do you mean?'

'Poison!' Pipe gave a wide grin. 'A few years ago everyone was at it, poisoning each other right, left and centre. The moment anyone took a dislike to a person, they slipped a little something into their food and . . .' She stuck out her tongue and rolled her eyes up. 'Last rites – if the priest had time to catch you before you expired.'

'This happened here at St Germain?'

'Oh yes, the place was positively crawling with poisoners. So, by keeping the royal kitchen separate they hope the common little poisoners won't accidentally knock off the rightful King of England or his heir. It'll just be us or the appalling old nigmenogs like them inside.'

Wackland came over and inspected the vegetable pots swinging from their hooks over the flame.

'Help here, wench!' he bawled at Alpiew. 'The stewed salads are ready. They must be drained.'

A liveried valet came into the kitchen and nodded in Wackland's direction, who summoned Pipe to help Alpiew.

The valet cupped his hand and whispered in Wackland's ear. Wackland nodded and dismissed him.

'Uh-oh! He's from the royal household,' said Pipe, sotto voce. 'I know that look of Wackland's. There's trouble ahead.'

Wackland moved silently to a corner and picked up a large stick. He brought it back to the centre of the room and slammed it down on the big table, causing all the pans and bowls to rattle about.

'Now! Turn!' He eyed everyone in the kitchen. 'Empty out your pockets.'

Alpiew stepped forward with the others and pulled her pocket inside out.

'Step out of your boots and shoes.'

'Has something gone missing, sir?' Pipe was unlacing her boots.

Wackland crashed the wood down again. 'No talking.'

'But not everyone who's been here today is still here, Lord Wackland,' said Pipe. 'There's someone missing. He swaggered off into Town, if you remember. Right after he'd gone upstairs and come back here to the kitchen seemingly richer, sir.'

'You're new here, aren't you?' A plump little woman slumped down into the chair opposite the Countess. 'I'm Lady Whippingham. Call me Lucy.'

As darkness drew in and a slight chill nipped the air, the company had retired to the music room to drink and chat. The Countess had a comfortable chair near the fireplace and, on the other side of the room, Virginia, ignoring the Countess, stood flaunting herself, chattering away to two men, wearing her smile so wide you could see practically all of her perfect white teeth.

'And that fat thing over there's my husband.'

Remembering the episode she had overheard through the door, the Countess suppressed a grin as the woman pointed at one of the men, a fellow in a huge yellow wig.

The Countess gave him the once-over. He was as thick about the waist as the squab castrato opera singer she'd seen last year at the May Fair; his periwig was large enough to load a camel and he had bestowed upon it a bushel of powder; his sword-knot dangled on the ground, and his steinkirk was most disagreeably coloured with snuff from top to bottom. And yet the Countess could see that Virginia and another young girl were flirting wildly with him as though he was the handsomest gallant in all of France.

'Whippy is such a big baby. Aren't you, Whippy? With your big bellikins!' The blonde girl was fingering Lord Whippingham in some pretty intimate places. 'Who's a nervous ickle boy?'

The Countess didn't like to ask Lady Whippingham about the other girl, as she seemed to be on very intimate terms with her husband.

'The blonde slut in the cheap muslin dress,' said Lucy Whippingham, as though reading the Countess's mind, 'is an orphaned trollop called Aurelia Brown, of all things, who chases after old, fat men who she believes might sponsor her.'

Sponsor! There's a new word for it, thought the Countess, writhing in embarrassment.

'She's only been here a week. And of course she's picked the wrong one in my husband. He's as niggardly a pinchpenny hunks as ever sewed up the opening of his purse rather than pay the poor-rates collector.'

'Virginia and I are looking forward to many exciting romps together,' said Aurelia, putting her arm round Virginia's waist. 'It is so wonderful to have someone else like me here.'

'Oh yes. We are going to have lots of fun.' Virginia gave a little clap. 'I adore France, so far!'

The Countess crossed her fingers. At this rate the girl would be paired off in no time. If only the child didn't get too closely involved with Aurelia nor give away her virginity in a romp. That must not happen before she got a contract drawn up and a ring on her finger, or the Countess would certainly lose her fee.

'That other man is the Doctor, is he not?' said the Countess. 'He's rather good looking. Is he married?'

'I hear you were set upon on the highway, Countess, and all your money taken.' Lady Whippingham turned back from the group to look the Countess in the eye. She took a huge slurp from her bumper of Rhenish wine, then lowered her voice: 'Don't think you'll be any safer in this place than upon the highway, my dear. The chateau is a positive thieves' paradise. People don't even balk at stealing from the Queen, who is practically revered as a saint around here, so I doubt they'd search their consciences much if it came to thieving from mere mortals like us.'

'I have no worries any more on that score, Lucy,' said the Countess in a conspiratorial tone. 'You see, I have no more to lose. The wretches took the lot.'

'The worse for you,' said Lady Whippingham. 'For now every time something goes missing you will be one of the first they look to. Then there's the poison-pen letters.'

Virginia had joined Aurelia chucking Lord Whippingham under the chin. The Countess winced. What was the point in that? she wondered. Why flirt with a man who was already married?

Nearby the Doctor was laughing.

Lady Whippingham shifted uneasily in her seat. 'I gather you've already been winnowed by the pious Prude, and now you're up in the paupers' quarters with me and Whippy.'

'Indeed. Being beholden to her I think is quite the worst aspect of having been robbed.' The Countess took a gulp of wine.

'I suspect she's the letter writer, to be perfectly honest. She's always so busy nosing around in other people's business. Advising us on adultery and every kind of fornication her withered-up mind can imagine.'

The Countess sighed. Her imagined trip to France was nothing like this hothouse of intrigue and bigotry. 'All things together, I have to say I am beginning heartily to wish I could go home.'

'Home?' said Lady Whippingham, with a cocked eyebrow. 'Alas, this is your home now.'

The Countess looked blank.

'Oh, dear. Has no one told you?'

'Told me what?' The Countess felt uncomfortable at Lucy Whippingham's gloating stare.

'You say you are a writer?' Lady Whippingham sat back in her chair, squinting at the Countess through half-closed eyes. 'Might I suggest you are not in fact a Jacobite refugee at all?'

It seemed to the Countess that Lady Whippingham's voice carried a threatening tone.

'Don't mistake me,' said the Countess. 'I am Jacobite through and through. It will be a great day when the Stuart family can regain the throne which is theirs by divine right.'

'I presume you are joking.' Lady Whippingham moved over and perched on the side of the Countess's fauteuil. She spoke in a whisper: 'Since the disastrous Irish campaign and the rout at the Boyne, James is finished. He'll never get the English throne back. Never.'

The Countess looked desperately around the room. Politics were never her strongest point.

Lady Whippingham hissed on. 'And now that the King of France has recognised William as King of England, and the little Dutch fellow seems to be keeping the peace quite successfully, I believe it would be folly to rock the boat with misguided attempts to put that miserable ineffectual old duffer, James, back at the helm, don't you?'

'Mmm.' The Countess shook her head. 'Of course not.' She seemed to remember now that in the old days, when her darling Charlie was alive, that slut Nell Gwynn had had a name for James: 'Dismal Jimmy'. And Nelly was usually near the mark. But the Countess felt it might be wiser to say nothing.

'Clearly it is impossible for those of us who have supported His Majesty over here for the last eleven years to expect that we could move home to England and swear allegiance to his usurper,' continued Lady Whippingham. 'But, as far as I can see, if we all just shut up about it, I don't know why we can't have a pretty decent life here in France.'

'Couldn't agree more,' said the Countess, anxiously glancing round the room for someone to rescue her from this impossible discussion. 'What time's supper?'

'You hear terrible stories,' Lady Whippingham pressed on. 'Only last month we heard of a man who had lived here in the chateau with us for two years. He decided to go back "home" to England. He'd lived a quiet life over here, never professed himself a Jacobite, done nothing wrong . . . or so he thought. But he was arrested within hours of arriving in London and taken to the Tower. We are waiting any day to hear the news he has been executed for treason.'

The Countess swallowed. The thought of dancing at the end of a hempen rope at Tyburn gallows wasn't quite what she meant by going home.

'Unless, of course . . .' Whippingham still eyed the Countess warily.

'Unless . . . ?'

'Unless you were sent over here by *them* in the first place. Unless you are one of King William's spies. Then it will be the officials here who will see you sent to the stake or the block.'

The Countess knew instinctively that this was a close call. Whichever side of the fence she plumped for, it would entail a long drop and a hard fall. Suddenly the idea of being at Isabel Murdo-McTavish's writing group seemed rather alluring.

'Well? Aren't you going to answer me?' Lady Whippingham peered at the Countess through her empty wineglass. 'Which is it, Countess? Jacobite or Orange spy? Because, whoever you are, I do not believe you are here as a genuine émigré.'

'Come along, madam!' The Countess grabbed Lucy Whippingham's glass. 'Let us fill our brimmers and drink to a long and happy life, wherever we are.'

She waddled away towards the drinks table, praying someone would engage her in light conversation en route.

The next thing she knew, Lady Whippingham was standing beside her at the wine table.

'That new pretty young girl with Aurelia, the one making love to my husband, does she belong to you?'

'Not exactly "belong" . . . I have been entrusted with Virginia's care.' The Countess poured two glasses and handed one to Lucy. 'I am here to help her find a new husband.'

'Really?' Lucy took a step back. 'What a strange idea. Who asked you to do that?'

'Her stepmother,' said the Countess. 'When she is safely betrothed, I am to collect a huge fee.'

'Back in London?' Lucy peered at her through half-closed eyes. 'You don't get paid till you arrive back in London?'

'Yes.' The Countess shuffled from foot to foot. Lady Whippingham's stare was making her feel very uncomfortable.

'Ah yes, that makes sense.' Lucy nodded knowingly. 'She wanted rid of the girl, and by sending her here to St Germain she could make sure the wench never came home, so stepmummy could keep daddy to herself. And by employing you to escort her, she could get her over here without risking her own safe return to England. What's more, she'll never have to pay you for your effort.' Lady Whippingham patted the Countess on the back and lurched forward. 'Poor Countess, you have been gullied. The stepmother has got rid of the child, and as a result *you* are the reluctant exile, condemned to a compulsory sentence of death by boredom here in this pious little back-biting court in the middle of nowhere.'

'What can you mean, Lucy?' The Countess took a gulp of wine. 'Why cannot I go home? I am a Londoner.'

'Spies, spies, spies. Unless you are working for King William, your presence here has you marked as a supporter of the rebel James. To stay at the King James's court at St Germain is as certain a life sentence as that imposed upon the mysterious prisoner at the Bastille.'

'Mysterious prisoner?' The Countess was baffled by Lucy's drunken onslaught.

'The man who has no name,' said Lucy Whippingham in an eerie voice. 'He is kept in a solitary cell in the Bastille, away from view of everyone, prisoners and warders alike, by means of an iron mask. No one knows why he is there, but his sentence is eternity – or so they say. We are the same – doomed to stay here as long as we live.'

The Countess found herself going hot and cold. She tried to gulp, but her throat was dry with fear. She swilled down another swig of wine. 'What did this mysterious prisoner do?'

'No one knows. It's all whisper and tattle. It is forbidden

to talk of him at court. Perhaps it is the mere invention of a drunken mind.' Lucy Whippingham gave a little hiccup. 'I heard a duchesse at Versailles whispering about it. But who knows, perhaps she is as addled as our dear Isabel Murdo-McTavish, living in a fantasy world of wolves and gingerbread houses, and glass slippers.'

The Countess wanted badly to confer with Alpiew. If what Lady Whippingham was saying was true – that by coming to St Germain they had effectively prevented their ever returning to London – what were they then to do?

'Look at that merry slut of yours.' Lucy Whippingham glanced across the room at Virginia. 'My husband appears to be preferring the fleering wench's company to Aurelia's. The little madam will not be happy with that! Your Virginia had best watch her back.'

The Countess thought that Virginia had best watch her back in more ways than one, for Lord Whippingham was busy fondling her rump.

'That Aurelia won't like the new competition from your pretty little ward. She's a sly creature. I've seen the sideways looks she gives to the men here when she thinks no one is watching.'

Aurelia was certainly scrutinising Whippingham's face now that he was preoccupied with caressing Virginia. The Countess didn't like the look of her at all. The girl had quite an evil glint in her dark sparkling eyes. She made a note never to cross her. 'The poor girl must have some friends here?'

'On the contrary, my dear.' Lucy Whippingham guffawed. 'The wretched girl looks down her nose at the women here as though we're all slimy creatures from the bottom of some bog.' She took another quaff of wine. 'She's quite definitely after something of the male variety. I suspect too that she has a preference for the older man, and 'tis my belief nothing will stop her getting one. I saw her trying her luck with Lord Wackland this afternoon in the garden. My goodness, he seemed agitated. But then, he's like Prude, one of those dried-up people – no juices, if you get my meaning. I should think he'd be horrified by a slut like her. He practically ran across the lawn to get away. I had to laugh.'

'Look,' said the Countess. 'She's making an attempt on the Doctor now.'

The Doctor was whispering into Aurelia's ear, while next to her Lord Whippingham was now chucking Virginia under the chin in a most embarrassing and flirtatious way. Lucy Whippingham slammed down her glass, wine splashing all over the table.

'I'm sorry, Virginia is behaving very badly,' said the Countess, wishing the floor would immediately open and swallow both her and her charge. 'Shall I take the girl up to her room?'

The Doctor edged away from the group and left the room.

'Don't be absurd. Let the girl at him. It will be fun.' Lady Whippingham nudged the Countess, gave a little yelp and clapped a hand on her thigh. 'Perhaps my dear husband is trying to enrol the pretty little thing as a muncher.' She downed the contents of her glass and guffawed.

'I'm sorry?' The Countess was lost in thoughts of how to escape from this appalling place without delay.

'I won't explain just yet about my husband and munching, but I gather he does pay well. Quite a few women here have offered their services. I've had a go, but it's not for me.' She elbowed the Countess in the ribs. 'I'm sure he'll get short shrift if he tries it on with your protégée, but, in the fullness of time, Countess, once he hears you need money, I've no doubt he will approach you and ask you too to munch.'

Wackland took a large flat iron spade and thrust it into an open oven. He pulled out a dozen or more bread rolls, and dropped them on to the table to cool.

As he turned away, Pipe's hand darted out and gingerly snatched one of the rolls, which she thrust into her pocket.

'May I have a word, please, Lord Wackland?' Dr Stickworth stood at the threshold.

Wackland barked out a few more orders, then smoothed down his jacket, adjusted his periwig and marched across to the Doctor, who settled on the bench near the fire.

Alpiew was on her hands and knees with a brush.

'There have been warning letters,' said the Doctor. 'I don't know exactly who received them, but it seems something will happen tonight.'

'What is that to me?' Wackland fingered the pin in his lapel and looked back to the kitchen. 'You see how busy I am.'

'Not *that* business,' said the Doctor, staring at the lapel pin. 'A death threat. A poisoning.'

'Do not come to me with this stuff.' Wackland stamped his foot. 'My kitchen is well run. There will be nothing coming from here with poison in it. I am confident enough to take a taste of every dish now, right under your eyes. Would you like to watch?'

'It's just what I heard.' The Doctor shrugged. 'That new girl, Aurelia, she got one of the threatening notes.'

'Don't tell me any more. I will deal with her. She's a troublemaker. Lady Prude will have her removed before she causes any more nuisance, believe me.'

'Here, let me help!' Pipe knelt down near Alpiew. 'What are they saying? Can you hear?'

Alpiew banged the brush against some pans to make a noise. 'Something about poison!'

'Enough of your gossip, Pipe,' Wackland called from the doorway as the Doctor left the kitchen. 'Fetch the red wine, place the bottles on a platter and take them through to the second antechamber.'

Alpiew saw Pipe take a surreptitious swig from one of the bottles as she gathered them up.

'Now, Alpiew, let's get these vegetables on to a charger. I trust I can leave you to add a decent garnish.'

Alpiew looked at the small bowls arranged on the table: fried parsley, cocks' combs, sliced carrots and lemons, and chopped tomatoes.

Pipe came close to Alpiew and whispered as she passed, 'Don't use the tomatoes. We'll eat them when old misery-guts has gone.'

Alpiew dropped the startling pink cocks' combs and slices of carrots at regular intervals over the chargers. Then she arranged small sprigs of parsley around them.

If there was poison flying about Alpiew urgently needed to get a message through to the Countess. She plopped a round yellow disc of lemon in the centre of the largest dish. When she realised that Wackland was staring at her and the bowls, she dipped her fingers into the tomatoes, ready to pretend to use them.

To her surprise her fingers came upon something at the bottom of the bowl that was clearly not a tomato. She waited till Wackland turned to attend to something else then pulled the item out.

It was a ring. Gold, with a ruby.

The table was set up in the next room and Pipe was laying large steaming dishes upon it. The Countess's mouth was watering, everything smelled delicious.

'Are you a meat or fish person?' whispered Lady Murdo-McTavish. 'Or do you yearn for the sweetmeats and puddings?'

'All of it.' The Countess licked her lips, it all looked splendid. 'I love food. But my appetite is somewhat moderated at present.'

'Why so?'

'I'm worried about dear Alpiew. Lady Prude whipped her away this afternoon, and I haven't a notion where to find her.' She didn't like to let on that the real reason was the news that they were trapped here at St Germain.

Pipe swirled in with a tray laden with bottles of wine, and laid them out on a credence table in the corner before heading back towards the kitchen.

'Ask that Irish serving wench next time she comes in. She was the Whippinghams' maid. No doubt they've put your Alpiew in the kitchen with her.'

'What happened to those Frenchmen who were here earlier?' The Countess hovered beside an empty chair. 'I thought they had come here to eat.'

'Obviously changed their minds.' Lady Whippingham strode to the corner table and poured herself another bumper of wine before slamming the bottle down. 'Pompous little farts, anyhow.' Lucy Whippingham caught eyes with Mademoiselle Smith, who was standing with Aurelia, examining the labels on the wine, and added: 'Though we must be grateful to the Marquis de Béchamel for occasionally experimenting upon us.'

Mademoiselle Smith turned and smiled. 'The Marquis is a difficult man, Madame. I agree with you that his behaviour is not the best. But he is a genius in the kitchen.'

'He is investing, I am told.' Lucy Whippingham flopped back into her chair and raised her voice. 'I believe he has a secret deal with my dear husband.'

Lord Whippingham shot his wife a black look.

'God alone knows what they get up to behind closed doors. But sometimes I wonder if my husband isn't open to anything.' She chortled into her glass.

The Countess glanced at Virginia. The irritating girl was still chattering away with Lucy's husband. The Countess pondered. Was the girl obsessed with middle-aged men? Since she had started flirting with Whippingham she seemed so merry. What was it about this fat, grubby man that had set the child constantly upon the grin?

'My lord husband,' screeched Lucy Whippingham, 'do get to the real point of your overtures, dear. Don't you have something you desire to stuff in this pretty girl's mouth?' She gave a hiccup and lurched towards the dining table, turning to wink at the Countess. 'Anywhere but the place designed for it!'

At this moment the main door swung open and Lady Prude

made her entrance, followed by a little pageboy, the door held open by two palace guards. All conversation hushed.

'Here she comes, the wicked old bitch,' muttered Lady Whippingham into her glass, before raising it in a shaky toast towards Lady Prude. 'Got any nice new penances, my Lady Prude, to offer our pretty new guest? I'm hoping you might have the exemplary life of some doleful saint to warn her off meddling with my husband.'

'*In nomine Patris* . . .' Ignoring Lucy Whippingham, Lady Prude crossed herself. '. . . *Filii et Spiritus Sancti, amen.*'

The Countess hung her head and followed the old routine while trying to keep an eye out. Virginia was smirking. Lord Whippingham looked bashful, and Lady Murdo-McTavish seemed deep in prayer. Swaying, Lady Whippingham stared at Virginia during the whole of grace, then turned on her heel and marched to the side table to be first at the food.

Mademoiselle Smith lined up beside Lady Whippingham, ladling food on to her plate.

Lady Prude looked down at the Countess's place. 'You do not carry your own caddinet, madam?'

'Let her have mine,' said Aurelia. 'I shall eat with my fingers, like the King of France.'

'You will do no such thing,' said Lady Prude, slamming her hand down to prevent the caddinet being passed across. 'This is the English court. Keep your own cutlery and we will get some for the Countess.' She nodded at Mademoiselle Smith. 'Run through to the kitchen, please, and ask Lord Wackland for a set of cutlery for Lady Ashby de la Zouche.'

The girl darted off.

The Countess decided that it would be better to make a friend of Miss Brown than an enemy. 'Have you been over here since you were born, Miss Brown?'

'Since I was three,' she replied.

'So you were educated over here?'

'L'Ordre de les Filles de la Vierge.' The girl beamed and

looked around the table. 'The Order of the Daughters of the Virgin.'

She rose and went to collect her food.

Isabel Murdo-McTavish leaned close to the Countess. 'There are some quite formidable convents over here which give impoverished girls an excellent education.'

The Countess looked at the girl, primly digging into the serving dishes, and hoped she didn't cross her, she seemed so confident. More than that even. The girl had an air of euphoria about her.

She looked to her ward: sulky and petulant in comparison. And clearly not averse to making enemies. Lady Whippingham was already giving her the evil eye. And Lady Prude looked none too pleased with her either.

'Virginia,' said the Countess, patting the empty chair at her side. She noticed that Virginia was clutching a knife and two-pronged fork, like everyone else. 'Why don't you come over and sit next to me for supper? I should be delighted to hear the adventures of your first day at St Germain.'

'I'll sit where I like, thank you, madam. You are not my mother, Countess, and now you have no money of your own and are dependent upon me, you are therefore little more than my servant. And as such I order you to leave me alone and keep your nose out of my affairs.'

'There you are!' Plate laden, Lady Whippingham flopped down into the chair the Countess was holding out. 'I knew she was a spoilt little twat! You'll have your work cut out trying to control her, Countess. And as for you, husband dear, she'll have your testicles for a moneybag before you can say "strumpet".'

'Decorum, Lady Whippingham,' hissed Lady Prude. 'And as for you, hussy, I will have you apologise to Lady Ashby de la Zouche, and you will sit next to me for supper. I should point out, Miss Franklyn-Green, that despite your mother's money I could eject you from this chateau whenever I want. It is my understanding that you are to be guided by the Countess and kept away from troublesome elements. I might suggest, Lord

Whippingham, that you are one of those troublesome elements, and I command you forthwith to keep a decent distance between yourself and Miss Franklyn-Green.'

'I'll not have you telling me what to do, you dried-up old hag,' said Lord Whippingham, draining his glass.

'However you like, sirrah. But I will remind you that, like the rest of us, you are dependent upon the pension kindly given you by His Majesty King James here at St Germain. He in turn is dependent upon the pension granted him by His Majesty King Louis at Versailles. I am friendly with and am well respected by both their majesties, whereas you and your little schemes are a laughing stock at both courts.' She sat and flicked open a napkin. 'I leave it at that, my lord. Now, I suggest you eat, while food is still available to you.'

Silently Lord Whippingham went to fetch his caddinet from the corner table. His wife snorted into her food as he passed behind her.

The Countess was longing to get to her paper and quills and set it all down. The Cues, she was sure, would be very pleased with her. Not only that, if she could encourage the helpful and charming bilingual Mademoiselle Smith, she might try to sell a French version to the *Mercure Gallant* and be famous all over Paris. Then she would have money enough to get away from this sanctimonious place and these boorish, self-righteous people with their petty hothouse lusts and jealousies.

Pipe gave Alpiew a grimace as she came back into the kitchen. 'Sounds as though there's much excitement over supper tonight. I could hear raised voices all the way back here.' She flopped down on a bench. 'Where's Old Misery? Gone off chasing the stable-boys?'

Alpiew tipped her head. Wackland was only in the walk-in pantry putting back some jars of seasoning.

'Here, I'll have some of those –' Pipe looked at the tomatoes and winked at Alpiew. She plunged her hand into the bowl and thrust the tomatoes into her mouth.

Alpiew watched, wondering if she'd used some sleight of hand and popped the ring in too.

Wackland swirled into the room.

Pipe sat down and started tying her bootlace.

Alpiew felt sure she had spat out the ring and was now hiding it in her boot.

'No time for sitting, Pipe,' snarled Wackland. 'As Alpiew has worked so hard on her first day, perhaps you would be so kind as to show her how properly to clean the fireplace after herself. It's a filthy mess.'

'A caddinet of cutlery, please,' called Leonora Smith from the doorway. 'For the ancient English lady with flaky paint and a red squirrel on her head for a wig.'

'Less of your badinage, miss.' Alpiew winced. She didn't like to hear the Countess laughed at. She grabbed a knife and spoon. 'Shall I take them in, Lord Wackland? 'Tis my lady the insolent wench means.'

'Absolutely not.' He snatched the cutlery from Alpiew and handed it to the girl. 'Now run along, Mademoiselle Smith.' He swung round to Pipe. 'Don't stand there, gawping. Show Alpiew her duties and then please take in the next tray.'

Pipe gave an inward groan and marched over to the fireplace.

They both knelt.

'Mademoiselle Smith?' hissed Alpiew. 'What kind of name is that?'

'You have to take all these –' Pipe slowly pointed at the metal poles, the dangling hooks, and the cauldrons while murmuring, 'There are so many people over here descended from the English. Remember there were thousands of them during Cromwell's time, and another lot when His Majesty came here. They left their offspring everywhere.' She gave a cough. 'And after they've had time to cool down, out in the courtyard, you wash them down and put them . . . back.'

'Where is she placed in the hierarchy?' Alpiew whisked her brush into the corner.

'She is halfway between us and them. She is staff, so sleeps in our quarters, but passes for straggler, because she is no doubt the daughter of some aristocrat who gave his life fighting for the King or somesuch. Her skills as a translator, though, mean she is called everywhere; she even works up on the second floor sometimes. She is the lower-division Prude.'

She giggled, and Alpiew laughed with her.

As Alpiew laid down her whisk broom, Pipe took a deep breath. She was suddenly very pale. 'She had a decent education – if you call a French convent with the laughable name Daughters of the Virgin an education. Those places more often than not are simply brothels with nuns.' She raised her voice again. 'And while you're waiting, you sweep out the grate, and make sure the fire is –' She dropped the broom, and grabbed at the front of her bodice. Her eyes rolled up into her head and she fell to the ground, her head hitting the flagstones with a loud crack.

Alpiew knelt at her side and tried to loosen her stays. Pipe writhed about for a second before starting to foam at the mouth.

'What are you doing down there, woman?' Wackland bent over Pipe's thrashing body. 'If she is indisposed, Alpiew, then you must needs take in the tray of stewed salads.'

'But, sir . . .' Alpiew gaped down at Pipe. She had heard Wackland talking of poison only minutes before, yet here he was, behaving as though nothing was wrong. 'She is ill!'

'Ill!' Wackland struck Alpiew a blow across the back of her head. 'I won't have talk of illness in my kitchen.'

Alpiew turned, ready to slap Wackland back, then saw that he seemed pale and shaky himself.

'In a minute . . . or two . . .' he gasped '. . . the girl will be better. Now, get that tray into the antechamber.'

'But –'

'I will deal with it. Leave me.'

'But I don't know where to go.' Alpiew hovered. His chopping-changing reactions worried her. 'Surely it is better if I stay here and look after Pipe?'

'It is not your job to give me orders in my own kitchen!' White and swaying slightly, Wackland pointed with one hand and with the other pulled open his cravat. 'I said *leave me.*'

'I find France is still a splendid place for the finer things of life,' said the Countess, munching on a slice of chicken-and-pork pie. 'I was over here as a youngster, during the Puritan times at home. I remember it so well. It is such a gay and bright country. So full of vigour. I have to say I am really looking forward to the balls and masquerades, the fêtes and fireworks.'

Lady Prude tutted.

Mademoiselle Smith had served herself and now sat demurely eating her meal.

'You'll be lucky,' Lady Whippingham slurred. 'The only decent balls round here are on the billiard table, and there's more Puritanical action here than ever there was in England in Cromwell's time.' She polished off her bumper of wine and sloshed more into the glass.

'It is true that times have changed, Countess.' Lady Murdo-McTavish wiped her mouth. 'We do not see much festivity any more. But we make up for it in other ways. Writing, music . . .'

'What do you mean?' Lord Whippingham laid down his fork and bellowed. 'We're kept busy from dawn till dusk. We're expected to be marshalled off into clubs and boring occupations that we're not interested in. We watch each other play billiards, we troop to the music room where someone is squawking out an aria that we have heard a hundred times already. We have our hobbies: playing cards, writing silly stories, learning the lives of the wretched saints, making . . . machines. We go for walks in the gardens and woods, we drink: coffee, tea, wine, every kind of wormwood water and alcoholic tincture to try to make us forget how miserable we are . . .'

'There is a masquerade being held for us next week, if you please, Lord Whippingham,' snapped Prude. 'Both of their majesties are very aware of the necessity for small pleasures in this sad life of exile from our homeland.'

'Oh yes, and masquerades! And if, like me, you don't dance, you sit sweating behind the face of a gargoyle or a wild animal while watching an interminable parade of clodhoppers prancing about to an interminable round of the Cushion Dance, Friday Night, Merry Andrew, Furbeloes and Apricocks, Mad Moll, The Ladies' Delight and any number of irksome capers until the final moments when we troop sullenly around in a line to a quadrille. And only then, at last, are we allowed to indulge in the one item of solace in this dismal place – sleep.'

While Lord Whippingham blustered on, the Countess noticed Isabel Murdo-McTavish methodically slipping bits of food from her plate into a napkin on her lap.

'Nonsense! You mustn't believe him, Countess. We are happy here,' snapped Prude. 'Every saint's day is celebrated with much style and exuberance. Tomorrow, for instance, is the feast-day of St James the Less. And I'm sure next week's masquerade will be enormous fun.'

The Doctor entered. He held the door open for a mousy-looking little woman with a large curved nose, and a pouty red mouth.

'Ah, here we are, I'm afraid. Late again!' He drew up a seat next to the Countess. 'You're new. What fun! How's supper? I'm Stickworth, by the way. Dr Stickworth.'

The mousy lady sat at his other side.

'Delicious.' The Countess noticed Alpiew enter from the other door, bearing a laden tray. She flapped her napkin, trying to get her attention, only to see that Alpiew too was trying to get hers.

'I practise physic the civilised, English way. Over here it's nearer to the more fantastical side of witchcraft than medicine as we know it: all herbs and diets and surgery! I stick to the good old English way: clysters, purges, sweating, applying leeches, cupping, blood-letting. Nothing foreign or unnatural.'

Stickworth winked at Aurelia, who blushed and downed her wine in one gulp.

'Alpiew! Pardon me, Doctor –' the Countess looked towards the corner – 'that's my woman, Alpiew.' She lowered her voice. 'Taken from me by you know who . . .' She rolled her eyes towards Lady Prude.

The Doctor gave an understanding grimace.

Alpiew moved closer to the Countess.

'Excuse me –' Alpiew nodded briskly and addressed Stickworth – 'did I hear you say you are a doctor? Only, Pipe has been taken ill. I'm frightened that she may be poisoned.'

'Poisoned?' Lady Whippingham repeated loudly. 'I say, there's a bit of excitement! It's a while since there's been a poisoning here at St Germain.'

Silence crashed round the table as everyone laid their fork down. Lord Whippingham, pale as a ghost, scraped his chair back. 'Come along, Stickworth.' He was making for the door to the kitchens, grabbing at Alpiew. 'Pipe, you say? Hurry, man.'

'Perhaps the Marquis was right about serving potatoes for dinner.' Mademoiselle Smith followed Whippingham and Stickworth. 'Maybe the French are correct, and they are poison.'

'Bless us and save us!' Lady Murdo-McTavish rose too. The Countess noticed how, with a deft swoop, she dropped her napkin full of food into an open bag at her feet and carefully kicked it under the table, out of sight, then made for the door. 'Pipe, poisoned!' she wailed. 'What kind of a fool can have done that?'

'Who or what is Pipe?' said Virginia, biting into a hunk of pie. 'And why would anyone want to poison it?'

'She's an impish little Irish girl who works in the household department,' said Aurelia, digging into her food. 'Quite pert and funny for a servant wench.'

'I suppose I'd better go and see what has happened to her.' Lady Prude wiped her mouth and slowly rose. The Countess noticed that her hands were shaking. 'It's bound to be a lot of fuss over nothing.'

'Can I come? I've never seen a poisoning.' Virginia followed Lady Prude out, leaving the Countess, Lady Whippingham, Aurelia and the mousy lady with the nose alone around the huge square table.

The Countess looked to the door. If someone was poisoned, she felt she should help. Or at least go and look around.

'Don't go chasing after them,' said the lady with the hooked nose. 'They always make such a to-do, because there is nothing else to entertain them here but creating dramas.'

'Pipe is like a child to Lord Whippingham. People always make a fuss about children.' Aurelia spoke quietly into her plate. 'Do you have children, Countess?'

'My play, my writings . . . but never any infants of the human species, no.' The Countess sighed, trying to cover her relief at the thought of not having the patter of tiny feet echoing through her life. 'But I have Alpiew. She is as good as a child to me.'

'Your husband, has he any?'

'I imagine he's got one in every port from here to Zanzibar, to be frank. But we have been separated for many years, so I know nothing of all that.'

Having finished off the food on her plate, Aurelia went back to the serving table for more.

'Are you the Doctor's wife?' The Countess turned to the little woman with the huge curved nose.

'She should be so lucky!' Lady Whippingham snorted. 'Her husband is a picture. He has to be seen to be believed.'

'I am the Duchesse de Charme.' The mousy woman smiled. 'My husband is the Duc de Charme.'

'How charming.' The Countess thought of the fluttering, teetering dandy with his bangles and beads. 'It's remarkable!' She hoped her face didn't reveal her true feelings, but her mouth had opened so wide a chunk of paint fell from her chin and landed on her lap. '. . . you married a . . . a . . . Frenchman!' In a fluster of embarrassment she decided to follow the others to the kitchen. 'I hope you don't think me rude, but I really should go and see if there's anything I can do . . .'

'All this talk of poison has made me feel quite ill,' said Lady Whippingham. The Countess couldn't help but notice that a sweat had broken out all over Lady Whippingham's face causing her make-up to run in thin red rivulets flowing outward from her lips.

'Take a deep breath,' said the Countess, fearing the woman was about to faint. She whipped out her fan and flapped it towards Lady Whippingham.

Someone was pulling at her skirt. She spun round as Aurelia, plucking at the fabric, lurched forward. 'Oh, madam. Oh lord!' The girl grabbed at the table, bringing her plate and cutlery crashing down around her as she slid from her seat. 'Oh, Countess, help me.' Aurelia, paler than putty, her eyes staring wide, gripped at her stomach. 'Oh my God! The fire in my belly.' She stretched her hand out like a claw and grabbed again at the Countess's dress. 'Help me, please. Oh God, I am dying.'

The Countess looked down at the girl. Her complexion was certainly white as any paint, and her lips were a strange hue: purple, verging on black. As she went into a fit, her huge dark eyes seemed to vibrate in their sockets.

'Don't worry.' The Countess reached for a glass and napkin and dabbed the girl's face. 'It is probably the fright, together with the wine . . .'

Aurelia battled with her, writhing about and grabbing hold of the Countess's hands.

Lady Whippingham looked much improved and was fanning herself as Aurelia slid from her chair to the floor, her body racked now with violent convulsions. A froth oozed from her mouth.

'God!' wheezed Lady Whippingham. 'Someone has done her in.'

'Help ho!' The Countess ran to the door and, crying out for assistance, looked back as Aurelia shuddered violently and then lay still. 'Duchesse . . . fetch someone . . .'

Shivering, the Duchesse rose, but she seemed rooted to the spot.

Aurelia's lips were moving slightly. The Countess bent low to hear her.

Her voice was barely audible, but she seemed to say: 'Wackland's buttered bun.' Then her body arched and went into spasm for a moment. 'The buttered bun,' she murmured again, then lay still.

The Countess laid her shaking fingers against Aurelia's neck, trying to feel for a pulse. The girl's mouth opened and green liquid spurted out.

'Oh, no, no,' said Lady Whippingham. 'Please God, no.' She pulled a piece of paper from her pocket and flung it on the floor. 'The letter was true.'

The Countess picked up the scrappy note and looked at it. There were only four words, written in an erratic hand: 'Tonight I will strike.'

FOUR

*Nonpareil — a kind of small
sugar-plum*

S tickworth knelt over Pipe and placed his hand on her
forehead. She lay still.

'The girl has a good strong pulse.' He rolled up his
jacket and placed it under her head. 'Is she accustomed to taking
fits, Whippingham?'

'Never while in my service. Well, not to my knowledge.
And you know in England we lived in close proximity with
our servants. If she had taken fits, I'm sure I would have
known . . .'

'She is burning up, but I think she will recover. See! Her
colour is returning.' He lifted Pipe and laid her on the huge
table. 'Some air, there.'

Alpiew threw open the outer door, and fanned it until a cool
breeze whipped the flames in the fireplace. 'Is that all right,
Doctor?'

'News of this must not go beyond this room.' Stiff as a
pikestaff, Prude gripped the edge of the table. 'We must not
worry His Majesty unnecessarily. If the Doctor says she will
recover, we must leave it at that. This scare MUST not reach
the Royal Household.'

'Might it have been something the child has eaten?' Lady
Murdo-McTavish peered at the sacks around the floor and jars
on shelves.

'I think the best we can do is return to the dining table.' Stickworth pursed his lips and took a deep breath. 'Or disperse and leave the poor girl to a bit of peace.' He turned fiercely towards Wackland. 'I fear, sir, that you sometimes drive your underlings too hard. This is not Versailles. There is no army of servants here. Do not fool yourself. You have a handful of people doing the work of hundreds.'

'I try to keep standards up.' Wackland raised an eyebrow. 'Does that disturb you?'

A piercing scream vibrated through the room.

'Good God,' said Stickworth. 'What on earth . . . ?'

Alpiew was already running through the antechamber leading to where she had left the Countess.

She burst into the room to find the Countess kneeling on the floor cradling Aurelia's head, Lady Whippingham in a sweat fanning herself, and the little Duchesse standing behind her, howling like a banshee.

'We were diverted from the real scene of the crime,' muttered the Countess into Alpiew's ear. She thrust the note into Alpiew's hand. 'Put this safe. Quickly. Now we must observe. You watch the men, and I the women.'

With a hand from Alpiew she hauled herself to her feet as the rest of the company spilled into the room.

Lady Prude did not appear to notice the corpse on the floor. She strode over to the Duchesse and slapped her into silence. 'What will His Majesty think?' she said, and turned on the Countess. Only then did she see Aurelia. Her hands flew to her mouth and she lost her balance, falling against the table.

Lady Murdo-McTavish and the Doctor stood frozen in the doorway staring down as Lord Whippingham shoved past them and pulled out a chair. He reached out for a glass of wine with a glance to his wife, slopped back in her chair. 'Drunk again, is she?'

'It looks like an apoplexy.' Dr Stickworth knelt at Aurelia's side and felt for a pulse. 'I think I should bleed her.'

'Bleed her?' said the Countess. 'After she is already dead?'

'Who says she is dead, madam?'

'It seems pretty clear to me she has been poisoned. I've seen it before. The convulsions, the ooze from the mouth . . .'

'Poison here?' hissed Lady Murdo-McTavish. 'Not today.' She plunged her hand into her pocket. The Countess wondered whether the Scotswoman did not have a copy of the same note that Lucy Whippingham had just produced.

'Poison, indeed!' The Doctor loosened his cravat. 'I cannot imagine why you mention poison, Countess.'

'Good God!' Whippingham spat a mouthful of wine back into his glass. 'Why would anyone want to poison that pretty little girl? Or any of us, and it come to that.'

The Countess and Alpiew both cast a sidelong glance at Lady Whippingham, still seated and slowly fanning herself. There was a shadow of a smile playing on her lips.

Wackland came into the room.

'Let's not leap to conclusions, everyone.' Beads of sweat lined the Doctor's brow and he wiped them with the back of his hand. 'Poison is not the only cause of sudden death . . .'

'It can't be from my kitchen,' snapped Wackland. 'I oversee everything. Anyhow, if there was contamination from the food, you would all be affected . . .'

'Poor child,' said the Duchesse, kneeling and stroking the dead girl's forehead. 'She was so full of mischief, and now . . .'

'Perhaps an autopsy is in order,' said the Countess. 'Then perhaps you can reassure us, Doctor. Once you have ascertained that the cause of death was not poison we can all feel safe, and Lord Wackland need not feel he has to justify his excellent kitchen.'

'Have I some sturdy men to assist me?' Stickworth looked about the room. Wackland and Whippingham shifted uneasily from foot to foot. 'I don't mean to help with the autopsy,' he shouted. 'I mean to help me carry the girl to a room with a lock upon it so I can get on with it.'

'Enough!' Lady Prude clapped her hands together. 'Might I suggest that the gentlemen get on with their unpleasant duty of removing the body, and the Doctor makes whatever investigations he can, while we women go to the chapel and pray for the poor woman's soul.'

'One minute!' Dr Stickworth stood up, and clicked the outer door shut. 'I think Lord Whippingham and I can manage. Lord Wackland should have a small talk with you.'

As the men bent down to carry out Aurelia's corpse, the ladies started muttering between themselves. The Countess surreptitiously picked up a napkin and filled it with all the rolls on the table, including the half-eaten buttered bun from Aurelia's plate.

'This is most unfortunate.' Lord Wackland clapped his hands for silence.

He looked around the room. The Countess noticed that his hands were shaking. 'I hope you will all maintain discretion. This unfortunate child's death could have dreadful repercussions for us all, as you know. So, no gossip, please. Mistress Alpiew, would you please return to the kitchen.'

Alpiew shrugged and made her way out. Virginia started sobbing and made to follow her. Wackland blocked her path.

'That is the door to the kitchen, madam. You are heading the wrong way.' He nodded towards the Countess.

'It's that ruddy Frenchman and his fancy sauces,' slurred Lady Whippingham. 'Cock's-comb sauce, entrails sauce, pea sauce . . . Whatever next? Why can't we have a simple English gravy?'

'The Marquis tastes everything he prepares,' said Mademoiselle Smith quietly. 'I assure you, his food is entirely safe.'

'You heard the Doctor!' Wackland raised his voice and the Countess thought he might hit Mademoiselle Smith. 'The child died of an apoplexy.'

'Bit young for something like that, wouldn't you say?' snarled Lady Whippingham. 'Why, the girl was young enough to be my daughter. Whoever heard of a child that age suffering an apoplexy?'

'Enough!' Lady Prude stepped between Wackland and Lady

Whippingham. 'There is no point quibbling about this matter. The Doctor is in charge and the best thing we can do is retire to the chapel and pray for the poor girl's soul.'

Isabel Murdo-McTavish stooped and picked up her bag from under the table.

The Duchesse and Mademoiselle Smith pulled their mantillas from their pockets and left the room.

The Countess followed, walking along with Virginia. She put her arm round her, but Virginia wriggled away.

'I could try to arrange for us to go home to London . . . ?'

'You go, if you like, you interfering harridan. Though I doubt you'll make it to London in one piece.'

'But if it is not safe here . . .'

'I'm safe, madam, believe me.'

'But . . .' The Countess felt a rising panic. She couldn't leave Virginia here alone, and yet, even if the girl came, where would they go? If what Lady Whippingham had told her was true, they could not return to England.

'You go where you like, madam. I want to stay here at St Germain.' Virginia jerked away from her. 'And no one is going to take me away from here until I decide to go.'

The Countess sat on her bed. She could not sleep. Her head was spinning from the events of the last two days.

Lady Prude had taken prayers for an hour and then dispatched everyone to their rooms. Although the Countess had urgently wanted to see Alpiew, it was impossible without making a scene. She had decided that the most important thing was to fade into the shadows, to remain as inconspicuous as she possibly could.

Pigeons shuffled about on the roof. Apart from that it was silent.

Checking that the buns were safely wrapped and hidden under the bedclothes, she put a wrapper on over her nightclothes and left the chamber, determined somehow to find Alpiew in this labyrinthine building.

Through the thin walls of the wooden garret corridor she could hear snoring. She tiptoed down the stairs and made her way through the antechambers leading towards the main staircase. At the top of the stairs she paused. She could hear low voices murmuring below. A man and a woman. She craned forward to listen.

The echo caused by the high ceiling and stone walls let her catch clearly only the odd word, some in English, some in French: shop, *papier*, *difficile*, tomorrow.

There seemed to be some parting exchange, then she heard the great door quietly open and close, then footsteps, coming towards her up the stairs.

She stepped back into the shadow and pressed herself into a doorway as a man walked briskly past.

He came so close she had no difficulty in seeing that it was Lord Whippingham.

She waited in the doorway until the footsteps were gone, then tiptoed down the stone steps and made her way through the dark billiards room.

She opened the door to the fatal antechamber in which they had eaten the previous evening, stepped inside and quietly clicked the door shut behind her. Then she froze. She could hear a rustling in the corner. She couldn't see a thing in the dark shuttered room, but she was certain someone else was in here.

She held her breath, and realised the other person must be doing the same.

The minutes ticked away, neither the Countess nor the other moving. The Countess was getting more accustomed to the darkness, but she could only make out dim shapes: the table, the chairs. The other person must be crouching, perhaps under the table. She began to wonder how long she could go on standing against the door, not moving, barely breathing. What if the two of them stayed there all night till dawn broke and the room flooded with sunlight? Perhaps she should make a break for it and stroll casually across the room and out through the far door.

No, there was only one thing to do, and that was to face up to whoever it was, challenge the lurking unknown.

She made ready to run, and silently prepared the door handle, all set to make a hasty exit should it be necessary.

She cleared her throat, and spoke in a forthright whisper: 'I know you're there. Come out and explain yourself.'

The unidentified person let out a strange sound, muffled and low. Was it sobbing? A rustling under the table and suddenly the person was standing right beside her. The Countess could feel the warm breath against her décolletage. She prepared to flee.

'It's me,' said Alpiew. 'What are *you* doing here?'

They both grabbed on to each other and let out sighs of relief.

'What a day!' whispered the Countess. 'It's been a veritable nightmare.'

'How do you feel about leaving France, madam? Going home?'

Quietly they pulled out chairs and sat.

'If we go right away they'll think *we* killed her,' whispered the Countess. 'Besides, I'm told that after a sojourn here at St Germain it's difficult to get home to England without being arrested the moment you arrive and marched off to the Tower for treason.'

'What?' Alpiew's voice burst through the quiet. They both went ssshhh and sat silently listening for a moment.

'I'll explain when we get out of this dreadful place. What will we do for money? We won't get far without a pistole between us.'

'We could try to find your friend the Duchesse de Pigalle,' said Alpiew. 'Perhaps we could work for her until we have enough money to get us home. Do you know where she is?'

'She owns land at the foot of the hill called Mont Martre. I presume she built her wretched school there.'

'We'll find a way to survive. We always do.' Alpiew shifted her chair to face the Countess. 'Who do you think killed her? I expect it's something to do with the thefts that are going on here. There was a ruby ring stolen tonight, and it was in the kitchen. I've spent hours searching to find it again, but it's gone, so someone in there has got to be involved.'

'The theft of a ring?' The Countess tried to put that theory into her own hypothesis. 'Then perhaps it is someone who works in the kitchen, for as she died Aurelia talked of "Wackland's buttered bun". I have all the bread rolls,' said the Countess. 'They're tucked up in my bed. Tomorrow I'd like to take them to an apothecary or someone in Town who might be able to analyse them.'

'I watched him make them this afternoon. There was certainly nothing about his manner to suggest there was anything wrong with them. But he did seem very perturbed when Pipe fell into a fit. I wonder whether Pipe's fit was staged for cover, to get everyone out of the room while the poison took effect?'

'This place is full of very odd people. That drunken Lady Whippingham didn't seem at all perturbed that her husband's doxy had met such an end. In fact she was smiling as they carried the girl out. But then she had had a threatening note.' The Countess crawled about, feeling under the table for Isabel Murdo-McTavish's bag. 'I saw another woman slopping her food into her bag. She must have *known* it wasn't fit for eating.'

'When you think about it, everyone seemed nervous this evening, as though they knew something was going to happen.'

'Perhaps others had the warning note, too. But who is to believe what in this dismal place?'

'I wouldn't trust any of them, milady.' Alpiew poked about under the table. 'I'll see what I can do to go to Town tomorrow too. Perhaps once there I'll find a way to get us enough for a fare to Calais.'

'The way I'm feeling, I'd walk it,' said the Countess. 'Barefoot and naked.'

'Me too. What of Virginia? Should we take her?'

'The girl tells me she wants to stay.' The Countess sighed.

'And frankly, if that's what she wants, maybe we should leave her here. We have only been paid our expenses, after all.'

'And that was taken from us on the road.'

'Moreover, it seems the ghastly Mrs Franklyn-Green knew perfectly well she was sending not only her daughter but you and me into perpetual exile.'

'We will get home.' Alpiew shuddered. 'We'll find a way.'

'I'm going to write about the characters here, Alpiew. Perhaps there'll be some printer in Town who could use it for the local news-sheet.'

'I have done so already!' Alpiew plunged her hand down into her cleavage and pulled out a sheet of paper. 'Here – I daren't leave anything hanging about back there in the servants' dormitory. Everyone's forever poking about into each other's things.'

The Countess took the crumpled note and crammed it into her pocket. 'I'll do my best to sell it tomorrow.'

'In case we fail to meet up, milady, shall we plan to make our escape tomorrow night? Let us meet at the foot of the great staircase and fly.'

The door flung open and candlelight flooded the room. Neither had heard the approaching footsteps. 'Aha!' Lady Prude held the candlestick before her, her shadow dancing upon the wainscot. 'What conspiracy is hatching here?' Her hair was wrapped in a night-cloth, and she wore a long velvet wrap-over gown. 'They say inevitably a murderer will return to the scene of the crime.'

'It's nothing like that.' The Countess rose and looked her in the eye. 'We were both hugely upset by what happened this evening. We wanted to speak to each other. Despite the hierarchy which rules here, Lady Prude, Alpiew is no mere servant to me. She is my friend and confidante. I needed to speak to her.'

Lady Prude looked them both up and down. 'Perhaps I will take you at your word, Countess.' She held the candle aloft. 'Back to your beds now. It will be a long day tomorrow. Preparations for Aurelia's funeral will have to get under way immediately.'

75

'Why the haste?' said the Countess, making to leave.

'The weather is hot, madam. It would be inadvisable to leave a corpse hanging about.'

'Do you know the result of Dr Stickworth's investigation?'

'Yes, Countess.' Lady Prude took Alpiew by the arm. 'The girl died of an apoplexy. Just as the Doctor surmised.'

Before they went their separate ways, Alpiew's and the Countess's eyes met. They knew Lady Prude was lying.

The Countess pushed the door open and flopped down on to her bed. She took a deep breath and lay back.

'Dreadful, isn't it? The whole business is grim beyond description.'

The Countess sat bolt upright.

Lady Murdo-McTavish struck a light with her tinder-box and lit a rush candle. 'I'm sorry if I startled you, Countess. I couldn't sleep, and thought I'd come and talk.'

'Ur, yes . . .' said the Countess.

'Where did you get to at this late hour?'

'I was . . .' The Countess racked her brain for a reasonable excuse to cover her tracks. 'I was out using the close-stool.'

'But there is one here in the room.'

'I know, but I prefer not to foul the air at night.'

'I'm much the same. Especially at times of stress.' Lady Murdo-McTavish leaned forward. 'Countess, Virginia has told me all about your exploits in London. Apparently you have some reputation tracking down murderers. I'm sure you must have a theory. Do you really think Aurelia was poisoned?'

The Countess paused, then decided to keep to the official line.

'No. I suspect it was an apoplexy.'

'But you said . . .'

'I know nothing of medicine. But there had been such talk before dinner of poisonings here in the past that my imagination ran wild.'

'I suppose you're right. Where would one get poison, for a

start?' Isabel Murdo-McTavish shrugged. 'No one from the chateau would go to the poison woman in Town nowadays. Not after the other cases. The *gens d'armes* rifled the woman's rooms and took all the names in her address book. Everyone in it was apprehended, and most of them executed. No one's going to risk that again.'

'So, Isabel, were you here during the last spate of poisonings?'

'Of course not.' Lady Murdo-McTavish laughed. 'That was when the French court was here at St Germain. It was King Louis's mistress at the bottom of it all. A saga of love philtres and getting rid of rivals – you know the stuff. Almost unbelievable in its twists and turns. Much weirder than we writers dream up for our fictions.'

We writers! The Countess winced. Perhaps it was preferable talking about murder than Lady Murdo-McTavish and her writing.

'I knew it was going to happen,' said Isabel Murdo-McTavish. 'I had a note.'

'"Tonight I will strike"?' asked the Countess.

'How on earth did you . . . ?'

'You weren't the only one to receive such a note, Lady Murdo-McTavish.' Despite herself, the Countess wanted to find out more. 'Who do you think sent you the note?'

'That would be impossible to say.' Isabel Murdo-McTavish leant back. The Countess suspected she did not want this conversation to go much further. 'Notes pass around constantly here. There are so many intrigues.'

'Does everyone get them?'

'I get them, and I know of another who does. For years I've had those ones. They may be anonymous, but they might as well have been signed. This last week, however, the notes have been different. Different hand, different style. And I am certain they are from a different person.'

The Countess couldn't help wondering if Isabel wasn't referring to a sort of blackmail. 'You think all this trouble is to do with Love? From my experiences of my only day here, there is not much love between anybody.'

'Not on the surface. All love-making, even a little agreeable flirtation, is severely proscribed in this melancholy place. Though, to my mind, in the whole of Cupid's realm there is nought more beautiful, more dangerous, nor more inspiring than the sad people who live here in this chateau.' Isabel Murdo-McTavish sighed. 'Do you think it was Lucy Whippingham? Do you think she killed the girl for flirting with her husband?'

'I think we should leave it to the officials here to decide.' The Countess didn't want to be dragged into anything. As long as the day passed without incident, by this time tomorrow she would be on her way. She climbed into bed.

'Lady Prude tells me your play was entitled *Love's Last Wind*.'

'Mmm. That's right,' said the Countess, snuggling into her pillow. '*Love's Last Wind*.'

'I wish I had known you then, for I think it would have carried better with a different title. I would have suggested something more ætherial . . .'

'The night is almost gone, Isabel. Are you not tired?'

'Gone! That's the word. *Gone With the Wind*. That has the ring of success to it.'

The Countess rolled over. *Gone With the Wind*, indeed! It was a pity that Isabel Murdo-McTavish couldn't take the hint and be gone with the wind herself. You could see why the woman had never been published. The Countess gave a wide yawn. 'Ah me, Morpheus beckons!' She lay back on the bed. 'Excuse me, Isabel, but a strange overpowering wave of tiredness has suddenly hit me.'

But Isabel Murdo-McTavish ploughed on regardless. 'I gather you write *The Grand Cyrus*-type stuff, Countess: *romans à clef*, scandal sheets, etcetera. I was thinking of going into that field myself, but I feel it's on the way out. The fairy tale is the future, I believe. I tread in the hallowed footsteps of Monsieur Perrault and Madame D'Aulnoy.'

78

The Countess feigned a snore. Would the woman witter on all night?

'Puss in Boots, Tom Thumb, Cendrillon, Little Red Riding Hood, The Blue Bird . . . I plan to wander through the woods and quiz all the old women who live in tumbledown shacks in the middle of nowhere with only rats and cats and squirrels for company, until I have my own collection of folk tales. Perhaps one day you will join me?'

To her infinite delight, the Countess felt herself sliding softly into sleep.

Alpiew arose at dawn to light the kitchen fire. Shortly afterwards a great banging on the doors presaged the arrival of a cartload of refugees. Alpiew sighed her relief as Wackland directed a surly-looking boy to the post of turnspit.

'Lord Wackland, sir,' said Alpiew, 'as Pipe is still not well, and it will be necessary for certain items to be brought in from the market, might I propose myself for the job?'

'Pish, woman!' sneered the maître d'hôtel. 'You have no French, and no experience.'

'Not true, sir. I was marketing maid for the Duchesse de Pigalle.'

Wackland cocked an eyebrow. 'Olympe Pigalle? The darling of the courts of France and England? She must be a century old.'

'Olympe Athenée Montelimar, Duchesse de Pigalle.' Alpiew stared him out. In fact she had shopped at St James's Market *one* morning for Pigalle, but how was he to know that? 'And she is in her mid-sixties, I believe, sir. Though to some of her younger admirers she only admits to thirty.'

'How is she?' Wackland gave a knowing smile. 'Still the same eccentric Olympe?'

'Much as usual, sir. Fencing practice at dawn in male attire, her London house doubles as a menagerie, she gambles till the early hours, always in a sequinned mask . . .'

'All right, Mistress Alpiew.' Wackland gazed around the

room at the gawping newcomers. 'To work, you lot, if you want feeding. I will give you a list. Cheapen everything you can, and get it delivered. It is now six o'clock. I will expect deliveries to start rolling in by eight.'

When the Countess awoke she found Lady Murdo-McTavish lying asleep upon the other bed, so whilst she had the chance she crammed the dinner rolls into a reticule and made a dash for it. It was her intention to get out into Town and spend as little time with these dreadful people as possible before her escape this evening. She shoved her quill, some ink and paper into her bag and made her way out of the chateau.

'Countess, did you sleep well?' The Duchesse de Charme grabbed the Countess by the elbow as she walked out on to the parterre. 'My husband and I tossed and turned all night with worry.'

'I know, the whole business is too frightful to contemplate.' And rather than get embroiled in another whodunit session, she picked up the cue from the Duchesse. 'I haven't had the pleasure of meeting your husband yet.'

'Monsieur the Duc spends much of his time at Versailles. There are two kings in such close proximity, but obviously it is more useful for him as a Frenchman to ingratiate himself with his own monarch.' She lowered her voice. 'Should we add: paying court to the King who actually *has* a throne.'

'Do we never even get a glimpse of His Majesty King James on our floor of the house?'

'Not really, except when the French King pays his devoirs. I gather King James spends most of his time with his children or in prayer,' said the Duchesse. 'Since the catastrophic Irish expedition, the Boyne, the rout at Aughrim . . .' She crossed herself. 'Have you ever met King William the Usurper?'

'I myself am not partial to Dutchmen as a whole, but I did meet King William once, and he seemed pleasant enough, although short. And Dutch.'

'Pleasant, yes.' The Duchesse gave a knowing nod. 'I had heard the same. Are you walking into Town?'

'I thought I'd take a look at the shops.' The Countess hoped she could shake the woman off. She had things to do in Town and did not need company. 'I remember the place only vaguely from my days as a girl when my family were in that other exile.'

'Then I shall walk with you,' said the Duchesse, linking arms. 'I myself was too young to be a refugee of the Commonwealth years, but my parents, of course . . .' She pulled herself closer and spoke in a low voice: 'Why have they buried that girl hugger-mugger?'

Back on to the wretched death of Aurelia. The Countess did not want to commit herself to any opinion. 'I don't know the customs over here . . .'

'She was buried before dawn this morning, with precious little ceremony, and we are all forbid to talk of it. Personally, I am sure she was poisoned.' The Duchesse squeezed the Countess's arm and steered her across the bustling road towards the centre of Town. 'Truthfully, Countess, don't you?'

A flock of geese waddled across their path, a white-smocked boy driving the flapping creatures forward with a cane.

'It could be anything,' said the Countess, side-stepping a steaming pile of horse manure. 'I am no medical expert.'

'I am sure whatever happened it was intentional. I received a note yesterday afternoon, you know . . .'

Not another! The Countess wondered whether every woman in the chateau had had one.

'My theory, Countess, is this: I think that someone at the chateau – and I might add, someone at *our* end of the chateau – bought some poison and polished off that poor girl.'

The town was buzzing. Wagons laden with barrels of wine, bundles of hay, and crates of vegetables rolled up the rue de la Paroisse.

'There is something most disturbing about the whole business, I agree. What of Aurelia's family? What will they make of it?'

'That's the thing.' The Duchesse looked about her as though worried she might be overheard. 'She was an orphan.'

A farmer turned into the main road. He was driving a dozen sheep before him. The Countess took a step back to make sure her feet were not trampled. 'Still no reason to pretend she didn't exist at all, I would have thought.'

'Yes, but you see, Countess, Stickworth and the men are agreed that the news of a poisoning must not get to Versailles. For, if it does, justice will be swift and arbitrary. Someone will be beheaded or burnt at the stake and we will all be sent on our way. Louis is not happy with the English rebels any more. He is only looking for a way to disperse us. This could be just the excuse he has been waiting for.'

'Disperse the English? Where to? Lucy Whippingham tells me no one can return home to England and expect a warm welcome.'

'We couldn't go home, no. We would all be displaced. We should have to become itinerants, wandering from country to country, begging on the clemency of others, dependent on no one taking sides with King William.'

'But surely *you* would be all right, Duchesse? You are married to a Frenchman.'

'Yes,' said the Duchesse.

'Court life here is certainly different from the old days.' The Countess thanked God she was shortly going to get away from the place. 'Lady Prude, for instance, does seem singularly without charm. Very masculine. Her face needs only a set of mustachios and she would make a striking fellow.'

'She keeps the place together, in her way. I like France, but I would love to go home – whoever is king in England.' The Duchesse manoeuvred her way past a row of itinerant lace sellers. 'It's when you see the tawdry stuff which passes for ribbon nowadays that you miss the French Huguenots. You must see a lot of their wonderful silk goods now in London.' She paused to finger a ribbon seller's wares. 'It's odd, isn't it? On the whim of a pair of Kings, thousands of French

Protestants were exiled to England and thousands of English Catholics exiled to France.' She moved on, pushing into the thronging street market. 'I think the English got the better bargain, for the French are superior cooks and surpass us at fashion. Whereas we English, what are we good for?'

'You? Are you new here?' A passing woman draped all in black grabbed on to the Countess's sleeve. 'Would you grant me a pension? I am a poor widow and my funds ran out . . .'

'Thank you, Madame Gardner –' the Duchesse pried the woman's fingers loose – 'the Countess is no more in a position to lend money than you are.' She marched the Countess away. 'I'm sorry about that, Countess. Poor woman, she approaches everyone for money. She's been wearing those weeds for ten years. She is poor, true, but no worse off than many others here.'

'Is there an apothecary hereabout?' The Countess gazed at the swinging row of shop signs, searching for a Galen's Head or Unicorn. She rued the moment she had ever agreed to come here, and was thankful she would soon be gone. 'There are some trifles I require.'

'I imagine it's old Mère le Sage you're really looking for, is it not?' The Duchesse pursed her rosebud lips and gave the Countess a penetrating look. 'The expert on secret matters.'

'I'm sure I don't know who you mean.' The Countess did her best to look ingenuous, but only succeeded in smudging her eyeblack so that it smeared up as far as her brows.

'The poison woman. She works in there –' The Duchesse indicated a dark doorway, set slightly back from the road. 'I saw you take the bread rolls from the dining table last night.'

'I was peckish.' The Countess gave a girlish smile. 'I always like to have a little something to eat in bed.'

'Mmm, of course.' The Duchesse pursed her lips again and the Countess was aware how plump and red they were. Like a cherry. She was a strange-looking woman, to be sure, with that little red mouth and the great hooked nose. 'And I like a bit of hemlock to get me off to sleep too. In you go. I won't tell anyone, but you must let me know what you find out. If there is a poisoner on the loose, I want to be warned.' The Duchesse gathered up her skirts and swished off into the crowd, turning and calling, 'Good luck to you, Countess.'

Alpiew had had a good morning. Many of the market traders seemed to speak tolerable English; many were English refugees. It was a relief to be out of the claustrophobic court kitchens and strolling through a pretty town on a sunny day. She was highly amused by the shop signs of France. Whereas in England you could see a row of Unicorn's Heads, Cross Keys, and Civet Cat and Three Herrings, here you found *Au faune qui boit, Le Chien qui fume, Le boeuf sur le toit*, which plainly from the paintings were the deer who drank, the dog who smoked and the bull on the roof. What on earth these things might signify she did not trouble to discover, but useless as the phrases might be in daily conversation they did give her her first French lesson.

She had already fulfilled her duties, and now intended chasing around after any ways of making money quickly so that she and the Countess could get away. There was always something, and that something didn't always have to involve sexual exploits. She could sell her hair, perhaps, or run around delivering letters or messages for the afternoon.

Unfortunately most of the notices pinned up in shop windows were in French with no accompanying illustrations, leaving her none the wiser.

As she crossed the main road she noticed a gaggle of women bowling along towards her. These women looked to Alpiew as though they were on their way to work, so she tagged along in the hope they would lead her somewhere she could offer her services for the afternoon.

The women turned off the street into a dark alley. Alpiew stayed close. They all trooped into an unmarked doorway and disappeared along a long, unlit corridor.

Alpiew hung around outside for a moment, then smoothed her skirt down and her hair back and prepared to enter. She pushed the door open, but some people were coming along the narrow hallway in her direction, so she stepped back outside to make way.

A well-dressed woman, laughing and looking very pleased with herself, came out into the alley. 'It's so exciting,' she called to someone behind her. 'I adore that we can romp secretly like this.' She turned and looked back along the passageway. 'And all those girls sucking and chewing! To think that we can make ourselves rich from such a thing. You are a genius, my dear.'

Lord Whippingham stepped out into the light. He was grinning from ear to ear. 'My dear lady, I am delighted to be able to pleasure you so.'

Alpiew held a handkerchief up to her nose, hoping it would look natural and would prevent Lord Whippingham from recognising her as he passed.

'Where did you find all those dreadful women? I doubt at the Court of le Roi Jacques.'

'Now there is a thought!' Whippingham gave a little laugh. 'I tried it out yesterday on my wife. She was not amused!'

'I am impressed with the girls you are using.' The woman eased herself out of the door. 'They have picked up the tricks of the trade very quickly.'

'You should know by now, this town is full of desperate people who will do *anything* for a few sous.' He pulled the door shut. 'Now, good lady, let me see you to your carriage, and in a few days we will behold the beautiful product of our splendid union.'

'Everyone who is anyone at Versailles will be begging us to satisfy them.' The woman threw back her head and spread her arms. 'The great Sun King will tremble at our feet. How could he resist?'

Laughing, the two linked arms and made their way out into the street. Alpiew was torn: should she follow the joyous fellow? Why? She and the Countess would be leaving tonight. If the nasty slubberdegullion was up to no good, it was none of her business. And anyhow, within hours she would be away from here and by the morning the whole thing would mean nothing to her.

However, out of curiosity she couldn't refrain from taking an investigative peek inside to see where they had come from and, more to the point, to find out what they were at.

At the end of the dark corridor was a door. Through it she could hear a humming noise, like a score of voices murmuring. She turned the handle. The humming stopped. The room was crammed full of women, all poorly dressed, all sitting. As one, they instinctively covered their mouths. One leapt from her seat and filled the doorway. She wiped the back of her hand across her lips and ran her tongue over her teeth.

'Yes?' she said, then spat sideways into a bucket just inside the door. 'What do you want?'

'I wondered if there were any jobs going?'

'No,' said the woman. 'Now, we're busy, so off you go.' She slammed the door in Alpiew's face.

The Countess mounted the dark rickety staircase to Mère le Sage's shop. The door at the top was decorated with cabalistic symbols, so she was certain the Duchesse had directed her to the right place.

She knocked and a high-pitched voice squawked '*Entrez!*' while a dog barked enthusiastically.

She pushed the door open.

Although it was daylight, the shutters were drawn and the room was lit by a number of smoky tallow candles. The interior was much the same as any London astrologer: bats pinned to the ceiling, silver stars on the wall and stuffed creatures baring their teeth from every shelf in the place. At the Countess's knee a black dog joined in the general snarl.

'*Tenez*, Lucifer!' The woman sitting behind the huge black-and-gold table was old and lined. As she spoke, the dog sat back quietly. Her wispy hair was held up in a sparkling scarf, and her sallow skin was so wrinkled she resembled a walnut with the black eyes of a rat.

'*Asseyez*,' snapped the ancient woman.

'English,' said the Countess, gingerly lowering herself on to the precarious three-legged stool. '*Anglais.*'

'I understand,' said the woman. Her accent was slight, though she substituted her '*r*'s with '*w*'s. 'What is it that you desire? Bigger breasts, thinner thighs, to bewitch a man until he is in love with you?'

'You speak very good English,' said the Countess, momentarily considering whether she might not try one of the spells for longer legs or thicker hair.

'For eleven years now the English have been my only clients, bar a couple of demented locals. If you want the trade, you adapt. Besides, it was easy for me; it only took one simple potion to give me the gift of tongues. So, what do you desire?' The old woman peered across the table. 'A new head of hair? To grow taller?'

The Countess wondered whether the woman was reading her mind. 'There has been some strange activity at the Court of King James . . .'

'Amaze me,' snapped Mère le Sage.

'Last night at the chateau a young woman died.' The Countess tipped the bread rolls on to the table. 'I believe she was poisoned.'

'Really! Another poisoning at the chateau after all these years!' A bony hand snatched out and grabbed one of the rolls. 'They did not buy any poison from me. I stopped selling poisons many years ago. And you suspect the bread?' She peered at the rolls. 'This one has a bite taken out of it, so I presume . . .'

The Countess nodded.

'Did she die quickly?' Le Sage was peering closely at the roll. 'Convulsions? Oozing from the mouth?'

'All of those. It was so sudden. We were barely sat down. She started eating and was dead in less than five minutes.'

The ancient woman picked up the roll and tossed it in the air. With one bound the dog leapt up and swallowed it whole.

'But . . . Evidence!!! I need that roll . . .' The Countess gaped with horror as the dog licked his lips and looked keenly towards the table, ready for another.

'What is it you really want from me?'

'The buns,' said the Countess. 'I need to . . .'

'Not firmer thighs? Or perhaps a little potion to see off a rival? Or do you want to enhance your sexual allure?'

Feeling like a fish in a bowl at a Royal Society aquatic exhibition, the Countess wished her mouth would stop opening and closing.

'Once I could provide a nice stealthy concoction to bring the sturdiest among us to a swift quietus. Sadly, I don't dabble in that area any more. But I would make a fortune if I could provide a poison as efficacious as you describe.' Her eyes seemed to stab at the Countess's thoughts. 'Perhaps I should draw up your horoscope. A journey over water? Am I right? That is what you desire. But how often have you been told: desire leads us to temptation, and we all know where temptation leads us.' The seer turned to her dog with a smirk. 'Don't we, Lucifer?'

'I only wanted to know about the bread rolls,' said the Countess, rising. 'That's all.'

'Yip, yip, boy!' Mère le Sage grabbed the remaining rolls one by one and threw them to the dog. 'Yip, yip! Isn't that good and tasty?' She leant back in her chair and threw the Countess another piercer. 'Does that answer your question? A dog might die at once, but a human would linger a while longer.'

The Countess was already at the door.

'I won't charge you this time. I know you have no money. Those nasty boys, what a horrid trick to play. But that's all it was. A prank with a twist. Good morning to you. And *au revoir*.'

Back in the kitchen, Alpiew was pleased to see Pipe, fit and well, sitting at the work-table taking a cup of small beer.

'How was Town?' said Pipe. 'I'm glad you had a chance to get out.'

Alpiew told her about the room full of women. She decided

to keep the bit about Lord Whippingham to herself. 'What do you think is going on in there?'

'I should think it's a Jack House. That's what most property owners round here do to make money these days.'

'Jack House? What's that?'

'English refugees, like you and me, don't always get a bed when they turn up here, as you know. Madame Prude doesn't always agree to provide a home. So they go to Town and rent a room. Well, at the start it was that, but so many have come, and the town hasn't got any bigger, so now they pay per person for shelter and somewhere to lay their head at night. I've heard that some tiny houses have seventy or eighty occupants.'

'Who gets all the money?'

'The courtiers at Versailles.' Pipe tipped the end of her nose. 'They can't believe their luck. They bought houses here, because this was the French Court, and they wanted to ooze their sycophancy within the orbit of the King of France. But when Louis and his court moved to Versailles, their houses lost all their value. Some had borrowed to buy here; they'd put all their country lands and chateaux in hock to do so, and now had no hope of recouping. Lucky for them, the Netherlander took over the throne in England, King James fled here, and suddenly there was a new way of making money out of those empty, unsellable properties – renting rooms to Jacobite refugees from Britain.' She slammed the leather cup down. 'I imagine poor Catholic runaways are providing many a noble equipage to impress the French King.'

'Those women looked depressed, that's for sure. But it's strange,' said Alpiew. 'It seemed to me that they were in there eating, but there was no smell of food. And they all had a look about them. An air of desperation.'

Mademoiselle Smith bustled into the kitchen.

'Please can we remove all the potatoes before the Marquis gets here. I don't want him shouting at me if he gets to hear about last night's . . .' Her voice drifted off.

'Aurelia was an old friend of yours, wasn't she?' asked Alpiew. 'It must be awful for you.'

'What on earth gave you that idea?' Mademoiselle Smith was rifling through the boxes, searching for potatoes. 'We knew each other, yes. Because we are both here at the court. But I have only known her a week, like everyone else.'

'I thought you were at school together?' Alpiew decided to help in the potato hunt. 'I was told you went to school at the Order of the Daughters of the Virgin?'

'I was. But if she really was there, I don't remember her.' Mademoiselle Smith gave Alpiew a strange look. 'Maybe she was there, for all I know. Perhaps in another class.'

Alpiew dived under a bench and pulled out another box. 'So you didn't know her before?'

'Are you insinuating something?' Mademoiselle Smith stood up and wiped her hands down the sides of her skirts. 'Are you accusing me of . . .' She flopped down on to a bench. 'I didn't do anything to her. I tell you, I never saw the woman until last week. She was nothing to me.'

'Here –' Alpiew hauled out a crate. 'Here are your potatoes. But I say it is a dreadful waste if you throw them out. There are hungry people in this town, and this box could feed a lot of them.'

From her seat at the work-table, Pipe sniggered.

The printer's shop was more demure than the Cues' set-up in London. There was no filthy yard up a dark alley, nor a hot dirty room with Mr Cue, black with ink, rolling out paper and lining up print. All of these messy activities must happen behind the scenes. The St Germain printer's shop stood in an elegant street, and the sign hanging above the door was a beautifully painted figure of St Martin and a quill. The Countess brushed a wisp of hair from her forehead and stepped inside. A sprightly man in a satin suit stood behind a polished mahogany counter.

'*Parlez Anglais?*' The Countess felt nervous addressing this chic little fellow in his powdered periwig and satin suit.

'But of course,' said the man with an ingratiating smile. 'This is St Germain. The alternative capital of Great Britain. We publish an English paper for the refugees.'

The Countess pulled the writings out of her reticule. In these surroundings her tattered and ink-dashed papers looked filthy and amateurish. With a coy, apologetic wince she slid them over the counter. 'I wonder if you will buy some news about the English court at the chateau?'

'Certainly.' The man thrust a pair of eyeglasses upon his nose. 'News from England I pay more for. If you have any of that, I can give you a better price.' He skimmed down the page and slid it back. 'Nothing in there to amuse, I'm afraid. Old news, all of it.'

'But . . .' The Countess gaped down at the paper in horror. She needed the money. 'I could scratch out some stuff about London. We were there only a couple of days ago . . .'

'Not for me. I'm sorry, style not polished enough. We don't tend to publish much by amateurs.'

'But I . . .'

'Good day to you.' The man had whipped round the counter and was holding the door open for the Countess. 'Maybe you should try a little sewing, or handicrafts to dawdle away your time here.'

The Countess opened her mouth, but decided to say nothing more as she stepped out into the busy street.

She felt a tug on her sleeve. 'Would you grant me a pension? I am a poor widow and my funds . . .'

Alpiew sat outside the kitchen door on a stack of crates. The sun was shining, and she was happy. Only a few more miserable hours and they would be on their way. It was the quiet time of the afternoon and Alpiew wouldn't be needed for half an hour. She had been looking for the Countess but found she was still out, so for her remaining ten minutes she was going to lounge about and get herself geared up for a long walk tonight.

Her face was burning and so she shifted the crates nearer to the door to get out of the direct sunlight. She positioned herself tightly into the corner. She didn't want to get a red peeling face and sore arms.

She curled her feet up and shut her eyes.

A dog somewhere started yapping.

She swivelled round a bit more and ducked her head in against the door to avoid the sun catching her neck. She let herself drift off for a minute.

'You handled it all wrong . . .'

Alpiew smiled to herself. Inside she could hear Lady Prude giving Wackland a ticking off.

'You should have let me deal with her.'

'But she's my own flesh and blood.'

'Really!' Lady Prude gave a scornful laugh. 'You should have thought about that years ago. Not now when she is come back to haunt you.'

'I was young . . .'

'We were *all* young then, sirrah. Now, if you know what's good for you, you will let me put an end to it once and for all. Have you seen her?'

'No. The arrangement is I leave letters in the confession box in the parish church.'

'Why have you not tried to talk to her face to face?'

'Because she will not see me, unless I "point her to the guilty bitch"!'

A resounding crack echoed round the kitchen. It sounded to Alpiew as though Lord Wackland had been slapped.

'She missed her target last night.' Lady Prude spoke in a hoarse whisper. 'We are lucky it is only that orphan girl dead. It could have been anyone.'

'It could have been you, you mean?'

'You would have liked that, I am sure.' Lady Prude gave a sob, then was silent for so long Alpiew wondered if she hadn't left the kitchen. 'Don't upbraid me because *you* did what you did. You should have followed your own heart, and not lived out your whole life blaming me for your own vaulting ambition, you pitiful pot-boy! God damn the day I ever laid eyes upon you.'

Alpiew could hear scuffling.

Lord! They must be fighting. She was tempted to peep round the edge of the door, but decided it was safer to stay put.

'All right,' said Lord Wackland. 'Do what you will.'

'I will lure her here. Leave it to me. The confessional. I will write to her.'

The Countess felt her cheeks burning from the walk across the parterre. She slipped into the main door and tripped up the stairs. The cool of the stone was delicious after all the heat outside.

She knocked at Virginia's door and entered. Virginia was sitting in front of the looking glass staring at herself. She groaned when she saw the Countess.

'Oh, you! Why can't you leave me alone?'

'Because your mother entrusted me with your care.' The Countess settled at the end of Virginia's bed, her feet dangling. 'In the light of last night's horrid events, I wondered whether you might like to leave.'

'I *told* you once: I don't want to go anywhere.' Virginia opened a pot of addition and smelled it before smearing some on her cheeks. 'I don't know why you carry on with this charade. My stepmother has no intention of paying you, because you cannot get to London without risking your life as a St Germain Jacobite traitor.' She sat back and looked at the effect of the make-up, then scrubbed it off again with a handkerchief. 'If I were you, I'd settle down and try to enjoy myself.'

'Wouldn't you care to see your father again?'

'My father's wife has made a prize booby out of you. It is amazing the things a man will do for a woman. He let me go. May I remind you, as you will never be paid, you have no job looking after me, unless you are doing it for love.' Virginia smirked as she peeled open a pack of Spanish papers and applied some rouge to her cheeks.

'So you are content to stay here?' The Countess was bewildered not only by her own worries, but by the changeable temperament of this girl. 'I thought you hated France. Listen, Virginia, if I offered you the chance to get back . . .'

'Will *you* listen, you old hag!' screamed Virginia. 'Yes, I said I hated France. But that was before I came here. I now see that it is a most civilised place, and here at least I am free from subjection to the whim of that termagant who married my father. If only I could be free of your malicious pestering as well, you rat-eaten social climber.'

Without a further word the Countess rose and left the room.

As she made her winding way up to the garret, the temperature became steadily warmer. She flapped her fan. What a wretched, selfish, horrid child! And what a devilish woman that smiling, ingratiating Mrs Franklyn-Green had been. The Countess despaired as the questions whirled round in her head: How were they to get any money to get them home? How were they to get into England without being taken as Jacobite spies? How were they to survive?

She hoped her room was not like an oven. She planned to have a little rest to prepare for tonight's escape.

If Virginia wanted to stay, at least the chateau was as respectable an address as you could get. The Countess had fulfilled her side of the bargain, and all for the price of the journey here. Virginia was right. Her stepmother hadn't paid her and clearly had no intention of so doing.

Halfway up the garret stairs, just as she was turning these thoughts over, the Whippinghams' door opened, and Lucy came out. She looked agitated, and was hauling a bulging bag.

When she turned and saw the Countess she kicked the bag back into the room, closed the door and leaned on it.

'Well met, Countess! How goes it?'

Surprised by this hearty welcome, the Countess flapped the fan a bit more. 'Very hot,' she said, reaching the top step, wondering what Lucy was hiding. 'I am still astonished by the death of that poor girl last night.'

'Don't talk about it.' Lucy grabbed the Countess's elbow and whispered: 'It was a mistake. It could have been any of us. That's the thing about poison. You can never be sure where it's from and where it will end up.' She looked around to make sure the coast was clear. 'It isn't over. Keep your eyes open at all times.'

'I will,' said the Countess, breaking free of the woman's grasp. 'If the heat doesn't get me.'

'Going to have a little lie down?' Lucy put her hands behind her again, grabbing the door handle, and beaming.

'I hope so, yes.' The Countess had to squeeze to get past, and Lucy Whippingham made no attempt to move out of her path.

The Countess went into her room, popping her head out of the door, ostensibly to give Lucy Whippingham a wave. She waited a while until she heard Lucy's door open again, followed by scuffling, then silently applied an eye to the chink she had left ajar, and watched Lucy dragging the heavy bag down the stairs.

Alpiew sat on her bed in the staff dormitory. What a relief to think that she would never have to sleep in here again. As she had done the messages this morning, she had been given a quarter-hour break before the onslaught of supper.

The shutters in the long room were closed against the bright afternoon sunlight. A couple of people lay asleep in their tiny truckle beds. Early or late shift workers, Alpiew presumed. Quietly she gathered her few things together, ready for her exodus tonight. She lifted each of her feet and inspected her shoes. Fine for working in a hot kitchen, but no use at all for walking in ditches and hiking across fields. She pulled her boots from beneath the bed. They were more the figure for tonight. She loosened the laces and started pulling them on. But as she tried to slide her foot into the second boot her toes were crushed before reaching the end. An old stocking, she thought as she plunged her hand inside. To her amazement, jammed up against the toe was a moneybag.

'What time is it?' Mademoiselle Smith spoke from a nearby bed.

Alpiew thrust the bag into the palm of her hand and wrapped her fingers round it.

'Have I overslept?' Mademoiselle Smith lifted her head from the pillow. 'I must be back in the kitchen for four o'clock.'

Alpiew went to the window and peered out at the clock. 'You'd better rush.' She slid her hand into her pocket in as casual a way as she could, and dropped the moneybag inside. 'You have only three minutes.'

'*Mon Dieu!* If I am late into the Queen's apartments no one notices.' The girl sprang from the bed, and pulled on her shoes. 'But the Marquis is a different matter. Typically French. He goes into a royal rage when I am late.'

'How is the Marquis taking the news of last night's . . . ?'

'Don't continue,' snapped Mademoiselle Smith. 'We are not discussing this matter with the Marquis.'

'I thought . . .'

'Don't think,' said Mademoiselle Smith. 'And don't drag me into this trouble. I've had enough of it all.'

When she was gone Alpiew made her way to one of the spiral staircases where she could not be watched, and pulled the moneybag out again. She tipped the coins into her palm. English coins. Not quite as many as when the bag had been taken from her, but it was unmistakably the Countess's bag. The very one stolen by masked bandits at gunpoint on the road to St Germain.

The Countess was busily putting the few things she planned to take with her together in a small drawstring bag.

She would go down to supper, to make things look normal. Claim a slight stomach upset, and avoid the food.

She did not trust Dr Stickworth's findings. And if a poisoner was on the loose she had no intention of being an accidental victim. Lady Whippingham was right: poison was such an unpredictable weapon. A poisoner could never be sure they hit the right target unless they poured the stuff down their victim's throat. So despite the fact tonight's supper might be the last sight of food for some time, she would do without.

Hopefully, Alpiew would smuggle out some fresh vegetables or fruit and they could eat by the wayside. She knew they didn't have a penny to their names, but what did that matter, really? They had two pairs of legs, and their wits. Somehow she and Alpiew would make their way to Paris, and from Paris they would find a way to get home. And once they stepped on to England's shores they would work out how to prove they were loyal subjects, and not spies.

'Going somewhere?'

The Countess jumped and turned. The Duchesse de Charme stood at the door.

'Oh, you gave me a start,' said the Countess, resting her plump hand on her heaving chest. 'I was just looking for my rouge.'

'I'm bored out of my wits. Do you fancy a hand or two of lansquenet before supper? Isabel and my husband are down in the gaming room.'

'I'm sorry, Duchesse, as you know, I am out of funds. I would not make a good player this evening.'

'Don't worry,' said the Duchesse. 'We take notes of credit. You could write IOUs against your funds in England, if you like.' She gave a little laugh. 'But how silly. Why presume you will lose? Isabel tells me you are good at the table. Perhaps you will make yourself enough to get out of this garret.'

The Countess smiled. Of course! Why had she not thought of that? If she won tonight she and Alpiew could take a stagecoach from Paris and travel home in style.

'I'm right behind you, Duchesse,' she said, tucking the bag up under her pillow. 'Let play commence.'

*   *   *

The Countess tried not to grin as she laid down a livre on the queen of hearts. 'I face.' Her voice displayed more reserve than she felt.

Across the table Isabel screwed up her eyes as she laid down a stack of coins.

'I raise you ten livres.' She grabbed a pen, scratched a note and pushed it across the table to the pile of stake money. 'And my castle and lands in the Borders.'

'Anyone seen Whippy?' Lucy Whippingham put her head round the door. 'He keeps vanishing on me. God alone knows what trouble he'll get himself into.'

The Countess trembled as she looked down at the IOU. She had noted the run of cards and knew she was still in with a great chance. What if she won? But she could only win with a similar stake. She glanced down at her own note: *My house in German Street, St James, with the blue door.* Her fingers stroked the edges of her scrawled pledge.

'He was with the Doctor earlier,' said Isabel. 'I saw them going upstairs.'

'Oh, that Stickworth is a bugger.' Lucy Whippingham groaned and poured herself a quick bumper of wine. 'He's always taking Whippy off when I want him.' She downed the drink in one and slammed out of the room.

'Did you hear? The Queen had a little win on the French lottery,' said the Duchesse. 'Not a great deal of money – fifty livres or something like that. Better than nothing . . . She is donating the money to the poor.'

'I wish she'd donate it to poor me,' said Isabel with a laugh.

The Countess dipped her quill and hesitated, leaving it hovering above the IOU.

'It's just ink on paper, darling,' the Duchesse de Charme whispered in the Countess's ear. 'It's not as if any of us are ever likely to be going home. And even if we do . . . well, who knows what remains of our estates by now?'

The Countess's heart was thumping. She had every intention of going home, and felt sure she could prove she was not a

Catholic spy once she reached Dover. And if she did get past the border controls, and the court spies in London, why, how wonderful it would be to have vast acres of land in Scotland. And a castle! And as the Duchesse had pointed out . . . if not, what matter? Who at this table would ever be in a position to claim against her?

'Double paroli,' she cried, defiantly thrusting forward her note staking her London house against the king of clubs. 'Sept et le va.'

The Duc, acting as banker, pulled another card from the box. 'Ah, Hector, knave of diamonds. Countess, you lose.' He pulled the cash and notes of credit towards him, and shuffled the cards, ready to start again. 'Place your bets, please.'

The Countess lurched forward, but realised it was too late. There was no way out but to raise her stake and win her house back. She hastily scrawled another IOU and slid it forward.

Isabel Murdo-McTavish picked it up and squinted at it as she read aloud: 'My steward, Godfrey, and my woman, Alpiew.' She smiled. 'Well, there's a bet! What can I think of to raise against that one? A hundred head of Highland cattle?'

After dinner was served and the kitchen cleaned, Alpiew was dismissed for the night. She made her way out of the back door towards the dormitory block in the stables. But before going in to pretend to sleep she decided to have a reconnoitre.

'I'm too hot to sleep just yet, Pipe,' she called, striding across the main courtyard. 'I'm going for a quick walk. See you in a short while.'

Pipe gave her a wave and went inside.

Alpiew marched along the main street looking for a road sign that said Paris. It only took her a few minutes to find it. She strolled back towards the chateau, and decided to walk over the panoramic terrace and watch the river.

Just as she turned into the parterres she saw the Doctor walking swiftly in her direction. She ducked down behind a potted orange tree. He marched past with such determination

Alpiew could tell he was in a temper. The crunch of his boots ground into the gravel.

She waited for him to disappear into the chateau before moving, but as she rose she saw something slumped on the grass. Was it a body?

Her heart thumped as she tiptoed nearer.

It was a woman. Alpiew could make out the fine fabric of a mantua, a splayed arm, a pair of slippered feet, the skirt riding up.

She drew near enough to touch and see. Holding her breath, she stooped to take a closer look.

It was Lucy Whippingham.

Alpiew gasped. What should she do? Run for help?

Just as she reached out to feel for a pulse, a hand grabbed her by the ankle.

'Sticky?'

In her shock Alpiew fell backwards and tumbled on to the grass.

'Don't leave me, you bastard. We could be so happy. You said we could. What better time to escape from this nest of spies and poisoners than now?'

'Are you all right, madam?' said Alpiew. 'I saw you across the parterre and thought you must have taken a tumble.' When she bent over Lady Whippingham again she could smell fumes of strong waters on her breath. 'Perhaps I could help you inside again?'

'Go to hell!' Lucy Whippingham groaned and rolled over on to her back. 'Leave me alone. I shall stay here all night until I am carried away by wild beasts.' She waved her hand in the air. 'Didn't you hear me, you impertinent trollop? Go away.'

Alpiew rose and turned.

If the woman wanted to sleep out on the lawn that was her business.

Alpiew was only grateful that this time tomorrow she would be well away from St Germain and all its inhabitants.

*   *   *

It was almost midnight when the Countess finally managed to get back to her room. She flopped down on the bed. What was she going to tell Alpiew? That she'd made a total fool of herself? That she'd gambled away everything, including her house, Godfrey and Alpiew herself? She let out a long sigh and gripped the bedclothes. The Duchesse was right. It was just a game. She and Alpiew would be gone from this awful place in an hour or two, and they would never set eyes on these appalling people ever again. Only an hour and the bell would toll one, and it would be time to make her way to the main staircase and meet Alpiew and escape. She tried to swallow, but her throat was too dry. She rolled over, gazed up at the sloped ceiling and let out another sigh.

From under the bed she heard a slight sound, rustling, scratching.

Rats!

She lay still and held her breath. Silence.

Then she definitely heard a breath, and it was far too heavy for any rat. She cleared her throat to appear unconcerned, and swivelled sideways. Then with a sudden movement she lowered her head to peer beneath the mattress.

As her eyes met two other eyes her wig fell off and both she and the stranger under her bed let out a muffled scream.

'Who are you, my lad?' she hissed at the boy. 'And what are you doing under my bed?'

'Don't tell on me, please.' The eleven-year-old boy was cringing as he slowly slid across the polished floorboards out into the room. 'I didn't know anyone actually lived up here in these dismal rooms.' He stooped and picked up the Countess's wig and laid it gently on her lap.

'I won't tell. Cross my heart,' she said, gazing at him in disbelief as she popped the wig back on to her almost bald pate. Though she had never set eyes on the boy standing before her in a night-shirt and jacket, his features were so like his parents' she knew exactly who he was. 'But what are you doing hiding up here in my room? Is it a game?'

'I've had enough of everyone,' said the boy, perching on the bed beside the Countess. 'Downstairs it's always the same, day after day: nothing but battle, war, invasion plans, battle, war . . . What I am supposed to do when I grow up and go fighting to get my country back.' He let out a long, weary sigh. 'I've had enough. It would be another thing if I was really out there, hiding in caves, running from the enemy, but we do it all on a table-top, with toy soldiers.' The boy gave a huge yawn. 'Do you realise how boring it is?'

The Countess nodded. She remembered well enough the tiresome way her own parents had plagued her with their ideas of what she would do when she became an adult. 'Does your father know you are disgruntled?'

'My father? You have to feel sorry for him, really, poor old thing. But just because he was disappointed and lost his throne, does it mean that I have to spend all my days playing soldiers on a baize-covered table, charting out strategies on paper and learning the names of the towns of England, Scotland and Ireland.'

'And what would you prefer to be doing?'

'Dressing-up games. Doing plays. Fishing. Chasing through the woods with the other children. Anything. Can you imagine?' The child gave a sniff and threw his arms up. 'I came up here to explore. I wanted to see whether I could move about in the chateau undetected. For surely, if I can't do it here, how will I ever do it in a place I have never even seen, like London?'

'Tell me, which name do you go by? James, Francis or Edward? Or would you prefer me to stick to protocol, Your Royal Highness? Though I don't fancy having to get down on my knees just at the moment.'

'Stay where you are, please.' The Prince of Wales smiled and laid his hand in the Countess's. 'Perhaps you can be my secret friend. Could you get me a spinning top or a shuttlecock? Or maybe some marbles. I could sneak up here every night and play with you.'

'I would if I could.'

'You have some bad problems, I think. I could hear you whimpering in your bed.'

'Did I really whimper?' The Countess gave a chuckle and patted the boy's hand. 'And well I should. I have got myself into an almighty mess here. But . . . can you keep a secret?'

The boy nodded.

'I'm leaving this place tonight.'

'Where are you going?'

'Eventually, I hope, to London. Home.'

'London! How exciting. But how on earth will you get there?'

'By road, then by boat, then by road again.'

'You are not going through Ireland or Scotland first?'

'No.'

'And where will you sleep on the way?'

'If I had the money, I should sleep in posting houses, taverns and inns.'

'How wonderfully clever you are.' The boy pressed his long fingers to his plump lips. 'Why did my father not think of that?'

'It's easier for me than it would be for your poor father.'

'I have it! It's simple.' The boy stood and rubbed his hands together, his eyes gleaming. 'Why not take me with you!'

'Well . . .' The Countess spluttered a little before rising and tapping the boy's shoulder. 'I would love to, Your Royal Highness. But you must see that it would be impossible.'

'I think you don't understand what I'm telling you.' The prince pushed his jacket back and stood, hands on hips, his white night-gown hanging down to his ankles. 'I spend *hours* every day with my father trying to work out a way to get back to London. But he seems to think we have to go to Ireland or Scotland and fight battles, and sleep in bushes and caves.' The boy pursed his lips together, deep in thought. 'But your plan seems better to me. Why complicate things if one can simply take a ship across the Channel?'

The Countess tried to explain how politics made things

different for royal people. How King William, the new King of England, would not allow him, a rival claimant to the throne, to land in Great Britain without a fight. And how perhaps the situation would one day change, and the Prince himself would be able to travel on a simple ship to Dover, as she hoped to do.

'You have a very old head on your young shoulders.'

'Old? Really?' The boy turned and looked at himself in a glass on her bedside table. 'You're going to go, and leave me with nothing but those wretched toy soldiers.'

'Many children like to play with toy soldiers.'

'I don't,' said the boy.

'So pretend.' The Countess laughed. 'To please your mother and father, pretend to like the table-top battles.'

When the bell tolled the third quarter after midnight the Countess picked up her drawstring bag and prepared to leave.

'Why are you leaving in the middle of the night?'

'Because I can't face explaining to Lady Prude.'

'Oh, I understand. I'm frightened of her too. I'll show you a secret side door, which isn't guarded at night. It's the way the servants get in and out to their dormitory.' The Prince pulled the door open. 'It's lucky I met you really, for the sentries at the main door would have told on you.'

'We have to pick up my friend at the foot of the great staircase.'

'Let me help you.' The boy took the Countess's bag and peered each way along the dark corridor. 'Follow me,' he said.

They found Alpiew hiding in the shadows near the stairs, and together they tiptoed through galleries and passageways till they reached the secret door. The Prince pulled back a pair of bolts and turned the huge iron key.

'Before you go –' he unclipped a button-pin from his jacket – 'here is a present. A memento of us.'

'What is it?' The Countess peered at the tiny object, identical to one she had noticed Lord Wackland wearing on the collar of his jacket.

'Look –' The prince gave it a slight twist, revealing a minute piece of parchment.

'GBKJPHI?' Alpiew read aloud. 'Is that French?'

'God Bless King James, Prosper His Interests. It's a secret button for our allies to wear.' He pressed it into the Countess's hand. 'Travel safely, friend,' he said, handing the Countess her bag. 'Oh! You never told me your name.'

'My very close friends call me Ashby. But you can only do that if you take my advice, and *pretend* to like the battles!'

The boy opened the door and Alpiew ducked through it out into the open.

'Farewell, my friend Ashby,' said the prince as the Countess followed her. 'And if we meet again you can call me by my new secret codename.'

'And what is that, pray?' The Countess turned and smiled at the boy. He peeked through the crack as he shut the door. 'You can call me the Old Pretender.'

Alpiew grabbed the Countess by the arm and together they ran out across the stable courtyard towards the darkened streets of St Germain and the road to Paris.

Neither noticed the curtain pulled back in the large window above them, and so they did not see the face pressed against the windowpane, patiently watching them go.

Owls hooted, and strange squawks came from the hedgerows as they stumbled along the Paris road in the moonlight. Luckily the night was bright and warm.

The Countess opened her mouth several times to tell Alpiew about the gambling catastrophe, but she lost her nerve each time.

'Now that we're well out of Town I can tell you something.' Alpiew pulled out the moneybag and dangled it before the Countess. 'You'll never guess what I found in my boot.'

'A moneybag?' The Countess gave it a glance and carried on walking. 'Is there any money in it?'

'You don't seem to realise what I'm saying – it's not just

money. It's *our* money. Our own lost moneybag. The very bag that was stolen from us on the highway.'

They both stopped as Alpiew showed the Countess the mark on the leather, just above the drawstring. The Countess peered inside. 'Is all the money there?'

'Not quite all, but nearly. Certainly enough to get us a stagecoach to Calais, a boat to Dover, and food and lodgings along the way.'

The Countess decided in the light of this good news not to sully the moment by revealing the details of her disastrous wager. 'Let's not have it happen again. We know that the French roads are every way as bad as the English ones. If we were set upon by footpads we could lose it all again. If anyone in a coach goes past I think we should put out our hand and hope for a lift.'

'I'm not sure, madam. What footpads would set upon two women walking a path like this in the mid of night? Sure, only vagrants would be on foot at this time. People not worth robbing.'

'Whatever you think. Perhaps there will be no coach – but if there is, let's risk it.'

They trudged on for a good ten minutes before, to the Countess's delight, the distant sound of a coach rumbled towards them on the highway in the direction of Paris. They stepped off the road and leant back into the bushes, waving their hands towards the driver. As the coach neared them it slowed down and a man stuck his head out.

'*Mesdames?*' he said. '*Où allez-vous?*'

'What's he saying?' whispered Alpiew.

'English,' said the Countess. '*Anglais.*'

'You go in Paris?'

They nodded and the man pushed the carriage door open.

'How *charmant!*' The Countess tried to step forward, but Alpiew tugged at her sleeve. 'Don't be silly, Alpiew. What harm can there be in arriving safe in Paris without tired legs or the threat of footpads stealing our moneybag a second time?

Monsieur,' she said, holding out her arm, *'merci.* Thank you so much for your kind offer. Come, Alpiew.'

The man slid along to make way for the two women and spread a rug across their laps.

'Tray genteel,' said the Countess. *'Merci.'*

Alpiew pressed the moneybag well down into her pocket and stared out of the window at the shuttered houses and trees along the roadside. At least this way they might be in time for the daily coach to Calais which would leave shortly after dawn, and thereby save a whole day. She shut her eyes and gently nodded off to sleep.

There was a bright glow on the horizon as the coach entered the city by the Porte de Versailles. The Countess gazed out at the city with its steeply angled slate roofs and circular towers with conical candle-snuffer domes. If the coach dropped them anywhere in the centre it shouldn't be too hard to find a staging office where they could book a place on a stagecoach to Boulogne or Calais. She looked over at the kind gentleman. He seemed familiar. He was dressed head to foot in black and wore no expression as he too gazed out upon Paris. She noted that he was gripping a sealed letter.

Alpiew was asleep.

A shudder went through the Countess again at the thought of the wretched card game. Please God, don't let those beastly women send a messenger to London to claim the house before she and Alpiew got home.

The coach took a turn and rattled as it moved from dirt track on to cobbled streets. Alpiew opened her eyes and prodded the Countess, flashing her eyes to indicate they should ask to be set down.

'Monsieur, descender, seel vous plait.' The Countess smiled and pointed towards the window. 'Can we get out here?'

The man gave a courteous smile in return and pointed a finger forward. He was going to let them out a bit further along, they gathered.

The Countess read the street signs as they progressed through

Paris. The tiled façade of the Tuileries Palace and the adjacent Louvre Palace twinkled with early-morning candles, while the rising sun reflected gold from the hundreds of window panes on the east side. Flaming torches lit the quais along the sparkling Seine, which were busy with fishermen and barges unloading. Horses snorted as they climbed up from the riverbanks pulling stacked wagons into the bustling city. Notre Dame stood nobly on the dark island to their right. The coach lurched across a busy junction and turned into a small side street: rue St Antoine. Mmm. That was a familiar name. The Countess racked her brains. Where had she heard it before? The road ahead widened. But the signs still said rue St Antoine. She hoped the man was not going to go straight out of Paris through the next city gate, which must be coming up soon. She noticed too that his cheek had started twitching. He was certainly nearing his destination, she felt. He had that determined air about him. She looked out again as the coach slowed and the horses turned in through a large open gate headed with trophies of arms. The very hunched street inside the gate was lined with small shops, the swinging signs above the doors indicating barbers, cobblers, poulterers and cheese-mongers. A drawbridge ahead was down, and the coach passed smoothly over it. The Countess looked down at the dark muddy moat and a shudder ran through her. Rue St Antoine . . . why was the name so familiar? The coach slowed and the driver spoke to someone at ground level. A row of guards raised their hats and covered their faces with them.

A shadow fell across the coach, throwing them into gloomy darkness again. 'We could get out here,' said the Countess, beginning to have her doubts about the man's intent. What if he were some Bluebeard luring them into his murderous castle? He nodded and smiled again, but his eyes were cold. She gripped on to Alpiew's sleeve and gave her a shake, while looking out and up. Ahead stood a black building, its walls stretching up about a hundred feet, almost obscuring the slowly lightening morning sky. The lofty towers were topped with battlements. What kind of place was this?

The carriage door was held open by a uniformed sentry. He too shielded his eyes with his hat.

The Man in Black turned and tipped both Alpiew and the Countess on the shoulder with his letter. *'Pour vous,'* he said.

With trembling hands the Countess took the letter and gazed down upon it. The crackle of a nearby link seemed deafening as she read in the flicker of its light. Amid a jumble of French she could certainly see both her own name and Alpiew's.

'Lettre de cachet,' said the man, *'du Roi Louis XIV.'*

'What is happening?' said Alpiew, ready to run for it.

'Bienvenue, mesdames,' said a smartly dressed man standing near the sentry.

'Rue St Antoine!' said the Countess, climbing down from the coach with a dawning recognition. *'Lettre de cachet!* Oh lord, Alpiew, what unmitigated horror has befallen us?'

'But what does it all mean, madam?' Alpiew looked about her at the guards lined up to welcome them to their new home, all hiding their faces.

'It means, my dear girl, that by order of the King of France we have been brought to a dreaded place where people have been known to enter but never to leave. This is the most feared prison in all of France, nay, all of Europe . . . the world. This lowering edifice, Alpiew, is His Majesty King Louis XIV's personal prison. This is that most feared and formidable of fortresses. We are about to enter the Bastille.'

FIVE

A la Parisienne — a particular way of making pies, after the mode of the city of Paris

They were taken to a windowless guardroom where they were stripped of their belongings.

'Will someone tell me why we are here?' said the Countess, gesticulating wildly. 'What have we done?'

The guard ignored her and pulled the contents from her bag, depositing them slowly upon a large oak table. 'We are English citizens,' she cried. 'English.'

A nearby turnkey stood waiting, his huge bunch of keys dangling from a large leather belt.

'I demand to see the Ambassador. Eeengleesh Ambass-a-dorrr,' she added, hoping, by changing the pronunciation and raising her voice, to make herself understood. '*Moi*, friend of *roi*. *Ami de roi* –' She mimed a crown and made small kissing motions. '*Amour, amour.*'

'*Cette femme*,' said the guard, pointing at Alpiew, '*elle est votre bonne?*'

'*Oui*,' said the Countess, grasping desperately at any word she knew. '*Elle est bon.*'

'*Non.*' The guard mimed scrubbing, and rolling up his sleeves. '*Servante? Domestique?*'

The Countess remembered the fate that had befallen them at St Germain and shook her head violently. 'My *ami*,' she said. 'Friend.' She grabbed Alpiew's hand and grasped it. '*Ami*.'

The turnkey grunted and scratched his posterior. The guard looked at the two women, raised his eyebrows and nodded to the turnkey, who seized Alpiew and marched her towards the door.

'No,' screamed the Countess. '*Non. Non domestique. Ami.*'

Growling and howling, Alpiew beat her free fist against the man's side, but he hauled her out of the guardroom as the Countess flopped down against the table in despair. She rolled her eyes up, and slid slowly down on to a chair, hoping that a feigned faint might bring in someone more civilised, like a physician, to help her.

The guard plunged his hand into the Countess's bag and ran his fingers round the lining. He stared into the bag, knotted his eyebrows together and gave a little grunt. '*Qu'est-ce que c'est?*' He pinched his fingers together and pulled out a ring. He peered down at it for a few moments, then called out for the sentry at the door. '*La bague perdue!*'

The Countess opened one eye. A ruby ring. How in heaven's name had it made its way into her possession? The guard held the ring out towards her, and she leaned forward, peering at the thing. The ruby sparked in the flickering light. He nodded towards her, asking if it was hers. She shook her head. 'Never set eyes upon it in my life.'

The Man in Black, who, in the light of the prison guardroom with its torches and candles aflame, the Countess recognised as the man she had seen lurking at St Germain, fixed his eyes on the ring.

'*Oui*,' he said, snatching it from the guard. '*C'est ça.*' He turned to the Countess. 'The ring of the Queen.'

'The Queen?'

'Queen Mary of England. Wife of James.' He held it up to the candle and the ruby flooded with blood-red light. 'How you say: stealed.'

'Why have you brought us here?' cried the Countess, hysteria rising. 'We never stole anything.'

The man gave her an enigmatic look and left the room.

Alpiew was led up and up a spiral staircase and thrown into a cell. The door slammed behind her. As she ran back to hammer against it she heard the key turn and a number of bolts shooting into their sockets. She was not going to be beaten. She'd been in prison before and in tighter squeezes than this. First to get a lay of the land, find out the customs and regulations of the place, and then come hell or high water she would get out, taking the Countess with her. She put her hands on her hips and turned back to face the accommodations. To her surprise even in the grey light of dawn it was rather bright and airy, an octagonal room with two comfortable-looking beds and a large table. Much better in fact than the conditions she'd had to put up with in the servants' quarters at St Germain.

The stone walls of the room were decorated in chalk with every kind of symbol: suns, moons, pentacles, eyes ... As she perched on the side of her sagging bed it became obvious who had done the interior decorating.

Her cellmate, a woman with long wild grey hair wearing a silver cloak, was sitting on a chair by the window, seemingly in a trance. Around her lay cards and twigs and strange totems – small statuettes and little china eyeballs – all arranged in a row and seemingly glaring at Alpiew.

Alpiew addressed the woman but received only a shriek by way of reply. She peered over towards the unbarred window and the sight of a bird winging past made it quite clear that that method of escape was unlikely. She flung herself down on to the bed and gazed up at the whitewashed ceiling. She would not be beaten. One way or another she would find a way to get out of the place and safely home to England.

* * *

The Countess was flung into a dark room and the door banged heavily behind her. She too surveyed her accommodation.

To her surprise it was unlike any prison cell she'd ever seen in her life. Hers was also a well-appointed room, also octagonal, decently furnished, and clean. There was a large oak table with a candlestick and a couple of well-carved easy chairs with brocade pads and cushions.

It was too dark to see much, but she could make out a glimmer of daylight coming round the edges of a silk curtain at the window. She strode over and pulled it back, flooding the room with dull light.

A walk-in fireplace was stacked with expensive-looking books.

The stone floor was covered in good-quality Turkish carpets, and there were two beds: a small truckle bed with a satin pillow, and a huge poster bed, complete with hangings to match the curtains and chairs. The truckle bed was empty. On the other was a fine woollen blanket covering a growling hump.

'*Fous l'camp!*' shrieked a gravelly voice from within the bed. '*Salope!*'

The Countess winced. One thing she knew from previous incarcerations was that the first rule of prison life was not to upset your cellmate on the first day. She might not understand much French, but she knew her fellow-captive had not just told her to make herself at home. She wondered what had happened to Alpiew and why they had both been brought to this place. Surely no one could think they had killed Aurelia? Perhaps after Lady Prude had found them together in the fatal antechamber she had reported them.

And what was the Queen's ring doing in her bag? She let out an involuntary gasp.

The woman in the bed sat up, throwing her blanket to the floor, her carrot-red hair standing up on end, her lips smeared with blood-red paint. '*Merde!*' she squawked, rubbing her eyes and staring at the Countess. '*Zut alors! C'est un rêve!*'

'Lord help us!' cried the Countess, recognising instantly her dear friend, Olympe Athenée Montelimar, Duchesse de Pigalle.

'Ashby, darling, can it be you 'ere in ze Bastille?' Pigalle squinted at the Countess and rubbed her eyes. 'Or am I 'aving a bizarre nightmare?'

'Yes, Olympe, it's me.'

''Ow? Why are you 'ere, incarcerated in a French gaol and not at 'ome in London?'

'It's terrible, Pigalle. I have no idea why we are here. But it seems that Alpiew and I have been implicated in deception, theft and possibly murder. They've taken Alpiew away I know not where and . . .'

Pigalle leapt from the mattress and staggered to the door, holding her finger to her lips. She listened for a moment then made her way back to the fireplace. She slid a pile of books to the side and pulled a few bricks from the fire-back.

The Countess followed and watched her as she called into the sooty void. Pigalle had a short conversation in French with a man who sounded not too far away, then a more distant woman joined in the exchange.

'*Merci*,' she yelled, cramming the bricks back into position. '*À bientôt*. Alpiew is right up at the top of the Bertaudière Tower, sharing a room with a witch.' Pigalle sat at the table. 'Which is good. We can see her soon.' She pushed some pieces of paper to the side. 'We will get our breakfast any minute.'

'Breakfast?'

'The food in here is excellent.'

'Oh, Pigalle, but why am I here at all?'

'They are always very slow here in telling you why you were chosen for a personal letter of recommendation from the King of France confining you to ze Bastille. I think zey want you to work it out, and so often thereby zey find out a number of other crimes. Some prisoners of the Bastille have been put away at the request of their families because zey are insane or obsessed with sexual endeavours. Others are here for treason against His Majesty, or other things like zat. Perhaps you have been doing a little of zat scandal-writing you do, *non?* Something detrimental to ze King of France?'

'No,' said the Countess in despair. 'Nothing like that at all.' She hesitated before broaching the delicate subject of Pigalle's own imprisonment.

'*I* called ze King's favourite, Madame de Maintenon, a fat ugly ridiculous pontificating whore.' Pigalle looked pensively up to the ceiling. 'Or maybe it was because I put ink into the holy water font, which in these sanctimonious days is tantamount to heresy.' She laughed, baring her long yellow teeth. 'Still, whatever it was, it did ze job. I got into ze Bastille. Here I am to prove it.'

'You *want* to be in here?' The Countess was puzzled; she seemed to have spent much of her life doing anything to get *out* of prison. She had never met anyone who tried to get into one.

'*D'accord.* Look at it. I have my own furniture and things around me. Ze food is good and on top of zat you get a nice allowance . . .'

'Allowance?'

'*Oui!* While we are kept at His Majesty's pleasure he pays us according to our status. Some goes towards the food. As I am a Duchesse, I get thirty livres, as a writer you will get ten.'

'Ten!'

'I see you are amazed. But perhaps you understand now why I am here. In ze winter ze place is reasonably warm, and once you get to know the inner workings ze company is fantastic. Some of ze most interesting people in France are in here. It is a great experience.'

The bolts slid back, and a humpbacked gaoler came in with a tray of food served on good-quality earthenware plates, and steaming leather mugs of coffee. He laid the tray on the table and exchanged a few words with Pigalle, who grabbed a book from the fireplace and handed it to him.

'*Pour la sorcière.*' She made a few spitting motions in the Countess's direction, and the guard left. 'Best not to let them in on anything. They don't like to let friends share a cell.' She grabbed a spoon and ladled the food to her mouth. 'He thinks I detest you as *une putain anglaise*.' She screeched with laughter, and took a great slurp of coffee. 'Ooh la la! How marvellous. My darling Ashby is in here too. It's wonderful, like a marvellous party.'

There was a book of cards on the table so Alpiew gave them a quick shuffle and played a game of pairs while her thoughts raced.

The witch had danced around the table, shrieked a bit at the sight of the food, then gone back to her seemingly endless vigil at the window, occasionally peeking out from her tangle of grey hair to cackle in Alpiew's direction.

When she quietened down, Alpiew tiptoed across to the chair and sat quietly. Her head was spinning with the events of the last few days. Why had she and the Countess been apprehended? And how had the Man in Black known they would be tramping the Paris road in the middle of the night? And what about the money? How had that mysteriously reappeared in her shoe at St Germain? The prison guard had taken it from her when she was searched. If this was anything like English prisons, she doubted she'd ever see it again. But how had it made its way back to her and why? The obvious thought was that Virginia had taken it by some miraculous sleight of hand. But Virginia was outside in the ditch being held at gunpoint when Alpiew had handed over the money. And the man who took it had jumped straight on to his horse and ridden away. It was hardly as though some stranger could have picked it up at the roadside and handed it in. There was no name and address tag in the bag and when they were robbed they were a good hundred miles away from St Germain. Yet last night the moneybag was returned to her very boot in the servants' quarters of the Court of King James.

A bolt slid back and keys rattled. Alpiew slid the cards to the side of the table. The humpback guard slouched in with a grunt and threw a book down on the table. Alpiew watched him as he lumbered out and slammed the door behind him. She picked up the book and opened it. John Bunyan – *A Pilgrim's Progress*.

Why on earth had he given her this? The book bore a pencil inscription: 'This might come in useful.'

This was the strangest prison she'd ever been in in all her life. Whoever heard of a prison where the rooms were more comfortable than your own home and warders doled out books?

She flicked through. She'd seen the book often enough in London. Godfrey quoted from it now and then. She remembered one of his leery looks while he read her a passage about 'the Delectable Mountains'. Which reminded her. She ran her fingers round the low neckline of her mantua and pushed up her substantial cleavage. No harm in letting the guard have a good look at that. It wouldn't be the first time she had used sex as a means of getting what she wanted. When the chips were down, her delectable mountains could make themselves very useful.

She let the book fall open at a few well-thumbed pages, then turned to the beginning and started to read: '*As I walked through the wilderness of this world . . .*' In the margin was scrawled 'in extremis'. It is a puritan tract, thought Alpiew. She flicked on until page 12 where, beside the line '*The name of the slough was Despond*' she found the word 'Company'. She flicked on and by the time she reached the line '*Then I saw that there was a way to Hell, even from the gates of Heaven*' on page 133, she had a whole set of instructions about a secret tunnel, which she would certainly try.

As the evening bells of the Angelus rang, the warder came into the Countess's room.

'*Allons!*' he grunted.

Pigalle indicated that she should follow him.

'What can it be? Why does he want me?'

Pigalle gave a massive shrug and slopped after her.

'Are you coming too, Olympe? Thank God for that.'

They walked along a stone corridor and the warder threw open a large oak door.

The Countess stepped into a vast room, brightly lit with wall sconces and chandeliers. It was packed with chattering people.

'*Bienvenue à la Bastille.*' The Governor, dressed in formal evening wear, complete with the blue sash of the Order of Saint-Esprit, greeted the Countess. 'It is not often we welcome *foreign* writers. You will find plenty of your colleagues here: satirists, playwrights, journalists.'

A man in the corner popped the cork of a bottle of champaign and poured.

'So I would be pleased if you would join me again, for a dinner party later in the week.' He gave a little bow and stepped away. 'I leave you to enjoy your evening.'

The Countess gave a coy smile as he wandered off towards a table groaning with food. 'What on earth is going on?' she hissed to Pigalle. 'Is this a prison or a social club?'

'I tried to explain before, darlink, but you didn't listen to me. Zis is your welcoming party. You find in this room some of the most entertaining people in all of Europe. It is marvellous here. I adore ze Bastille.'

The Countess squinted at the gathering. There were a small group of musketeers in full fig, lords, ladies, even a bishop, and . . . Alpiew!

'You see, it is ze *crème* of society!'

'Milady!' Alpiew ran to the Countess grimacing, while she inspected the elegant crowd. 'Murderers and robbers all, I suppose. Duchesse, what a surprise! Are you just visiting for the party?'

'I am here like everyone else for upsetting the King of France.' Pigalle grabbed a cupful of champaign. 'No one is in ze upper rooms of ze Bastille for murder or robbery or any of those unpleasant things, Alpiew.'

'But I thought we were in here for poisoning some girl at St Germain.'

'I told you, darling, zis is the King's personal prison. I would imagine zat your crime is none of those you have mentioned.

118

If you had poisoned zat cow Maintenon, or another of Louis's favourites, maybe. But no – ze Bastille is not for zat kind of thing. Are you sure you have not written something bad about ze King of France?' Pigalle laughed. She stopped and lurched forward to whisper to the Countess: 'You didn't really murder anyone, did you?'

'Certainly not.'

'Zat is disappointing, Ashby!'

'No doubt at our trial,' said Alpiew, 'we can defend ourselves against what must surely be trumped-up charges.'

'Sorry, my dears. When it comes to ze Bastille you know perfectly well there are no real trials or judgements, again only ze whim of the King of France. Unless you are one of the poor wretches who has committed a murder – which you will know soon enough, as murderers and thieves are generally tried within a day of their arrival – you have been brought in here at his caprice, and ze only way out is ze same.'

'But . . .'

'This is some rum prison, to be sure,' said Alpiew, passing the Countess a glass of champaign. 'I have to say I prefer being incarcerated here than being free at St Germain.'

'Did you get ze book?' Pigalle chomped into a juicy sausage. 'It is ze route to our chamber, should you wish to pay a visit later tonight.'

The Countess nodded eagerly. 'We do need to talk, Alpiew.'

'Why wait?' said Pigalle, marching off towards a handsome *gens d'arme* with a sparkling smile. 'I have my own business to attend to.'

'Our world gets smaller every day,' said the Countess, leading Alpiew into a corner. 'First we find that by staying at St Germain we have all but exiled ourselves from England. Now it seems there is no way out of this prison but by royal permission.'

They sat slightly away from the crowd.

'Was it that child who reported us, do you think? The Prince of Wales?'

'Apart from him, who else knew we were leaving?' Alpiew

took a swig from her glass. 'Perhaps he thought we should have better lodgings here.'

The Countess shuddered. She didn't like to think she'd been betrayed by a Stuart, the very nephew of her dear dead Charles.

'Virginia?' Alpiew looked carefully at the Countess. 'Did you tell her?'

The Countess gulped. Alpiew had been right all along. She never should have been tempted by that awful woman and her spoilt stepdaughter.

'You're right, Alpiew. It's comfortable here, but it's still a gaol. We were best to work out who would desire our incarceration and why.'

'Who planted the money in my shoe?'

'And the Queen's ring in my bag?'

'The Queen's ring?' This was the first Alpiew had heard of it.

'The ruby ring you told me about – it was in my bag when the guard searched it.'

'Who poisoned that poor unfortunate girl Aurelia Brown?'

'Ah yes.' The Countess gave her wig a scratch, reducing the height of her forehead by an inch. 'With us out of the way, the guilty party can safely pin it on us. From what I gather no one will know we are in here, so it will look as though we absconded. I believe that, technically speaking, we have now vanished from the earth. And what's more we could be left here, invisible to the world, forever.'

Alpiew drained her glass and banged it down on a nearby table. 'Suddenly the cramped old kitchen, with Godfrey snarling and farting in a corner, seems ever so attractive.'

'Oh, Alpiew, I am so sorry. It is my fault for bringing us over to this godforsaken country.'

'Never mind that.' Alpiew took the Countess's hand and patted it. 'We will get out. I'm willing to use whatever means to escape, and then I will go on my knees to the King of France. Or whatever position he desires!' She winked and smiled. 'We will get safely back to German Street, milady, and one day we'll laugh about this mad Gallic escapade.'

'I haven't told you the worst part . . .' The Countess bit her lower lip and cringed. 'I lost the house in a card game.'

'You bet your house?'

'And Godfrey . . .' The Countess felt herself shrinking as she braced herself for the rest of the confession. 'And you.'

'You staked *me*?' Alpiew stared at her mistress. 'In a card game?'

The Countess gave an imperceptible nod. 'I thought I would win us a castle in Scotland and a hundred head of Highland cattle.'

Alpiew took a deep breath before responding to this.

'And which of those vultures now owns me, pray, madam?'

'That awful Scotswoman.'

'The writer, with the ribbons?'

The Countess nodded again. Her head was bobbing like a cheap wooden toy at Bartholomew's Fair.

'Right.' Alpiew rubbed her hands together. 'So we really MUST get out of here, and I shall have to win myself, Godfrey and your house back.' She rose, pulling the lace cuffs of her sleeves up to the elbow. 'Let me at her with her book of cards. I know every sleight of hand there is. I can pull out five aces from any pack. Six, if necessary.'

'But what if they get to London and claim the house before we get there?'

'If what they've told you is true, madam, they have as much chance of making a hasty return to London without being captured and forced to do the hempen jig as we do. You know me, milady, I can out-trick the best street conjuror in Covent Garden Piazza. But first we must make our escape and go back to St Germain.'

'I was lucky,' said Pigalle, lounging back in an easy chair, 'my husband died before I ever had children. He was so protective of me, as I believe all Frenchmen are of their women. And he thought ahead of how he would feel if we had daughters. He warned me he would have all their teeth removed in case zey became too attractive to men. *Zut!* What a madman! The very wenches on his estate he forbade to milk the cows in case by performing that action they were encouraged to entertain impure thoughts.' She chuckled to herself. 'But I had decided not to have children long before I met him, after some wicked fortune-teller told me I would die in childbirth.'

The Countess gave a wan smile. She was not listening. Her thoughts were filled with the problem of how to escape, how to win back her house, Godfrey and Alpiew, and how to get home to England without taking the jump from a gallows.

'Ze trouble I had to go to after I left him. I couldn't return to France or I would have been arrested for desertion, so when I wanted to travel from London to Rome to see my dear friend Queen Christina of Sweden on her deathbed I had to go by way of the Low Countries, Germany and Switzerland. *Ma foi!* What an excursion zat was. Much of it on ze back of a donkey. And the Swedish paillasse went and died before I arrived, even though I had prepared a last love scene between us.' She gave a little sigh, and wafted her taloned hand. '*Alors,* was there ever a merrier woman than I when I heard zat my *salaud* of a husband had fallen off his horse-drawn plough and drowned in a pool of cow dung.'

'Olympe, dear,' said the Countess, as though continuing the conversation, 'you know I love your company. But I have to get out of here. Help me, please. And why don't you come too?'

'Ashby, darling.' Pigalle started smoothing what had once been her eyebrows, but which were now mere pencil lines. 'It's so lovely in here. How can you . . . ?'

'We're in prison, Olympe. We have lost our freedom. However pleasant the company, the food, the warmth . . .'

'Ze pay! Your allowance here must be more than you get from those miserly printers – and here you have to do nothing for it but sit and chat with an old friend.'

'Olympe, please. You *must* help me to get out.'

'No, Ashby, please don't go, don't leave me . . .' Pigalle fell to her knees and grabbed at the Countess's skirts. 'I *cannot* leave. I have to stay in here. You cannot imagine ze trouble I am in . . .' She started sobbing. 'In here at least I am safe. Please stay with me.'

'Oh, darling, what has befallen you?' The Countess stroked her friend's hair. 'I thought you had a lovely new school.'

'I inherited ze land at the bottom of ze hill, Montmartre – The Martyr's Mount, you see, because it was where St Denis was beheaded. Ze place was a wild wilderness, save for a few windmills higher up and a chalkpit. So I put up some buildings, and set up an academy for girls in ze style of Madame Maintenon's academy St Cyr.'

'How could something as noble as that land you in here?'

'I arranged for ze girls to learn cookery, embroidery, painting and other feminine activities. All was going well, ze school was over-subscribed, we had a waiting list! But a nasty mob of gangsters turned ze place into a high-class bordello and gambling den, serving ze lowest of the low.'

'Oh dear,' the Countess sighed. 'But I suppose there is a profit in that too?'

'Ashby! You joke, no? The Pigalle Academy teaches girls to become experts in the Postures of Aretino and forty ways to pick a pocket. Fathers everywhere are baying for my blood. Ze repulsive gang of criminals have made ze honourable name Pigalle into mud. Say "Pigalle" and people think "sex"! Can you imagine, darling? Now zey say I must sell zem ze place or zey will kill me.'

'But Olympe, dear, it is simple. Sell!'

'In ze terms of ze inheritance I *cannot* sell until I die. So if I die it is all right for zem. Instead I did ze next best thing, and got myself incarcerated in zis place, where you are as good as dead, but you still can eat, and sleep and have a laugh with your friends.'

The Countess thought about it. In the Bastille no names were used, the guards on the way in had covered their eyes.

It was as though all the rules here were designed to make sure that you ceased to exist. The comfort and pay and good food were no doubt all part of the design – so that once inside you didn't want to escape.

The thought sent a shudder down the Countess's spine. What a terrifying way of controlling your enemies. Making them cease to exist. And, worse, lulling them into acceptance of it.

'But surely, Olympe, the obvious thing to do is to escape with me, then get out of France quick. Go back to your lovely home in London and you will be fine.'

'And how can I do zat? How can I get to England without travelling through France, where my face and name are known to all.'

The Countess gazed at her friend with her shock of red hair, her tall spindly frame, her long yellow teeth, and realised she would indeed be hard to disguise.

'We'll get you out. It's a deal – you help me and Alpiew to get out of here, and we will get you safely back to England.'

Alpiew shuffled and dealt herself another hand of patience. It was well after midnight. Following the party everyone had been taken back to their chambers and locked in. The witch, who had declined the invitation, sat with her head propped against the window, gazing out into the moonless night. Alpiew wondered if she was checking for passing broomsticks.

She couldn't believe that the Countess had done such a terrible thing as write out those chits, but now it must be rectified. She threw the cards down and flung herself on to the bed. Perhaps they were better to get out of here and then hot-foot it straight back to London, and if anyone should ever turn up claiming the place, they could deny all knowledge of it and swear they'd never set foot in King James's Court at St Germain-en-Laye.

There was a rattling of keys and bolts slid back. What now? A ball, perhaps, or a masquerade?

The turnkey slouched in, and two guards behind him led in a cloaked woman, her head bowed.

'*Anglais!*' the turnkey growled. '*Une Écossaise pour vous.*'

Alpiew gave a little grunt, and rolled over. She hadn't a notion what the man had said. The turnkey and guards left the room, the door slammed after them, and a new prisoner sank on to the seat on the other side of the table.

'Weren't you in the kitchen at St Germain?' cried the prisoner, throwing back the hood of her cloak. 'I never forget a face. It's Alpiew, isn't it?'

Alpiew looked up. She controlled her urge to jump up and cry out, for before her sat Lady Isabel Murdo-McTavish.

'So this is where you both got to,' said the Scotswoman, pulling off her gloves. 'I presume your mistress and companion Lady Ashby de la Zouche is detained here too? I tell you, there was much talk when you both disappeared in the middle of the night. The whisper was that you had absconded with a lot of money and jewellery, that you were spies sent by Whitehall to murder Aurelia.'

Alpiew decided to let her continue babbling. Perhaps she'd learn something useful.

'So this is the famous Bastille! When I realised they were bringing me *here* I trembled from my poor wee scalp to my bunions. But it doesn't look so bad, does it? At least together we can take our minds off the horrors of imprisonment. Who knows, together we might even write a great book about life in gaol.' She unfastened her cloak. 'We could call it *Crime and Punishment.*'

'With a name like that it would never sell.' Alpiew scowled and tried to weigh up the woman who had won her at cards. 'Why are you in here? Have you come to collect your spoils? What's the game, missus?'

'A man in black was waiting for me in my bedchamber when I arrived there after supper tonight. He led me down to a waiting coach, without a word. Then tapped me on the shoulder with some French letter. An arrest warrant, I presume. I suppose they now think I killed that ghastly Aurelia.' She got up and walked around the room. 'Perhaps everyone from our set is here.' She nodded a smile towards the woman in the window and mouthed the words: *Who's that?*

'No idea,' said Alpiew, taking a seat at the table, gathering up the cards and shuffling them again. 'Don't you feel even the slightest bit embarrassed to be sharing a cell with a woman you possess through sharp practice?'

'I've never set my eyes on that banshee in all my life,' said Lady Murdo-McTavish.

'I mean me.' Alpiew studied Lady Isabel Murdo-McTavish, weighing up her prey. 'I am Alpiew, remember? You won me at cards with my lady.'

'No, no, it wasn't like that.' The Scotswoman blushed. 'I don't . . . It's nothing to do with me . . . I . . .'

'Spit it out. What are your terms? I would like to belong to no one but myself. Frankly, I imagine my lady must have been extremely flustered to even think she was in a position to use me as a stake. I am no slave. I am a freeborn woman.'

'You don't understand. I can't talk about it. And anyhow, what does it matter now we're in here? Will they burn us at the stake, do you think?'

Alpiew was trying to work out this conundrum. Was Lady Isabel planted in the cell to encourage her to confess to something and report back to the authorities? It seemed too much of a coincidence that they had all three been thrown into the Bastille within a day of each other. And what was this mad prison all about? No one was in here for murder or thieving or any of the crimes you found in English prisons. And it was run more like a coffee house or pleasure garden.

'The man at the door said I might visit the library, which is apparently quite well stocked, even with books in English.' Isabel sighed and flopped down opposite Alpiew. 'I have my quill and some paper, so perhaps, with all this enforced time I will write a great book.'

Alpiew gasped. There was a link between the three of them.

They were all writers. And what was the Bastille used for in the main? To teach writers who had displeased the King of France a lesson.

'Have you written anything lately?' Alpiew tried not to sound too interested.

'Oh yes . . .' Lady Isabel brightened up. 'It is a tale about a princess who pricks her finger and falls asleep for years and years . . .'

'No, not stories – satire. You've written nothing about the King of France? No scandal sheets? No lampoons?'

'I don't think any of the French princesses ever pricked their fingers . . .'

'In London we write a sheet of society gossip for a journal. You haven't written anything like that?' Alpiew was trying to recall the details of the piece she and the Countess had tried to sell. What if it had made remarks about the King, meaning sad old James Stuart, but someone had thought they meant King Louis?

'Folk tales are my speciality. I wander the woods and hamlets talking to wise old women who tell me the stories passed down through generations. I record them for a new generation, so that they will never die.'

'And none of these concern a great French King or someone called Louis?'

'No.' Lady Murdo-McTavish shuffled uneasily. 'I'm sorry, Mistress Alpiew, but I don't know why you are being so brusque with me.' She pulled out a handkerchief and wrung it in her hands.

'Will you give my lady back her house, or do I have to win it from you?'

'I can't do that. It was won in fair competition.'

'It's only a leasehold, you know. You can only keep it as long as she lives; after that it will revert to the Crown.'

'The ownership of her property is nothing to do with me.'

'Do you know who poisoned Aurelia?'

'Of course I don't.'

'You called her ghastly.'

'She had only been at St Germain a week, but she came prying. Asking me questions about my husband.'

'Like what?'

'How long I knew him. Who he had known before I met him. I couldn't understand what she was getting at. I hate talking about him, you see. It's all a very unhappy memory for me. So I turned the quizzing back upon her, asked her why she'd come to St Germain, was it just to poke about in other people's business? She said she had come to St Germain to be with Mademoiselle Smith.'

Alpiew sat back. What a turn! When Mademoiselle Smith denied all knowledge of Aurelia.

'She was horrible. Staring at me with those piercing black eyes.' Isabel Murdo-McTavish started to cry. 'You can't imagine how frightened it made me.'

'Frightened you! So her death must be a relief?'

'On the contrary. Now she is dead, I am even more terrified.'

'Why?'

'Because whoever killed Aurelia made a mistake. It was *me* they were trying to kill. I am sure of that.'

'What on earth makes you think they wanted to get you?' Alpiew fanned the cards out and shuffled again. 'Have you cheated so many people they're all after you?'

'I have had threats. Letters telling me that I will die.'

Alpiew looked up and appraised the Scotswoman.

'Who from?'

'How would I know? Some madman.'

'Or woman.'

'Perhaps.' Lady Murdo-McTavish wrung her hands. 'At first I thought it was her – Aurelia. I got the first threatening note the day she arrived. And she wandered about as though she'd been among us all her life. Her enigmatic visage never cracked, with its pristine mask of addition, the white ceruse, her immaculate ash-blonde curls snaking around her neck, beautifully contrasting with the blue veins painted so delicately upon her bosom. The most perfect make-up I have ever seen. Right down her neck, and her breast. Even her hands. So few people at St Germain bother to paint their hands. She was like a player in the theatre. We're all so tired and bored with each other that she seemed an amusement at first. But I didn't like her. She was cold, and those black eyes . . .' She shuddered before continuing. 'I felt they were ever searching, prying. Seeking out the secrets of my very soul.'

'So what did they say, these threatening notes?'

'"You will die for disposing me." Things like that.'

'Have you disposed of *me* yet, or am I still in your ownership?' Alpiew sat back in her chair. 'You make a habit of disposing of people, do you?'

'I thought it must be a mistake – "disposing me". It made me think they were written by someone French, who didn't properly understand English.'

'Perhaps it was someone like me who you won at cards, and then sold on?'

'I'd never . . .'

'Go on.' Alpiew dealt a hand. 'I play for myself and the Countess's home. I stake two hundred livres.'

'There are two ways out of the Bastille,' said Pigalle, sitting up in bed, sipping a warm brandy. 'We write a creeping letter of apology to that strutting megalomaniac, Louis, keeping our fingers crossed that it is not intercepted by anyone, most of all his bitch of a mistress, and wait for his reply, freeing us. Or we break out.'

'You make that second one sound so easy, Olympe. What do we do, stroll out of the front door?' The Countess was climbing into bed, in a red silk night-gown lent to her by Pigalle.

'I take your point. We need to discuss this with someone who knows.' She leapt out of bed and pulled on her shoes. 'If I do escape, I will have to travel everywhere in disguise, of course, but . . . Come along.'

'Where are we going now?'

'We need to speak to the expert.' She walked into the fireplace and climbed on to a stack of books. 'I have never had occasion to visit him till now, but I know where he is. They moved him today. You can always tell. Follow me!' cried Pigalle, tucking up her skirt, exposing her spindly legs and red-heeled shoes. The Countess watched as Pigalle pulled herself up the chimney and her feet slowly disappeared from view.

'But, Olympe . . .' The Countess winced as she prepared to follow. Pigalle was so thin, whereas she had a healthy *embonpoint*. She climbed daintily on to some books and gazed up into the long, thin chimney. What if she got stuck?

'Ashby – come on!' Pigalle's voice rasped with a hollow echo from the void.

Gripping on to an iron spar, the Countess hauled herself up into the darkness. Ahead of her Pigalle was crawling along a tunnel radiating from the main chimney at a steep angle. Taking a deep breath and murmuring a quick prayer, the Countess followed. After a brisk crawl the light ahead grew stronger as Pigalle cleared the tunnel and dropped from view. The Countess shuffled along after her and peeked meekly down into a candle-lit room. She crossed herself again, took a deep breath and jumped. She landed in a sooty bundle at a gentleman's feet. She staggered to her feet, brushing herself down and wishing she was not wearing such a provocative night-dress. She pushed a stray hair out of her eye, only to realise that her wig was somewhere back in the chimney.

'Hello,' she said, gazing with awe at the man. 'Or is it *bonjour*?'

'*Buongiorno*,' said the man, fully dressed in a beautiful blue velvet suit, his long white hair tumbling out on to his shoulders. He tossed back his cloak, revealing a beautifully turned calf, and held out a hand. 'Might I help you to a chair, madam?'

But the Countess stood rooted to the spot, unable to utter

or move, for though she could see the man's eyes sparkling in her direction, his face was entirely covered by an iron mask.

'That's a spare ace, Mistress Alpiew, that I believe you are keeping up your sleeve.'

Alpiew threw the card down. 'And you, Lady Murdo-McTavish, have secreted the king of clubs somewhere about your person.'

'I'd say we were equally matched, wouldn't you?'

'Equal as sharpers, perhaps, but not in duplicity.'

'I've told you before: I am not to blame for your lady staking her house.'

'Enough of your crafty flim-flams.' Alpiew picked up another card from the deck. 'From what I've heard we could be stuck here in this room till one or other of us dies.'

'With only the banshee for company.'

The witch, still staring into the night, gave a little shriek and sank down on to her chair.

'You've set her off now,' said Alpiew as Lady Murdo-McTavish rose from the table. 'We'll never get any rest if she gets into a state, believe me.'

'There are only two beds. Where am I to sleep?'

'Well, you're not sharing with me.' Alpiew pulled the other spare cards from her sleeve and gave a sigh. 'What use is my lady's London house to you? Tell me that.'

'All right.' Isabel Murdo-McTavish threw her arms up and wailed. 'I'll tell you. I am, like you, a wily card-player . . .'

'You mean cheat,' mumbled Alpiew, not really liking to admit it of herself.

'I picked it up from my late husband. He wasn't as good as I am, and thanks to him I lost my fortune – all of it – before we came into exile. Then, to add to my humiliation, once we were settled at St Germain the wretched man died of a clap, leaving me penniless. You've seen how it is there. Dog eat dog. I earn my keep. I gamble and I win. But all that I win goes directly to someone else, and in turn they provide me with income enough to stay at St Germain. There you have it. Yes, I won your mistress's house and you and some personage called Godfrey, but they are all signed over now to another.'

'Who?'

'That I cannot tell you, and even if I could I wouldn't, or all the many years I have been playing the game will have been pointless for I will lose everything.'

'How can someone have control of your life like that?' Alpiew thought hard. Who among that sinister set of ghouls could be manipulating the Scotswoman? 'Why don't you just leave St Germain? The world is a big place.'

'I cannot leave.' Lady Murdo-McTavish put her fingers to her lips. 'You wouldn't understand.'

'You *have* left, madam. Look about you. You are detained at His Majesty's pleasure. You *have* left whatever you thought kept you at St Germain.'

Suddenly Lady Isabel threw herself on to Alpiew's bed and sobbed loudly into the pillow.

'Lord, madam,' said Alpiew, rising and throwing down her handkerchief. She didn't like the idea of sleeping on a pillow damp with another's tears. 'Here are such unaccountable choppings and changings the devil himself couldn't tell what to make of them.'

It's love, she thought. The Scottish muse was enamoured with some married cove at St Germain. Though which of those whining, sighing, ogling fops and coxcombs would inspire such a love, she could not imagine. 'And he won't know where you are now, will he?' she said quietly. 'Your love will think you've left him anyway.'

Lady Murdo-McTavish wailed, and in doing so set the witch in the window off into an inharmonious caterwauling.

'I hope this will work,' said the Countess, her head up the chimney as she swept piles of soot from obscure ledges into a rolled-up cone of paper torn from one of Pigalle's books. 'I suppose you have enough face cream and butter to mix it up with?'

'I think I'm in love with him,' said Pigalle, staring into the candlelight and reaching for a quill. 'I shall write him a billet-doux. Who knows, perhaps ze fellow will be freed one day, and he could come to live with me in St James's. We could hang his mask on the wall. It would make a gorgeous *objet* of décor for my salon.'

'How much soot will we need, do you think, Olympe, to blacken our faces, necks and hands?'

'"Dear Mysterious Prisoner . . ."' Pigalle's quill hovered above the page. 'I wonder what he has done zat he will not reveal his name even to *us*? "You must allow us to repay your kindness . . ."'

'When I have collected enough soot, Olympe, should I start tearing the sheets to make the ropes, or would it give the gaoler too much of a clue if he notices that our sheets are gone?'

'It must be hard for him to see out of zat terrible iron contraption,' Pigalle mused to herself. 'So I must remind him . . . "I am tall with an admirable figure."' She scratched and dipped. '"My eyes are rather large, but I never open zem fully, a charm which gives me ze sweetest tenderest look possible."' Pigalle tried out the doe-eyed look and was impressed by the impression in her hand-glass. '"My throat is well-modelled, my hands divine, my arms passable (zey are perhaps a little thin) but I am consoled for zis misfortune by ze pleasure of having ze most beautiful legs in ze world." Zere!' she said with a flourish. 'If he does not come and visit me in London when he gets out, call me Aureng-Zebe.'

'Have you ever wondered, Olympe,' said the Countess, emerging from the chimney with black hands and a smutty face, 'if he is such an expert in escaping, why has he never tried himself?'

'Never mind about zat,' snapped Pigalle, hastily sealing her love letter. 'We must hope zat Alpiew comes soon, for we don't want to leave her behind.'

Alpiew gave her bed to Lady Isabel and sat up at the table until the Scotswoman was asleep, whiling away the time flicking through *Pilgrim's Progress*. The witch never took her eyes from the dark sky.

The candle guttered, and Alpiew blew it out.

Before the witch had time to accustom herself to the change, Alpiew dashed for the chimney and prepared for the long crawl.

As she approached the turning which led to the Countess's chimney, she called ahead in a low whisper. Four hands appeared in the light below, and helped her down.

'Thank goodness,' said the Countess. 'We thought you would never come.'

Alpiew rubbed her eyes. Was it smut in her eye or was the Countess turned black?

'Here –' cried Pigalle, thrusting a bowl full of a black cream at her. 'Spread zis over your face, neck and arms. We are still knotting ze sheets.'

'What is happening?' Obediently Alpiew smeared the black unguent over herself. 'Why are we turning Hottentot?'

'We are breaking out, of course,' said the Countess, stamping on one end of a ripped sheet while she pulled at another to tighten the knot. 'We have so little time, for once the sun starts to rise 'twill be too late.'

Pigalle was busily tying an end of sheet to a bedpost and running back and forth from the chimney to the bay, piling up books.

'Do you know what you're doing? There's a moat down there, isn't there, and guards with dogs?'

'I have meat,' said Pigalle, dangling a linen bag. 'Hurry now.'

'Thirty, thirty-three . . .' The Countess was winding the sheet-rope and counting. 'Thirty-six, thirty-nine.'

'Where will we go to?'

'Sshsh!' The Countess shook her head. 'Forty-five, forty-eight.'

'Three times table is a very hard one,' hissed Pigalle, wrapping a dark cloak round Alpiew's shoulders. 'We need sixty feet, and he told us our arms were about three foot long.'

'Sixty!' cried the Countess. 'And a bit to spare.'

Pigalle threw open the window, grabbed the loose end of the rope and tossed it out. 'I am tallest so I will go first.' She climbed up on to the ledge and teetered for a bit, before turning, clinging to the rope and lowering herself. 'Wait till you hear me in ze water, then follow.'

Her ginger mop of hair disappeared below the window ledge. The bed gave a creak and the rope tightened. The Countess leaned out, watching her friend.

'It's a long way down, Alpiew.'

There was a clanking sound and Alpiew spun round, hoping the bed was not about to collapse. 'Madam!' She stared in horror as another clank and a rattle came from the door.

The Countess turned as the door opened, revealing the Governor and two warders.

Beneath the window a splash.

'Mesdames!' cried the Governor, staring at their blackened faces. 'Are you both turned Mulatto to welcome me?'

'We were enacting some scenes from the famous play *The Empress of Morocco*.' The Countess closed the window, and stepped gingerly away from it. 'And hoped it would give our performance a little more veracity.'

'And what is this?' The Governor pointed at the taut line of knotted sheet.

'That is ...' the Countess gazed at it and stammered, 'it is ...'

'It is the sail of the royal ship the Empress travels upon,' said Alpiew, falling into a curtsey at the Countess's feet and speaking in a sing-song tone. 'Your royal majesty of majesties, come light upon yon noble barge and leave bold Euphonio's curse behind ye!'

The Countess looked down at Alpiew in horror. What was the wench babbling about? No character called Euphonio appeared in *The Empress of Morocco*.

There was a squealing, splashing sound coming from outside the window. Alpiew was nodding up at her to continue.

The Countess grabbed a book from the table, ran to the window and flung it out. Another splash. Another squawk.

'Thus,' the Countess declaimed as loud as she could, 'thus I fling the remnants of my maidenhead into the vasty deep of the Barbary Sea, before *I am removed by my keepers from this place* to somewhere . . . I know not where.' She threw her arms wide and hoped for further inspiration in the art of poesy. 'Come, Gaoler! Take me whither thou goest.'

'You English are funny dogs, all the same.' The Governor shook his head. 'I am sure, ladies, your performance was dazzling, but I have more serious business with you now.' One of the warders handed him a letter.

'I hold here a *lettre de cachet* in the names Countess Ashby de la Zouche and Mistress Alpiew.'

Alpiew took a deep breath. The Countess gulped.

'It declares No True Bill, and so, by order of His Majesty, Louis King of France . . .' Both shut their eyes and winced. 'I must take you from His Majesty's Prison of the Bastille and deliver you back into the hands of my friend.'

From the shadows behind him emerged the Man in Black.

SIX

*A la Royale — a particular
way of preserving
cherries as it were after the
royal manner*

The sun was rising as the coach pulled out of Paris.

Alpiew and the Countess sat in silence, occasionally catching eyes and raising their eyebrows. They dared not speak.

Both entertained thoughts of gibbets and gallows, of burnings at the stake, of beheadings with silver swords and blunt axes, of the rack and the wheel. Both winced at the thought of Pigalle, in the moat of the Bastille, blacked up and floundering.

After about an hour rattling along country lanes, the coach came into a town of wide boulevards and elegant newly built houses.

The Countess had never seen a town like it. 'Where is this place?' she said, pointing out of the window. '*Ici, où?*'

'Versailles.' The Man in Black gave a little inclination of the head.

'Versailles!' The Countess turned to Alpiew. 'My God, this place has changed since I saw it in the fifties. It was a tiny hamlet, then, and look!'

The coach swung round a busy market square and into a wide tree-lined avenue.

'Louis had a little hunting lodge out here. His chateau. I went there once to a party. Draughty, poky little place.'

The coach rolled across a bit of scrub and through a portal made up of two obelisks before passing through a wrought-iron gate and into a huge cobbled courtyard.

The coach made a sharp turn and jolted to a stop.

'*Mesdames* –' the Man in Black indicated the carriage door, which was being held open by a smartly liveried lackey – '*le chateau du roi, Louis quatorze.*'

'Odskilderkins!' cried Alpiew, stepping out and looking around her at the vast but gracious building, a redbrick C wrapped around a black-and-white chequered courtyard, with its hundreds of windows and gilt roof leads sparkling in the morning sunshine. 'This is some rum lodgings.'

'Fan me, ye winds!' The Countess teetered out into the sunlight. 'I think Louis has put up an extension or two since I was last here.'

'*Allons!*' said the Man in Black, hastily entering through a side door.

The Countess and Alpiew followed him up an ornate marble staircase crowded with gabbling hordes of elegant people waiting for entry to the royal apartments. The crowd parted as the Man in Black swept up, led by a pair of Swiss Guards. Alpiew stopped to gape at a pair of sedan chairs, tilted precariously mid-staircase, primped ladies sitting proudly inside, their chairmen bullying to be the first on to the loggia at the top of the steps. The Swiss Guards barked an order and the chairmen fell back, flattening a few elderly men in the mob behind them.

They passed into the vestibule, while the Man in Black pushed on through the guardroom, which was lined with rows of empty sedan chairs. Chattering chairmen, lifeguards and a press of primped and painted courtiers formed a mob trying to get into the next room.

'What a place!' Alpiew tugged the Countess's sleeve. 'Did you ever see the like?'

In the ornately decorated white-and-gold room, a babble of

courtiers fluffed up their wigs, drew their sword-knots smartly to the side, and adjusted their sashes, while gossiping with women dressed in a rainbow of silk and brocade. Instinctively, the Countess's hand flew up to her face. Such make-up! White as alabaster, rouged cheeks, bird's-egg blue shadowed eyes and mouths slashed in crimson. And that was just the men.

The Man in Black stood back and let the Countess and Alpiew go first. As they passed into the next room they heard a general guffaw behind them. '*Anglais! Anglais!*' cried the crowd. 'Bizzzzzaaarrrrrrrre!'

What have they to laugh at? thought Alpiew. They're wearing enough paint to plaster a kitchen wall.

But all thoughts of the cruel laughter behind them were dispelled at the sight of the next room they entered.

Alpiew gasped. The Countess stood open-mouthed gaping at it.

'Sure, 'tis the eighth wonder of the world!' Alpiew twirled, gazing round and up. 'Whoever has seen such a room except in dreams?'

'All those mirrors! And all huge.' The Countess was trying to count them, totting up the cost. 'I didn't know they could make looking glasses so big.'

'It makes the proposed looking glass in the German Street front room seem rather piddling, does it not, milady?'

'This room must have cost hundreds of thousands of pounds.'

Some in the crowd around them started to titter into their sleeves. The Man in Black silenced them with a look. When he felt the Countess and Alpiew had expressed sufficient awe, he led them onwards, striding towards one of the mirrored alcoves. He knocked quietly at a secret door set within the wall. The crowd hushed. People nudged one another, jealous, as the door was opened and the Man in Black ushered the Countess and Alpiew inside. The Swiss Guards waited outside in the Hall of Mirrors.

The three passed briskly through a room where a dozen sombre courtiers sat round a table, busily scratching at papers and sealing letters. The Man in Black raised his little finger and scratched at the next door with a long curved nail. He then bowed to Alpiew and the Countess and left them.

The door slowly opened.

They entered a billiard room, empty but for a guard. In the corner behind the billiard table stood a screen. On the mantel an ornate clock ticked loudly.

'What's happening, milady?' hissed Alpiew, giving the enigmatic guard the once-over. 'I've never seen such a magnificent place in all my life.'

'It's not a dream, is it?' The Countess spoke loudly to make sure that if anyone was listening they heard her. 'It makes St James's Palace look like a dog kennel.'

The Countess shuffled. She didn't like the way the guard was smirking at them. Alpiew started laughing.

'What's funny?'

'I doubt but he doesn't speak English, madam. But here we stand in this awe-inspiring place and, maybe you have forgotten, but we are both still carbonadoed from last night's escapade.'

The Countess looked down at her blackened hands and cleavage. This in a place where, from the look of the ladies they had passed, the more impressive the equipage, the whiter the paint. 'Oh lord, Alpiew. We are standing in the private apartments of the most puissant monarch in the world looking like a pair of Newcastle coalmen.'

The far door opened and a man entered, holding a large packet of papers. He nodded at the guard who left the room, shutting the door behind him.

'Welcome to King Louis quatorze's cabinet des secrets.' The man laid his papers on the billiard table. He spoke perfect English. 'I presume you are grateful to His Majesty for your release?'

'Very,' said the Countess, deciding not to remind him that His Majesty had had them banged up in the first place.

'First, you can tell me about this –' He whipped out a piece of scrawled paper. 'What does it mean?'

They took the paper and read it.

'Scurrilous!' The Countess left it to Alpiew and wiped her hands, leaving a black streak on her skirts.

'Filthy!' Alpiew was looking very carefully at it, holding the paper close to her face. 'Who wrote this scurvy smut?'

'You did,' said the man, glaring at Alpiew.

'I did not.' Alpiew lowered the paper and handed it back. 'It looks like my hand, I'll give you that. But it is forged. See where the writing wavers between the letters. Look at the tails on the "d"s and "g"s. That is where the writer shows himself up as a falsifier of not quite the first water.'

'You are observant, madam.' The man inspected the paper. 'And level-headed. Many people would have been sent into a panic in such a situation. It was handed in to one of His Majesty's servants. Presumably to expedite your instant imprisonment.' He laid the paper down and rubbed his hands. 'His Majesty realised his error and released you from the horrors of the Bastille. But nothing comes free in this world, mesdames, as I am sure you know. So, in return, His Majesty desires me to hire you ... er ...' He stopped and looked down, shuffling through the papers. 'Tell me, Countess, what do you know of the man they call the Mysterious Prisoner of the Bastille?'

'I don't know of whom you are speaking.' The Countess did not want to get the pitiable fellow into any more trouble than he already was.

'Are you sure?' Their inquisitor looked the Countess in the eye. 'A man in an iron mask?'

The stillness behind the screen was overwhelming.

'I repeat: I do not know to whom you refer.' She had no intention of talking about the tunnels in the chimneys, and how else would she have known about him? She wrung her hands. All this talk of the Mysterious Prisoner reminded her again of poor Pigalle. 'Apart from the Governor's reception, I had only the company of Alpiew and my dearest friend, the Duchesse de Pigalle ...'

A snuffling sound came from behind the screen.

'His Majesty has commanded me to employ the pair of you to act as informants at the Court of St Germain.'

'Spies, you mean?' Alpiew felt her heart skip a beat. This was more like it. A proper job.

'You will store your information carefully. *None* of your findings will be written down and left around. If you must write things down, keep them about you. The place is a hotbed of thievery, as I gather you experienced for yourselves. We are satisfied that Queen Mary's ring was placed in your bag to incriminate you and cast the light away from the real villains who loiter in the Stuart court. The theft was reported to us, as was a hint of where to find the missing ring. Clearly someone at the chateau wanted you out of the way. Have you any idea who that might have been?'

'I don't know about them wanting us out of the way, mister,' said Alpiew. 'But I can tell you we heartily wished ourselves out of the way.'

The Countess jabbed her in the ribs. 'I think what Alpiew means is that we were not pleased to be separated.'

'We were also informed that someone, a writer by repute, had been libelling His Majesty. Naturally we do not look kindly upon that sort of thing, especially among a group of people dependent upon His Majesty's charity. But a later report indicated that we had picked up the wrong writers, and that another lady was the one guilty of writing defamatory stories about His Majesty.'

'Isabel Murdo-McTavish!' The Countess laughed. 'Unless His Majesty is a squirrel or a woman who lives in a gingerbread house, I think he can count himself safe from the whiplash of her pen. The woman writes fairy tales. And I would suggest that whoever reported her must be in a similar trade, for it is as unlikely a prospect that Lady Murdo-McTavish could write political tracts as that the plays of the Elizabethan hack Shakespeare should one day be performed at the Comédie Française.'

The man stared closely at the Countess, and scribbled a note to himself.

'Be that as it may, madam, in the course of our own explorations we have discovered that you two have a good reputation in London for investigation. So you are to go to St Germain and investigate for the King of France.' The man picked up a piece of paper and read from it. 'His Majesty wants to know a number of things: 1) What happened to the girl Aurelia, and why? He is very keen that another poisoning scandal does not sully his reign. 2) Who are the thieves? 3) Whether any of the Jacobites among the company have plans to raise armies or plots against King William, who, you may know, is now acknowledged by our King as the rightful ruler of England. 4) Why certain French lords insist on dining at St Germain, when it is well known the cuisine here at Versailles is infinitely superior.'

'I can answer you that last question now,' snapped the Countess. 'The answer is peas.'

'Peas?'

'You know, little round green things. Eaten on a knife.'

The man laid his papers on the billiard table and leaned forward. There was a creaking behind the screen.

'In order to both please and flatter His Majesty, the courtiers feel that while in his chateau they need to eat peas by the bucket-load. But then, not being as fond as His Majesty of those smaragdine legumes, they have need afterwards to retire to the next room to exgurgitate.'

A chortle from the corner.

'What is that snickering noise?' The Countess pointed at the screen. 'Why does not the titterer disclose himself to us as it is clear we know him to be there?'

Another laugh from behind the screen, followed by a short whisper.

'Why have you darkened your faces to come here?' asked the man.

'We were acting . . .' said the Countess. '*The Empress of . . .*'

'Escaping, sir,' said Alpiew. 'We were escaping from the Bastille. And we'd have done it, if we hadn't been interrupted with his letter de cachay.'

'Oh lord! Olympe!' The Countess went into a fluster. 'You must know too, sirrah, that we are very worried about our friend the Duchesse de Pigalle, who we left thrashing about in the moat.'

The giggling behind the screen erupted into full-blown laughter.

The man leaning against the billiard table tried to cover the sound by feigning a coughing attack. 'The gentleman who took you to the Bastille and brought you here is His Majesty's Private Secretary. You will see him oft-times at St Germain. He may not be addressed by you, but will contact you when necessary.'

'Grateful as I am to His Majesty, I'm not going back to those kitchens to work for that Wackland fellow again,' said Alpiew. 'I'd rather go back to the Bastille.'

'If it is His Majesty's pleasure you can be sent to the gallows, for all I care. His Majesty could always prepare for you another of his favourite *lettres de cachet* . . .'

'Back to the Bastille again?'

'No, no. This one would suit you very well, I'm sure. It sends you to a convent.'

'For a retreat,' said the Countess. 'How lovely – all that silence.'

'No. To join the order. Indefinitely. You would both become nuns. In a silent order.'

'Oh lord, madam!' Alpiew pulled the Countess's sleeve. 'Not that. Anything but that!'

'So I'm sure you see that if you know what is sensible in planning a long and happy life you will go to St Germain and do as you are asked. Countess, you will stay at the chateau in the same rooms as you had before.'

'Not the garret!'

'Yes, we feel that there you are most likely to be at the

centre of things. Madam Alpiew will be lodged in rooms in a townhouse. That way you will be free to look around the chateau without being under the orders of the St Germain staff. Remember, we will be watching you both. As I am sure you know we have been doing so since you first arrived at King James's court.' He looked at the mantel clock. 'You have a limited amount of time. Today is Sunday. His Majesty gives you until Friday night to return here with the answers.'

'Why Friday night?'

'We have had information that there will be a Jacobite atrocity and it will take place on Friday night.'

'And if we can't find what you want?'

He shot Alpiew a forbidding look as he strutted towards the door. 'A coach will pick you up at dusk from the chequered courtyard. You will find your bags waiting for you with the guards at the outer door. In the meantime you are invited to look around the royal domain of Versailles. On a sunny day like this, you will find the gardens refreshing, with many a private shady nook.' As he opened the door for them, he handed them a note. 'Study this. One of our spies came across it in a room in the chateau at St Germain.'

'Whose room?' asked the Countess.

'Someone we suspect of being a spy. But that is not information we feel inclined to share with you. You may not take it away with you, but it will be part of your job to decipher the riddle. Possibly it will relate to the other questions.'

The Countess tumbled against Alpiew in an attempt to curtsey as the man called after them: 'I think it would be wise for you to join one of the St Germain clubs. Preferably the writers' group.'

'But . . .'

'Do we get paid for this employment?'

The door closed behind them.

The midday sun beat down relentlessly on the parterres as the Countess and Alpiew walked away from the chateau.

They made their way down stone steps and sat under the spray of a magnificent fountain, looking back in awe and wonder at the huge palace.

The Countess undid the seal on the letter and read:

L.S.

Resurrection

Epiphany

Friday Night

Apocalypse: Death of the exalted whore.

'Well that's as clear as the Thames on a foggy night.'

'I don't understand. If there's such a rush on, why don't they cart us back to St Germain right now?'

'I think we are first meant to take in the extent of His Majesty's domain – and therefore his power.'

'Oh lord, madam, I hate being spied upon.' Alpiew looked over her shoulder. 'Do you think someone is listening to us now?'

'Not unless one of the golden nymphs in this fountain is real.' She peered forward to take a closer look at the figures basking in the sparkling water. 'Hey day, what's going on here? The women are all taunting that marble maiden up top, and most of them are turning into frogs. See, Alpiew, some of them are already fully frogs.'

'Perhaps that's what His Majesty will do to us if we don't crack his mysteries.' Alpiew dipped her hands into the fountain and washed the grease and soot off. 'Who was laughing boy behind the screen?'

'The private secretary fellow who's been following us about, perhaps?'

'No. It is someone much taller. I could see two humps of black hair sticking up like horns. Is the King of France tall?'

'Very. Oh, Alpiew, there are so many questions. We had better get it all sorted out before we are separated again. What a humiliation to have been arrested and imprisoned. They will all take us for criminals now, mark my words.' She fanned herself with the mystery letter. 'Good lord but it's hot.'

'Milady, remember, unless we tell them, no one will know we have been in the Bastille. How can they? Even the guards at the entrance were forbidden to look at us, and to the ones inside we were a pair of numbers. I think we should tell the whole frightful crew we've been into Paris to see a sick friend.'

'Someone will know.' The Countess smiled and winked at Alpiew. 'The one who reported us in the first place.'

'Oh yes. Of course.' Alpiew threw her head back and let the sun warm her face. 'I love this place. And at least we are free again.'

'Oh dear, poor Pigalle. I do hope she survived the swim, and made it out into the world.' She held her hand to her mouth. 'I promised to protect her from some villains who were chasing her. Now I think on't, perhaps it's better if she's been caught and locked up again.' She too dipped her hands into the cool water and splashed it over her soot-streaked face. 'How will I eat at that dreadful place? I'll suspect every mouthful to be noxious. It's all very well for those young rakes to come to St Germain to avoid peas – what will I do to avoid food? I shall be as thin as a whip by the time we return home.' She let out a little wail. 'Phough, Alpiew, I shall have to be part of the wretched writers' circle.'

'The Scot is in the Bastille. So you may take over her domain and make it your own.'

'Indeed and indeed.'

A passing woman, teetering on high heels, stared at them, laughing. Alpiew put her hands on her hips and glared back.

'Well, madam?' she challenged, and seeing no response to her English continued: 'The devil, madam, are you in a fit to laugh at us because we are a little grey-faced?'

The woman muttered something incomprehensible in French.

'Spit your venom, Madam Toad!' Alpiew grabbed the Countess's arm and led her away. 'My lady and I have taken a little too much sun, not to mention too many Frogs.'

People were spilling out into the gardens, strolling along the paths; some were already rowing on the lake, others sitting in shady groves that radiated from the main paths.

'Let's find another quieter fountain, madam, and wash this filthy smut from our faces. Maybe we can find some seats in the shade and curl up for a little nap. And no doubt there will be food somewhere inside. We must eat our fill while we can, even if it is only peas.'

They strolled along, past more beautiful fountains, and found a solitary spot tucked away in a dappled walk near the fountain of Bacchus, with his black grapes and drunken gold cherubs.

'We must lay our hands on a Bible,' said the Countess, 'so that we can study the details of the Epiphany and the Apocalypse, and try to work out that riddle.'

The Countess took the paper from Alpiew and scrutinised it. 'If I am not mistaken, this note is writ by the same person who wrote the ubiquitous vengeance notes.' She screwed up her eyes and squinted down at the paper. 'Do you know, Alpiew, it looks to me more like a list of things to do, or a shopping order than a riddle.'

'How long do we have? Four days. Where do we start, milady?' Alpiew bit her lower lip. 'What do we look for?'

'Smallest things first. The jewellery.'

'I saw the ring. I know Pipe hid the ring in her mouth and then caused a fuss to distract everyone. Also she seems to go everywhere, with no questions asked. Not only that. There's something about the girl I don't quite trust.'

'I agree. Only saw her half a second, but she is too pert

for my liking.' The Countess was peering along a leafy walk which ended in another ornate fountain. 'Look – who are they?'

A row of orderly young women trooped into the path, striding in step towards them. They were all dressed in uniform brown skirts and whalebone bodices, with white caps, collar and lace cuffs. The eldest wore blue ribbons, then came yellow and green and finally red.

'My word, what a formidable bunch,' said Alpiew, stepping back to let them file past.

'They are the girls from St Cyr.' Mademoiselle Smith was standing beside them, apparently having appeared from nowhere. 'I saw you by the Latona Fountain. This afternoon the Marquis is making a demonstration for the girls. I am free until tomorrow. So I am meeting up with an old friend to stroll through the gardens.'

'Was *your* school like that?' Alpiew was still watching the martial line of girls pass. 'Like a military academy?'

'Oh no!' Mademoiselle Smith laughed. 'It was supposed to be, of course, but I'm afraid our outfit was a very second-rate place.'

'How do you mean?' The Countess thought back to Pigalle's talk of the school she had started. 'More like a brothel?'

'Most certainly not. But we didn't have ribbons, and awards, and trips to places like Versailles.' Leonora Smith looked hard at the Countess. 'Were you in some kind of accident? Only you seem to have a few smuts on your skin.'

'Ah yes,' said the Countess. 'We were watching one of the gentlemen here demonstrate a new flying engine and it exploded and . . . Alpiew and I were about to wash ourselves down in this fountain.'

'You'll get all kinds of diseases from that filthy water. It's piped in from miles away. There is no river near the Chateau of Versailles, you know. Come with me and I'll take you round to somewhere you can really wash yourself down.'

'How kind of you, Miss Smith.' The Countess pulled Alpiew

away. 'I'm glad you have a friend here. I suppose you must be rather lonely at St Germain now that Aurelia . . .'

'I am shocked at her death, certainly. But, as I told Alpiew, I barely knew her. I had only talked to her twice.'

'We were wondering what Monsieur the Marquis made of it all.'

'He doesn't know.' Leonora looked very serious. 'But I'm sure he would blame it on potatoes. If the mad English insist on eating poisonous tubers he believes that sort of thing is inevitable. Now, if you follow me, I can lead you to the kitchens and after you have washed yourselves, you can taste some fare fit for a King.'

As the shadows lengthened the Countess and Alpiew, pockets stuffed with bread and cheese, bags bulging with fruit and pastries, made their way to the side door to find their coach.

'*Bon soir, mesdames!*' Baron Lunéville, the tall French gentleman who regularly came to St Germain to escape the dreaded peas, stood before them. He had a dejected air about him.

'You come St Germain?' said the Countess, thinking that if she left a few words out the sentence would be easier for a Frenchman to understand.

He shook his head and wagged a finger. '*Pas aujourd'hui.*' He leaned towards them in a conspiratorial fashion. '*Le Roi!*' He rolled his eyes up. '*Interdit!*'

The Countess felt guilty. Perhaps she had caused this ban on Versailles courtiers popping across to St Germain to escape peas.

He slouched away as a coach rumbled towards them.

They picked up their bags.

Roger stepped down from the postilion's seat and held the carriage door open as the Duc de Charme, resplendent in a silver satin suit with fluttering cherry-red ribbons and enormous puffs of lace, still wobbling precariously on very high heels, lurched down on to the wooden cobbles.

He caught sight of Alpiew and his eyes lit up. 'Eet's my

tam-tam girl!' He teetered over to her and raised his hands ready to pat her cleavage.

'Oh no you don't, you impertinent popinjay.' Alpiew raised her fist and threw a punch at the perfumed peacock. 'Last time you played upon my bubs as though they were a set of African drums I told you I'd give you a dowse in the chops if you tried it again, so don't say you weren't warned.'

The Duc de Charme's eyebrows almost touched his hairline, and his mouth was a perfect 'O'.

'My lord!' cried Roger, trying to grab the Duc as he staggered backwards, battling against the angle of his shoes. 'Oh, my lord Duc!'

'Is someone going to help me out of this infernal coach? I'm stifling.' A pale woman with dark brown hair was leaning out of the carriage. Alpiew recognised her at once as the woman she had seen with Whippingham the day after Aurelia's death.

'Ah well.' The woman gathered up her skirts and jumped without help, almost losing her balance too as she hit the ground. She whipped out her fan and flapped. 'It is too hot. Versailles is hell when it's like this.'

The valet glared at the woman as he steadied the Duc.

'Come along, my lord,' cried the woman, grabbing hold of the Duc's elbow. 'We shall be late.'

The Duc addressed Alpiew, his eyes fixed on her cleavage: 'I was only admiring your formidable *poitrine*, madam.' He was upright now, busily untangling the ribbons, which were caught in his blue sash and hooked up in the ringlets of his enormous wig, which in turn was caught in his diamond earrings. 'Eet ees a compliment. I love women with the big front.' He rolled his hands in front of his lacy cravat, then gathered his fingers together and kissed them. '*Parfait!*'

Alpiew scowled. The Countess caught her arm before she lunged forward again.

'Ooh la la!' said the Duc, fire in his eyes. '*Les fauves!*'

Like an apparition, the Man in Black glided between them. In silence he looked the Countess in the eye and pointed towards the coach.

'We are to travel in the Duc's coach?'

'Eet ees not mine,' the Duc giggled, grabbing his ebony-and-silver cane with a flourish that set his bracelets jangling. *'Allons.'*

He wobbled into the chateau, with the mystery woman a few steps behind.

As the Countess climbed up into the coach, the Man in Black put out his hand.

'What's he want now?' said Alpiew.

He did a little mime of writing.

'I hope you've got it memorised.' The Countess pulled the riddle from her bag and handed it back.

'You know me, milady. It's inscribed in my brain.'

The valet jumped back up on top, as the Man in Black slammed the coach door, and the horses trotted off.

'Phwoagh.' Alpiew fanned the air inside the coach. 'That fellow wears more perfume than all the whores in Covent Garden. That woman with him, she's the one I saw with Whippingham. Is that his wife, the Duchesse?'

'Harrumph!' The Countess slumped back and screwed up her mouth. 'It most certainly is not. Why, the wench was young enough to be his daughter. The Duchesse is a strange-looking little thing. She has a great hooked nose reaching almost to her pouty red rosebud lips.'

'Easily recognisable, then?'

'Yes, you can't miss her,' snapped the Countess. 'She looks like a parrot eating a cherry.'

'And does she laugh at his effeminacy?'

'Au contraire. She appears to dote upon him.'

'Fancy a beribboned Jack-a-Dandy like him being surrounded by doting women!'

'Ah yes,' said the Countess. 'It's a French thing. Their idea of masculinity seems to be the converse of ours.'

Alpiew gazed out at the elegant town streets. 'The trouble

with solving a poisoning is that the murderer doesn't even have to have been there at the deadly dinner. They could have been in the kitchens. They could have been asleep upstairs. They could have come from outside the chateau . . .'

'Yes, Alpiew, dear, I get your point.' The Countess rubbed her hands together and gritted her teeth. She didn't want to hear pessimism at this stage. If they applied themselves to this job they could be away in a fortnight. 'So what do we know? Whom do we suspect?'

'Everyone,' said Alpiew. 'What a bunch they are.'

'Is there anyone apart from Lady Whippingham who had a motive to kill the wretched girl?'

'You think it was Lady Whippingham? Why? Because the girl was flirting with her husband?' Alpiew pondered. 'It doesn't seem enough to me. Anyhow, I told you, she seems to be carrying on with Dr Stickworth.'

'Perhaps they did it together. A doctor would certainly be able to lay hands on poison.'

'And as we said before, milady, poison is not a precise method. Who is to say whether they did strike but hit the wrong target? Lady Murdo-McTavish is convinced it was meant for her.'

'Poison . . .' The Countess sat back and thought. She tried to remember all the poisoning cases she had read about. 'It's a coward's weapon.'

'Or a voyeur's,' said Alpiew. 'You lay it, then sit back and watch the consequences.'

'Come to think on it, why were none of the rest of us afflicted? Why was Aurelia the only one to suffer, when we all ate the same meal?'

'You were there. Try to remember. What did she eat and drink?'

'She drank some wine. But everyone had wine. I did too. She even went back to the table for more.'

'And what did she eat, do you recall?'

'That's the strange thing. She ate exactly the same things as I did.'

'There must have been something she ate and you did not, surely?'

The Countess felt rather uneasy. She didn't like anyone to think she was greedy, but . . . 'You know how I pick at things, Alpiew. Well, I took a little of everything there. Just to try it. I had a little of *every* single dish. So whatever she ate, she cannot have tasted anything I did not.' She wiggled uncomfortably. 'It was all so tempting.'

'All right then.' Alpiew couldn't help smiling at the Countess's confession. 'Perhaps your stomach is better designed for the stuff. But now I think on't, another thing comes to mind, milady: if a person has laid poison I reckon that they'd be a bit ginger about eating at the same table, just in case they poisoned themselves. Was anyone picking around at the food?'

'Yes – you have hit it. There was a person at the table who took her food and secreted it.' The Countess sat up, grabbing Alpiew. 'Isabel Murdo-McTavish.'

'Damn!' Alpiew banged her fists together. 'I wish I had known about that. I could have quizzed her last night. She told me she thought Aurelia was ghastly.'

'Everyone thought Aurelia was ghastly. Let's face it, she *was* ghastly. God rest her soul.' The Countess crossed herself.

'So all of the women of a certain age, apart from Lady Prude, received a note? And Lady Prude is involved in some intrigue or other with Wackland,' said Alpiew. 'I heard them quarrelling like husband and wife in the kitchen.'

'Lady Prude? She is in the same age group as the others.' The Countess rubbed her finger across her lips, leaving a red smudge up to her nose. 'Yet Aurelia also received a note. And she was, like Mademoiselle Smith, only about sixteen or seventeen years old.'

'So every woman except you, Mademoiselle Smith and Lady Prude got one of these threatening notes?'

'Those who received the notes may describe them as threatening, Alpiew, but think: what did the notes actually say?'

'"Tonight I will strike."'

'Indeed. It's a warning rather than a threat, wouldn't you say?'

The coach lurched over a hump in the road, and Alpiew was bounced along the seat until she was practically sitting on the Countess's lap.

'Lady Murdo-McTavish is up to something,' said the Countess, pulling herself free. 'But we know where she is now, so we are safe from her.'

'Nonetheless, Countess, you must be vigilant. You must not eat anything at table in St Germain.'

'You want me to watch all that delicious food slide down people's gullets and not taste any of it?' The Countess let out a wail. 'I shall be a walking skeleton.'

'I will get fresh food in the markets each day and bring it to you.'

'But if I am seen to be avoiding the food, should there be another poisoning I will be the chief suspect.'

'Then do as Lady Murdo-McTavish does: slop your food into a bag when no one is watching you and throw it away later.'

'Harrumph!' The Countess sank back into her seat and wailed. 'Why did I ever believe that wretched girl's stepmother's promise of money and drag us over here to this godforsaken country?'

Alpiew bit her lip and refrained from saying 'I told you so.'

'I *will* eat. And I will eat before them, and I will eat like a king.'

Alpiew waited.

'Eat like a king,' the Countess repeated, clapping her hands together. 'That's it, Alpiew! The King of France eats with his fingers. But at the fatal supper I thought I would miss out on the meal altogether because I hadn't brought my own caddinet. Do you see? Prude sent for a spoon and fork for me. Every person at St Germain has their own set of cutlery.'

'You mean . . . ?'

'Yes. The most likely source of the poison which killed Aurelia was her own caddinet.'

'And a person could smear poison upon a fork and spoon at any time of the day except mealtimes.'

'I must get a caddinet of my own, just to be safe.'

'No,' said Alpiew. 'There are fingers poking everywhere. Even if you slept with the thing under your pillow, I still wouldn't feel safe for you.'

'Food poisoning. Everyone is confined to their rooms with a flux,' said the Countess as quietly as she could even though they were standing outside in the lime walk with no other person in sight. 'I shall definitely starve to death.'

It was midday. The Countess had arrived at the chateau shortly after supper, and made her way straight to her old chamber, where she ate a little of the food she had purloined from Versailles and slept comfortably enough. She rose with the bells and made her way to the chapel only to find everyone from her end of the chateau remaining in their rooms with a dose of diarrhoea.

'Have you seen Virginia?' asked Alpiew.

'I peeped into her room. She was fast asleep. Or pretending to be.'

'And what of the others?'

'I told you.' The Countess held up her fan to shade her eyes from the glaring sun. 'They've *all* been poisoned this time.'

'What did they eat?'

'Oysters.'

'If they eat oysters in May no wonder they've got a flux.' Alpiew was delighted to find her accommodation was in a comfortable townhouse opposite the chateau. From her window she could watch the comings and goings. 'Has anyone escaped the illness?'

'Prude.' The Countess looked about her again. 'She was there in chapel this morning. Cornered me on the way out, trying to find out why we had left without informing her. And begged me to keep up my interests and join one of the little groups. I narrowly avoided being recruited to her Hagiographical Society.'

'When does the writers' circle meet?'

'This afternoon. But I doubt anyone will be there, on account of the flux.'

'Then it will be a perfect time for you to fulfil your royal obligation, milady. You will have the club all to yourself, what with the Scottish sharper banged up, and the others glued to their close-stools.' Alpiew looked about before whipping out a pencil and some paper. 'Let's quickly write our lists, then I will burn them in the fireplace at my lodgings.'

'Right.' The Countess trotted over to a shaded bench on the terrace facing the river valley.

'Lady Whippingham, Lady Prude, Mademoiselle Smith, the Duchesse de Charme and Isabel Murdo-McTavish . . .' Alpiew scratched down the names. 'Who else might have wanted the girl out of the picture?'

'It's odd,' said the Countess, 'but everything about this feels wrong. I can't put my finger on it, but . . . something doesn't add up.'

'I agree. And what of Wackland and his buns?' Alpiew sighed. What a situation to find themselves in. Their only hope of escape lay in solving a crime that seemed to have no logic to it. 'Let's go wild and run through everyone and allot them a reason, however ridiculous.'

'All right.' The Countess splayed her fingers and counted off the dinner guests one by one. 'I suspect Virginia has a month's mind for Lord Whippingham. If she is serious about finding a husband here and had decided upon him, might she have tried to dispatch a rival . . .'

'Criminy, madam, what can women see in that fat, snuff-covered windbag? And anyhow, she'd have done better to polish off his wife first, surely?' Alpiew scribbled down the name Virginia. 'I would still like to know what it is that smutty fellow gets up to with all those women in those rooms in Town. I'd like to get my hands on a magnifying telescope and follow Whippingham when he next wanders round the streets.'

'Dr Stickworth. He took the autopsy and, in my opinion, covered up.'

'Lord Wackland is in charge of the kitchens where the food came from.'

'The Duchesse de Charme was so upset she screamed and screamed. Oh, Alpiew, where can this lead us?'

Alpiew scratched out all the names. 'You are right.' She chewed on the end of her pencil. 'You know, I still think it is connected with that ring which ended up in your bag.'

'So let us imagine who here has reason to thieve . . .' The Countess threw her arms up in despair. 'Practically everyone. Servants resentful of their position or who want a little more besides their miserable perqs. Those with no money, which seems to be everyone concerned. Certainly all the people who live up in the garret, and therefore all the people at dinner.'

'Countess, Countess!' Virginia came running towards them, her face streaked with tears. 'Thank goodness you are back!'

Alpiew jammed the paper into her pocket, while the Countess rose to greet her charge.

'What on earth is wrong, child?'

'I have to go home.' Virginia collapsed on to the bench, sobbing. 'You were right. This is a horrible place. Please take me away with you . . .'

'You seemed happy the other day.' The Countess put her arm round the girl's shoulders. 'What has brought about this change? Are you suffering from the flux?'

'I must leave St Germain,' Virginia wailed. 'I need to go back to England. Now.'

'I'm afraid we can't, child. You know we cannot arrive in Dover without some proof we are not Jacobite spies.'

'My father will vouch for me. I know he will. He knows King William. He sells him candles and things. Wholesale.'

The Countess looked to Alpiew.

'We have no money, Virginia, to get us even as far as Calais,' said Alpiew following another train of thought. 'Remember, our money was stolen on the highway.'

'You do have money. I know you got your money back. 'Twas I arranged to have it put into your shoe by Mademoiselle Smith.'

'I suspected as much.' Alpiew glared at the girl. '*You* stole our money. But how?'

'I did not steal anything. I said I had the money restored to you, not that I took it. It was stolen by as arrant a knave as ever stole an innocent maiden's heart. I took it from him to make sure you got it back.'

'Who?'

'A man who knows neither principle nor honour. A man who has been bewitched by a whore old enough to be his grannum.'

'Bewitched?' Alpiew was ready with her pencil. 'And what is the name of this dastardly fellow?'

'I can't sully my lips by mentioning his name. As far as I am concerned, he is dead.'

'Dead?' Alpiew glanced at the Countess, who raised her eyebrows by way of reply.

'Interesting. A dead thief, messing about with an elderly witch.' The Countess picked at a black stain on her skirt. 'So what is your role in this decidedly unheroic tragedy?'

'The rake-hell has broken my heart.' The girl slipped down off the seat and sprawled out, face down on the grass. 'Oh God, I wish that I was dead.'

'I knew that boy John was trouble from the moment I first set eyes upon him.' Pipe lay sprawled out on the barrels by the kitchen door. 'Mr Confidence, I called him. And, lookit, didn't that girl Aurelia take ill within a day of the fellow turning up here? Lord Wackland was fooled by his sultry looks and his flashing smile, and he stopped concentrating and that's why everyone's been poisoned. Also, during the spalpeen's short time here things have gone missing. And now the rogue has done a disappearing trick.'

'I lost you some way back, Pipe.' Alpiew wanted to make sure about what she was hearing. 'You think that the boy who was turnspit before I arrived is a poisoner? Are you referring to the current collection of cases of the flux?'

'No.'

Alpiew perceived that Pipe was blushing.

'The other thing – the girl.'

'Aurelia? But I thought they said that she had died from an apoplexy?'

'That's what they *said*.' Pipe looked around then crooked her finger, summoning Alpiew closer. 'But only because they're scared what will happen if the news of a fresh spate of poisonings reaches Versailles.'

'So who has told you John is a poisoner? Wackland?'

'No. The Doctor is certain it was poison. I heard him whispering about it with Lord Wackland. It's me that thinks *John* is the poisoner. And a thief. Just look at the timing of events. The confident lickspittle arrives here, all bedraggled and covered in dust (he'd ridden hard, fleeing from some other trouble, to be sure), and begging us for succour. Wackland gives him a job, but he's always peeping here and prying there, and so full of self-assurance. Next thing he's all on the grin, and flinging his money about. Then poof! Like a conjuror at the fair he's gone. But that's not such a clever trick either. In fact, Alpiew, to tell true, I *know* what happened.'

'Yes.' Alpiew cupped her ear. 'Tell me.'

'Who do you think the scoundrel has chosen to run off with?'

'An old wrinkled hag, by any chance?'

'Accraw, Alpiew! And they call me wicked-tongued!' Pipe threw back her head and laughed. 'She's not *that* bad, you saucy thing. No, it's possible that John the handsome charmer has run away with the Caledonian Thalia.'

'Who on earth . . . ?'

'Why, Lady Isabel Murdo-McTavish, of course. Both she and John were missing from their beds yesterday morning and haven't been seen since.'

'But ... I wouldn't have thought ...' Alpiew hoped there was more, as she knew perfectly well where the Scotswoman had disappeared to. 'Do you really think that is likely?'

'I did think so but ...' Pipe seemed to doubt her own words. 'It is either the Scot or, well, perhaps it's a mere coincidence, but the very same morning it appears that, without so much as a word to her husband, my master ...' Pipe looked about to make sure they were not overheard. 'Lady Whippingham has also disappeared, and with a bag of my lord's money! And knowing how John seemed able to lay his hands on money all the time, do you think he may have absconded with my Lady Whippingham?'

'My father's new wife is a whore.' Virginia knotted her hands and flopped back against the bench. 'But she's a young whore. A taunting strumpet, and she wanted me out of the way. I realise it now, but then it seemed such a good opportunity to get away from her and having to watch her fawning over my father, forcing him to do this and buy that.'

The Countess gazed out at the Seine, sparkling in the sunshine, and winding into the distance on its convoluted way to the sea. While the girl babbled on she let her mind drift off.

'John was such a handsome boy. He was my father's groom. But he wasn't just a servant. He had class. And I loved him, and let him love me. Anyway, when my father's strumpet suggested I go to France to find a husband, I was desolate. John told me he'd follow me, wherever I went. I didn't think he would, but he did. He arrived in Calais on the first ship that left Dover after ours. He met a couple of friends who came for the frolic, as he called it. They watched us at the inn in Calais. They saw us all getting into the coach.'

'Oh yes, I see.' The Countess snapped out of her reverie. 'And he and his friends made themselves known to you by frightening us out of our wits and stealing our money.'

Virginia nodded and sobbed simultaneously. 'I myself did not realise it was him at first, but he was the one with the pistol, who pulled me out of the carriage. When he held me in that wood, he whispered to me that they would ride on ahead and he would meet me here, at the chateau.'

'I wonder at you, Miss Franklyn-Green, that you did not make your friend give us back our money right away, and in full.'

'That should have been a sign to me that he was not such a nice person, I agree. But I did take the money from him . . .'

'. . . what was left of it . . .'

'And had it placed in Mistress Alpiew's shoe when she was asleep.'

'And the ring?'

'Oh lord, Countess, I did not realise those wicked boys had taken your ring too . . .' She wiped her nose with the back of her hand. 'I'm so sorry.'

'There, there . . .' The Countess pulled out a handkerchief and handed it to her. 'So now he's run away. Did he have money of his own?'

'I gave him a little of mine, but . . . I suppose the witch will keep him now, and . . .' She broke into uncontrollable sobs. '. . . And I will go home to Daddy.'

'Come, come, you mop-stick ninny. It will get better. There are some follies like stains, that wear out of themselves.' The Countess put her arm round the girl. 'And one of those follies is Love.'

'It was like this, you see. John went into Town, and everyone knows it's easy to buy poison or love potions or whatever you like here in France. And then he came back and my guess is that he smeared the poison round the girl's plate.'

'Tell me, Pipe – for in your position you must see a lot of things –' Alpiew watched her closely – 'why would John want to do a thing like that?'

'I don't know *why*. Perhaps there was money involved. Perhaps she was blackmailing him.'

'But you never saw John with Aurelia?'

'No, but . . .'

'I see. Because you were afflicted by the poison too, were you not?' Alpiew decided to press on, push Pipe into a corner, hoping that she would trip herself up. 'Did John poison you too, is that what happened?'

'No.' Pipe wiggled uneasily. 'Wisht, Alpiew, I suffer from the falling sickness. When I have a little too much excitement the fits take me.'

'Excitement, like stealing rings?'

'I don't know what you mean.'

'What makes you think John left with Lady Whippingham? Who is to say they didn't all three of them go off alone?'

'Virginia had a month's mind for the big lubberly fellow. She was always hanging around him. She told me he'd gone off with an older woman. And as two older women disappeared on the same day . . .' Pipe sniffed. 'I know things. Lady Whippingham probably had a hand in the killing too, if you think about it. It would be in her interest.'

'Why's that?'

'If you don't know that, I can't be telling you. It's not right.'

'A love affair, I presume?'

'Oh yes. Lady Whippingham certainly had a month's mind for the Doctor.'

'Really?' Alpiew recalled the sorry picture of Lady Whippingham, tear-stained and drunk, rolling about on the grass while Dr Stickworth strode away. 'Does her husband know?'

'Pshaw, Alpiew, and accraw, my blind girl. Why should he care? He has an amour of his own.'

'Lord Whippingham has a lover? Someone here at the chateau?'

'To be sure. Lord Whippingham has a passion for Lady Murdo-McTavish.'

'Is it reciprocated?'

'There's something going on.' Pipe knotted her eyebrows in thought. 'I've noticed them whispering together. Sometimes she has tears in her eyes; sometimes she seems to be imploring him . . . to leave his wife, I suppose.'

'Everyone here seems to be chasing after each other.' While Pipe was in the mood to gossip, Alpiew decided to capitalise on it. 'Lord Wackland, for instance . . .'

'Oh no,' said Pipe. 'Wackland's a weird one. You never see him with a woman.'

'But I thought he had something with Lady Prude.'

'Prude!' Pipe laughed loud and long. 'Wackland restricts his company to the male of the species. Mind you, Prude is as near as you can get in female form.'

Alpiew tried to align this with the quarrel she had heard between them.

'Do you know what? I suspect they all took a shine to that John. Wackland has been very tense since he went. Perhaps they are all gone off together. It's Lady Murdo-McTavish running away which makes no sense. None of us can quite get to the logic on that one, for with the wife out of the picture the field would have been clear for Lady Murdo-McTavish to set herself up with my Lord Whippingham . . . But whatever went on between them all, the poor desperate man has taken to his room. I'm telling you, since Lady Murdo-McTavish left, Lord Whippingham is desolate.'

'Perhaps he misses his wife?'

Pipe threw her a scornful look.

'Perhaps he is forlorn at the death of the girl? Perhaps he has a flux?'

'The folk who ate the oysters have a flux. Believe me, Alpiew, Lord Whippingham took to his room the moment he found that Murdo-McTavish had gone.'

Alpiew gaped. Could it be that Lord Whippingham with his snuff-coloured cravat was the secret passion Isabel Murdo-McTavish had described to her with such a winsome and desperate air!

'Lord Whippingham didn't eat the oysters?'

'Whisht, I am so tired of all this talk of oysters. There

was nothing wrong with them.' Alpiew noticed a rising flush spread across Pipe's cheeks. 'It's not my fault. Lord Wackland is responsible for checking everything, and if he thought something was wrong he shouldn't have served them. They looked all right to me. But in my opinion oysters are pretty horrible-looking things. I can't think why anyone lets them in their mouths.'

'You bought them, I presume? At the second-hand food market – and charged Lord Wackland the full price?'

'They were fine.' Pipe wiggled uneasily. 'They looked the same slimy grey colour they always look.'

SEVEN

fricandoes — a sort of Scotch collops, well larded and well farced

T he Countess took a seat near the door. She found out from Pipe where the writers' circle met, but there was no one here.

She was pleased that Lady Murdo-McTavish was banged up in the Bastille. She doubted she'd have had the courage to meet her eye.

Why on earth the Court of Versailles should want her to nose in on this little group of amateur writers, she couldn't imagine. Perhaps they feared the writers were going to publish Jacobite pamphlets, or panegyrics upon the King of France himself. She took a sheet of paper from the pile of writings on the table and glanced at it.

Love by Mademoiselle Leonora Smith

Of all the passions that may be said to tyrannise over the hearts of mankind, love is not only the most violent but the most persuasive. It conducts us through storms, tempests, mountains and precipices with as little terror to the mind and as much ease as though through beautiful gardens and delightful meadows. The nameless little tender proofs of affection exchanged between two persons whom a sincere regard for each other will enable them to aspire to the highest . . .

Well that should pose no problems for the French court. Or for anybody who wanted a little something to get them off to sleep. She tossed the scrawled essay back on to the table and picked up another piece.

The Princess lay in a death-like sleep, for many years. During that time the Prince came every day, bent low over her prostrate body, kissed her lips . . .

Oh dear! She gave a sigh. What banal rubbish. Fit only for children. She read on:

Prince Charming crept away from his wife and made his way to the Sleeping Princess. She was asleep, as she had been for years, and so as usual he undressed himself and ravished her.

Phough! What nauseating stuff. The Countess continued reading:

Still asleep, nine months later she gave birth to his child, and when that child bit her nipple with its sharp teeth she finally awoke . . .

Good lack, who wrote this filth? She flicked to the end of the story: *Isabel Murdo-McTavish*. Pshaw! Well, what could be expected? From what Alpiew had told her the woman seemed capable of anything. And if in a fit of jealousy at Lord Whippingham's interest in the young girl Aurelia . . . well, then . . .

'It's a fascinating piece of folklore, don't you agree, Countess? I scribbled that one the night before I was carried off.'

The Countess dropped the paper as though it was on fire. Standing in front of her was Lady Isabel Murdo-McTavish.

'Isabel!' She tried to look nonchalant. 'You're back?'

'We each hold one another's secret.' Isabel put her finger to her lips and sat at the table. 'But now we are on a mission, no?'

The Countess looked about her. No one else seemed to be present, but with all the spies she'd heard of, how could she be sure of anything? 'I've come to join the writers' group, Isabel. Where is everyone?' She fanned herself, pulled out a chair and sat, trying to look blasé. 'What exactly do we do at these meetings?' She pulled out a quill and dipped it in the centrally placed jar of ink. 'Is no one else coming?'

'I lied.' Isabel leant towards the Countess and whispered: 'It's usually only me and sometimes Leonora Smith. I let Prude think there are lots of others, so she won't interfere. But it's lovely keeping it down to two or three, then we can really analyse one another's work in great detail.'

'Come along, Isabel.' The Countess poised her pen over a blank page. 'I'm all aflame with creativity. Let's write!'

'A little piece together, do you think?' Isabel picked up a blank sheet of paper. 'Do you know, Countess, my little sojourn has inspired me with the most wonderful tale. While in . . .' she lowered her voice again '. . . you know where, did you hear tell of a Mysterious Prisoner?'

The Countess tried to look interested and ignorant at the same time, and succeeded only in going cross-eyed.

'I am going to write a story about him. They say he was put in there because he bears a strange likeness to the King. My theory is that the Mysterious Prisoner is the King's bastard twin-brother, hidden from sight. But there lies the interest of the story: which one is the *real* King of France?'

Convinced that behind some screen all this was being noted down for the King himself, the Countess gave a little cough and wiggled her quill around. 'Shouldn't we just get down to writing something?'

'What do you think, though? Do you think there is a story to be told about the man in the iron mask?'

'Who's to say?' The Countess shrugged. 'But I doubt it would take. I mean, what have you? A man is in prison, no one knows who he is or what he's done or whether he'll ever get out. What interest could there be in that?'

Lady Murdo-McTavish leant close and whispered: 'Tell me, Countess, how did you explain your absence to Prude? She's so full of pride, and such a snob. I wouldn't want her to know I'd been . . .' she lowered her voice further '. . . in *there*, for fear she'd discriminate against me. You know how riddled with prejudice she is. In fact at one point I thought she would make a good study too. I planned to write a panegyric upon her. And I designed to call it *Pride and Prejudice.*'

'*Prude and Prejudice* has a better ring to it.'

'There's no need to mock me, Countess. I know I am not a professional like you, but at least I try.'

'Tell me, Isabel –' the Countess tidied the papers before her and pushed them away – 'you know all about the writers' group, of course, but what of the other societies? Have you attended any of their meetings?'

'I went once to the Hagiography Society – my, what a depressing bunch! Prude told us the life of St Agatha, patron saint of bell-ringers. The lady reviled the advances of some Roman general so he tortured her and cut off her breasts. The poor woman still carries them around heaven on a plate! Then the silly guild of bell-ringers adopted her because sign painters depicted the breasts so badly in their pictures, people mistook them for bells.' She leant back in her chair and guffawed. 'I didn't go back the next week for Saint Wilgefortis, the patron saint of bearded ladies. I didn't think I'd have the fortitude to keep a straight face a second time.'

'What about the engineers' group?' The Countess now tried to steer her where she really wanted her to go. The subject of men. 'What do they get up to?'

'Nothing much, I think. I suspect it's like my fictional writers' circle.' Lady Murdo-McTavish started doodling a heart on the blank page. 'They're all wind. They spout off about flying engines and horse-less carriages, but they never seem to have anything to show for all their frequent meetings and secrecy.'

'Secrecy?'

'Their gatherings are deadly secret. Locked doors. Only the chosen allowed to attend. Perhaps they really are on the verge of a Eureka, but I doubt it – look at the sorry members: Lord Wackland, Dr Stickworth and Whippingham.'

'Lord Whippingham is a member?' The Countess watched Isabel's face closely.

'Staunch. He cannot abide being left out of anything that might make money.'

'Money. I see.' The Countess made a mental note that perhaps he was in the card-playing, property-stealing game. 'He's popular with the women, I am told.'

'Whippingham? Really?' Isabel drew a row of spades and diamonds. 'I can't imagine who told you that.'

'Virginia, my ward.' The Countess put pen to paper and drew a row of hearts too. 'She has a month's mind for his lordship.'

'Then the girl must be cracked.' Isabel gaped at the Countess. 'That fat filthy lump? Who would want to have anything to do with him? Poor Lucy had to keep herself fuddled to the point of inebriation to bear touching his blubbery body. Phough! A pox on him! He's been sniffing about me for years. I wouldn't touch him with the mast of a forty-foot ketch. The smelly whoremonger.'

The Countess wondered whether the lady was protesting a little too much. Though maybe she was a brilliant actress, for her declamation seemed to bear the strange ring of truth.

'I thought the Duc de Charme was one of that set?'

'My lord Duc has far too much self-interest. He is a genuine engineer, and tends to work towards the most revolutionary ideas – travel by air with balloons, or by road with horse-less carriages.'

'He is a demented dreamer, you mean?'

'Slightly so.' Isabel laughed. 'But he is a very kind and considerate dreamer.'

Hi jingo, come again! Perhaps Pipe had got it wrong, and in fact Lady Murdo-McTavish had a fancy for the finical, fluttering fop. The Countess had seen it a hundred times before when women ran after such dandies as would never spare a thought for anything but the latest fashions and whether a pink silk cravat was modish enough to go with the colour of their over-powdered and prinked peruke.

The Countess doodled a few more hearts, then wrote down John, in capitals, darting looks at Isabel to see her reaction to the name, to make sure that one of Pipe's conjectures was wrong.

'John!' Isabel shook her head as she dipped her quill into the inkpot. 'I am surprised you don't think John a name too usual for fiction, Countess. 'Tis the fashion nowadays to use names like Philander, Bellamour and Clerimont.'

'I was thinking of the handsome English groom who worked in the kitchens here and has absconded without a word to anyone.'

'You know the names of the staff? How intriguing. Were you doing research for a project about the lower classes? Oddly, it is a subject which has always fascinated me. I have a wee idea for a story about social division. I wonder what you think of it. It concerns a young man who is born in the clutches of poverty until a mystery benefactor, a woman living alone in a decaying, cobwebbed . . .'

The Countess feigned a coughing attack rather than have to listen to the whole saga.

'Come, Countess, I have no great expectations of today's writing session. This room is hot and stuffy and not beneficial for a person suffering from a chin-cough.' Isabel tossed her quill down and rose from the table. 'No one else will come to the circle today. They're all glued to their close-stools. Let us go out into the sunshine together and do the thing writers do best.'

The Countess shuddered at the thought of what this might be.

'I hope you have on a pair of sturdy shoes, for we are going deep into the forest.'

Lady Murdo-McTavish grabbed a few pieces of paper and thrust them into a side-pocket. 'You should take some too, Countess, for we will be making copious notes.'

With some trepidation the Countess took some paper. Into the forest? Alone with a scribbling madwoman, who could possibly also be a cold calculating murderer? She thought not.

'I promise you, Countess, today you will see and hear things you will never forget.'

Alpiew felt as though her hair was standing on end as she browsed the pages of the Bible. All she knew of the Apocalypse was that it concerned four horsemen.

> *I am the Alpha and Omega, the beginning and the end . . .*
> *And he had in his right hand seven stars, and from his*
> *mouth came out a sharp two-edged sword.*

She sat at the back of the chapel. Shafts of sunlight piercing through the mist of earlier incense gave the place an eerie feel. She shivered and flicked over a couple of pages.

> *Because thou art lukewarm, I will begin to vomit thee out*
> *of my mouth. Because thou sayest I am rich and made*
> *wealthy, and have need of nothing and knowest not that*
> *thou art wretched and miserable and poor and blind and*
> *naked . . .*

Alpiew started to copy out bits like this that seemed to have a bearing on the business around her.

> *The fearful and unbelieving, and the abominable and*
> *murderers and whoremongers and sorcerers and idolaters*

and all liars, they shall have their portion in the pool burn-
ing with fire and brimstone which is the second death.

'Might I ask you what you think you are doing?'

Alpiew had been so wrapped up in writing she had not noticed the approach of Lady Prude, who now stood before her, arms folded, one foot tapping. 'Well? What do you think you are doing in here?'

'I am reading the Apocalypse of St John.' Alpiew gently shut the book and holding it out for Lady Prude to see, she staggered to her feet. It hadn't seemed quite so heavy when resting on her knee.

A glint came into Lady Prude's eye. '"Who is worthy to open the book and to loose the seals thereof?" Certainly not you, Mrs Alpiew. You are a mere scullery-maid and have no business in the Chapel Royal.'

'I only wanted to . . .'

'Get back to the kitchens at once, woman,' barked Prude. 'I shall have words with Lord Wackland for being so slack with you.'

'I do not work there any more, madam.' Alpiew thrust the huge Bible at Lady Prude, causing her to lose her balance. 'Nor do I live in the chateau. I am visiting the chapel only to read the Bible, an occupation I would have thought you would have applauded.'

'I am amazed that a mere menial like yourself *can* read. Or are you lying to me, Madam Pert, to cover some other misdeed?'

'I have no necessity to answer to your nosiness, Lady Prude.' Alpiew made her way towards the aisle. 'I have accommodations in Town now, so I am neither beholden to you, nor obedient to the irrational whim of Lord Wackland.'

'In that case, Mistress Malapert –' Lady Prude laid the Bible down on a nearby pew – 'you have no business in the chateau at all, and certainly none in the chapel.' She pointed towards the door. 'So I suggest you find the nearest way out. I shall certainly have words with your mistress about this episode.'

Alpiew's triumph at cheeking Lady Prude was tempered with irritation at her own impetuosity. For now how would she ever get her hands on a Bible? And those wrathful words of fire, spat out by St John in the Apocalypse, clearly held the key to the King's riddle.

The Countess was beginning to think Lady Murdo-McTavish planned to walk all the way to Calais, they seemed to have trudged so far into the forest. She had lost sight of the chateau ages ago, without managing to communicate with anyone. No one, not even Alpiew, knew where she had gone, or with whom. She looked about her. Nothing but trees, stretching out as far as the eye could see. Oh lord! She felt her heart skip a beat. So far away from civilisation, who could hear her scream?

'We're almost there.' Isabel started fumbling about in her bag.

What was she looking for? A knife, maybe? Or a pistol? The Countess hoiked up her skirts, ready to run.

'Keep up.' Isabel was striding on, heading towards a row of ramshackle buildings, which were hidden behind a gloomy thicket.

She has walked all this way to show a row of pigsties! The Countess forced a smile while her mind raced. What was she up to? Why had she brought her here? To tell her pornographic stories? Or was her purpose more sinister? 'How much further?' The Countess's voice came out as little more than a croak.

'We are here.'

The Countess took a deep breath, but despite the fact they were in the open air the place exuded a foul stench. She put a handkerchief to her nose. 'What is that smell, Isabel?' The Countess braced herself. Was this a charnel house, where Murdo-McTavish and her besnuffed or beribboned paramour disposed of bodies?

Isabel advanced on the first of the low tumbledown structures. 'It is the smell of hardship and abject poverty.' She pushed open the rickety door and advanced. 'You go in first.'

The Countess turned to run, but Isabel grabbed her by the wrist and spun her round. 'I hope you're not turning coward on me, Countess?'

'Not at all.' The Countess forced a wan smile, and hoped the wild thumping of her heart didn't show through her corset. 'Why should I be frightened?'

Again Isabel plunged her hand into her bag. The Countess braced herself for the pistol shot.

'Inside!' Isabel's face was stern and tense. 'Let's get it over with.'

Holding her breath, the Countess turned and ducked through the low entrance. Even as Isabel Murdo-McTavish pushed her roughly inside, the Countess clenched her fists and prepared to scream.

Alpiew had really got her bearings in Town. It was a small place and though the names around her were sheer gibberish it was easy to see from the picture of the sow that *À la Truie qui file* was a shop that sold cooked meats and *À l'Écrevisse* was a fishmongers. She'd also managed to work out which were the Jacobite houses from the groups of English speakers coming in and out.

When she was well acquainted with the thoroughfares and alleyways, she loitered near the entrance to the alley where she had seen Lord Whippingham and the woman. She'd worked out that the French had slightly different mealtimes than the English, and as suppertime drew near, she returned to hide in the doorway.

As she'd expected, a gaggle of women came out. She fell in with them, listening out for the English among them.

'Come to my place for a bite of supper?' A short, rosy-cheeked woman stepped out into the street, slinging a hessian bag over her shoulder.

'You joking?' said her fair-haired friend with a sneer. 'I've had enough. That's the pity about this job. It puts you off your prog.'

'It doesn't affect me. I could eat a horse. Mind you, I'd rather turn kinchin mort than have to wade my way through all those journals again.'

Alpiew skipped a step to keep up as the two women broke from the main gaggle and turned into the crowded main street.

'Kinchin mort? Don't make me laugh, Sarah. You'd no more suit the life of a vagrant than I would. Cony-catching would be more your game. I've seen how nimble you are with a book of flats.'

'Flats? Not done much of that since I left the chateau. No one in this town's got any money for card-playing. It's all show here. I think I'd earn more night-walking.'

Alpiew stepped out into the path of a hay wagon and threw herself out of the way by colliding with the two women.

'Here, watch it!' The blonde had snatched the rosy-cheeked woman's bag and was swinging it like a weapon. 'You on the foist, you tawdry maux? She's a nim, Sarah, mark my words.'

'Sorry,' said Alpiew, stumbling as she tried to keep up with them. 'I was in a daydream. I'm progging. Not eaten for days. I'm new here, see. Looking for a job.'

'Cutting purses or lifting from shops?' Kate blocked Alpiew's path. 'There's always jobs going for bung-nippers.'

Alpiew dug around for some more of the cant she'd heard exchanged by the thieves who loitered around Covent Garden. The language of the criminal underworld was almost as incomprehensible as French. 'I've gulleyed a few cullies of their nabs in my time, but I was hoping for a proper job.' Alpiew prayed that she had just admitted to pick-pocketing and not something utterly immoral or unspeakable. 'But I see that's unlikely over here when you don't speak the lingo.'

'There're jobs for the London Jacks.' Kate tapped the side of her nose. 'But they're only for them what's in the know.'

The Countess stood inside the filthy hovel. Nothing was as she had expected. The place was not a tumbledown deserted animal pen, nor a hideout where Lady Murdo-McTavish kept the bodies of her victims.

It was a family home.

Seven dirty emaciated children played upon the mud floor, while a gaunt woman in rags stirred what looked and smelled like a pot of water, which was precariously balanced upon a meagre fire made of green sticks. Pulling a loaf of bread from her bag, Isabel stepped inside.

The woman turned and wiped her skeletal hands down her skirt before holding them out, palms up. The Countess couldn't help noticing that the bones of the woman's shoulders stuck out like drumsticks as she tore the bread and dropped hunks of it into the pot to make a water gruel.

Isabel started pulling out other pieces of food from her bag.

The children leapt up and grabbed on to Isabel's skirts. She gently stroked their thin, patchy hair.

'*Merci, merci!*' they whimpered as their mother tossed them bullets of bread, which they gulped down. '*Ange de dieu!*'

Isabel gently pulled herself away and left the hovel. The Countess crept out behind her.

'What has happened to these people that has reduced them to such destitution?' The Countess felt guilty for fanning herself earlier against the smell. 'I have never seen anything like it.'

'They are not the only ones. There are families like this everywhere. Out of sight of the great chateaux, but they are hereabouts, never too far away. Come along.' She strode on further into the woods. 'The hamlets and villages all around Paris are bursting with such horrors. Men are found daily lying dead in ditches, their mouths green from eating grass; some are so hungry that when their children die of hunger, they eat bits of their poor wee skeletal bodies. Babies are abandoned under trees, their mothers hoping that some rich hunter will pass by and pick up the child out of pity, or if not, they pray that their own child will die of cold in the night, and pass out of this miserable existence.' Her voice started to waver. 'It is a national disgrace.' She looked warily about her. 'I hope we are safe here, but it is not done to speak out against the unpardonable creatures who have brought about this horror of inhumanity.'

'I'm so sorry.' The Countess apologised even though Isabel couldn't possibly know what for. She felt impotent and stupid. 'Tell me, Isabel, how has it come to this for these poor souls?'

'The weather has done the French people no favours. Poor harvests, floods, summer storms, icy winters – all have taken their toll. But in my opinion the King and his courtiers are to blame. These starving people dare not even help themselves by growing a cabbage in the dirt outside their shacks, for once they produce food they must pay the dreaded salt tax. They are penalised for helping themselves. They are destitute, yet they pay more tax than all the parasitic painted fops and dames flouncing around Versailles . . . I could go on, but what is the point?'

'Why did she have so many children, that poor woman?' The Countess looked back at the ramshackle home. 'She must have foreseen that she would never have enough money to provide for them.'

'You might ask.' Isabel gave a sardonic laugh. 'The powers from above promise them a cash reward once they produce more than ten children. It is tempting for them. Many make the attempt, but no one gets to ten. And by seven they are so exhausted it only takes a nudge to kill them. How long do you think that poor woman will survive?'

'A reward is promised for giving birth to so many children?'

'His Majesty needs boys to grow up and be soldiers.'

The Countess felt dizzy with the horror of it all.

Ahead of them another shack leaned precariously against a great oak tree.

'Come along, Countess. "Let us not be weary in well-doing: for in due season we shall reap, if we faint not." I've heard that sanctimonious bitch, Prude, say that. Much she knows about well-doing.' Isabel pulled open the rickety door and entered the next hovel.

Inside, lying on a strange carved bed, was an old woman, her skin as brown and wrinkled as a prune.

'Isabel,' she cried. Her low, husky voice bore a heavy French accent. 'I thought you would never come.'

'I brought a friend, Madame Severin.' She sat on the edge of the bed and brought out more scraps of food. 'Like you, madame, my friend the Countess here was once mistress to a King.'

'Charles.' The Countess gave a wan smile. 'Of England. Back in the sixties.'

'A few years after me, then. Louis was a child of sixteen. I was on the staff. He came to me to lose his virginity. He was not so cruel and self-important when he was a boy. But always the practical joker.' The woman plucked at her threadbare sheets. 'Now it is not so amusing.' She gnawed at the chicken leg Isabel passed her. 'So, Isabel *chérie*, have you your pencil ready?'

Isabel drew up a stool and sat near the old woman's pillow. She whipped out a small shagreen-bound book and pencil and, as the woman started speaking, she made notes.

'Once upon a time,' said Madame Severin, 'there was an old woman, and she had as many children as there are holes in a sieve . . .'

Alpiew hunched round a small table in a tavern with her new acquaintances.

'Well, I could sneak you in,' said Kate. 'But it's top secret. You're meant to get vetted by this posh mort. She's the fence.'

'It's a stolen goods place, is it?'

'I wish it was!' Sarah laughed. 'No. We have to do something quite disgusting all day. Bad enough to put you off your food.'

'I know about all that. I used to work Covent Garden,' said Alpiew, nonchalant. She'd never been a prostitute in her life, though she had occasionally used sex to get what she wanted. But then, what woman hadn't?

'You see,' said Sarah with a knowing leer, 'what we do is Oriental.'

'No, Sarah, it's not. It's Chinese.'

'Really?' Alpiew had heard all about weird foreign practices. 'I've worked in the Flogging Houses.'

'Flogging!' Kate laughed this time. 'That's easy compared. Frotting, fellicating – I'd do them easy on any filthy old bastard rather than this. They're over quicker, for a start.'

'And the money's better.'

'So what is it?' Alpiew couldn't imagine, unless it involved animals or stools – and she didn't mean the ones milkmaids use.

As Kate was about to open her mouth, Sarah shushed her into silence.

'We can't tell you. Only *we* know, or we won't get the bonus when our services get taken up by the King of France.'

'I was as shocked as you, Countess, the first time I encountered a shanty.' Isabel pushed back the lappets from her frontage, and let the sunlight fall on her pretty décolletage. They sat on a sunny knoll overlooking the Seine, leaning against a great tree, and for the first time since they'd met, the Countess could clearly see Isabel Murdo-McTavish for who she was: a beautiful, kind woman with a fine figure. Quite a catch for a beau of any age.

'I can't believe there's nothing we can do about it.' The Countess looked down at her hands, which were still shaking, and her mind flooded with images of the misery she had seen that afternoon. 'Does no one but you try to bring them aid?'

'Queen Mary used to take special collections for the poor. But word came down from Versailles, and so she stopped. Now she dabbles in the French lotteries, and when she has a win she donates the winnings.'

'What about Prude? Won't she help us get some charity to them?'

'Don't be absurd! The woman is so wrapped up in her

poisonous piety that she is blind to real goodness. Her only desire is to please King James and the court upstairs, and to get promoted into the Royal Household, and she won't do that by rocking the boat. Anyone can see that Louis is tired of James now, so everyone at St Germain has to tread particularly softly around the subject of French politics. We don't want to be exiled a second time. If we were to be ejected from France, where would we go?' She pulled a deck of cards from her pocket and started shuffling them. 'As it is, we are all dependent upon Louis. Every one of us.'

'How can that be?'

'King James fled England and arrived here with nothing, just the clothes he stood up in. He can't raise taxes in a foreign land. He has no money of his own, so the Royal Household is maintained by a charity grant from the French King. And to tell the truth, I think Louis is beginning to regret having given James sanctuary when William seized the English throne. Especially now that it is clear James will never get it back.'

'The bickering of three kings affects so many lives,' said the Countess. 'Three Kings! Fan me! That's it!' She instantly regretted having shouted in front of Isabel Murdo-McTavish, who started and dropped her cards. Epiphany was the presence of Three Kings. And it was clear to the Countess that all the Jacobite wranglings were concerned with the fate of three kings: two of England and one of France. 'I mean, how terrible that with three kings involved there is still this deprivation here.'

'No one can blame William, though. He sits safely across the Channel. The poor in his country are not reduced to indigence.'

While Isabel crawled around gathering her cards the Countess tried to recall the wording of the King's riddle. Something like: L.S.; Epiphany; Friday Night; followed by the Apocalypse and then the Resurrection.

'I am sorry about the business with the card game, Countess. I wish I hadn't done it to you now. We really are kindred spirits. When you first arrived I thought you were one of *them* – rich and uncaring. Or so high up the social scale it wouldn't matter that they're poor as church mice.'

She shuffled her deck.

'Won't you tell me who owns my house, Isabel? Please, just give me a chance to get it back?'

'I can't do that.' Isabel flicked cards into a line on the grass as she spoke. 'Really. I can't.'

'Why let Alpiew know enough to tantalise if you won't tell the rest?'

'We were safe in the Bastille. I didn't think I'd ever be released. You've heard the stories about that place.' She laid down the ace of spades and stared at it. 'I wish now I hadn't told Alpiew at all.'

Isabel's eyes locked with the Countess's stare, and the Countess could see a great sadness in them.

'But I will get it back for you, I promise.'

Alpiew sat at the back of the dark church.

Evening Benediction was over and the altar boys were preparing for Mass. How she wished they'd all go off somewhere and leave her to nip up and peruse the row of Bibles sitting on a huge oak shelf near the choir stalls. As the parish had so many English speakers, and as she'd noted that many of the listed priests had Irish names, she was depending on the fact that there would be an English version among the French and Latin ones.

She remembered that Wackland and Prude had talked of leaving notes in a confession box in this church. She had wandered round the church with all its side chapels and found various boxes, one for St Anthony's bread, one for restoration of the church roof, but none marked confession box.

Alpiew watched as, one by one, heads bowed, people came to kneel in front of the altar and pray.

Two inscrutable nuns passed, their flapping veils fanning her. It was hot, and she would have been happy to employ a troop of nuns to waft around her all day – the St Germain equivalent of Nubian slaves.

A woman dressed all in black followed them up the aisle. She stopped at a pew and addressed a praying man, her hand held out. He shook his head and she came up to Alpiew and thrust her hand out. 'Would you grant me a pension? I am a poor widow and my funds ran out . . .'

'I'm sorry, old love,' said Alpiew. 'I would if I could, but . . .'

The woman pulled a piece of paper from her sleeve and squashed it into Alpiew's hand. Not quite knowing how to react, Alpiew smiled, nodded, and put the paper into her pocket, with a mumbled 'thank you'.

The woman said, in a voice too loud for church, 'Mark!' and moved on to someone at the back of the church.

Matthew, Mark, Luke and John, thought Alpiew. And John's the evangelist I'm after today, thank you, madam.

The altar boys genuflected in unison and exited into the vestry. Alpiew scuttled up the aisle and mounted the steps to the bookshelves. She tugged at the first huge Bible. Latin. She slammed it back. Three more Latin versions, then one marked *Douai*, which to her delight was in English. She heaved it over to the lectern, turned the pages to the Apocalypse and read.

> *These things saith the First and the Last, who was dead,*
> *and is alive: I know thy tribulation and thy poverty, but*
> *thou art rich.*

She wished she could find a way of scribbling these bits down without being too noticeable.

> *Fear none of those things which thou shalt suffer. Behold,*
> *the devil will cast some of you into prison that you may*
> *be tried: and you shall have tribulation for ten days.*

She smiled to herself, crossing her fingers and hoping that their tribulations did only last ten days, and then they'd get safely home. Home! They'd have to sort out that little problem too before they left or heaven only knew what would happen.

I know where thou dwellest, where the seat of Satan is: and thou holdest fast my name, and hast not denied my faith.

Perhaps that was a coded way of referring to the St Germain court, and how everyone there had followed the King into exile for the sake of their religion.

To him that overcometh, I will give the hidden manna, and will give him a white counter, and in the counter, a new name written, which no man knoweth, but he that receiveth it.

A white counter? A gambling stake perhaps. Alpiew began to fear that the thing was so over-written and vague that it all had a myriad of possible hidden meanings, and probably meant nothing at all.

These things saith the Son of God, who hath his eyes like to a flame of fire, and his feet like to fine brass.

Well, that ruled out anyone she knew.

Looking up to the top of the next page, she glanced into the church and saw another penitent making his way to the pews: Lord Wackland. And she could see he had tears rolling down his cheeks. He knelt and lowered his head.

Alpiew's eyes darted across to the corner of the church and watched an old woman limp up to a dark curtain and go through into another room.

She lowered her gaze and stood stock still, trying to make herself invisible behind the thin upright of the lectern.

Stooping to keep her face well and truly hidden, she briskly read on, praying that he wasn't here for some endless prayer session.

I have against thee a few things: because thou sufferest the woman Jezabel, who calleth herself a prophetess, to teach, and to seduce my servants, to commit fornication, and to eat of things sacrificed to idols. And I gave her a time that she might do penance, and she will not repent of her fornication. Behold, I will cast her into a bed: and they that commit adultery with her shall be in very great tribulation, except they do penance from their deeds. And I will kill her children with death.

'Mistress Alpiew?'

Alpiew cringed behind the book, wishing a bit of apocalyptical smoke would vanish her away. She grabbed hold of the Bible and turned a wad of pages, so he would not see which page she was reading.

'I thought you had left St Germain?' Wackland stepped up beside her. She kept her eyes fixed on the open page. But that only made her laugh aloud as her eyes ran along the line. *'And the men of Sodom were very wicked . . .'*

'Oh, Lord Wackland. What a surprise!' She slammed the cover shut. 'How are things at Poison Hall?'

'I didn't have you down for a Bible reader.' He picked the book up, placed it back on the shelf and grabbed her by the hand. 'Or a gossip. As you well know, there has been no poisoning. Aurelia was suffering from an apoplexy.' As they walked up the aisle he made the sign of the cross.

Emerging into the sultry heat of the afternoon Alpiew tried to ape him with her free hand.

'You know as well as I, Lord Wackland, that that is a mere puff, to quieten the spies from Versailles.'

'I see you are not a Catholic!' He spun round to face her. 'Why did you come here? Are you sent by the Court of William the Infidel?'

'I, er . . .' She wiggled free from his grasp, trying to work out what she had done to give herself away. She took a shot at one possibility: 'You had hold of my right hand or I should have

185

used that to cross myself. I didn't wish to leave the house of the Lord without blessing myself.'

'Where is John? Is he with you?'

'I know nothing of John, sir, and even if I did 'twould be no business of yours. I am not a dependent of the chateau now.'

She turned and walked briskly away, but couldn't help noticing that he stayed there, alone in the middle of the empty square, watching her until she had turned the corner.

She strode through the town stepping in rhythm and found that an old ditty came to her head, one that was told her by a Covent Garden rake one drunken night:

> *And now we find to our Sorrow*
> *We are overrun*
> *By sparks of the bum*
> *And peers of the land of Gomorrah.*

'They have a language of their own, the cards.' Isabel laid the pack down card by card.

It was evening, and still no one was about in any of the antechambers. The Countess sat next to Isabel on a settee by the window in the worsening light.

'French packs are prettier, but I'm attached to this one. My mother gave it to me. I carry it everywhere.'

'Do you read destinies in the cards?' Having spent the afternoon with her, the Countess found herself feeling increasingly fond of the woman. 'What will become of us all, trying to survive in this terrible place?'

'Pick three.' Isabel spread the pack and the Countess pulled out the cards and laid them face up.

'King of hearts. Hearts is a good suit. It represents a liberal man. The French call this card Charles.'

'You are making it up!' The Countess blushed and gave Isabel a coy smile. 'You must already know of my past. Where does it say that that card represents Charles?'

'It doesn't represent King Charles. On French packs the court cards are all named. There's David, Alexandre, Lancelot, Hector, Judith, Cesar, Rachel, etcetera . . . and Charles is the name of the king of hearts.'

'He was that.' The Countess gave a wistful sigh. 'He was a king of hearts, you know. Not like . . .'

Isabel held her finger to her lips. 'Now.' She picked up the next card. 'Seven of diamonds. Aha, Countess, this signifies an unexpectedly recovered debt.'

The door opened and Pipe came in carrying a taper to light the wall sconces and candelabra. She gazed at the Scotswoman, as she held the wavering flame over the candles.

'I raise you a sept et le va, madam.' Isabel threw a card across the table as though they were at play. The Countess took the hint and quickly gathered up a handful of cards.

'I mase you.' She picked a card from the pack and stared intently at her hand. Pipe swiftly departed, the closing door setting the candles guttering.

'Can't be too careful.' Isabel swept the other cards out of the way and resumed her reading. 'The ten of diamonds. Diamonds are almost always good cards. Ten indicates a journey or change of residence.'

The Countess refrained from saying she didn't want a change of residence, only to get home to German Street. 'Will we go back into the woods tomorrow to visit those poor needy souls?'

Lady Murdo-McTavish held her hands up to silence the Countess and whispered, 'After supper, with loaded bags, we could sneak out. It will be too difficult to leave together. At midnight I will wait for you at the edge of the forest, where we sat this afternoon.'

Before Isabel had a chance to move the cards, the door slammed open and Lady Prude burst in. She stood, aghast in the doorway. Without speaking she marched to the table and gathered up the cards.

'Satan's picture-book!' she cried, throwing cards in the air and stamping on them as they landed. 'Why are you here? Why are you here? Shame on you!'

'What is wrong, Lady Prude?' Isabel sighed. 'I can sit where I wish and with whomever I desire.'

'But you . . .' Lady Prude appeared to gather herself. 'How often have I warned you? You and your ungodly practices will bring doom upon us all.'

Isabel scooped cards into her lap as Lady Prude took a handful and tore at them, trying to rip them in half.

'Go away! Go away from here, I say!'

'Calm yourself, Lady Prude.' The Countess rose and grabbed the hysterical woman's hands. 'I assure you there is no Satanism going on in here. Lady Murdo-McTavish was simply explaining to me the historical references in the court pictures: Charles, Lancelot, Hector and the others.'

Lady Prude burst into tears and, flinging the cards away, ran from the room.

The Countess turned to laugh, but Isabel's face was frozen in horror as she looked down upon the table.

In the centre lay one single card, the nine of diamonds.

'Oh no. Why must that one be left behind?'

Her hand quivered as she gathered up the other cards lying on the floor. The Countess helped her.

'But you said diamonds were good.'

'Not the nine. Not to a Scotswoman. The nine of diamonds is a card of very bad omen. They call it the Curse of Scotland.'

Alpiew waited in the alley for a while before trying the door to Lord Whippingham's house of ill repute.

To her surprise, the place was locked up. Whoever heard of a joint like this not working nights? But then, she was used to Covent Garden hours. At night in St Germain everyone was quietly tucked up in their homes.

It didn't take long for her to pick the lock and get in. Once in the long hall she cursed herself for not bringing a lantern. She groped her way in the black, and tried the end door.

Locked, of course. For Alpiew, picking the lock took a little longer than usual, but she did it, and fumbled clumsily into the room.

The moon shone into a window and she could make out a couple of rows of chairs. As her eyes grew accustomed to the light she noticed stacks of newspapers in the corner and a line of buckets under the windowsill.

She plunged her hand into one of them and pulled it out again pretty smartly. Her hand was now smeared with a slimy grey matter. She smelled it. It had no smell. She decided not to taste it.

She started singing the song that had been running round her head all afternoon:

> *'We women are quite out of fashion*
> *Poor whores may be nuns*
> *Since men turn their guns*
> *And vent on each other their passion.'*

In the corner near the door was a stack of serving trays, and next to it a pile of decorated boxes. They looked like tea caddies, or jewellery cases.

She put out her hand to touch them but the whole lot tumbled down. And as she lurched forward to catch them she stumbled over a chair and fell on her face. She cursed and brushed herself down. She didn't see the door open, or the man who walked in, until she reached out and touched his riding boot.

At half past eleven the Countess crept along in the dark to the main staircase. She tiptoed down the stone stairs, but just before she came to the door she heard a 'hist'. Isabel must have changed her plan, she thought, and turned to look into the shadows under the stairs.

'Hello?' She stepped nearer to the shadow. 'Isabel? Is that you?'

'Are you running away again?' Prince James stood in his nightshirt with his hands on his hips. 'I helped you escape out of here once. Why did you come back?'

'Your Royal Highness . . .' The Countess did a little curtsey and had to grab a pillar to regain her balance. 'I am going out on a secret assignation. You and I know all about secrets, don't we?'

'A woman of your age?' The Prince squinted and looked the Countess up and down. 'I am astonished.'

The Countess suppressed the urge to slap the boy, and straightened her wig.

'You are enjoying your war games now?'

'Ah yes. Upon your advice I have become the Old Pretender.' He gave a great sigh. 'But oh how I wish the Royal Household mixed more with the ordinary people like you. I hear that life in your part of the chateau is more exciting even than life in stories. While I sit around praying and playing table-top soldiers all day, I'm told downstairs is all excitement and murderings, robberies and every kind of debauchery.'

'Oh?' If life up in the Court of the King was more boring than the life of the refugees downstairs, God help them. 'Who told you that?'

'One of the servants, of course. They know everything that goes on.'

'Might I ask what you are doing up and out of your bed, sire?'

'I'm on a secret mission.' The boy looked round, to check no one else was near. '*Cave speculator!*'

'Oh yes, sire, we must watch out for spies, you are right.' The Countess was going to ruffle the Prince's hair, but she checked herself. 'You do know I won't tell on you, but you must be sure not to tell on me.' She held out her hand, and they shook.

Boys and their games! She smiled as she made her way out into the garden, leaving the true blood heir to the English throne lurking in the murky shadows.

*   *   *

Lord Whippingham stooped and helped Alpiew to her feet.

'How did you get in here? The place should have been locked.' He was looking at her intently. 'I have seen you before. Do you work here?'

'I worked at the chateau once.' Alpiew tried to look and sound like the girls she'd met in the street. 'I wanted a job here, see. That's why I come knocking. Wondered if there was room enough in your set-up for another wheedling trull?'

'What set-up do you mean, exactly?' Whippingham stooped and picked up a half-dozen boxes.

'You know . . .' Alpiew angled around, hoping for inspiration. 'Girls. Sucking . . . Whatever?'

'I'm sorry.' Whippingham smiled and, cradling his painted caddies, nodded towards the door. 'We have a full complement at present. I shall accompany you to your lodgings.'

Alpiew couldn't believe she was being let off so lightly. She was expecting to be given a good thrashing and dragged by ear to the nearest constable, or whatever was the French equivalent. Instead, here she was being walked home. 'Did you have the flux yesterday with the rest of them?'

'Lucky for me I detest oysters.' Whippingham laughed. 'And I've been rather busy for the last couple of days.'

'How is your wife, sir?'

'Oh,' he blustered, 'a flux. Like everyone else.'

'Really?' said Alpiew. She stumbled on a loose cobble and grabbed out at Lord Whippingham's sleeve. Rather than trying to help, he swerved away, protecting his armful of boxes.

When she regained her equilibrium, she ran her eyes up and down the snuff-smeared fellow and decided that she still didn't trust him one bit, was very suspicious of his precious boxes, and certainly didn't want him knowing where she lived. 'Cannot I help, sir, by carrying some of your boxes?'

'No thank you, Miss Pert.' Whippingham veered away from her. 'I can easily manage. Where are you staying?'

'Near you,' she said. 'In the chateau.'

As they strode up the street Alpiew marvelled at the man's strength, carrying so much and not even needing to stop for breath.

'It must be dreadful for you, Lord Whippingham.'

'Why would you think that?'

'I heard that your wife had gone missing.'

'Really? Who told you that?'

'Shortly after Isabel Murdo-McTavish's disappearance.'

'Isabel is back, though. So that means nought.' Whippingham's step faltered and his voice wavered. 'I am sure my wife is capable of looking after herself while she has the funds. She'll be back, mark my words. She's been a little upset of late.' He regained his composure, and his step increased. 'You must know, though, that in any case, our marriage had long grown stale as a chancery case.'

At the chateau, the guards opened the main door and Whippingham nodded briskly.

'Busy night for you, my lord,' said one, a burly Scot. 'In and out, in and out.'

Whippingham shot him a look. Alpiew felt sure the two soldiers were sniggering into their chin-straps.

'Impertinence!' muttered the noble lord as he balanced the boxes more evenly and started up the great staircase. 'They will never know the business of Engineering.' He gave a little cough. 'So, Mistress Alpiew, I thought you had left St Germain. Didn't you and your Countess do a moonlight flit?'

'My mistress had sudden and urgent business in Paris. My lord, I think we have need of a candle to light our way.' Alpiew didn't like the way Lord Whippingham seemed to rub himself against her on the dark staircase.

'I can feel my way,' he said.

Not over me, thought Alpiew, pulling sharply away just as, emerging from the shadows, a cloaked, hooded figure came down the stairs towards them. Even in the black, she instantly recognised Lady Prude.

Alpiew stooped as though to pick up something which had fallen, and prayed Lady Prude's eyesight wasn't as good as her own.

Whippingham, turning slightly away as though to hide the boxes, bid Lady Prude a very good night.

Without even casting a glance in his direction, Lady Prude swept past them. It was as though she was a ghost, passing on a different plane.

Alpiew realised she would never have found out the way to the garret without Lord Whippingham. She was about to thank him, when from the door at the top of the spiral steps came a stifled giggle.

Lord Whippingham started coughing, as if to cover the sound. He tapped the door with the back of his hand and the laughter stopped.

'Shall I open it for you?' Alpiew reached out for the handle.

'No!' he barked. 'That won't be necessary.' Flustered, he shuffled the boxes about. It was clear he was not going to open up till Alpiew was gone. 'Thank you. Good night.'

Alpiew backed away and wandered up the corridor. Which was the door to the Countess's chamber?

She listened at the first door. Silence.

Then she heard a sound like a cane swishing through the air. She turned back. Whippingham was still there, smiling and nodding. He gave a nervous cough. It was obvious he was not going to enter his room until she was gone.

But Alpiew didn't want to march into the wrong room. 'Don't want to wake her,' she whispered, wondering why the man wouldn't just disappear and leave her to explore. She put her hand on the nearest door handle.

'Good lack, madam!' Lord Whippingham coughed, and dropped one of his boxes. 'Do you need me to come and turn the handle for you?' He gave her a knowing look.

Alpiew removed her hand and crossed the corridor, facing two more doors. One, two, buckle my shoe. Without a sound she turned the handle of one and peeked inside.

'Ah! I understand,' she heard Lord Whippingham mumble as she tiptoed into the chamber.

Even with no light Alpiew could make out the mess of papers, books and quill pens. This must be the Countess's chamber. But no one was at home.

Somewhere nearby a bell tolled midnight.

Alpiew pulled out her tinder-box and lit a candle. The cramped room seemed cosy in the flickering light.

Alpiew smiled. Knowing her, the Countess would have wangled her way into the royal apartments and she'd now be sitting entertaining the crowd with tales of King Charles and the good old days.

Alpiew picked up a book that lay open on the bed: *The Last Remains* – Poetry by Sir John Suckling. She unlaced her boots and hauled them off, then puffed up the pillow, sprawled out on the bed and started to read.

> *I prithee send me back my heart,*
> *Since I cannot have thine;*
> *For if from yours you will not part,*
> *Why then should'st thou have mine?*

Well, not quite her preferred literature, but at least it would be an improvement on *The Pilgrim's Progress*.

There were lines scratched in the margin, and underlinings all down the page. Perhaps the Countess was going to start a new line as a poet.

She flicked back and forth through the book for a while then returned to the beginning.

> *Why should two hearts in one breast lie,*
> *And yet not lodge together?*
> *O love, where is thy sympathy,*
> *If thus our breasts thou sever?*

Next to this verse was scrawled in capitals 'I mean it.'

She felt a sneeze coming and reached into her pocket for a kerchief. With it came the note the woman had given her in church.

She flicked it over.

'*Cave. Cave puella pulchra.* Your mistress is in grave danger.'

EIGHT

Bouillans — little pies made of the breasts of roasted capons or pullets minced small with calves udder, bacon herbs &c.

The Countess knew she was very late. And in the dark, once she walked under the trees and the moonlight was extinguished, she was not so sure-footed. She had heard the midnight bell toll a good fifteen minutes before she reached the meeting point.

Isabel was not in position.

She sat down on the grass for a while. Perhaps Isabel had been delayed as well.

In the distance the sparkling river was brilliantly lit by the moon. The Countess sat transfixed by the sheer beauty of the view for a long time.

Then the thought struck her. Perhaps Isabel had gone ahead. Perhaps she was now already at the shanties, dropping her food parcels.

She gathered her cloak about her and set off into the forest.

An owl shrieked and then she heard an animal call nearby. The wild howling of a fox, she hoped, and not some huge hairy monster coming to catch her and eat her.

She glanced around into the black void surrounding her

and shuddered. Ghostly shadows played among the trees. She started to panic. What if there was a maniac lurking here, or a pack of wild beasts, waiting behind a tree to tear her to shreds? Her pockets were full of chicken and sliced gammon, for God's sake. She knew she must be laying a tasty scent for all meat-eating animals within miles.

Another owl hooted and she leapt a foot into the air. Peering ahead, she trotted on, trying to see a clearing, or indeed *anything* that would help her find her way. But all she could see was trees.

Flustered, she stood still for a moment. She couldn't see the chateau or the shanties.

She turned again. A full circle.

She was utterly lost.

She hesitated for a moment then turned back on herself and wandered off the same way she had come, praying all the while that she would find the terrace of the chateau.

Something – was it a rat? – scuttled away through the leaves near her feet. She gave a little shriek and lost her balance, tumbling helplessly into a large toadstool growing from the base of a tree. Her face was now smeared with the noxious stuff. She plunged her hand into her pocket for a handkerchief and found only a mess of cold meat and cheese. She stumbled on, wiping her eye with a greasy, food-smeared hand. What if she never found her way out, and only managed to go deeper and deeper into the forest, wandering in circles for eternity? She tried to pull herself together; after all, no forest reached to the end of the world. Somewhere she must come back to the edge and to humanity.

She made another decision on direction and strode off.

But she hadn't gone five steps when racing footsteps hurtled up behind her.

She spun round, only to lock eyes with a wolf, his teeth bared in a vicious snarl and his long fangs dripping with blood.

Where was the Countess got to? Alpiew looked again at the

note the old woman had shoved into her hand in church: '*Cave. Cave puella pulchra.*' What could that possibly mean? Alpiew presumed it was in French, as it certainly made no sense to her. 'Your mistress is in grave danger.'

Alpiew wished she knew where the Countess was.

She picked up the poetry book and looked again at the marked verse.

> *O love, where is thy sympathy,*
> *If thus our breasts thou sever?*

'I mean it.' What could that signify? Alpiew took a closer look at the writing. It was small and neat, nothing like the Countess's scrawl.

She looked at the frontispiece: 'With all my love, darling, forever.' Strange! Who can have written that to the Countess? She flicked over to the next page. 'I M-M. Her book.'

Oh lord.

She looked about the room again.

The cloak hanging on the back of the door was not the Countess's. Nor was the hairbrush, nor the pots of addition.

She was in someone else's chamber! She threw the book down and leapt from the bed. Scrambling to the floor she pulled on a boot, praying that she would get out before she was discovered. She fumbled under the bed for the other boot, and her hand fell on a piece of paper. It was a letter, consisting of only four words:

I will be avenged

The Countess didn't move a muscle as she stared into the wolf's eyes.

'Nice doggy,' she said in a voice high enough for opera. '*Bon chien.*'

The wolf gave a low growl in basso profundo. His lips quivered as he pulled them further back over his long sharp fangs. The Countess watched as the fur on the wolf's back rose, forming a dark ridge. His pale glassy eyes stared coldly into hers.

Barely moving, the Countess slipped her hand into her pocket, grasped a handful of cooked meat, and threw it so that the wolf had to back up to get it. He took only a step, then turned back, still eyeing her warily and baring his teeth. She noticed a lick of pink drool dangling from his angry maw. She threw another handful, and then another.

He yelped and leapt forward each time her hand shot out.

'Food!' she said softly. 'Yum, yum! Miem, miem!' she added, hoping that he'd understand it in one language or the other.

But the wolf did not budge.

After an unblinking staring competition, during which he snarled, giving the air an occasional nonchalant sniff, he stooped, still keeping an eye on her, to lap up the scraps of food.

She fumbled about in her pockets for more, pulling it out and dropping it as calmly as she could. Her hands were quivering like aspen leaves. The wolf darted about, polishing off the ham, then the chicken, then the cheese, then a piece of tongue, before lolloping back to where she stood. Then he growled and bared his teeth again.

'Oh, you're a hungry boy, aren't you?' she said, as he took a step towards her.

Frantically she pulled the last piece of bread from her bag and dropped it by her feet.

The wolf picked it up and chewed hard, then gulped it down. A string of spittle swung from his jaw. He looked up and let out a growl even lower than before. His eyes seemed aflame.

Baring his teeth into an angry snarl, he poised himself to leap.

The Countess made a desperate prayer.

With a bound the wolf lunged up at her neck. She grabbed

one of his paws and tried to beat him off, gripping the scruff of his neck and pushing him away. She could feel his hot wet mouth snapping at her, smell the rank bestial stink of his rancid breath.

She swung her head this way and that, trying to evade his fangs. She kicked out, and stumbled backwards, his weight adding to the impetus.

She was going to fall. Then what would happen, with him on top of her attacking as she floundered among the bracken? She knew she wouldn't stand a chance. She tumbled backwards, taking small panicked steps, trying to maintain her equilibrium.

The wolf was now hanging from her shoulders. The moment she hit the ground she knew she would be finished. She felt his teeth pressing against her neck, his drool dripping down her cleavage. Still teetering in reverse, her back smacked into a tree. She pulled her arms round, ready to use the leverage to shove the animal away, when, without a sound, he suddenly tumbled down on to his back and lay at her feet. Pressed hard into the bark of the tree trunk, panting, the Countess gazed at the wolf sprawled at her feet, twitching on the bracken.

A dull froth oozed from his mouth. He lifted his head for one last snarl and then, with a whimper, he lay still.

What was happening? Was the creature dying? The Countess stood stock still, staring down at the creature as the last breath rattled from his lungs. He was dead all right. But how incredible! It was as though she was Hercules and had just dispatched the Nemean Lion.

She sidled gingerly away. What if there were a pack of his wolf friends lurking behind the trees ready to come out and take their revenge?

Fired with a new energy, the Countess grabbed her skirts and ran like the devil, finally staggering out into the moonlit parterres of the chateau just as, from high up in the garret, a piercing scream shattered the still of the night.

Alpiew had just laced her second boot when she heard the

scream. It came from somewhere very near at hand. She threw open the door and ran along the corridor.

She could see a woman standing in a doorway, her hands up, holding the sides of her blonde head. She was illuminated by a flickering candle from within the chamber. As soon as she saw her profile, Alpiew remembered the Countess's description of the Duchesse de Charme.

'Good lack, madam!' Lord Whippingham burst out from his room. 'Do you want to wake the dead with your infernal hollering?'

Alpiew reached the Duchesse and spun her around. Her hands were bloody, and her face frozen in utter horror. Her bulging eyes stared down at the floor beside the bed.

This was certainly the Countess's room. Her things were everywhere. Alpiew's heart flew into her mouth. A solitary candle in a chamber-candlestick illuminated the room. Alpiew crept softly in.

On the floor before her a woman lay sprawled out, face down in a pool of blood.

The Duchesse was still screaming.

'Calm her,' Alpiew cried to Lord Whippingham. 'And fetch the Doctor. Quickly!'

Alpiew knelt down and turned the woman round.

It was Isabel Murdo-McTavish, her ghostly face contorted into a wild alarmed stare. Her bodice had been cut open and her clothes torn from her body.

Alpiew felt her neck for a pulse. Nothing.

Feeling faint, Alpiew sat back to take a breath. Her hand rested on something soft and slimy. She glanced down. It looked like offal from a butcher's stall at Smithfield Market. She turned back to look at Isabel's body. The poor woman's stomach had been slit open, and the organs slung out on the floor. And lying either side of her head was a severed breast.

NINE

Zests — certain chips of orange and lemon peel cut long-wise, from top to bottom, as thin as it can possibly be done

Puffing, the Countess clambered up the staircase. Servants holding candelabra bearing dozens of guttering candles fought the draught on the stairs, and a crowd of people was squeezing into the garret corridor.

She saw Lord Wackland, pulling on a velvet jacket, coming from Lord Whippingham's room.

Pipe was cowering against the banister.

'What on earth is going on, Pipe?'

'Horror!' Pipe covered her mouth. 'It's Lady Murdo-McTavish. A lunatic's been at her with a carving knife. Roger has the weapon.'

'She's dead,' said the Charmes' valet. 'Dead.'

'Don't go any further.' Wackland came reeling back along the narrow corridor. He reached out to catch the Countess. ''Tis no sight for a woman.' His pallid face was dripping with sweat, his hands shaking. Before him, on the floor, lay the knife. The blade and handle were dark with clotted blood.

'Let me through,' said the Countess, shoving the valet out of her path. 'She was my friend.'

'Make way! Make way there! The Duchesse has fallen into a swoon,' Whippingham shouted as Alpiew and the bejewelled Duc carried the prostrate Duchesse de Charme along the crowded corridor. 'Fling open a casement. Let us have air!'

They laid the Duchesse in Isabel's empty chamber, and while the flustered Duc tried to revive his wife with a bottle of hartshorn, Alpiew fought her way back to the Countess.

'Oh, milady, I thought at first it was you. We found her in your room. It's too awful.'

They both stood in the doorway, watching the Doctor carefully covering the body with a pair of sheets.

'Alpiew –' the Countess glanced quickly around the room and lowered her voice – 'were those like that when you found her?' She pointed down into the pool of blood near Lady Murdo-McTavish's waist.

'The playing cards? Why, yes.'

A pack of cards was roughly spread out around the body, but two cards were separate from the rest. Isabel's lifeless fingers rested upon them.

'Your eyes are better than mine. Tell me which cards she is touching.'

'The queen of spades, milady, and the knave of diamonds.' Alpiew glanced down at her bloodstained hand. 'I must wash my hands.'

The Countess stepped back for her to pass.

'Come with me, milady.' The Countess knew from Alpiew's tone of voice that she meant something more significant. 'You should sit down.'

She hauled the Countess into Isabel's room and, while Alpiew rinsed her hands in the china basin next to the close-stool, she indicated the letter she had seen on the floor earlier.

While the Countess pored over the note, Alpiew dried her hands and stooped across the bed. 'Excuse me, Monsieur le Duc, I'll just get that book out of your lady's way, shall I?'

The Duchesse's eyelids flickered as Alpiew slid the poetry book from under her skirts.

'Suckling,' murmured the Duchesse, reaching out for her husband. 'Easy Suckling. Oh God!' She sobbed and sat up, grabbing on to the Duc's lacy sleeve. 'Save me, Antoine! Save me from hell.'

Ribbons dangling, earrings jangling, the Duc pressed his weeping wife close to his spangled chest.

'I must get through.'

The Countess recognised Lady Prude's imperious voice booming along the hallway. She and Alpiew watched at the door as, whey-faced, Lady Prude strode along the corridor attended by four palace guards.

The Doctor was leaning out of the room where Isabel's body lay, gasping for breath. 'Clear this area, for Christ's sake!' he shouted. 'And open some damned windows.'

'Enough of your blasphemy, Dr Stickworth.'

'Words! How can you worry about words at a time like this?' He tore off his blood-soaked cravat and tossed it away. '*This* is blasphemy, what has happened *here*. And no amount of piety can ever repair the damage. Good God, woman, step off your sanctified pedestal for a minute, can't you?'

As the guards carried Lady Murdo-McTavish's body down to the chapel, everyone stood in a hushed horror. Even after her body disappeared down the dark shadowy stairs, the silence lingered.

Until from behind the end door came a muffled squeal. All heads swung round to look.

'That room is vacant.' Lady Prude glared at the door. 'What on earth . . . ?'

Everyone, the Countess well to the fore, huddled together and pressed onwards.

Another low groan.

Pipe pressed her face into Lord Whippingham's cravat, Stickworth and Wackland took a step forward, while Lady Prude signalled to the Countess and Alpiew. Steeling herself, the Countess gripped the handle and flung open the door. The Charmes' valet, Roger, held up his candelabrum, flooding the dark room with dancing light.

Lady Prude gasped and reeled back, covering her eyes.

On the bed in the corner of the chamber lay Virginia. She was totally naked and straddling her manfully was the missing groom, John.

TEN

*Pot-pourri — a hotch-potch,
or dish of several sorts of meat,
first larded and fried in lard
to give them a colour, and
afterwards stew'd in broth
with white wine, pepper, salt,
a bunch of herbs &c.*

'C ave puella pulchra,' repeated the Countess for the
fifth time, smoothing the note out against her knee.
'Beware of the beautiful girl. The beautiful girl. Are
there any beautiful girls here?'

'Mademoiselle Smith? Pipe, in her wiry way?' said Alpiew at the
other side of the table in her new room. 'Virginia? How is she?'

'The very picture of confidence. I sat with her this morning
and tried to tell her about the birds and the bees, but she laughed
in my face and told me I was plain jealous.' The Countess threw
her arms up. 'He certainly looked a lusty fellow, and sure of
his prowess. But if she is looking for a husband, to play at
prick-in-the-belt with a groom . . .' The Countess trailed off.
It was not her responsibility.

'So, madam, she is not much affected by the death of Lady Murdo-McTavish?'

'I wonder if the child doesn't exist in a world all of her own. We talked on the subject for only a moment, then she was back extolling the virtues of her black-haired beau.'

Alpiew wrote down the name Virginia. 'And our other beauties are Pipe, and Mademoiselle Smith.'

'If you say so. None of them would have been considered beauties when I was young. Too spindly by half. A man likes some flesh to lose himself in.'

Alpiew pulled out her notes and laid them out before her. 'I keep finding this phrase in the Apocalypse: "I am the Alpha and the Omega." What does that mean?'

'It's Greek, Alpiew. They are the first and last letters of the Greek alphabet.'

Alpiew jotted down A and Z.

'No.' The Countess leaned forward, took the pen and scratched out A and Z. 'The capital letters appear *comme ça* –' she jotted A and Ω – 'and the lower case look like this –' She added an α and a ω.

Alpiew stared down at them. 'So either way the A is much the same as it is in English.'

'Similar, yes.'

'Does it mean anything else?'

'It is generally thought to be symbolic of first and last.'

'Ah yes.' Alpiew sucked the vane of her quill. 'It said that in the Bible. "I am the Alpha and Omega, the first and last." Why did you want to see those playing cards, milady?'

'Only yesterday evening Isabel told me they all meant something.' The Countess sat in the window seat of Alpiew's room, staring out at the chateau across the busy square. 'I'm still shaking, are you?'

'I wish we could just run away from all this, milady. Go home.'

'What can we do? Last time we tried to make a dash for it, look what happened.'

The hawkers and street vendors below them cried out their wares both in English and French; horses neighed under the weight of their wagons; children bowled along playing catch.

'I can't believe such a terrible thing has happened, and yet the world just carries on as normal.'

'Don't the French raise the hue and cry after a murder like we do in London, madam? Where are the constables? The Justice? Will nothing be done, and another poor woman buried and the whole business forgotten about, like it was with Aurelia before her?'

'The cold-blooded butchery of it.' The Countess saw again the image of Isabel Murdo-McTavish lying in a pool of blood and her hand flew to her mouth. 'We must make a plan of action. For as soon as we can delve to bottom of the affair, then we can leave this grim place before we ever reach Louis's Friday deadline.'

'Amen to that.' Alpiew was busy sharpening her quill with a penknife.

'Someone over there is not quite right in the head, and we are the only people who seem to care a fig about it.' The Countess stamped her foot on to the carpet. 'It's ridiculous. People are dying and yet everyone treads softly around the matter so as not to rock the political boat. What kind of a place is this?'

'Tell me about the playing cards, madam.'

'Isabel told me earlier yesterday that every card has a meaning. Seeing the pack spread out like that, with two court cards set apart, made me wonder.'

'But, milady –' Alpiew laid out pieces of paper in a neat row – 'she could not have lived after those atrocities.'

'You have clearly never read the Lives of the Saints, Alpiew. St Denis walked three miles carrying his head under his arm, St Cecilia lived on for three days after being boiled and then all but beheaded. These things happen.'

'Headless men walking about the streets?' Alpiew popped a biscuit into her mouth. 'I've never seen one.'

'You've never seen *Africa*, that doesn't mean it doesn't exist. I'll have one of those. I'm half-starved.' The Countess leaned forward then hesitated as her finger touched the plate. 'Pshaw, Alpiew, I am forgetting about the supper last night. Whoever killed Isabel made two attempts.'

'Two?'

'They'd have got me too, but we slipped all of our food away from the table. Didn't eat a morsel. Either of us. I fed mine to a rabid wolf and killed it.'

'A rabid wolf?' Alpiew gave the Countess a sideways look and decided not to ask. 'Do you think the poisoning of Aurelia and Lady Murdo-McTavish's murder are linked?'

'Who's to say? But someone definitely made an attempt to dispose of the pair of us last night. We were the only ones at supper. I'll bet that the killer was certain he should have succeeded with Isabel after she'd eaten, then when she didn't keel over at the dinner table, the poisoner went up to her room to check, and . . .' She sat back and took a deep breath. 'Oh, wasn't it terrible! The poor woman.'

'But she wasn't in her room. I was. She was in your room.'

'Yes. That puts another complexion upon things.' The Countess looked to Alpiew, then leant her cheek against the cold glass of the window. 'Why should anyone here want to kill *me*?'

Alpiew deflected the question. 'What are they doing at the chateau this morning?'

'Praying, of course. As if that will make any difference.' The Countess munched on the biscuit. 'One thing's got to be said for the French, they make an excellent Savoy.'

'Let us start at the beginning, madam. Aurelia falls down dead of poison before your very eyes. Most of the assembly have left the room . . .'

'Been lured from the room?'

'Perhaps – by Pipe.' Alpiew was jotting down names in a great chart. 'Everyone claimed they had been getting threatening notes. We have seen some of them so at least we know it is true that ladies Whippingham and Murdo-McTavish received one.'

'Then the girl was spirited away by the men, and buried with little or no ceremony.

'Next thing we are in the Bastille, Queen Mary's ring secreted among my things,' the Countess continued the thread. 'Then Isabel too arrives in the Bastille. We are all writers, and we are all there at the whim of the King of France, who has been warned against us by an informer. Then you and I are released. Barely a day has passed and Isabel is also released, only to come back here and be brutally murdered, after someone has made an unsuccessful attempt to poison both of us.'

'Back again.' Alpiew dipped her pen. 'Reasons to kill Lady Murdo-McTavish?'

'That's hard to say.' The Countess sucked at the end of the Savoy. 'She was, quite rightly, against the social system in this country. That could mean trouble. She wrote fairy tales . . .'

'Is that an incitement to murder?'

'*Chacun à son goût.*' The Countess popped the whole biscuit into her mouth, shrugged, and started on another biscuit. 'Isabel was a good-looking woman. Perhaps it was an amour? You say Lord Whippingham acted strangely when you talked of her leaving?'

'*D'accord!*' Alpiew stuck her tongue into her cheek and twirled her pen between her hands. 'I've picked up a bit of the lingo myself, milady.'

'I find his charms hard to see, but then I think of my own husband and wonder at the choice I myself made. It was a wise man who first said that Cupid was blind.'

'In my opinion, madam, he's not only blind but half-witted.'

'*L'amour! L'amour!*' The Countess sighed. 'Religion aside, the cause of almost all the misery in the world.

> *'In all amours a lover burns*
> *With frowns as well as smiles,*
> *By turns.'*

'Not to mention the poem that I found marked on Lady Murdo-McTavish's bed, milady:

> *'"I prithee send me back my heart,*
> *Since I cannot have thine;*
> *For if from yours you will not part,*
> *Why then shouldst thou have mine?"'*

'Sir John Suckling!' exclaimed the Countess. 'Well there's a coincidence! Suckling himself died by poison in Paris.'

'Oh criminy, madam!' Alpiew dropped her pen as she spoke the next verse. 'It didn't mean very much when I first read it:

> *'"Why should two hearts in one breast lie,*
> *And yet not lodge together?*
> *O love, where is thy sympathy,*
> *If thus our breasts thou sever?"*

'In the margin against that verse someone had scrawled: "I mean it."'

'I see.' Not wanting to appear greedy, the Countess snapped a biscuit in two and nibbled at half. 'Put that together with a note that read: "I will be avenged", and I think we can be sure someone truly set out to rid the world of Isabel. For a start, the second poisoning attempt was no mere smearing of caddinets. That food I gave to the wolf knocked him stone dead in seconds. It must have been heartily laced with something very powerful.' The Countess crunched into the second half of the sponge biscuit. 'Thank God we didn't hand it around those starving peasants. It would have been the Black Death all over again.'

'Madam, we sit here surmising that someone set out to murder Lady Murdo-McTavish and Aurelia before her, but so much points to you as a victim. I was given that note in church. Believe me, you are in danger too.'

Though her palate was dry at the thought that someone was trying to kill her, the Countess thrust another half-Savoy into her mouth and sucked.

'Perhaps it is someone with a larger grudge – against the English, or Catholics, for example, or supporters of King James.' Alpiew scratched a few more words on her list. 'Perhaps they would kill everyone at St Germain one by one.'

'You are right.' The Countess swallowed with some difficulty. 'The chateau is something of a honeycomb, and we should presume that we are all targets while we are here. Oh, how I wish we had two strapping handsome bravos to mind our safety while we get on with discovering and delivering the information to the King.'

'I still have a suspicion of Whippingham and that workshop of his. What is it he does with those girls?' Alpiew scribbled down his name. 'He is hiding something. Last night there was something he didn't want me to see. Something . . . or someone in that bedroom at the top of the stairs.'

'And his wife has disappeared. Perhaps she is dead too.' The Countess laid down her half-eaten Savoy. 'It's quite enough to put you off eating.' She pulled out a pack of cards she had taken from the games room earlier that morning. 'What do we have? A pair of cards, some poetry, and a phrase: "Wackland's buttered bun." The buttered buns, the buttered buns . . . Perhaps I misheard that child Aurelia as she lay a-dying, Alpiew. The buttered bun? What does that sound like?'

'Shuttered shun? Guttered gun? Odso, milady, look! You can say that without moving your lips.'

'The queen of spades and the knave of diamonds.' The Countess moved across to a seat at the table and spread out the cards. 'Who do they look like?'

'Fluttered flun? Nuttered nun!' Alpiew held out her hands in triumph. 'It was a mad nun!'

'This queen carries a flower and this knave a halberd.' The Countess slammed the card down. 'Look, Alpiew.'

'So? What are you saying? That she is a gardener and he a guard?'

'Do you know, Alpiew, perhaps there are two people involved in all this. But before we proceed we must learn the language of cards.' The Countess peered at the rest of the pack. 'It is time for us to visit a professional prognosticator.'

Mère le Sage pressed her fingers together and lounged back in her chair, staring at Alpiew, who stood behind the Countess on the other side of the consulting table. 'You won't be searching after the treatment for bigger breasts, I presume?'

Alpiew lunged forward to take a shot at the old woman.

'Alpiew!' The Countess gripped Alpiew's arm and gave Le Sage a benign brown-toothed smile. 'We are neither of us here for a treatment, madame. More of a consultation.' She whipped out the two playing cards. 'Explain me these.'

'I raise you trente et la va.' Mère le Sage swept the table clear. 'How much do you stake?'

'You misunderstand. We need to know the meaning of these cards. Whom do they represent?'

The old woman snatched the cards and laid them face up on the table. 'In my opinion . . .' She pulled out a magnifying glass and pored over them for a moment. 'They represent the queen of spades and the knave of diamonds.'

The dog, who was lying on a large embroidered cushion under the window, shuddered and gave a sleepy growl.

'Lucifer has a great dislike of flats.'

'Flats?'

'Gaming cards. I myself employ only the Major Arcana.'

'We're not interested in members of your staff, madame.' The Countess tried to sound more civil than she felt. 'But these cards are of great import.'

'Queen beats knave? Twenty-three?' Le Sage took the cards and aimed them at the dog. 'Lucifer!'

'Thank you, madame.' The Countess snatched them back before the dog leapt. 'I've seen that trick before.'

Alpiew was not in the mood for this tease. She walked about the room, and let her mind drift back to the possibilities, leaving the Countess to deal with the bizarre old woman in her own well-mannered way.

'Are you going to pay me?' Mère le Sage let out a cackle. 'Otherwise what care I for you and your cards?'

The Countess dug into her pocket and laid down a coin.

'Are you here to buy poison? I have told you I do not handle the stuff, whatever the profit. I plan to keep hold of my head.'

The Countess pointed to the cards. 'Queen of spades. Knave of diamonds.'

'The suits are low,' muttered Le Sage. 'Spades ranks lowest in the pack; diamonds just above it. Diamonds signify delay, quarrels and annoyance. Spades are the worst suit of all. Spades are always trouble. They bring grief and sickness, and . . .'

'Not –' the Countess's hands flew to her mouth – 'death?'

'No.' Mère le Sage shifted uneasily in her chair. 'I was going to say loss of money.' She pocketed the coin and sat, arms crossed.

The Countess laid down another coin.

'Chuttered chun,' murmured Alpiew. 'Sputtered spun.'

'And the queen and the knave, what do they signify?'

'Guttered gun.'

'A woman and a man, of course.' Le Sage was warily eyeing Alpiew. She leant forward and whispered to the Countess. 'Your woman is an *engastriloque*?'

'No,' huffed the Countess. 'I assure you she has all of her faculties.'

'Really?' Le Sage was still eyeing Alpiew.

'Shuttered shun. Duttered Dun.'

'Mère Le Sage, please. My consultation!' The Countess

rapped her knuckles on the table-top. 'Queen of spades? Knave of diamonds?'

'The first a malicious and dangerous woman; the French name this card Pallas, after Pallas Athene, sometimes too it is named for Jeanne d'Arc. The second a mischievous man, named Hector after either the Trojan hero or Lancelot's brother, we cannot be sure.' Le Sage spoke distractedly, eyes on Alpiew striding back and forth. 'How long has she been doing this?'

'Walking up and down? About two minutes.'

'No, I mean practising to speak out of her belly with a stationary countenance.'

'Guttered gun. Guttered gun,' Alpiew recited. 'Guttered gun.'

'See, it is a marvel. She's not moving her lips!' Mère le Sage was pointing joyously at Alpiew. 'I could make use of a good ventriloquist at one of my séances.' She leaned in to speak intimately with the Countess. 'But why does she need to acquire such art to talk of a leman?'

'She's never mentioned a lemon,' snapped the Countess. 'She's talking of a buttered bun.'

'That's what I said. A leman, a paramour, an illicit mistress, a clandestine strumpet. A buttered bun.'

'I don't know why I didn't think of it.' The Countess marched along with Alpiew close at her heel. It was sweltering hot, and flies buzzed around the various piles of animal dung in the centre of the street. 'Everyone used the expression about ten years ago. It was the most voguish phrase in London.'

'But, remember, most of the people here in St Germain left London at the revolution, in other words about ten years ago. They may not have moved with the times, but don't you think it odd for a phrase like that to come from the mouth of a young girl educated here in France?'

'Unless she had been brought up among other ex-patriots.' The Countess stepped back as a large coach filled to bursting with newly arrived Jesuits attired in the customary long black gowns trundled past. 'And if Aurelia said it in order for everyone around her to understand that she had been poisoned by Wackland's illicit mistress, the question remains as to who that is.'

'Pipe would have us believe that Wackland prefers boys. Perhaps Wackland's boy was after Aurelia and Wackland took his revenge?'

'Alpiew, dear, if I didn't know better, I'd think you'd been seeing too many Jacobean plays. Why would he take revenge on Isabel for something a boy had done?'

'We say boy, though we mean male. Perhaps Wackland's leman is Lord Whippingham. He was there on the scene both times. And there is a mystery about that grubby cove. Who was hiding in his room last night? Someone was definitely in there waiting for him to come back with his damnable boxes.'

'Yes, Alpiew, I understand. I myself saw Wackland coming out of Whippingham's room last night pulling on a jacket.'

'Lord, madam, we are very near Whippingham's strange place.' Alpiew grabbed the Countess by the hand and scuttled along the street, turning abruptly into a tiny alley. 'This is it.' Alpiew stood before the front door leading to the room that housed Whippingham's mysterious enterprise. 'I know that by day at least he keeps scores of women in there, and by their own confession they're doing something worse than fellating.'

'Is there anything?' The Countess slid her tongue round her front teeth as she brushed away a distant and unwelcome memory. 'And upon whom are they performing this indelicate act?'

'That's the mystery.' Alpiew folded her arms and leant back against a low windowsill. 'But there are buckets full of something sticky inside there too.'

'Please, Alpiew, if you continue I shall exgurgitate.' She fanned herself. 'Do you know, I overheard some word apropos of this subject pass between the Whippinghams just before Aurelia partook of her last supper. The detail escapes me, but it was something about his lordship wanting Lucy to slip something into her mouth. He told her she had the wrong kind of teeth for the job. But tell me, Alpiew, what are the right kind of teeth?'

'I have been told that the secret was to have no teeth at all.' Alpiew had heard talk on a similar vein among the molly boys in Covent Garden. 'Toothless gums. In terms of dental equipment, Godfrey would be ideal for the job.'

'In God's name how should I know something like that?' The Countess's fan was flapping like a butterfly. 'I'm sixty years old.'

'Let's tiptoe along and burst in. We should get a good eyeful, even if it's only a few seconds' worth.'

'I dread to contemplate it, but you are right. Come on.' The Countess snapped her fan shut and marched forward. 'You look left; I'll look right.'

At the first doorway they both took off their shoes and crept up the long corridor. They listened at the door for a moment. That same humming and spitting sound. They grimaced at one another.

Then, on a mouthed count of three, they burst into the room.

The twenty chewing girls stopped, their mouths bulging.

After a moment's silence one girl spat into a bucket. Then the others all spat into theirs.

'Can I help you?'

The Countess recognised the woman she had seen getting out of the coach at Versailles with the Duc de Charme. Close to, she was very impressed by her painstaking make-up. A beautiful pale Venetian ceruse, with a delicate tracery of veins painted on her décolletage, and slightly rouged lips. A masterpiece of powder and paint.

'Good morning, madam . . . ?'

The woman was blocking their view now and edging them out of the room. Alpiew craned her neck, trying to get another decent squint.

'I am Lady Anastasia Ashby de la Zouche, Countess of Clapham, Baroness . . .'

'Yes?' The woman shifted forwards and clicked the door shut.

'I am a particular friend of the Duc de Charme and His Majesty.'

'Mmm?'

'And you are . . . ?'

'Mademoiselle Bontemps.'

'Well, Mademoiselle Bontemps, my husband, the Count, is particularly fond of that thing which you offer . . .' The Countess gave a playful little wink. 'And for a special birthday treat I wondered . . . ?' She left the sentence dangling.

'Chest?'

'Oh no.' She gave a winsome smile. 'He has Alpiew for that.'

'Tray?'

'I'm sorry?' The Countess leaned forward, a hand cupped round her ear. 'Un, deux, tray, you mean? I am not that generous. I think one session will suffice.'

'Would you please tell me what you want? A caddy? Come along. If I'm not in there watching the girls, they get sloppy. Believe me, Countess, you cannot trust these masticators.'

'He is *that* too, but how in heaven's name did you know?' The Countess was feeling quite bewildered by the woman's raw audacity. 'Just tell me how much you charge and what exactly you offer for the money.'

'Excuse me, Mademoiselle Bontemps . . .' Alpiew wished she could get another glance at what she thought she'd just seen: a roomful of women cramming their mouths with torn-up pieces of newspaper. She thought back to the stack of ornamental boxes she'd seen piled up in the room last night. Maybe the boxes were a cover. And if they asked to see a box now it would at least give them a chance to peer through the open door once more. 'Her ladyship would like to take a peep at a caddy, please.'

The woman slipped into the room and shut the door behind her.

'It's as strange as a snowball in August, madam,' Alpiew hissed. 'I know what they're doing. They're chewing up newspapers and spitting it into buckets.'

'Perhaps it's the lampoons against the King. It's certainly a safer way of disposing of them than simply tearing them up.'

The woman returned with an armful of large painted tea caddies.

The Countess took a black one decorated with flowers.

'Fan me, ye winds!' She handed the box to Alpiew. 'Look at this!'

Alpiew took the box.

'Lord, madam.' She opened it and looked inside. 'How is it so weightless?'

'That, mesdames, is the trade secret.' Mademoiselle Bontemps gave a furtive smile and seized the box back. 'Our products are lightweight but durable and strong. Excellent for travelling, and useful for elderly servants. The trays, for instance, are an exquisite –'

'Yes, yes, yes,' said the Countess, taking a red one to inspect. 'But where's the sex?'

'I'm sorry, Countess? We are a papier moulé merchant. And we have just received a huge order from the court at Versailles, so time is precious.'

'Papier Moulé?'

'The new-found Oriental process for creating *objets d'art*.'

'You mean this isn't a brothel?' said Alpiew, disgusted.

'Certainly not.' Mademoiselle Bontemps snatched the beautiful caddy back from the Countess. 'And if you think you can come nosing around here, trying to steal our method, you are mistaken. Good-day.'

She strutted back into the workroom and slammed the door behind her.

The Countess sat back against a tree, gently wafting her fan against the sultry noon heat.

'Whippingham is a queer cove, to be sure, milady. We may

have misunderstood the meaning of "munching", but there's more he's hiding away. You mark my words.'

Alpiew sprawled out on the grass, chomping on an apple. A fly buzzed around her, she swatted at it with her handkerchief.

'The queen of spades –' the Countess was laying out playing cards on the grass – 'that is the Buttered Bun, I presume. And the knave? Any man who commits murder is certainly a knave.'

'You know, milady, you say *knave* of diamonds, but people who I know would say Jack.'

'Jack? Jack of diamonds!' said the Countess. 'Is there a Jack amongst us?'

'The little Prince.'

'Why yes, James Francis Edward. He, and his father, Jacobus Secundus.'

'And to the locals this is the court of le Roi Jacques.'

'I doubt that the deposed King of England and his eleven-year-old heir have been out on a murdering spree amongst their most loyal subjects. Or rather, their loyal Jacobites. Remember, Alpiew, their nickname is the Jacks.' She flicked the two playing cards between her fingers. 'Jack could be so many things: Jack Horner, Jack-a-lantern, Jack Tar – perhaps he's a sailor!'

'Or Jack Sprat, and he's a dwarf.'

'Jack-in-a-box, he leaps out on people. Jack Frost, he's cold.'

'Jack-a-Napes, he's a cheeky fellow. Jack Ketch, he's a hang-man.'

'Stop, Alpiew! There are too many of these Jacks. Apple Jack, Black Jack, Cheap Jack. The very use of the word Jack has opened more possibilities, than we could ever explore.'

'Jack of all trades. I have a friend called Jack in Covent Garden; he's one of those.' Alpiew laid the gnawed core of her apple down. 'One minute – his real name is John. Jack isn't only Latin for James, remember. It's English for John.'

'And we have a very shifty John hereabouts. A man who's

willing to terrify the life out of us and steal our money for a jape. And he was here at the chateau. Where he went in between-times might be a mystery, but on both occasions he was only yards away from the site of the murder.' The Countess held out her hand for a lift up. 'Oh, Alpiew, I fear we have been barking up quite the wrong tree, for right under our noses we have a knavish Jack and a *puella pulchra*. We need to find Miss Franklyn-Green and her cohort the highwayman.'

Virginia was sprawled out on the bed in her well-appointed bedchamber, fully clothed this time, and sobbing.

'Lord, child, what an up-and-down creature you are,' said the Countess, perching on the bedside. 'It's always laughter or tears with you. What has happened now, pray?'

Virginia squawked an incomprehensible sentence into the pillow.

The Countess nodded in Alpiew's direction and she tiptoed discreetly out of the room.

'What is it, Virginia?'

'I am tired of this stupid place.' The girl rolled over on to her side, spluttering. Her face was red, and her eyes had puffed up to a startling degree. This was no little tantrum; the child must have been crying ferociously for hours. 'It has grown exquisitely dull and I shall be heartily glad to leave it.'

'Pshaw, girl, things can't be so bad.' The Countess smoothed her hand along the green brocade bedcover. She wondered how things could possibly get any worse, but saying that was not going to get her anywhere with this howling girl. 'John may be only a groom, but he's a fine figure of a man. I wouldn't mind a romp with him myself.'

Virginia shuddered and groaned before breaking into a raucous wail.

What on earth could be worrying the child? The Countess thought of the sight of them hard at it last night and suppressed a smile. But when she remembered the look of astonishment on Prude's face, she couldn't help but laugh aloud. 'I presume it wasn't your first time a-swiving?' The Countess vividly remembered her own youth and wondered whether the girl was upset because she had given away her virginity. 'No one actually does what they say they do when they talk about sex, you know. Everyone has a try at the old romp-a-bed before they are married, I wouldn't worry about that. Unless, that is . . .' She crossed herself. If the girl was with child that would put entirely another slant on the matter. She'd either have to get Virginia married off very quick, pay a visit to Mère le Sage and have the problem dealt with using herbs or whatever was the current French method, or take her off into the country declaring that she had been struck down with a tympany, to explain the swelling abdomen. Then, when the nine months brought forth their bouncing fruit, they could palm the baby off on some barren wife who needed an heir to keep her claim on the family wealth. The Countess gripped the brocade and prayed it couldn't be true. Things like that might be easy enough to facilitate in England, but in France? Lord, what a mess! She reached out and gently stroked the wailing girl's hair. 'Good lack, child. What a crying out is here! 'Twill all come right in the end. Whatever has happened, I will be as good as a mother to you.'

The girl wept on. The Countess took her limp hand from the pillow and patted it. 'And as I said, John is a fine figure of a lad.'

After a few quivers, Virginia rolled over on to her back.

'He is no such thing.'

'I've seen a few in my time, and I tell you, from all that I saw last night . . .'

'No. John is not who he pretends to be.' She wiped her nose with the back of her hand. 'He confessed it all to me last night, after everyone left us. The whole affair has been a lie.'

The Countess winced. She could guess what was to follow. The man was married, or worse.

'John is no groom.' Virginia's eyes wrinkled up again and her mouth opened lengthways, making her resemble an ancient

Greek tragic mask. She let out a heart-rending wail. 'He's a wealthy heir!'

'I'm sorry?' The Countess thought she must have misheard. 'He's a what?'

'He's rich. And he is Viscount Ventnor,' she howled. 'But when his father dies, he'll be a duke.' She turned and with another wail plunged her face into her pillow.

The Countess swallowed hard. How could the girl be disappointed by news such as this! Her own husband had passed himself off as being the scion of a rich family; it was only after they were married that he had confessed he was in fact descended from a long line of impoverished sutlers, and that he'd been awarded his much-vaunted knighthood in a case of mistaken identity on the battlefield of Worcester when he was only a lad of thirteen.

'Come, come, you buffle-headed creature,' cooed the Countess. ''Twould be far worse if the pretence was reversed and you had been cozened of your maidenhead by a groom pretending to be a lord.'

'But, Countess, if he could lie to me thus? He was so convincing.' She sobbed again.

'Did he tell you why exactly he was pretending to be a groom when he is clearly a member of one of the highest families in the land?'

'He was acting, he said. To see if he could convince anyone he was who he pretended to be.' Virginia's body shook, and she banged the pillow with her fists. 'The duplicitous, double-dealing Judas! How can I ever trust him again?' She sat up and wiped her cheeks with the back of her hand. 'He was so convincing as a groom. So all he has proved is that he is a liar and a trickster.'

Alpiew lurked around the corner until the assembly came out of the Chapel Royal of the chateau. When the crowd had gone she crept inside to get another look at the Bible.

The place reeked of incense. She checked carefully that no

one was loitering in the corners, then nipped up the altar steps, hauled the great book from the stand and carried it over to the front pew.

She turned a few pages, and realised that, perching here with her back to the door, she was a sitting duck. Whoever entered could see her but she could not see them. Lady Prude for one was always hovering around the place.

She saw a little wooden structure with an open door. She looked inside. It was something like a night-watch Charlie's box, with a comfortable wooden seat and a little ledge where she could easily rest the great *Douai* Bible. There was even a conveniently placed candle sconce.

She carried the big book over and placed it on the stand in the box. She took her seat, struck a light and closed the door behind her.

Snug, cosy and safe, she opened the great book at the Apocalypse of Saint John.

> *I am Alpha and Omega: the Beginning and the End. To him that thirsteth, I will give of the fountain of the water of life, freely. He that shall overcome shall possess these things. And I will be his God: and he shall be my son. But the fearful and unbelieving and the abominable and murderers and whoremongers and sorcerers and idolaters and all liars, they shall have their portion in the pool burning with fire and brimstone, which is the second death.*

Alpiew was so carried away noting this passage down that she only heard the footsteps, echoing along the stone-flagged aisle, when they were too near for her to do anything.

She hastily extinguished her candle and sat still. What if whoever this was needed to come in here? How would she explain herself?

She held her breath and winced as the footsteps stopped momentarily then slowly approached her tiny wooden cell.

She heard a noise, like brass sliding on brass, a curtain opening.

There was a fumbling sound and a rustle of silk from the other side of the wooden partition, then a murmured 'Father? Father?' It was a woman's voice, with a tremulous quality to it.

Alpiew could vaguely make out the silhouette of a woman through the tightly woven brass grille in the partition. She couldn't decide whether to fling open the door and make a run for it. She edged her feet round, ready to bolt.

'Father? Please may I make my confession?'

Confession? Oh lord! Alpiew wiggled about, wishing she could escape. This huge thing must be the confession box.

Alpiew lowered her voice and tried to sound priestly, even adding a slight Irish burr for veracity. 'Yes, child,' she growled.

'Bless me, Father, for I have sinned . . .'

Alpiew's eyes bulged out of her head with astonishment. Once the woman spoke a complete sentence it was obvious who sat on the other side of the grille. The penitent about to confess her sins was none other than Lady Prude.

'Now, Virginia, when did this declaration of John's social position actually occur? After the frightful events of the night, I presume?'

The girl's hands flew to cover her face.

'Tell me, child . . .' the Countess cooed. She wanted to know how long they had been together in that room, so close to the horrors taking place up the corridor. Whether they had heard or seen anything. 'You must have had quite a romantic evening together for it to result in such an explosive climax.'

'Not at all.' Virginia threw back her head and gave a sarcastic laugh. 'The pig came rushing in here to my room, all dishevelled, his shirt unlaced, his hands soaking wet, grabbed me by the hand and, without speaking a word, he dragged me up to the garret, kissing the back of my neck all the while. It felt romantic at the time. Now it makes me feel dirty.'

'Oh, yes. John had been away, hadn't he? You thought he'd left with an old witch. Did you know he was coming back?'

'I realise now that I never knew anything about him.'

'How did you get to know him so intimately, then? Explain me that.'

'He took a temporary position with my father's stables. He flirted with me, and I . . . well, I responded. And when I came here, he followed me to France, then he left me, then he came back.'

'But why was a viscount working as a groom for your father? Did he explain that?'

'I told you!' Virginia huffed. 'He wanted to see whether he could convince people he was a groom.'

'I'm sorry, Virginia, but why would he want to do that? Is he hoping to become a player? In which case he'd be better seeing whether he can convince people he is a lord. There are very few good parts who are grooms, believe me.' The Countess shook her head. What a puzzle. And how unhappy the poor child looked. She felt quite sorry for her. 'So where is the scoundrel now?'

'How should I know? I slapped him and ran away from him when he told me.'

The Countess couldn't help thinking Virginia was well rid of the man.

'Why did he tell you about it this morning in particular? Do you know?'

'He wanted us to elope.'

'Again?'

'I didn't know we were eloping the last time. I thought I was being sent into a lonely exile.'

'He cared enough about you to follow you here.'

'He wasn't following *me*.' Virginia's eyes wrinkled up and her lips turned inside out again. 'He was sent here with a message. I was a convenience.'

'A message – who on earth for?'

'I don't know. Some woman. That's another reason why I

don't trust him. I know there's some old woman over here; it's her that he's really come to see. I think he only comes to see me when he can't see her because she's with her husband or something.'

'Did he tell you her name?'

'He made me swear I'd tell no one. But after he's been so mean to me . . . I'm sure it's all right if I tell you. She's called Denise.'

'And where does she live, this Denise? Did he say?'

'I don't understand, Countess.' Virginia's face puckered up again. 'What is wrong with me? I'm not ugly or fat. Why doesn't he love me?'

'I am sorry to be the one to tell you, and after the horse has bolted at that, but Love, however omnipotent he may seem, abates much of his divinity when he comes to full enjoyment.'

'I told him to go away and leave me. To go to his precious Denise.' This set the girl off into another chorus of sobbing. 'And he *went!*'

'He definitely told you that this Denise dabbled in the black arts? You're not just guessing because you're jealous.'

'He himself called her a basilisk. And *I've* been to the theatre. I know that whenever a man calls a woman a basilisk in Act One, by Act Five he's calling her a virago, a shrew, a hag and a witch.'

The Countess sighed. She could only agree. Using the word basilisk to describe a woman was never a good sign in a man, especially as handsome and eligible a man as John, the erstwhile groom, the present Viscount Ventnor.

Alpiew gripped the book in front of her. Now the woman had started, what could she do? She had no notion of the papist rig-me-roles priests performed within the wooden walls of this strange box.

'Bless you, child.' Alpiew grabbed a handkerchief from her pocket and covered her mouth.

'I last went to confession earlier this morning, Father. But when I saw the door closed, I decided to come in again. For my soul is labouring under a great burden which I cannot hold in another moment.'

Alpiew opened her mouth, and shut it.

Lady Prude also hesitated, as though uncertain whether to proceed.

Alpiew held her breath.

The silence between them was palpable.

'Are you not going to ask me . . . ?'

'You are free to talk at your leisure, child,' said Alpiew, adding a 'bless you' for good measure.

She could hear Lady Prude's brocade mantua rustling in the darkness. Then another sound. What was it? A sort of wheezing.

Perhaps Lady Prude was suffering from asthma.

'I have been looking back on my life – should I say the stormy tumult, the perplexity of my past, and how I came to be here – and contemplating some grave errors I have made along the way.'

Alpiew winced. Lord, but this was an uneasy position to find herself in. She gave a grunt. 'Go on.'

'I was a fornicator,' announced Prude. 'I reformed, but now I believe I went too far in that reformation.' Lady Prude sniffed. Alpiew realised the woman was crying. 'Love is good, Father, is it not?'

Alpiew sat silent.

'Tell me Love is good, Father. Surely, if one person can sacrifice things for the love of another, it cannot be wrong in the Lord's eyes? And yet I have castigated those whose only sin is love. And as a result I have unleashed a terrible and true Evil into this place.'

She fell silent.

'It was all because of me.'

Silence again.

'I thought my nemesis was gone. But it has returned. Twice now it has come.'

Another long silence.

'I wish to confess the sins of my past, Father. When I was young I made a mistake. And that mistake is come back to haunt me.' Lady Prude fell silent. Then Alpiew could hear her sniffling, before she continued: 'I was a bigamist. And though it was easy enough at the time, now the wraiths of my past have risen up. I am compounding my sin with error upon error.'

Lady Prude cried quietly for a moment or two.

'Yes?' Alpiew hoped she could make Lady Prude carry on and explain herself more clearly.

'In order to protect myself, I gave false information. And this information has led to innocent people dying.'

Alpiew wondered for a moment whether priests ever asked for a detailed explanation. 'Mmmm,' she said in a knowing but judgemental way. 'Go on.'

'Once I realised what was happening and the girl died, I pointed the finger. I tried to make it better. I arranged for the object of my persecution to be locked up. I imagined she would be safe under lock and key. But somehow she managed to get free and came back here. Here, to this place where I had done everything I could to ruin her.'

'Why?' said Alpiew, not reaching the depth of tone she was after and covering with a little cough. 'What drove you?'

'Two things, Father. A false sense of decency caused me to persecute her. But by having her arrested I thought I was saving her life. You cannot imagine my anguish when I realised she had come back here. God help my soul.'

'Child . . .' Alpiew couldn't resist a quick question: 'You spoke of fornication . . . bigamy . . .'

'Yes, Father. But I saw the error of my ways, and have since devoted myself solely to the Lord and to my King.'

It was clear there was more she wanted to say. And Alpiew wanted to hear it. 'But . . . ?' she said.

'I turned about so far I was wrong. God help us, if it is true love drives the goodness in the world on, it must be allowed. Love must . . .' She broke off and Alpiew could hear her groaning with remorse, her breathing coming ever more laboured. 'What can I do, Father?'

Alpiew dared not utter.

'Please, Father. I know I was a sinner. I know I deserve your wrath. But pity me, whose only faults were too much selfishness and too little sympathy.' She was blowing her nose now. Alpiew stayed silent.

'I am frightened that these days of terror are not over.' A strangled quality came into Lady Prude's voice. '"For true and just are His judgements, who hath judged the great harlot which corrupted the earth with her fornication and hath revenged the blood of His servants at her hands." Please say something, Father. Perhaps I am jealous of others. Jealous of their love.' She sobbed again. 'Oh, Christ our Saviour, forgive me, I am confessing that a woman certainly died because of me. Perhaps two.'

'Died!' Alpiew's voice came out far too high. She swallowed hard. Then lowered her voice again. 'Did you play an active part in this death, my child?'

'Yes.' Lady Prude let out a smothered wail. 'I alone am guilty.'

ELEVEN

Farces — usually made of several sorts of meat and herbs chopt small and well season'd with spice; Of these farces there is a great variety, and some are distinguished by particular names, as godivoes, mirotons, poupetons, salpicons &c.

'And you see, Countess, I saw her coming down the stairs only minutes before the Duchesse screamed. She was wrapped up in a cloak and seemed much disturbed.' Alpiew perched against the Countess's side-table in her garret room. 'Perhaps she was running away from the crime.'

'Do you know, Alpiew, we may talk about horrors, of hissing snakes and gnawing worms, but I think that all human language cannot describe the torments of an accusing conscience.' The Countess pondered. 'But 'tis a pity you didn't take better pains to find out exactly what her role was. In my opinion, if she had physically performed the act of murder her confession would have been much clearer, or she wouldn't have confessed at all.'

'Do you think perhaps that Lady Prude was the writer of the threatening letters? She talked of persecuting someone, someone who she had also had locked up.'

'Someone had us locked up. And someone had Isabel locked up. But Isabel talked about receiving letters. Let's go and take a look for them.'

'So you gathered the letters were from Prude, criticising Lady Murdo-McTavish in some way?' Alpiew tried to recall the late-night conversation she had had in the Bastille. 'I rather thought she believed that Aurelia had written them. And they were death threats.'

'Well, let us find them and we shall see. Who knows? Isabel talked of two sets of notes in differing handwriting.' The Countess rolled over and reached down for her shoes. 'Bring that doormat over here, Alpiew, dear. The sight of the bloodstain frets me. I scrubbed it as hard as I could, but, lord, there was a lot of blood. See how it has soaked right into the wood.'

Alpiew slid the mat over to the bedside.

'Won't you be scared to sleep in here, on your own, milady? Why, we do not know if Lady Murdo-McTavish was murdered by mistake, and you are not the real target. She was killed here in your room. And you yourself said someone poisoned the food which only you two were to eat.'

'This puzzle needs solving speedily.' The Countess grasped Alpiew by the arm. 'Why was Isabel in my room at all? We were due to meet outside in the woods. I left a little early. Perhaps she thought I might still be here and was coming to tell me she would be late. Did her killer come here and kill her by mistake, or did Isabel come here for a purpose, perhaps to hide from her murderer?'

'Perhaps there was another reason. If she knew you were meeting her elsewhere, she would have known your room would be empty. Perhaps she came in here for some purpose of her own: to steal, to leave *you* a threatening note. Who knows?' Alpiew flopped down on the bed beside the Countess. 'Go through the events, slowly.'

'Isabel and I were chatting downstairs. Prude came in and had some kind of fit of fury because we were playing cards – well, in fact Isabel was teaching me a little cartomancy. But Prude was very strange and tense, her eyes startled and full of horror. But, not realising about the poison, Isabel and I stuffed the food that came through into our bags and walked upstairs together, our pockets and bags bulging.'

'Who brought in the food? Who served you?'

'A girl. I hadn't seen her before. Moorish. She hung her head, laid the food on the credence table by the door, and scuttled out.'

'Did you eat anything at all, milady?'

'Only a bread roll each,' said the Countess. 'So off we went, laughing and giggling like schoolgirls, with all this food in our pockets and bags, because the plan was that we should meet again later, when everyone was asleep. We had just reached the foot of the final staircase when she tapped her forehead and said she had to go back, she had forgotten something.'

'I wonder what that was.'

'I came here to my room. I got my cloak ready and sat on the bed until the clock struck the half-hour. Then, at half eleven, I tiptoed quietly downstairs . . .'

'You didn't go to fetch Isabel from her room?'

'No, that wasn't the plan.'

'So she may or may not have come up during that time.'

'I went down, and met up with the young Prince again. We talked for about a quarter of an hour and then I rushed out to join Isabel. I waited and waited. Then there was the wolf episode, then I came back and heard the scream which alerted you to the Duchesse discovering the body.'

'So how long was that after you'd last seen Lady Murdo-McTavish?'

'Over an hour,' said the Countess. 'Plenty of time for evil-doing.'

'Let's go and see if we can't find those other letters she talked of.'

They crossed the corridor and listened at the door to Isabel's old room.

Silence. Warily, Alpiew turned the handle, and sneaked the door open. The Countess looked up and down the corridor and they slipped inside.

'Criminy!' Alpiew shut the door and surveyed the chamber. 'What whirlwind has been through here?'

Every drawer was pulled out, and clothing scattered over the floor. The bedding was pulled back and a chair tumbled.

'Someone was looking for something.' The Countess twirled a full circle. 'And they decided to play safe.'

'Howso?'

'Where are the papers? I have seen her room; it was not unlike our way. Isabel wrote, she kept notes, she had stacks of papers – her fairy tales, her poetry, the offerings from her writers' circle. And see, Alpiew, there is not a scrap of paper left.'

Alpiew let out a little scream as the Duc de Charme rose to his feet from behind the bed. 'I had lent Lady Murdo-McTavish a book,' he said, waving the Suckling poetry at them. 'I wanted to have eet back.'

He smiled, bowed politely, and tottered to the door.

'Not so fast, mister. Why are you in here?' said Alpiew, dashing round to block his way. 'And what's that book to you?'

'Eet is our property.' The Duc shrugged. 'Eet belongs to my wife. I must return eet to her.' He pulled open the door and stood in the doorway. 'I might stop to ask why you are een here also. But I will not.' He left the room, taking a lingering glance at Alpiew's cleavage as he passed.

'Cheeky devil,' said Alpiew, making to go after him.

'Hold!' The Countess grabbed her sleeve. 'Calm down.' She counted to five under her breath. '*Now* let us follow him.'

'All right.' Alpiew peered along the corridor. 'But he is already gone out of sight, madam.'

'On those heels?' cried the Countess. 'He can't have got far. Come on. Quietly now.'

They tiptoed along the passage and were about to descend the steps when they heard an almighty ruckus coming from Whippingham's room.

'Get your hands off me, you popinjay!'

'I will have it. Now.'

There was an almighty sound of banging, as though tables and chairs were being overturned.

'All right,' shouted Whippingham. 'Much good it may do you.'

'Good. Now eet ees over. The end. No more.'

'Charme,' growled Whippingham, 'you are a perfect fool.'

'To be perceived as a fool by you, monsieur,' snapped the Duc, opening the door and teetering on to the landing, 'can only be a compliment.' Unabashed at their presence, he turned and smiled at the Countess and Alpiew. *'Mesdames! À bientôt.'* He bowed politely and lurched down the stairs.

'You'll never guess what!' Pipe sat sunning herself on a barrel at the kitchen door. 'All hell has broke out. First Lord Wackland was shouting at her, and saying the kitchens were going to shut down. He would not be responsible, and all this stuff. Then in came all these *gens d'armes* and they carried her off in a big wagon.'

A few yards away Mademoiselle Smith lay out, seemingly asleep.

'Slowly, slowly, Pipe. We are in a maze.' The Countess pulled up a stool and perched beside her in the afternoon sun. 'Who exactly was carried off?'

'Lady Prude!' exclaimed Pipe. 'Her hands tied behind her back like a common criminal, madam. The like I'll not be seeing again, I'd say. It would make you split your face laughing to see the figure she cut.'

'And if the kitchens are to be shut, how are the folk who live here to eat?' The Countess felt relieved and saddened at the same time. No more worries about being poisoned at communal meals, but no chance of any decent food either.

'His lordship says people can buy their own stuff and cook it in here themselves. He will not be blamed, he says, for any other trouble that may happen here.'

'I can't see many of that lot huddling over a boiling pot of broth,' said Alpiew. 'What will everyone do?'

'Lord Wackland says if they won't cook for themselves, they must dig into their pockets and go to eat at an ordinary or a coffee shop in Town.'

'What about the Marquis de Béchamel?' asked the Countess, hoping to be counted in on any experiments. 'Will he go on practising over here?'

'Oh yes,' said Mademoiselle Smith. 'Where else can he find so many eager guinea pigs? I'm expecting him at any minute.'

'The Marquis is cooking here tonight?' said the Countess. 'How wonderful.'

Alpiew gave her a kick.

'Tell them about the missing bracelet, Pipe.' Mademoiselle Smith rolled over and lay on her front.

'Oh, that,' Pipe shrugged. 'Another piece gone missing upstairs.'

'A pretty necklace, Lord Wackland said.' Mademoiselle Smith propped her face up on her hands. 'Sounded gorgeous. Composed of the finest sapphires and pearls, he said.'

Alpiew was busy scrutinising Pipe, who gazed down at the cobbles, knocking her boots against each other.

'Do you know where they took Lady Prude?' The Countess presumed, from the method of her arrest, that Lady Prude must have been taken away by whatever made up the St Germain constabulary, and not been whisked off to the Bastille.

'No,' said Pipe, leaping to her feet and rubbing her hands

with glee. 'But with any luck it means she'll miss this precious masquerade she's had planned for so long.'

'Surely that will be cancelled.' The Countess was appalled. 'Lady Murdo-McTavish only died yesterday and will be buried tomorrow.'

'"Life must go on," Wackland said. We've got to live as normally as we can.' Pipe sat back and closed her eyes. 'So, tomorrow night, upstairs in the grand ballroom, there will be a masquerade.'

'Pipe, you were the Whippinghams' servant, were you not?' The Countess tried to appear nonchalant. 'What is Lucy Whippingham's Christian name?'

'Are you joshing me, or what, Countess?' Pipe peered at her as though she was cracked. 'Why, Lucy Whippingham's Christian name is Lucy – Lucille. What else would it be?'

'She's never been called Denise at all?'

'No.' Pipe gave her another bewildered glance. 'Lucy.'

'What's the new girl called?' Alpiew decided to slip in something on another line. 'The Moorish girl?'

'Search me!' Pipe shrugged. 'I don't know of such a girl, but you know how it is in here, Alpiew. New people come and go all the time.'

'You weren't here last night?'

'As everyone was ill from the oysters –' Pipe gave a little cough and avoided Alpiew's glance – 'there wasn't much to do. I laid out a few plates of food, then Lady Prude came in. She was very agitated. Lord Wackland told me to take the rest of the night off. So I didn't hang around here.'

'Where are we to find masks, at such little notice?' The Countess was trotting on ahead of Alpiew, peering into every shop front. 'Everyone has got here first.'

A bell rang the hour.

'Should we be wasting our time on such a thing when we should be following the trail?'

'Pshaw, Alpiew! Firstly, what trail do you mean? What have

we but a finger pointing at everyone? Secondly, don't you see what an opportunity a masked ball can be? We will be hidden behind masks, so who will recognise us?'

Alpiew looked at the rotund little figure trotting along ahead of her and wondered who could ever mistake her.

'Besides, my dear, the shops will shut in a minute. Hurry along.'

Alpiew thought they'd do perfectly well with a piece of pasteboard and a ribbon, but the Countess was all for spangles and feathers and all kinds of sparkly things.

'Where on earth do you think they're holding Prude? The town isn't so big. We're sure to find the local lock-up.' The Countess put her hands on her hips and looked around. 'I wonder if they arrested her for murder?'

'Maybe someone else was in the chapel while she was confessing, and overheard it all.'

'Oh, phough,' panted the Countess. 'They must have raffling shops in this godforsaken town.' She stepped through a flock of particularly fat ducks and they all waddled together down the rue de Poissy. 'More so than in London, from the penury I've witnessed here. Keep your eyes skinned for the sign of the Three Golden Balls.' She stopped and peered in at another window. 'But my word, Alpiew, French milliner's shops are pretty. And look at those sumptuous fabrics next door in the drapers. If only one of us could sew, it would be so nice to buy some.'

'But we can't. You said yourself the shops are about to shut.' Alpiew hauled her away. 'I see a pawnbroker.' She pointed ahead. 'What do you mean to pawn, milady?' Alpiew looked her up and down as they walked. Surely nothing she had about her would fetch a shilling.

'To *buy*, Alpiew. 'Tis the easiest place to cheapen pieces of jewellery in a raffle-shop, so many don't ever have the money to come back for the pieces they've laid in lavender. There must be some pretty things available in a town like St Germain-en-Laye. And when we find some, then we can decorate ourselves.'

They were close enough to peer inside the window, when the black front door to the pawnshop opened and, pulling on his gloves, out stepped Baron Lunéville.

'Oh look, Alpiew!' cried the Countess. 'This is Baron Lunéville, one of the gentlemen who used to make the journey from Versailles to St Germain simply to get a decent meal.'

Lunéville jumped, then placed his open palm on his chest and smiled. '*Vous m'avez donné un choc!*'

The Countess beamed at the gangly Frenchman. 'How are the peas?' She mimed eating a knife-ful.

He lifted his hat and scurried off.

'Typical Frenchman!' exclaimed the Countess. 'So rude, yet always so well turned out.' She pushed into the shop.

The pawnbroker was inspecting a piece of jewellery through a magnifying glass as the Countess approached the counter. She opened her mouth to speak, then grasped Alpiew's hand and tugged it, never taking her eyes off the piece of jewellery in the man's hands.

It was an exquisite sapphire and pearl necklace.

'Odso, madam, who would suspect . . . ? I shall follow him.' Alpiew bunched up her skirts and dashed out, chasing up the street in the same direction Baron Lunéville had gone.

'*C'est très beau, ça,*' said the pawnbroker, still eyeing the necklace.

'A little *too "très beau"* for me, monsieur,' said the Countess. 'If you *parlez Anglais*, I would like some cheap goods; some unredeemed sparkles and spangles for use upon a masquerade costume.'

Alpiew dodged in and out of the traffic, trying to find Baron Lunéville. She had almost given up, when she saw him lingering in the doorway of a coffee shop. She pressed herself back into the entrance to a mews and watched him as he took out a fob watch and looked at it, then glanced up and down the street. He was clearly anxious.

After a few moments he relaxed. Alpiew followed his gaze.

Sauntering up the street was Roger, the valet. He greeted Lunéville warmly, then embraced him, a tad too long for Alpiew's liking. Lord, these Frenchmen!

Then without further ado the two men parted and walked off in different directions. Well, there was a turnabout! What had seemed the expression of a pair of lovers, Alpiew surmised, was in fact a bobbing of the booty. It could only be that. Something, presumably the cash from the sale of the stolen necklace, had changed hands before her eyes.

Alpiew made up her mind and switched to trailing Roger. He strode along looking straight ahead and arrived at the chateau within a few minutes. Alpiew held back; she would be too noticeable in the wide-open space near the front gate, but Roger made his way round to the side of the chateau, heading for the Cour de Cuisine.

Alpiew ran across the courtyard, narrowly avoiding being run down by a large wagon loaded up with barrels. She arrived in time to see him go inside.

Hastily she straightened herself up, and then slouched in after him. As she entered she noticed Pipe jam her hand into her pocket and say, rather too loud for veracity: 'The Duc and Duchesse are out on the terrace walking, Roger.'

Roger spun round, cocked an eyebrow, and pushed Alpiew out of the way as he left the same way he had just come.

'Never did like him much,' said Pipe, grabbing a pot full of water and slinging it on to a hook over the fire. 'Would you like a biscuit?'

'That's all right, Pipe. I'm not so hungry now.' She flopped down on the bench. 'You couldn't lend me a livre or two, could you? I can pay you back tonight when I see my lady.'

'Sorry!' Pipe threw up her hands. 'I haven't a sou to call my own, let alone a livre. All I can offer is a biscuit.'

The Countess had acquired a good supply of band-board, ribbon, a swatch of silk moiré, some ostrich feathers and a pot of assorted spangles.

She sat in Alpiew's room, arranging the items into their colours, while Alpiew scribbled away at her notes.

'As I always suspected, Pipe is a prig and a buzz.' She wrote so fast her quill sprayed ink all over her fingers. 'Yet, how she has acquired the services of a French baron from Versailles to fence her plunder, we have yet to discover.'

'Do you want the green moiré or the red shantung?' The Countess held up the two free swatches she had got from the shop by saying she needed to match them up to her upholstery.

'Prude has confessed to her involvement in these deaths. Or at least one of them.' Alpiew rifled through her Bible notes. 'And she quoted from the Apocalypse. Here we are: "True and just are his judgements, who hath judged the great harlot which corrupted the earth with her fornication and hath revenged the blood of his servants at her hands."'

'Whatever that might mean,' said the Countess, sucking the end of a piece of cotton ready to thread it into a needle. 'Was she talking of herself, do you think, or someone else?'

'Is Prude the queen of spades? Is Prude the leman, the buttered bun?' Alpiew sucked the top of her quill. 'And how on earth do I find out without entering Lord Wackland's bedchamber in the middle of the night?'

'Do you know nothing of the laws of Love, Alpiew? Meetings with mistresses are never at night. An illicit dalliance is far more likely in the middle of the afternoon. That line of action though is out of the question while her ladyship is banged up.'

'We only have a hunch that it is Lady Prude.' Alpiew drew a row of small diamonds on the page. 'We certainly have a knave, or a Jack, otherwise known as John.' Alpiew scratched them on to a piece of paper of their own. 'The groom – or rather Viscount Ventnor.'

'Poor Virginia! She dispatched him and to her surprise he actually went. Ah, young love! Thank the lord we are too old for things like that. I think the turquoise feathers will go well with the green, and you shall have these white ones.' The Countess laid out a row of large stiff white feathers, then started hacking at the pasteboard with a huge pair of scissors Alpiew had snaffled from the kitchen. 'I wonder if we will meet King James. I didn't like him, you know, Alpiew. He was only Duke of York when I saw him before, but he was a miserable hypocrite, always living a dissolute life while braying on about religion, quite unlike his brother, King Charles, who always . . .'

'Countess, please. Let us get on with this business.'

'Sorry.' Poking her tongue into her cheek, the Countess continued chopping. 'Life as a hanger-on at this desperate court is hell. I've never seen a place so full of pots jeering at kettles. And you know what they say – the whole timbre of any society always comes from the top. Do you have any old paper here, Alpiew, that I can use to line the back of the masks?'

Alpiew pointed her quill at a drawer by the window.

The Countess rooted about among the spare whalebones and busks for her corset, bodkins, hairpins and other female appurtenances. 'Do you have a pot of paste and a brush?'

'Of course I don't.' Alpiew shook the pen a few times and dipped it again. But when she applied it to the paper a great glob of ink spread over the page.

'Hey day!' said the Countess, pulling out a scrap of paper. 'Did you put this in here?'

'What is it?' Alpiew had upended the pen and was busy picking dirt from the nib with one of the Countess's pins.

'It's you, Godfrey and German Street.' The Countess held it aloft. 'It's the wager slip I exchanged with Isabel Murdo-McTavish.'

'How did it get in there?' Alpiew dropped the pen and spun round. 'Someone must have put it in here.'

'You don't lock up?'

'The concierge thinks it unnecessary,' said Alpiew. 'I have asked for a key.'

'I've never noticed a locked door keeping *you* out of anything before, Madam Pert.' She handed the paper to Alpiew. 'But this incident makes a first: being burgled so someone can give something back to you.' She passed the credit note to Alpiew. 'You keep it about your person.'

'I wonder where Lady Whippingham has got to? No one seems in the least concerned about her. Least of all her husband. Who is to say that someone has not murdered her while we were in the Bastille? No one seems to talk of her.'

'Your friend, the prig, mentioned an amour with the good Doctor, and you yourself witnessed something of an heroic drama between them.' The Countess sat at the table and pulled up some of Alpiew's notes. 'He is a strange, unaccountable fellow, that Doctor! Still protesting Aurelia's death was natural. Rather good-looking too. Why did Wackland go along with all that haste in burying the child? Surely not simply to protect the kitchens?' She fingered a small glass bead that had rolled across the table and flicked it over to Alpiew. 'You do think they *did* bury her, don't you? They wouldn't have kept her body for something unthinkable?'

'Not to do the business with a dead body, surely?' Alpiew reeled back from the table. 'Oh, madam!'

'I wasn't actually thinking of that, but now you mention it . . .'

'So what *were* you thinking of?'

'Anatomy. You hear of doctors digging people up to have a peep at their veins and hearts and bones and such, don't you?'

'And do you think Wackland joined him doing whatever anatomical thing he might have been doing?'

'Who knows? Men are sometimes so baffling in their ways. I did see Wackland last night. You must have only just found Isabel's body. He was coming out of Whippingham's room, pulling on his jacket. We have already touched on the possibility that he and Whippingham are . . .'

'. . . Sparks of the bum / And peers of the land of Gomorrah?' Alpiew grimaced. The thought of Whippingham and Wackland was too grim to contemplate. 'But if so, which of them is the queen of spades?'

'Alpiew –' the Countess was up and ready to depart – 'let us go over to the chateau and use the kitchen to cook up a little paste for our masks. We might even be lucky enough to cadge a little of Béchamel's fancy provender for our supper.'

'The servants would know if Wackland and Whippingham were playing husbands and wives with each other.' Alpiew crammed her things into her pockets and followed the Countess. She slammed the door shut. 'After all, they have to change the sheets.'

'What have sheets to do with it?'

'Sparks of the bum . . .'

'No more of that, miss. You know I have a delicate constitution.' The Countess took a deep breath and walked out into the street. 'Dr Stickworth!'

The Doctor was stepping up to the front door.

'Are you coming to visit Alpiew?'

'Sorry, Countess –' Stickworth coughed and looked about him – 'I was off in a daydream.' He looked up at the façade of the house. 'I didn't realise that you had a room here.' He patted his bag. 'I have a patient to see.'

'The Marquis is making an experiment in the kitchen,' said the Countess. 'We are going over to see if we can have a taste. Will you be coming?'

'I'm sorry, Countess, once I have seen my patient I will be riding into Paris for a meeting.'

'Anything interesting?'

'Medical matters, madam,' the Doctor laughed. 'Nothing of import. I would so much prefer a decent supper.'

'Anatomy?' said the Countess.

'An atomy of what?'

'No. Anatomy –' the Countess gave a tinkling laugh – 'the dissection of the human body.'

'I've been doing that all afternoon,' said the Doctor. 'Hearts, livers, entrails, all separated. Everything sealed and safe now, I'm glad to say.' He moved away. 'I shall be late.'

The Countess and Alpiew watched him disappear into the house.

'Did you hear that?' hissed the Countess, almost stepping out under a passing wagon. 'He *is* practising anatomy. 'Tis my belief he kept that child Aurelia's body for his own evil ends.'

'Jamais! Jamais! Jamais!' screeched Béchamel into a steaming pot. *'Ne jamais mettre de farine dans une sauce!'*

Pipe backed away holding a large pot of flour. Alpiew knew that while the Frenchman was experimenting she'd never get a word in with Pipe, so she rambled out of the kitchen leaving the Countess to make her paste.

'Je vais commence par une sauce blanche traditionnelle, composée d'amandes blanches et poitrine d'une capon. Mais sans les épices habituelles.'

'He wants a traditional white sauce.' Mademoiselle Smith flicked through her notebooks. 'No flour. Here – white sauce: blanched almonds, breast of capon, ginger, cloves, cinnamon and rose water, but without the spices.'

'Whisht, then why did he not say so? He kept muttering *"blanc"* at me, and flour was the only white thing that sprang to mind.'

'Mademoiselle Smith,' cried the Countess, picking up a spoon, 'perhaps I can help?'

'Monsieur Béchamel is particularly keen to create a new sauce to accompany peas for His Majesty at Versailles. He has been working upon the project for some time, and fears another will beat him to it. Or that the pea frenzy will pass. He is trying to persuade the King to create him chevalier de l'Ordre du Saint-Esprit, and believes he is in a race against time.'

'Ah! That is fine. You don't mind if I do a little something of my own?' The Countess sank down upon the bench near the big table. 'Pipe, my dear, I wish to mix up a little paste for our masks. Would you mind?'

'Des tripes?' screamed Béchamel.

'Tripe,' translated Mademoiselle Smith.

Pipe slammed the pot of flour on the table and slopped a white pile of tripe beside it.

'*Coupez!*'

'Chop it.'

Pipe set to work with a large chopping knife.

'Would you mind if I help myself?' asked the Countess, opening the flour pot.

'*Chawdrons!*' Béchamel thrust out his hand, while still stirring the pot.

'Lord, save us.' Pipe ran across the kitchen. 'Sure, the French don't cook up children in their recipes do they?'

'Not children – *chawdrons*.' Mademoiselle Smith sighed. 'Mixed entrails.'

The Countess felt her stomach heave slightly. Perhaps trying for a taste of the Frenchman's concoctions might not be such a good idea. Especially after the conversation she had just had with Dr Stickworth.

'Frenchmen!' Pipe fetched a bowl full of slithery indistinguishable animal matter. 'He is making a chitterling sauce.'

When she had finished slicing, she handed the bowl to Béchamel, who slopped the contents into a fry-pan, breathing deep of the aroma as they sizzled.

The Countess was rooting around under the counters looking for a pot. She pulled out a large black stew pot and carried it over to the table, then set about finding a large spoon.

'*Beatilles!*'

'Beetles,' squawked the Countess, leaning back. 'Well, there's a novelty for a sauce.'

'These are *beatilles*,' murmured Pipe, spilling a handful of mixed cocks' combs, livers and gizzards on to the table and hastily chopping them. 'He's making a sauce of all the things we usually throw away!'

'Will Monsieur Béchamel be attending the masquerade, mademoiselle?' The Countess ladled flour into the pot.

'I am certain that he will. He loves any occasion where people might praise him.'

Pipe turned and squinted at the Countess's saucepan. 'Did you find that under the counter?'

The Countess nodded.

'There is melted butter at the bottom.'

The Countess peered in and stirred the flour about, seeing the brown grease staining the lower flour.

'It was Monsieur's first attempt. I put in butter thinking he wanted to fry, but he did not, so I put it away to use another time when he does want butter.'

'No matter,' said the Countess. ''Tis only for a glue-paste.' She stirred the flour until the fat was all absorbed. 'You speak excellent English, mademoiselle. And I assume your French must be so too. Were you born over here?'

'*Et maintenant un peu d'épice.*' Béchamel ran around the kitchen picking up bunches of herbs, rubbing them and smelling, before grabbing a bunch of sage and dropping it on the table for Pipe to chop.

'We moved over here when I was six. A while afterwards my father was killed on the Irish campaign. My mother could not manage on her own, and feared with a small child she would never find another husband to keep her. So I was sent away to a charity convent. I think there were quite a few of us.'

Béchamel took a large spoon and ladled a small amount of the sauce to taste. '*Parfait.*' He pecked at the white creamy liquid and smacked his lips. '*Il faut attendre une heure, et le plat sera prêt pour le Roi. La sauce Béchamel est arrivée.*'

Alpiew was about to enter the games room when she heard Wackland's voice inside. He said: 'Don't forget to bring the instruments of torture.'

Alpiew stopped in her tracks and applied her ear to the door.

'And our dominatrix?' Whippingham wheezed at the word. 'The usual, I hope.'

'Lady Prude!' Wackland laughed. 'As long as she is free tomorrow afternoon. May we use your room again for our sport?'

'I don't see why not,' said Whippingham with a snigger. 'Now that the wife is safely out of the way.'

Alpiew couldn't believe she was hearing this. She dared not breathe for fear of missing a word.

'Stickworth will come too?'

Wackland laughed. 'Have you ever known him to miss one of our engineering meetings?' Alpiew felt as though Wackland had put the word engineering into inverted commas.

'Lucky Baron Lunéville!' Wackland gave a stifled laugh and she heard footsteps inside the room. 'The fellow hasn't got a clue what we have made up for him.'

'And we don't have too much time either. All must be ready for tomorrow night.'

Alpiew wiggled about, trying to get her ear flatter to the door panel.

'Madam?' The valet, Roger, stood beside her, scowling. 'Are you so low-bred a servant that you stoop to listening at doors for your gossip?'

'Roger!' Alpiew smiled. 'I heard voices and I wanted to find out whether it was my lady before I entered.'

'The easiest way of finding out who is within a room is to behave thus –' Roger stepped forward, smiling serenely, and pulled the door open. 'No.' He turned to Alpiew. 'Your mistress is not inside. Neither is mine.'

Lord Whippingham was standing by the fireplace and Wackland had gone.

'If you are looking for your lady, Miss Snoop, I suggest you try the kitchen. That is where you both were together a mere five minutes ago.'

When Alpiew reached the kitchen Wackland was sitting chatting amiably with the Countess and Mademoiselle Smith.

'To fetch water you need to go out and work the pump,' said Wackland. 'But I have excess of milk, if that would serve.'

'The least effort. 'Tis only for a paste for my mask.'

'The milk will not last till the morning.'

The Countess sloshed milk into the pot and stirred it about. She inspected the concoction. 'It doesn't mix too well.'

'Heat it for a few moments.' Mademoiselle Smith put the pan on to a hook over the fire. 'That generally merges the powder with the liquid.'

'They certainly taught you a lot at L'Ordre de les Filles de la Vierge.'

'Yes. Everything to do with making and mending and keeping house.' Mademoiselle Smith laughed as she stirred. 'The nuns wanted to be sure we caught a husband.' She carried the pot to a hook out of the direct heat of the fire. 'But nuns, being nuns, recognised that some of us had a chance and others didn't. There was one little girl – she was only about four, and she was half-caste – she didn't stand a hope, so after a couple of years they farmed her out.'

'To what?'

'Work, I suppose. She slept at the convent but was away every day. Then one day she didn't come back. The nuns told us she had died.'

'What a terrible story,' said the Countess. 'Poor little mite.'

'It's funny,' said Leonora Smith. 'You'd think so. But she was like a wild little cat, always spitting and scratching, so I'm ashamed to say we were not as kind to her as we should have been.'

The Countess lowered her voice. 'Have you seen the poverty here in St Germain, the people who live in tumbledown shacks and live on water gruel? I sometimes think it would be better for them to die than live a long life of pain and suffering . . .'

'But this child did not die. No, the nuns told us she'd died, because for them she might as well have done. But my best friend said she saw her a number of times, painted up like a trollop in Paris. She was down on the quays by the Seine, selling her favours.'

'What of the child's father? How could he simply leave her there?'

'He did.'

'I suppose he was some aristocrat who didn't want a smudge on his scutcheon?'

'Absolutely not. The nuns told us her mother was a mulatto, a servant, and she had died in childbirth. Her father was an English scullion-boy who kept her for a while then ran off with some fancy mistress. Mind you, the nuns told us she was dead when she wasn't.'

Deathly pale, Wackland lurched up from the table. He was staring at Mademoiselle Smith. 'Why have you come here?' His voice was croaky and rough. 'What is your business here at St Germain?'

'I act as a translator for people who move between this court and Versailles.' Mademoiselle Smith eyed Lord Wackland warily. 'Have I offended you in some way?'

'You are some plotter, aren't you? Some spy, some trouble-maker?' Never taking his eyes off Mademoiselle Smith, Lord Wackland reeled to the door. 'There is something afoot here, and I will know what it is. Now, out of my kitchen – all of you!'

He slammed the door after him.

'Come along. 'Tis almost bedtime. The man is overtired.' The Countess patted Mademoiselle Smith on the hand. 'He is having a temperamental fit, anyone can see that.' She rose and pulled a face at Alpiew. Then, leading the girl out, mouthed back: 'Alpiew, take my pot of paste to your room.'

'Where is it, madam?'

'Hanging over the fire.'

As they left, Alpiew hauled the pot from its hook and left for her room in Town.

'Now, Leonora, you are tired, I am tired. I suggest we both go and get a good night's sleep.'

'Why did he take me for a spy?'

'He was just agitated.'

'It is more than that.' Leonora grabbed the Countess's arm. 'I want to know what I have done wrong. Before the men arrived to haul Lady Prude away, she was going on and on at me to confess.'

'To confess to what?'

'She didn't say. She just kept on repeating and repeating, "Admit it. Tell the truth. No harm will come to you if you do. I know you were treated badly. I will make sure you get your just deserts . . ."'

Hauling the iron saucepot, Alpiew hurried over the road to her lodging. She pushed the front door but it was locked. She banged. No one came. She banged again, and hollered until the key rattled in the lock, the door opened an inch and the concierge peered through the crack.

'Madam,' said Alpiew, 'I am coming home to my room.'

'It's late,' said the woman. 'I'm tired of all this coming and going.'

'Madam,' snapped Alpiew, 'I went out, and now I am returning. What cause have you to complain of that?'

'There's been people padding up and down these stairs all day. Men in high heels, men with doctors' bags. You're not a prostitute, are you?'

Alpiew sighed. 'Do I look like a prostitute?'

The woman looked her up and down and made no comment. 'No cooking in the rooms.' She pointed to the pot. 'I don't want no fire burning the place down.'

'It isn't food. For your information, it is glue.'

'And I am the Queen of Nineveh.'

'Well, your majesty, might I come in?' Alpiew shoved the door.

'I'm only paid to take care of the rooms.' The concierge stood back and let Alpiew pass. 'I don't want to get blamed if the place turns into a brothel.'

'What is this racket?' A door on the first landing opened and a head popped out. 'I am trying to sleep. Some of us have work in the morning.'

'You!' Alpiew instantly recognised the woman who had given her the note in the parish church. She belted up the stairs and put her foot in the door. 'What work? I thought you had no funds? You're always pestering everyone for money.'

'That is my job, if you don't mind,' the woman shouted at Alpiew, while trying to dislodge her foot so she could close the door. 'Some go padding, or on the glim. I relieve people of their spare cash too, but at least I do it with good manners.'

'Why did you write the note you passed me in church?'

'I didn't,' said the woman. 'Passing notes is a sideline. It's a popular activity here in St Germain.'

'All right, you were told to pass it to me. So tell me, who paid you?'

'Will you leave me in peace if I tell you?'

Alpiew nodded.

'Lady Prude.' Alpiew withdrew her foot and the woman slammed the chamber door, shouting through it: 'The cheap-skate bitch! She only paid me fifty sous.'

The Countess mounted the stairs to the garret, humming to herself to save herself from feeling scared in the darkness. Images of Isabel lying dead on her floor flooded her mind. Every creak made her freeze, nerves jangling, as she stared about her in fear.

Turning into the garret corridor, she could see a flickering light coming from the crack under her door. She tiptoed along and put her ear to the panel. There was only the slightest of sounds from within. It sounded to the Countess like whimpering.

As she pressed her ear closer, she heard footsteps coming briskly up the stairs behind her. There was no light, so clearly whoever it was, like her, had no candle. She took a step back, pushing herself into the architrave of Isabel Murdo-McTavish's door.

It was Roger. He too noticed the light coming from her chamber, then listened at the door.

In one resolute movement he opened the door and went in.

There were sounds of a scuffle, and the moaning became

252

louder. After a minute the door opened again. Then the candle went out, and Roger came into the hall, carrying in his arms the prostrate figure of the Duchesse de Charme.

The Countess watched as gingerly Roger moved down the stairs, leaning his back against the wall for balance. The Duchesse lay limp, her head balanced against the ruff of his cravat. The Countess momentarily caught sight of her face. Like Niobe she was all tears, the tracks of which cut vertical lines down the Venetian ceruse with which she painted her chubby cheeks.

Waiting until the sound of Roger's footsteps had vanished into the distance, the Countess went into her room and re-lit the candle. Nothing had been disturbed. Nothing that is except for the mat with which she had covered the bloodstain. This was pulled back and creased.

The Countess put on her wrap and walked about the chamber. She could not sleep in here, that was sure.

She tiptoed along the corridor, checking on all the doors for candlelight or conversation. She reached the end door, the spare room, where only last night they had so cruelly interrupted Virginia's pleasures.

She let herself in and shut the door after her.

She lay on the bed and shut her eyes.

What a place! If only she had never taken the money from Virginia's stepmother. If only she were curled up warm in her own bed in the kitchen in German Street. She yearned for the comforting noise of Godfrey snoring and farting all night, for the simple joy of watching the dying embers of the kitchen fire as she slid gently into a warm sleep, safe among friends.

But just as she felt herself drifting off she was awoken by the creaking of floorboards outside the door.

Lord, help us! Someone was about to come in.

She slipped off the bed and slid underneath, pulling the skirt of her night-gown close to her so nothing showed.

The door opened.

She lay still.

253

Someone walked over to the bedside table. She could see a man's shoes. The door clicked shut. Another softer pair of feet moved towards the bed.

'Don't!' The whisper was an order. 'Light would give us away.'

The Countess put her face into her hands and winced. Who was this? Please God they were not about to start fornicating on the bed above her.

'That woman on the door makes it impossible for me to visit you at night, you understand?'

'It is easy enough for me to come to you.'

The mattress lowered as someone sat.

'Are you ready?'

'As ready as I will ever be.'

The mattress lowered further.

The Countess prepared herself for the worst.

Alpiew had retrieved the paste and placed it, lid firmly in place, in her garderobe, ready for the Countess to use tomorrow.

She itched to get home to London.

She stared out of the window across the Grande Place to the chateau beyond. The moonlight spilled down, casting long shadows from each of the corner towers. How formidable the place must have once seemed. A mighty fortress and stately home rolled into one.

A gang of half a dozen men reeled drunkenly across the square, hushing each other as they stumbled upon the cobbles, grabbing on to one another for stability.

Alpiew was about to turn and get undressed when she saw Lord Wackland running across the parterre towards Town.

Grabbing her boots and cloak, she blew out the candle and dashed down the stairs, determined to find out what business could bring him out of the chateau at this late hour. Before leaving she took care to jam the door with a piece of card, and hoped that the concierge would not rise and lock it after her.

* * *

'Go on.' The woman spoke, followed by a rustling of clothing. 'Show me your weapon.'

Bunched up under the bed, the Countess grimaced. What grisly activities were about to happen within her earshot?

'Oh!' The female let out a little gasp. 'Is it not too big for me to accommodate? See how it bulges through your breeches.'

'I am an expert, believe me. No one before has ever found any difficulties.' A further rustling of clothing. 'See!'

The lady sighed again.

'After so much protracted stimulation I fear reaching the climax may not, how shall I say, bring us to the pinnacle we desire.'

The Countess scratched an itch on her nose. All this word-play! Why could they not get on with the business they intended, and then in all probability they would fall asleep and she could make her escape.

'And the Jacks? How many others will come to join us?'

The Countess wanted to wail. It was going to be an orgy!

'I have decided we must keep it between the two of us.' The man gave a wheezing laugh. 'And eventually our victim, of course . . .

'Friday night,' whispered the man.

'Friday night,' echoed the woman. 'And you have made arrangements to spirit us away? I could not bear to be caught, for surely we will swing for it.'

'Those two women worry me. I thought at one point they would put an end to the whole business with their snooping.'

'Nothing can stand in our way. Not even two dead hags.'

'Dead?'

'If necessary.' There was another rustle of clothing. 'For the cause.'

The sound of a kiss.

'No gallows for us, you promise? No burning at the stake. I am too young to die.'

'And too beautiful.'

'I love you.'

'And I you.' Another kiss. 'I had best be gone now, before my absence is noticed.'

'And I must get back to the grand project.' The man laughed again. 'What fools we will make of them all.'

They stood and kissed for a long time, while the Countess tried to make out any detail on their shoes, but there was not enough light to perceive anything more than that the man's shoes had red heels and the woman wore satin pumps.

The Countess watched both pairs of feet tiptoe to the door and leave the room.

She relaxed and took a deep breath, not moving from her hiding place.

What was this talk of Jacks and victims and projects that you could swing for? And two dead hags. Who could that refer to? Not Aurelia and Isabel surely, as the man spoke of it as if it were a future event, not one already in the past. The Countess crossed herself, banging her elbow on the bed base. She was frightened to move, so she rolled over.

A bell tolled midnight.

The Countess lay thinking among the dust balls until she fell asleep.

Alpiew edged round every corner and watched Wackland stride onwards. Then, scuttling along in the shadows, taking refuge in alleys and doorways, she followed until he came to a stop.

He stood at the side of a dirty old building at the bottom end of Town. Head down, Alpiew sidled along until she was past him and around the nearest corner, but within hearing distance.

It must be the gaol. She had seen a barred window as she passed. And Wackland was talking urgently into it.

She could hear only the odd phrase:

'Why did you not tell me she was here?' Wackland was wheezing. 'I thought we had buried her.'

'So did I. Twice now. How could this be her?' Prude's voice was quivering. 'It all seemed so easy. Everything there for us on a plate.' Lady Prude gasped. 'Oh lord, I didn't mean that ... not literally, but ... I felt sure it was her. Dead again.'

'You should have made certain. You have the means ...'

'So do you.'

'You were the one who forced me ...'

'I can't believe you still throw that at *me*,' Lady Prude wailed. 'You didn't have to do everything I asked. She was yours, after all. Nothing to do with me ...'

A horseman galloped past up the main road, and the clattering of hooves drowned out their conversation. Alpiew held her breath and tried to hear through the noise. The rider turned the corner.

'If it had been her it would have all been over now,' Prude said, speaking hastily and in a tone Alpiew had never heard before. 'What are we to do?'

Some more murmuring.

She thought that Lady Prude was crying.

'... to know who I am?' Wackland's voice was shaking too.

'No!' Prude spoke with a steely edge. 'But she wrote that her father was a servant ...'

'The woman's identity – you didn't tell her that either?'

'Only hints,' Prude sobbed. 'And look what happened. You leave everything up to me.'

'I retrieved the papers from the Scotswoman's room. I was sure she had discovered us ...'

'Where have you put them?'

'They are burned in the kitchen fire.'

'Why are you so weak, Wackland?' Lady Prude let out a wail. 'And why do you not think? You alone can bring this catastrophe to an end.'

'Stop it!' snarled Wackland. 'Stop it!'

'I shall never forgive myself for what happened to Isabel

Murdo-McTavish. I chased about after her. I searched high and low.'

'She was a stupid woman,' Wackland mumbled. Prude whimpered in reply. Alpiew squeezed forward, getting on to her hands and knees and bending low so that she could peek round the corner at shoe level. She saw Prude reach through the bars, her hands grabbing at Wackland. He reeled backwards, then grudgingly patted the back of her hands.

'I cannot handle all this alone,' said Wackland. 'What can I do to get you released?'

'Don't even try it. I informed against myself. I sent a note to the gendarmerie informing them I was a thief, and when they came to question me I admitted it. If I can get others arrested to protect them, why cannot I protect myself? In here at least no one can get me, don't you see? I have made it easier for you. So tell her. Tell her the truth.'

Alpiew was aware of a foul smell. She sniffed. She looked down. Her hand was resting in a pile of dog-turd. Without a sound she lifted it, still craning forward.

'Does the girl know her mistake? Why is she still here?' Wackland spoke through gritted teeth. 'Are there to be more deaths? Am I a target?'

A coach rumbled round the corner, drowning out all sounds but its own. By the time it rolled down the hill, Wackland was saying: 'We must deal with it tomorrow.' He spoke firmly. 'She must be disposed of. What is that smell?' he said, pulling away. 'Someone is here.'

'Probably one of that snooping, impudent pair of liars from London.'

Alpiew rested back on her heels and pressed herself into the wall.

'I don't know what they're angling after, but I wish heartily to see the back of them.'

'I did try,' said Lady Prude. 'I still don't know how they sweet-talked their way out of the Bastille. I laid two trails leading to them: libel against the King of France and thievery.'

Alpiew crept up to a standing position.

'Hold. There is definitely someone there.' Wackland stepped towards the corner, and Alpiew scuttled along the street, praying she would turn the corner before he did.

She reached the end of the wall and swung round into the main road, then loped away down an alley, where she crouched in a dark entry behind a pile of boxes of rubbish until Wackland's footsteps receded.

Then, cursing the dog who had fouled the cobbles, she washed her hands in the public fountain before making her way home.

She climbed the stairs in the dark and as she was about to enter her room she noticed light spilling under the door. She knew she had extinguished the candle, so someone else had been inside, or was in there now.

She pressed her ear to the door and listened. Silence. She knelt down and tried to see what she could through the crack beneath the door.

It was when her face was squashed as flat as possible on to the floorboards that the door opened.

Alpiew was face to face with the hem of an expensive mantua. Before she had a chance to look up, the door slammed in her face.

Alpiew stayed on the floor.

Now what? She was not in the mood to sit out here and listen, nor to sleep on the stairs.

She rose slowly to her feet, listening out, but hearing nothing but the rustle of fabric.

She grasped the door handle and twisted it. Marching in as though she had no idea she had a welcoming party.

'Oh,' she said on the threshold, putting her hand to her bosom and giving a little skip. 'You surprised me.'

Mademoiselle Bontemps, the manager of Whippingham's papier moulé workshop, stood before her. She was alone.

'I was beginning to get frightened,' she said. 'You can't be too careful.'

A quick squint told Alpiew she had not searched the place, or, if she had, she'd been discreet about it.

'My word,' said Alpiew, flopping down on a chair. 'It's after midnight. What can be so pressing, Mademoiselle Bontemps, that it brings you here in the middle of the night?'

'Something weird is going on,' said Bontemps, perching on the side of Alpiew's bed. 'And it involves the Duc de Charme. Roger, as you know, is his valet. And as the manager of Lord Whippingham's papier moulé company I have encountered the Duc many times when we have shared a carriage to Versailles. He is much changed these last days.'

'How did you get into my room?' asked Alpiew.

'The front door was ajar,' said Bontemps. 'I knocked at this door and, when I got no reply, I tried it. I was terrified at every step, I have to say, fearing that I might stumble across another slaughter like last night.'

'How did you know where I lived?'

'Both Mademoiselle Smith and Roger told me. Everyone knows each other's business here in St Germain, you know.'

Alpiew took a seat at the table. 'What do you have to tell me that you think is of such interest that you come to me in the middle of the night?'

'Roger would have come with me, but he is on duty in the chateau. He feels it would be dangerous to leave the Duchesse at this time. Especially when the Duc is in such a strange mood. Roger says it is quite clear the Duchesse is in a very unstable condition. She is terrified of him.'

'You are telling me that you think the Duc is a killer?' asked Alpiew. 'He seems such a mincing, mollyish man, not at all like a murderer.'

'Roger dresses and undresses him. His body apparently is formidable. His muscles positively bulge through his rather firm skin. He has the body of a wrestler. And he has been very agitated since Lady Murdo-McTavish died.'

'He was close to her ladyship, was he not?'

'They seem to have spent a lot of time together, yes.'

'Roger told you this?'

'No, my friend Leonora Smith. She said the Duc was spending a quite unnatural amount of time with Isabel Murdo-McTavish. The day she went missing, he was running about the place everywhere, searching for her, becoming more agitated as the day wore on.'

'But what about the Duchesse?'

'He paid no heed to her. They just carried on right under the poor woman's nose. In front of her, more often than not.'

'You still haven't explained why you come to me with this tale?'

'Everyone says you and the Countess are investigators, sent to sort out the mystery.'

'Who is everyone?'

'Leonora Smith.'

'Why should such a subject ever come up between you?'

'Leonora and I met up at Versailles on Sunday. She talked about you, and told me in her opinion you and your mistress were some sort of spies. At first I thought you were come to find out the secret method of papier moulé, but now I believe it must be something else you are ferreting out.'

'There is one thing I have been wondering about the Duc and Duchesse, and you may perhaps be able to satisfy my curiosity. 'Tis usual for the wife to lodge at her husband's convenience; as the Duc is a Frenchman, how is it that he and the Duchesse stay at the Chateau of St Germain, with all its petty restrictions and piety, when they could stay on the Duc's estates or at Versailles?'

'Roger asked him that very question one day, after Madame Prude had given him a ticking off. The Duc became quite agitated and told him it was none of his business to inquire after such things. Then he calmed a little and said he lodged there to be near Lady Murdo-McTavish.'

Alpiew tried not to gulp at the audacity of the man. The dapper Duc and his plain little wife!

'How awful it must be to have your husband's infidelities

paraded in front of you like that,' she said. 'Perhaps things will be better for the Duchesse now Lady Murdo-McTavish is no longer amongst us?'

'Well, I see a problem there too. I've noticed that the Duc seems to be lavishing more and more attention on Leonora Smith.'

'Really! And what does Mademoiselle Smith think of that?'

'That's the thing, you see. She is utterly unwilling to discuss the matter. It really worries me. What if he has got rid of Isabel only to replace her with a younger, prettier model, my old school-friend Leonora Smith? And what if she is easily flattered and too silly to see that, if a man can murder once, he could do it again?'

Or, thought Alpiew, what if the Duc, anxious to replace one mistress, had plotted with her replacement? Perhaps the Duc and Leonora Smith had killed Isabel. It certainly made sense of the cards: the queen of spades and the knave of diamonds. Knave of diamonds would be an obvious reference to the Duc, with his sparkles and spangles.

'I am glad you came to me,' said Alpiew. 'I shall put your theory regarding the Duc to my mistress in the morning. In the meanwhile, I would be grateful if you could answer a few of my questions: Miss Bontemps, you said Mademoiselle Smith was your school-friend. What do you know of her?'

'We are opposite sides of the same thing.' Mademoiselle Bontemps smiled. 'I had a French father and an English mother, and Leonora is the other way round. She was born in France and is called Smith. I was born in England and am called Bontemps. And, with Fate's intervention, we both ended up at the same school. She was a little older than me, though.'

'So you were at school also with Aurelia?'

'Aurelia who?'

'You attended the convent of the Order of the Filles de la Vierge?'

'Yes.'

'But you know of no girl called Aurelia?'

'No.'

'Do you remember a half-caste girl? She died.'

'No, she didn't die. The nuns *said* she died. But they lied to us. That poor wild little mite. I feel sorry for her now that I am old enough to understand things properly. We were awful to her. But I suppose children are. We called her Pucelle, after the Maid of Orleans, as we thought she looked as though she had been burned at the stake.'

Alpiew winced.

'I know. She wasn't long at the school. And next time I saw her she was working as a prostitute in Paris, all daubed with layers of white addition, like a player at a fair.'

'How old was she then?'

'Only about twelve. It's terrible, isn't it? The nuns should have kept her. But no money, no shelter. That's how it goes.'

'One last question,' said Alpiew, rising and moving towards the door. 'What became of Pucelle, do you know?'

'Probably died of a clap at fourteen. It's what happens to these children. Or died in childbirth. There is little hope for street children in that occupation, I believe.'

Alpiew held the door open and Miss Bontemps walked slowly down the stairs.

As Alpiew watched her go she wondered how much of her tale tonight had been truth and how much lies, and what her motive was in telling her this stuff.

She broke a hunk of bread from her loaf and jammed a slice of meat on it, then flopped down on the bed to think.

Prude and Wackland.

The Duc and Leonora Smith.

And what of the Duchesse herself? It would have seemed to her that with her rival, Isabel, out of the way things might have improved for her.

Alpiew considered the fate of the mousy Duchesse, consumed by jealousy at her husband's affair with Isabel Murdo-McTavish, and how easily that could have driven her to murder. After all, she had been right there, standing on the threshold with the body still warm on the floor before her. If the Duc and Isabel *were* lovers, and the poor strange-featured Duchesse was the jealous wife, wasn't that a classic scenario for murder? A *crime passionnel*, to be sure. But nonetheless, a crime.

TWELVE

Turning — a particular way of paring oranges and lemmons. This term of Art signifies to pare off the superficial rind or peel on the outside very thin and narrow, with a little knife, proper for that purpose; turning it round about the lemmon or orange, so as the peel may be extended to a very great length without breaking

Alpiew was in the Countess's chamber shortly after dawn. The Countess was already up and back in her own chamber after her night sleeping on the floor of the spare room.

'Pshaw, Alpiew!' exclaimed the Countess after they had exchanged tales of their nocturnal experiences. 'Instead of getting simpler it gets more convoluted by the minute. So now we have three pairs and a single.'

A deep melancholy bell started to toll.

'The service is about to start. We had better go down right away. I feel sure Isabel's funeral rites will expose something among the congregation, though lord alone knows what.' She threw her black mantilla over her shoulder. 'Come along.'

'Oh, madam –' Alpiew patted her head – 'in my rush I have forgot my headgear. I will not be allowed into the chapel without.'

'Quickly! There will be something here we can make pass for a hat.' The Countess turned and started going through the chest. 'Hey day,' she said, rooting about at the bottom of her stocking drawer. 'What is this?'

She pulled out a small notebook and flicked through it.

'I believe this is Isabel's handwriting.'

Alpiew was pulling out stockings and whalebones, still seeking a black piece of makeshift headgear. 'Put it in your pocket and we'll go through it after the funeral.'

The Countess grabbed a pair of black silk stockings and started winding them round Alpiew's head. 'I shall make you a turban, like a Mussulman in a play. Hold still, child. 'Twill look like a hat, of sorts, and we can adjust the toes so they dangle down beside your cheeks to make a pair of lappets.' She snapped a whalebone over her knee, then arranged the pieces within the stockings to create a little *frontange*. She stood back and admired the view. 'Lord, Alpiew, in another life, I could have been a milliner. Come along.'

Feeling very self-conscious with two dangling toe-ends slapping at her cheeks, Alpiew followed the Countess running down the stairs.

After Mademoiselle Bontemps' revelations of last night, Alpiew was resolved to keep an eye on Leonora Smith.

'Countess!' Alpiew stopped in her tracks. 'Leonora Smith!'

'Yes,' said the Countess, having her doubts about Alpiew's headgear now she saw it in action, but deciding to say nothing. 'What about her?'

'Leonora Smith,' hissed Alpiew: 'L.S.'

'L.S.?'

'L.S.; Resurrection; Epiphany; Friday Night; Apocalypse: Death of the exalted whore.'

'And does that make it any clearer to you now, Alpiew?'

'Well,' said Alpiew, 'not exactly.'

The chapel was still hot from the warmth of all the people who had squeezed in for this morning's earlier High Mass, which had been attended by the King and all his courtiers. Clouds of incense hung heavy in the beams of sunlight that streamed in through the tall windows, while the magnificent organ played a mournful dirge by Purcell.

The Countess and Alpiew took seats in the back row.

In the centre of the aisle at the foot of the altar steps was Isabel's coffin, draped in purple and black taffeta and strewn with white lilies.

Much nearer the congregation, on a tall black credence table, stood three urns.

'What are they?' whispered Alpiew.

'Funeral urns,' said the Countess. 'It's a French thing. They get buried separately.'

'Separately from what?'

'The actual body.'

Alpiew pondered a few moments.

'So what's in them? Her favourite food, or books, or something?'

'Lord, no!' The Countess felt her stomach turn as she thought about the reality. 'In one urn is Isabel Murdo-McTavish's brain, in another her heart, and the last one contains her entrails.'

'How gruesome! Why did I ask?' Alpiew fanned herself with the Order of Service, and started regretting her headgear again. It was already bringing her out in a sweat. 'Where will they go?'

'Who knows, but she must have left instructions. The brain to Scotland, for instance . . .'

Alpiew gave a sidelong glance at Wackland as he slipped into the seat in front of her. She wondered, had he seen her running away last night? His inscrutable expression gave no clue as to his strange liaison with Lady Prude.

The Countess was leaning forward, clinging to the pew and staring down at passing feet. There wasn't a man in the place without red heels, or a woman not in satin pumps.

Leonora Smith walked up the aisle. She was pale as milk, her eyes staring. She looked about her, as though she was searching for someone hidden in the congregation. She edged forward slowly, gripping on to the pew ends to steady herself. Alpiew noticed that her hands were shaking violently.

When the altar boys had finished lighting the candles, just before the service began the chapel door was flung open again and Lady Prude, hands linked by a pair of shackles joined by a chain, walked up the aisle between two rough-looking gaolers. The three sidled along the front row, and knelt down as one.

The priest ascended the steps and started the service.

'It's very hot!' Alpiew plucked at her dress as the priest droned on. She was aware of tears of sweat rolling down the back of her neck. 'Cannot someone open a window?'

The Countess tried to take her mind off the oppressive atmosphere by letting her eyes keep straying up to the magnificent Poussin oil of *The Last Supper*, which hung on the wall above them. 'Is that a lapdog?' she said, squinting up. 'Fancy putting a dog next to Jesus! And who is that lying with their head on the table? Or is it John the Baptist's head? The light is reflecting against the varnish.'

Glancing round the room, Alpiew could see that everyone was suffering from the heat. Whippingham for one was as red as a beet. The Doctor took out his fob watch, just as the door opened again and Virginia crept in and took a seat at the back. Roger gave her a weak smile and shuffled along to make way for her. He was looking very pale, his forehead beaded with sweat.

The priest's monotone as he chanted away in Latin was making the Countess feel edgy too. She took another look at the painting. Astonishing – all those men in dresses lying on the table while they ate. And which one was Judas Iscariot, she wondered. Perhaps he was the mysterious figure in red, disappearing through the door.

She was grateful when the Duc de Charme wobbled up the steps to the lectern to make the eulogy.

Resplendent in black and gold, the Duc took his place next to the table that displayed the three urns.

'Isabel Murdo-McTavish was a beautiful, elegant, sharp-witted *femme galante*.' He spoke in a firm tone, looking down from time to time to check his notes. 'Eet ees more than a tragedy that a woman so full of life now lies dead beside me.'

'There's wormwood!' The Countess looked towards the Duc's wife. She was on her knees, her strange little face buried in her hands, her shoulders shaking.

'Isabel,' continued the Duc, 'was always the most amiable person in the world, *une femme vraiment belle*. She was frequently my companion. Een her presence the days passed like moments . . .'

Alpiew and the Countess exchanged a look.

'*La mort nous fait penser de la vie*. Isabel was a writer, and a genius at ferreting out the mysterious and the bizarre. Her mind, een many ways, was a mind before eets time. And as for her heart, eet was the tenderest, sweetest, most caring heart imaginable . . .'

The Duc stopped. He took a deep breath, blinking back tears, then started gulping and biting his lower lip. He looked down at his wife, and a kohl-stained tear rolled down his painted cheek. The silence in the chapel was broken only by the Duchesse's sobs and the flapping of Order of Service cards.

'She was a bright shining star among us. A woman who took her own route and who was afraid of nothing, including the censure of others.'

The Countess could see Lady Prude in profile. She maintained an unblinking stare at the catafalque.

A shaft of bright sunlight, streaming in through the high window, bestowed with a supernatural significance by the defining haze of incense that still hung in the air, struck the credence table, illuminating the three urns with a mysterious radiance.

With a jingle of earring, the Duc pulled out a black handkerchief and wiped the tear away, careful not to smudge the rest of his meticulously applied addition.

A deafening crack, loud as the report of a pistol, shattered the serene moment.

Stickworth and Whippingham, both veterans of the Irish campaign, instinctively ducked for cover, dragging to the floor whoever sat next to them.

The bewildered Duc put his hand to his bleeding cheek and staggered down the steps to his wife, looking about him for the cause of this sudden explosion.

As the congregation splayed out on the floor and along the pews, an intolerable stench pervaded the chapel.

The priest whipped the lacy cloth from the altar and, realising what had happened, threw it over the credence table.

In the heat, and with the assistance of a sunbeam, one of the sealed urns had exploded. Large shards of broken pottery had burst across the room, together with the fermenting entrails of the dead Scotswoman.

In the front row, Lady Prude was retching as, with her chained hands, she tried to pick pieces of Isabel Murdo-McTavish's decomposing guts from her wrinkled cleavage.

The Duchesse had risen and was screaming like a siren, her hands in the air, her face a picture of terror.

'*In nomine Patris,*' intoned the priest, repeatedly crossing himself, '*et Filii et Spiritus Sancti . . .*'

The altar boys were crawling about at his feet, picking up broken shards of porcelain and slivers of innards.

'Open the door, someone,' shouted Stickworth, coming up from under the shelter of his pew. 'Let in some air, before we all swoon.'

Wackland was already pulling open the heavy doors. Beside him, Roger, stomach convulsing as though he was about to vomit, wafted clear air into the chapel with his jacket.

'This is your doing, Stickworth, you fool!' shouted Wackland. 'You did not put sufficient preservative into the urns. No one should trust you with a corpse.'

'Isabel, rest, my darling, rest quietly,' wailed the Duchesse, wandering forward as though in a daze. 'I will have your sweetest heart again. Our hearts *will* live together.' She pulled the cloth back, picked up one of the undamaged urns and cradled it in her arms. Then she stooped to kiss it, murmuring:

> '"*Why should two hearts in one breast lie,*
> *And yet not lodge together?*
> *O love, where is thy sympathy,*
> *If thus our breasts thou sever?*"'

She laid her cheek upon the urn and sobbed.

While she was reciting, Whippingham strode up the aisle to the flustered Duc, grabbed him by his fluffy black lace cravat and spun him round to look at his wife. 'Do you not see what a fool you are, you prinked and powdered popinjay!' He pointed to the Duchesse. 'Look at your wife! And look at yourself, you sissified sybarite. No woman, I believe, would choose to marry a buffoon like you unless she designed making a fool of him in every sense of the word. Do you not know what a laughing-stock you are become?'

The Duc gaped in silence, shrugging his shoulders in a Gallic way.

'Must I explain in words of one syllable, you fat French fool?' barked Whippingham. 'Your wife and that Scotswoman played at the game of flats together.'

'Flats?' mumbled the Duc, blushing. 'They played cards? I knew that.'

'They were Tribades, my lord Duc. Lesbians. Whatever word you care to use for it. They were lovers, man.'

'Eet ees you that ees a fool. And a dirty fool at that.' The Duc pushed Whippingham away. 'Do you think I did not know? I love my wife and I want her to be happy. Eet is no business of yours, you filthy mongrel.' He advanced on Whippingham. 'My wife told me of the day you tried to ravish Isabel. Yet you think to insult me with your tirade.' As Whippingham stepped forward, the Duc teetered towards him, flicking him back with heavily ringed fingers. 'I do not shout to the world of how you humiliated *your* wife, jigging eet with every chambermaid and scullery wench een the town. Where ees Lucy now? Has she deserted you because you are dirty and disgusting? Or have you killed her een a jealous rage and thrown her body into the Seine? My wife loved Isabel. I am glad that for a moment my wife, who I love very much, found such happiness. Now get out of my way.' The Duc lifted his fist and with one punch floored Whippingham.

'Easy on, old fellow.' Stickworth stepped forward to hold the Duc back from lunging again at the stricken lord. 'Mustn't hit a chap when he's down.'

At this moment, with a resounding crack, Pipe fell to the floor, her body convulsing.

'Oh my God,' screamed Roger. 'Pipe is taking another fit.'

Lord Whippingham, blood dripping from his nose, was on his hands and knees crawling towards the door.

Stickworth grabbed a prayer book and jammed it between Pipe's teeth.

As the Duc tottered up the aisle to hold his wife in his arms, he paused near the Countess. 'You have your gambling stake back, madam, I trust? I myself secreted eet een your woman's room yesterday.'

The Countess gave a bewildered smile. What was the Duc de Charme doing with the note in the first place? She thought it better not to quiz him and silently watched him take his sobbing wife from the chapel.

'*Confiteor deo.*' Lady Prude was making an act of contrition as she was marched up the aisle by her gaolers. '*Peccavi nimis cogitatione, verbo et opere,*' she wailed, thumping her breast with both her linked fists. '*Mea culpa, mea culpa, mea maxima culpa.*'

Mademoiselle Smith rose and turned to face the melee. Then she started to chant in a high plaintive voice: 'Once upon a time there lived a Scottish woman, a poet and a wit, as clever as she was captivating, as beautiful as she was gay . . .'

'Lord, madam, I have never beheld such a scene in all my life.' Alpiew had her feet up on the table as she cut a new groove in her battered old quill. 'It was like Drury Lane on a benefit night.'

'Do you know, Alpiew, if a playwright put such a scene in a play the audience would think his mind was in a frenzy and, like the poor great bard, Nathaniel Lee, he would be dispatched instantly to Bedlam.' The Countess was sitting at Alpiew's window, arranging the pieces of her mask on a chair beside her, ready to assemble and stick it. 'I feel sorry for the poor little Duchesse. I have never beheld a more pitiful scene.'

'But what about that swine Whippingham? What a pig!' Alpiew threw her knife and quill down. 'This is no good. I shall have to go out and buy a new one.'

'Never liked the fellow,' said the Countess. 'I presume from Pipe's fit that she is one of his paramours. I wonder if he has dispatched Lucy?'

'Why would he need to – he had everything he wanted. She was hardly a bar to his enjoying himself.'

'And where does the Smith girl fit into it all? Why she

suddenly reared on her hind legs and started spouting all that nonsense, I cannot imagine.'

'I'll be about ten minutes,' said Alpiew, heading for the door. 'I'll get us a loaf too, and some small beer.'

'And some nice French cheese too.' The Countess looked about her. 'Alpiew, dear, where is my glue-pot?'

'In the garderobe.' Alpiew went out on to the landing. 'Mr and Mrs Cue should like this for a story, but how we get it to them without it being intercepted by His Majesty's spies, I shall never know.' She pulled the door shut.

The Countess heard her clattering down the stairs and out into the street. She laid the last jewel down and went over to the garderobe door, pulling the door open and thrusting her head inside.

She yelped with astonishment as, in a swirl of alcoholic fumes, from somewhere between Alpiew's cloak and her night-gown, Lucy Whippingham fell upon her.

'You are right, my husband is a swine,' slurred Lady Whippingham, stepping out of the garderobe and hiccuping. 'I am glad you can see that. You don't have a bottle of anything, do you? I could murder a brimmer.'

'Why are you hiding in Alpiew's garderobe?' The Countess was puffing, trying to maintain her equilibrium after the shock. 'And how long have you been here?'

'So the bastard was exposed at the funeral, was he?' Lucy flopped down on the Countess's chair. 'About time too. Do you really have nothing in the way of a drink?'

'Why are you here, Lady Whippingham?' The Countess stood over her, trying to look menacing. 'People think you are dead.'

'Good. That's what I wanted them to think.' Lucy laughed. 'I was hoping they'd blame either my husband or that bastard Stickworth.'

'What an extraordinary thing, Lady Whippingham! Why would you want that?'

'Stickworth killed that Brown girl as sure as poisoned eggs

are poisoned eggs. And if I disappeared I thought everyone would look at him again.'

'So where did you go?' The Countess was astonished by this, but did not want Lucy Whippingham to see her surprise. 'I saw you carry a bag downstairs. Dead people don't usually take their things with them.'

'Ah. You weren't supposed to see that.' Lucy peered about her. 'Do you have anything to drink?' She threw up her hands and flopped back into her chair. 'It's quite easy to hide in this town, you know. Practically every building is a Jack House like this one, with so many people coming and going. I stayed a night here, a night there . . . I came over here because I thought there must be a good view of the chateau from this house. I didn't realise this was your room.'

'It isn't. It's Alpiew's.'

'Well!' Lucy Whippingham's eyebrows shot up. 'There's an unconventional set-up.'

'Is this your resurrection, Lady Whippingham? Are you risen again yet?'

'I don't know about that,' said Lucy with a cough. 'But I'm bloody thirsty.' She gave a sniff. 'So poor Isabel got killed, did she? It had to be her or me. So I've escaped twice now. We both got the same notes the same afternoon, you know, Isabel and I: "I will be avenged." The day you disappeared, in fact.' She squinted at the Countess. 'I don't suppose you wrote them, did you?' She looked about the room. 'I'm starving. Do you have anything else to eat?'

'Else?' said the Countess.

'I polished off that soup you had in the garderobe. Rather tasteless and, in my opinion, it would have been better without the horrid little pink lumps, but I suppose after all this time I've got used to all this over-seasoned French stuff. Anyway, that girl keeled over at dinner and I decided it wasn't worth sticking around to see if the note was a serious threat or someone's pathetic idea of a joke. I told Isabel to go too. But she had her own reasons for staying, which you now know. Anyway, I packed my bags and got out of the ghastly place.' She smacked her lips. 'With people being poisoned in front of your eyes, I'm not surprised you do your own cooking, Countess, even if you don't have much talent at it. If I were you though I'd just leave St Germain altogether.' She picked up the two playing cards, the jack of diamonds and the queen of spades. 'What are these two doing separated from the rest of the pack?'

The Countess was poking around in the garderobe, looking to see if a scraping of her glue remained, but the pot was mopped clean.

'Trying to make a trick pack? Are you taking over from Isabel as court sharper? Poor old girl. If she'd have only asked him, I'm sure the Duc would have provided for her. He is a most generous man, for all his fashion sense. I suppose she was too proud.'

The Countess plonked the empty pot on the table. 'What were you saying, Lucy?'

'Nothing much,' said Lucy, putting the cards down. 'I was talking about your carreau valet and your pique dame.'

'My what?' The Countess hoped the conversation wasn't going to turn indecent.

'Carreau valet –' she held up the knave. 'And pique dame –' she slid the queen forward. 'It's what they're called in French. How did the dear Doctor take the news of my running away? Is he pining for me?'

'Dr Stickworth?'

'Yes, my old Sticky. I thought he would come away with me, but he is essentially a bastard, like all men.' She gave a disgruntled sigh. 'Do you think he knocked off that girl? I wouldn't put anything past him.' She peered into the empty pot, wiping her finger around to pick up a last smear of the contents. 'Who else can lay their hands on poison these days?'

'Why would you want anyone to believe Dr Stickworth had killed you, Lady Whippingham?'

'I gave him the chance to run off with me, and he spurned me, the swine. And now I find he has barely noticed I am gone.'

She sucked her finger. 'I suppose he was too entranced with his new piece to notice that I had gone.'

'New piece?' The Countess pulled her seat up to the table and sat on the unassembled pieces of her mask.

'The dear Doctor, my lover, has got himself some young girl.'

'Really,' said the Countess. 'You amaze me.'

'Sticky and I have been at it for years.' She guffawed. 'You don't honestly think I'd sleep with that fat, filthy husband of mine, do you? Look at him. His defects balance his possessions, and he wants more virtues than he enjoys. In short, he is a fat, indolent pig. Sticky, on the other hand, is a charmer. When he crooked his finger I danced after him, fool that I am. But he'd gone off me by the end. I could tell. I tried a few tricks to get his interest back, but nothing worked. I gather the new piece was much younger. A schoolgirl, practically.'

'Mademoiselle Smith?' ventured the Countess.

'How in God's name should I know? You don't think he was going to tell *me*, do you? I rather thought at first that it might be that insipid Aurelia. But he didn't seem unduly upset by her death, did he, so it must be the other one. The one who works with my husband and his revolting munchers.'

'There are more than three young women in the town of St Germain, Lady Whippingham. And a doctor can always find an excuse for a home visit.'

'Yes.' Lucy Whippingham gave a burp, and leaned back. 'I suppose so. Like looking for a needle in a bottle of hay.'

'Tell me –' the Countess made a gambit, hoping Lucy Whippingham might let out more gossip – 'is everyone over the road playing the round of Amour?'

'A doctor can find an excuse for everything.' Ignoring the Countess, Lady Whippingham grimaced. 'You don't think he took responsibility for the girl's body so he could practise a little bit of necrophilia, do you? After all, Aurelia would hardly have been in a position to say no to him by then.' She leaned back in her chair, fleering. 'Men!' she cried, throwing

277

her arms up in a dramatic gesture. 'I wouldn't put anything past 'em.'

'Love, I think, is the problem, not men,' said the Countess. 'How about your husband? Aren't you going to let him know you are safe?'

'Good lord, no. Let him stew. I doubt he's even noticed I've gone. He has a predilection for servants and gets up to some weird thing with the men too, I believe.'

'Really? Which way weird?'

'Never could squeeze it out of him. But he meets with Wackland and sometimes other men and they do something in the afternoons. He always comes back from those sessions looking rather flushed. Or in any case more flushed than usual.'

'Do you not love your husband at all?'

'Not any more. I did once, while our passion had the gloss of novelty, but I see him now with the eyes of custom. I have had the leisure to view him with consideration and he is undone by it. He provided well enough for me, I suppose, but by foul means.'

'How foul?'

'He did you over, for a start. He used to pay Isabel to knock people out at cards. She won him others' property and in return he gave her a pittance to live on. She needed the money, though, if she was to stay here and be near her funny little lover, the Duchesse.'

'You mean your husband took all the IOU notes?' Suddenly the fight she had witnessed between the Duc and Lord Whippingham at the top of the stairs the day after Isabel died made sense. The Duc was getting the note back from him. 'What a nasty game. I can understand why you no longer love him,' said the Countess. 'I had an *éclaircissement* regarding my own husband a few months back. Do you really love the Doctor, do you think?'

'I don't know. If I thought that he . . .' She took a deep breath. 'Perhaps.'

'I understand, Lucy. It only needs a tiny amount of hope to breed Love.'

'Ah yes, Countess. And, as I'm sure you know, the ideal breeding ground for love is boredom. Everyone over at the chateau is bored, ergo everyone is in love. And inevitably with somebody who is not necessarily available to them. But tell me this, Countess: what causes it, this love which we all prostrate ourselves to feel?'

'A rush of blood to the brain,' said the Countess. 'A disorder of the nervous system, an incipient madness?'

'And is it enough to drive a person to murder?'

'Oh yes,' said the Countess. 'It certainly is.'

Alpiew swung round the market in a few minutes, now she needed only to pay a visit to the brewer to pick up a firkin of small beer.

She had the strangest feeling she was being followed.

She loped along the row of stalls, stopping suddenly and pretending to pick up a piece of merchandise while stealing a quick glance behind her, but nothing was out of order. Wiggling past a flapping canvas side, Alpiew left the market and darted down a narrow alleyway. If someone was following her it would be quite clear here. She got three-quarters of the way down and stepped back into an even smaller by-passage and, holding her breath, looked back.

The alley was empty.

She exhaled and, as she took a step forward, a gloved hand came from behind her and slapped round her mouth, preventing her from screaming.

She was hauled backwards into the by-passage. Whoever had hold of her was very strong. She fought, dropping the bags of shopping as they skittered along. She tried to bite his leather-gloved hand, but he simply yanked her till she stopped.

Finally she was hauled into a dark, run-down house with broken windows and a tattered door, then hurled on to the dirty tiled floor.

Before she had time to turn, a black scarf was tied round her eyes.

'What do you know of the coming of Alpha and Omega?' A cultured male voice addressed her, while another two men held her still.

'Nothing,' said Alpiew. The little she did know she wasn't about to blurt out to men who had abducted her by violence. 'What is it?'

'Who are the three kings?'

'The Magi,' said Alpiew.

'Who did they visit?'

'They came to see the baby Jesus in the crib.'

The man laughed. 'Any more?'

'They brought gold, frankincense and myrrh.'

'Upon what day?'

'January 6th,' said Alpiew. 'The Epiphany.'

'I see you have had a good Bible education,' said the man. 'Now, let's stop playing. Who are the three kings?'

Alpiew remained silent.

'All right, I will tell you who they are. There is King James, erstwhile King of England, hoping to return; there is King Louis of France, his generous host; and there is the real King of England, King William, now reigning in London.

'Three Kings – and two countries. It's not a very good recipe, is it? Especially when there are lots of disgruntled fellows about who want one solution or another.'

Alpiew was trying to put this into the context of the riddle or list she had been given at Versailles.

'We both know something evil is about to be unleashed. And that people are already dead because of it. I am hoping that we can prevent the next strike.'

Alpiew didn't utter.

'The three kings. They *could* be Louis, James and William, don't you think? Three kings mutually bound by their differences. There is also a baby, Prince James, the heir apparent. William is not in the best health and has no children.

Meanwhile his sister-in-law, Princess Anne, seems incapable of bearing a strong male child to inherit the Stuart crown in England. So the pretty eleven-year-old boy over the road in the chateau is a precious cargo, wouldn't you say? Worth more than gold to some? A desperate threat to others.'

Alpiew's mind was racing. Surely this must be the answer to at least part of the riddle. Some of the anti-Jacobites must be planning to assassinate the Prince of Wales.

'Who killed Isabel Murdo-McTavish? And why? What do you know? Is there a connection? Our spies think there is.'

'I know nothing,' said Alpiew.

The gloved hand gently stroked Alpiew's cheek. Without being able to see this gesture Alpiew felt it was full of menace.

'Where is Lucy Whippingham? What is her husband up to now she is gone? Is he part of an anti-Jacobite plot? Is she perhaps the bringer of the Apocalypse? The English girls,' said the man, firing his queries at her back, 'who among them do you trust? Which of them do you fear? Certainly one of them is part of this.'

Alpiew remained silent, even when she was shoved from behind.

'The Order of Saint Denis – who at St Germain is a member?'

'Thank you for returning my mistress's moneybag,' said Alpiew. 'You who call yourself John. Would you be so polite as to tell me if that is your real Christian name, you thieving cove? Or should I say Viscount Ventnor?'

The man was silent now.

'I might remind you, sir, that I have seen you naked, playing at rump-pumping with my mistress's ward.'

The man's companions were sniggering.

'Also, you still owe us a few gold guineas.'

'Take off the blindfold,' said the man.

As the knot was untied, Alpiew found herself in a shuttered room. John, the quondam groom, dressed head to toe in black, towered above her.

'You are not as flighty as you look,' he said, pulling off a leather gauntlet and flinging it on to a rickety table, laden down with papers. 'I am really John, as it happens.'

'Why would a titled man like yourself work as the groom to a London alderman?'

'I needed to know that I was convincing. If I could convince one of those jumped-up City fellows, I'd easily convince the people here. And it was my good fortune while there to meet the girl who will be the future Viscountess Ventnor.' He sat against the edge of the table and glared at Alpiew. 'Is that enough for you? Tonight there will be a masquerade. I have information that there is also a catastrophe planned.'

'A catastrophe for whom?'

''Tis that we must discover.' John leaned forward and spoke right into Alpiew's face: 'You and the Countess will be there at the masquerade. So will I, and my friends, Gaston and Pierre. Together we will do what we must do. There will be a murder tonight, or perhaps it will be an assassination. You should remember you have been sent here to look after Virginia. If pandemonium breaks out you will be responsible for saving her. And if anything happens to her –' he lifted her chin and flicked it with his fingers – 'God save you from my wrath. Now, go.'

Gaston and Pierre opened the door.

'What about my groceries?' said Alpiew. 'They cost money, you know.'

Gaston held up her bag, the loaf still sticking up over the side.

'Here,' said John, grabbing a bottle of Bordeaux and dropping it into the bag. 'Have a drink on me.'

As the door slammed behind her, Alpiew brushed herself down.

Why the silly boy couldn't have just stopped her in the street and asked her those questions, she couldn't imagine. But she supposed he needed his hocus-pocus, just as he had needed to frighten them out of their wits on the highway in order to let Virginia know that he was in France.

She peered into the shopping bag. Everything did seem to be there still. After the shock she'd had, though, she wanted a treat, so she pushed into Veevils, a coffee shop opposite the fountain, which always had the most delicious-looking pastries on display.

While the shop-girl was wrapping two scrumptious cream cakes, Alpiew looked round the shop at the tables. In the corner, shivering and pale, sat Mademoiselle Smith. Seated next to her, with a protective arm around her shaking shoulder and the glimmer of a smile playing upon her lips, was Mademoiselle Bontemps.

Alpiew approached them. Mademoiselle Bontemps' expression took on a solicitous air.

'Mistress Alpiew –' she indicated an empty chair – 'would you like to join us?'

'I can't stay,' said Alpiew. 'My mistress is expecting me. Are you all right, Mademoiselle Smith?'

'She had a bit of a fright.'

'Didn't we all?' Alpiew thought back on the hideous events of the funeral and gave an involuntary shudder.

'Leonora was already in a delicate way, she tells me.'

Alpiew couldn't be sure, but it seemed to her that Miss Bontemps was about to burst out laughing.

'She's been awake most of the night.'

'It was awful,' whimpered Mademoiselle Smith. 'And when I had convinced myself it was all a dream and was on the verge of falling asleep again, she came back.'

'Who?' said Alpiew.

'A ghost. It glided past my bed.'

'In the staff dormitory?'

'That's right.' Leonora Smith cradled her saucer of chocolate in both hands and took a sip.

'The ghost of Isabel Murdo-McTavish?' Alpiew was beginning to think that Leonora Smith was as mad as March butter.

Leonora started keening. Bontemps rolled her eyes up, indicating that Alpiew had made a big mistake.

'Isabel would never have frightened me. She loved me. I know she did.'

'So who was this sinister apparition?'

'It was Aurelia.'

Alpiew wondered what plot they were really cooking up between them, these girls.

'Aurelia came back to visit you? Did she have anything interesting to say?'

'No. She didn't utter. She just floated through the room, her blonde hair piled high, wearing that same pale muslin mantua she wore the day she . . .' Leonora Smith tensed up.

'Go on.' Bontemps gave her a little squeeze. 'Tell Mistress Alpiew.'

'About half an hour later, she came back silently, the way she had gone, neither looking to the left nor right. She didn't say anything,' said Smith, 'but I know what she wanted.'

'Really?' said Alpiew. 'And what was that?'

'Before she died she told me she was searching for her mother. Well, she didn't say mother, actually, she said her father's woman. She must want me to continue the search.'

'Did she tell you who her father was?'

'No. She said he was a liar and a fake, and that she would discover him to the people who believed his pretence.'

'The apparition left this behind her –' Mademoiselle Bontemps passed Alpiew the lacy kerchief that lay on the table in front of her. 'On the floor near Leonora's bed.'

Alpiew glanced at the handkerchief and put it down. She snatched it up again and took another look. She could not believe her eyes. 'May I take it away?'

Mademoiselle Bontemps gave her a penetrating look. 'It would be better if you did not,' she said, pocketing it. 'Why would you want it?'

'No reason,' said Alpiew. 'My mistress is a great aficionado of supernatural phenomena. I'm sure she would love to have seen a tangible proof of the existence of ghosts.'

*　　*　　*

'How have we forgotten the notebook?' howled Alpiew, bursting into the room with her shopping. 'We must read it instantly.'

When she saw Lucy Whippingham, Alpiew stopped, and dropped the bag on to the table.

'Lady Whippingham! I am glad to see you well.' She pulled out the food. 'I hope you are hungry. I have bought us a little feast.' She put the wine on the table.

'Open up, woman.' Lucy fingered the bottle. 'I am dying of thirst.'

'Have you been to see your husband at all since you got back, Lady Whippingham?'

'I'm not really back yet. I am a mere spectre, so don't go telling on me.' Lucy Whippingham grabbed a leather mug and held it out for Alpiew to fill with wine. 'I am still in the nether realms of an uncertain fate, at least as far as those men in my life go.'

'Milady, we have an appointment this afternoon, remember?'

'Ah yes.' The Countess squinted at Alpiew, understanding.

'The mantua-maker!' 'The perruquier!' they said in unison.

'All those little things one needs to attend to before a masquerade,' said the Countess. 'We only have a few hours left.'

'There's a masquerade tonight? Well, well.' Lucy Whippingham slopped more wine into her cup and sat back. 'If it hasn't been cancelled in respect of Isabel, that can only mean one thing.'

'Yes?'

'That we are getting a surprise visit from the Sun himself.'

'Whose son?'

'No. *The* Sun. The brightest of heavenly bodies, that luminary orb around which we all dance.'

'The sun is going to come out at night?' said Alpiew, wishing she had a reflecting telescope. 'What a planetary phenomenon!'

'I'm sorry, Countess, I don't understand what this wench of yours is talking about.' Lucy gave a hiccup. 'You comprehend me, don't you?'

'Louis?'

'Incog., of course.'

'Well, it is a masquerade,' said the Countess. 'Isn't it *obligatoire* to be travestied?'

It was Alpiew's turn to be lost. 'Could one of you please explain this to me in simple English?'

'We suspect the French King will be coming to the party, Alpiew. So we'd better get ourselves decently attired. We don't want another of those letters he's so fond of issuing.'

'Certainly not, madam.' Alpiew grabbed her empty bag, thoughts of spending the rest of her life banged up in a convent sparking her into action.

The Countess threw a lump of cheese into some bread, and made for the door. Noticing the pastries, she stretched back to snatch one of those too before Alpiew yanked her out on to the landing.

They clattered down the stairs and out into the open. The sun was beating down, and the Countess visibly wilted as she stepped on to the cobbles.

'Phough! It's too hot for me.'

'There'll be a storm soon. Feel how heavy the air is.' Alpiew grabbed the Countess's elbow and steered her through the traffic. 'Well, what a time I've had of it. I was abducted by our old friend John the highwayman, who tells me that something will happen tonight at the masquerade.'

'Good lord, Alpiew, did he say what?'

'No, but things are falling into place. It's good that Lady Whippingham is alive and well, albeit in her spectral state. What's more, I have an Alpha Omega clue.'

'Tell!' The Countess stepped into the path of a horseman who pulled his horse up, narrowly missing her.

'When we are sitting.' Alpiew looked in both directions and regained her grip on the Countess's elbow. 'I need to draw it for you.'

They swerved round the back of a wagon piled with boxes full of chickens, rows of feathered heads sticking out between the slats, and narrowly avoided another, larger wagon coming from the other direction, laden with boxes marked *Pois*.

'Uh-oh,' said Alpiew. 'Is that short for poison?'

'Only as far as Baron Lunéville is concerned,' said the Countess, watching the wagon roll into the kitchen courtyard. 'It means there will be peas for supper at the chateau tonight. Talking of which, I do hope Monsieur Béchamel's sauce was more successful than my glue.' The Countess was digging into her pocket for Isabel Murdo-McTavish's notebook. 'Let's find a quiet spot along the terrace, to read. Somewhere in the shade.'

They crossed the parterres and wandered into the tree-lined pathways.

'I've seen this book before.' The Countess was flicking through the book. 'It's the shagreen journal Isabel had with her when we went into the forest together.'

'I wonder why it was in your chamber?'

'Yes, it is her notebook.' The Countess spread the journal open. 'See: "thre once ws a wmn" – that must mean there once was a woman, I suppose – "and she hd as mny chldn as thr r hles in a sve."'

'Is she writing in French or something?' Alpiew gawped at the page.

'No. It's a way of writing things down quickly.'

The Countess flicked on a few pages. 'Look, here is her last entry.'

'Her lst ntry, you mean,' said Alpiew. 'What's that?' Alpiew held her finger on the last word. '"Cnts."'

'I dread to think,' said the Countess.

'Countess?'

'Yes?' replied the Countess.

'No. Countess! Cnts is short for Countess.'

'Well, that's a relief,' said the Countess, squinting at the rest of the page. '"Smth n prst?"'

'Smith in pursuit, of course,' said Alpiew. 'Lord, madam, I begin to wonder why we bother with vowels at all.'

'Pish, Alpiew!' The Countess peered down at the book. 'With my title, without vowels I am a ruined woman.'

'Look –' Alpiew ran her finger along the scribbled lines as she read: '"Duc most understanding man. But I am frightened of Smith and her pestering. Found her in my chamber reflooring . . ."'

'That'll be rifling, Alpiew.'

'Oh yes, "rifling through chest. Must find new place to hide journal."'

'That's it, Alpiew. That's why Isabel came into my room. I feel sure this is the book she said she kept safe at all times. She didn't want Smith or anyone going into her room and reading it while we were in the forest. So she hid it in my chamber.'

'"Cannot allow Smith to upset Flora,"' Alpiew read on. 'Who in the devil's name is Flora?'

'Must be the Duchesse.'

'"Flora is sure I will run off and leave her alone in this godforsaken place. Doesn't believe my Bastille sojourn. Thinks I was with Smith. How can I reassure her?"'

'Good grief, Alpiew. Everyone was in love with Isabel. You don't think that nice Mademoiselle Smith killed her, do you, in a jealous rage?'

'Mmm, a jls rge. Could be.'

'So?' The Countess took the book and slammed it shut. 'Alpha and Omega?'

'All right.' Alpiew pulled a crumpled scrap of paper from her pocket, and scribbled on it. 'What does that look like to you?'

'Alpha and Omega. Lower case.' The Countess pondered. 'Or in fact, if you take it out of context, it could be AW.'

'Well AW or Alpha Omega appeared as a monogram upon the 'kerchief dropped last night by the ghost at the foot of Leonora Smith's bed.'

'I'm sorry, Alpiew . . .' The Countess gave Alpiew a worried look. Had she suffered a blow to the head to bring on this bizarre conversation? 'Are you feeling quite well?'

'Leonora Smith and the Bontemps woman claim that last

night the ghost of Aurelia Brown walked through the staff dormitory and dropped a 'kerchief with AW embroidered upon it.'

'But why would Aurelia Brown's ghost carry a handkerchief with the initials AW, I wonder?' The Countess mused. 'Can ghosts marry?'

A bell tolled three o'clock.

'Come along, madam. Look at the time – mid-afternoon. I'm hoping we will be right on the dot to interrupt a bit of male jiggery pokery.'

'I've forgotten,' said the Countess. 'What exactly . . . ?'

'The secret meetings in Lord Whippingham's room.'

'Pshaw, Alpiew! Now Lady Prude is arrested, surely the fun and games will be cancelled?'

'We should check to see what these so-called engineers get up to in any case.' Alpiew was striding across the parterre. 'With or without their dominatrix.'

'Nothing too exciting, please, Alpiew.' The Countess shoved the notebook back in her pocket and checked on her cake before following. 'I wouldn't like to lose my appetite before I eat that cream pastry.'

The two women tiptoed up the staircase leading to the garret rooms.

From behind Whippingham's closed door they heard a swish and a crack.

Alpiew, eyes bulging, turned to the Countess. 'What was that! I heard it once before, when I was coming up here on the fatal night.' She bit her lower lip, held up her skirts and trod softly until she reached the top landing.

Silently huffing, the Countess bent to listen. 'Someone is whimpering,' she whispered.

'Attention!' The female voice sounded strangely strangled. 'Plunge it in faster. At this rate we will never come to a climax before we must dress for the masquerade.'

The Countess frowned, and shook her head at Alpiew. 'Let's go. I dread to think . . .'

The whip cracked down again, followed by a high-pitched whimper.

'Sorry, Lady Prude.' Whippingham's voice.

The bed creaked in a regular beat.

'Good Lord,' hissed Alpiew. 'She must be released from gaol.'

'Keep up that rhythm, boys.' The twangy voice barked out a mad laugh as the whip hissed through the air.

'Ouch!' a male voice cried. 'That hurt!' They both recognised it as belonging to Lord Wackland.

'What are you frightened of, you big baby?' said the strange female voice. 'It's only a little prick.'

'Oh phough, Alpiew!' Spinning on her heels and lifting her skirts, the Countess made ready to run down the stairs. 'Let's be gone from here.'

Alpiew giggled. 'Now we know there is quite another side to Lady Prude, madam.' Alpiew squashed her ear flat against the door. 'But, my word, doesn't the excitement deepen her voice!'

The Countess tried to start off down the stairs, but Alpiew had hold of her sleeve.

'Please, Lady Prude.' Alpiew recognised the Doctor's voice. 'My apparatus has got stuck in the hole.'

'Then pull it out,' barked the woman, 'and plunge it in further along.'

'Pshaw, pshaw, Alpiew!' The Countess was repeatedly swallowing. 'What depraved diversion are they about in there?'

'Prepare yourself, madam.' Alpiew rested her hand on the door handle. 'We are about to behold the scene with our own eyes.'

'In, out, in, out,' snapped the dominatrix, lashing the air in rhythm, as the bed creaked. 'Keep it up, boys. I don't want you peaking too soon. In, out, in, out. Go with the natural rhythm.'

Alpiew flung the door open wide.

Seated on three wooden chairs facing the door were Lord

Wackland, Dr Stickworth and Lord Whippingham. Each was dressed in his shirt and breeches.

Standing on the bed, horsewhip in one satin-gloved hand, and sporting a fully painted face, was Roger, the Charmes' valet. He was wearing one of Lady Prude's mantuas.

On the seated men's laps lay an ornately embroidered man's jacket. Wackland had a needle in his hand, poised mid-air. Whippingham's needle was in the process of making a neat stitch in the collar. Stickworth's was caught in the middle of a tricky embroidery stitch.

'What?' said Alpiew. 'But this is . . .'

'An embroidery club,' said the Countess, stepping into the room with a smile. 'How lovely! And what a beautiful garment you have made, gentlemen.' She lifted the edge of the jacket and peered at the stitching either side of the fabric. 'Lord, what do I see here? Cross-stitch, Irish stitch, French knots, a lovely bit of passement filigree – so hard to pull off, I always think. I love the silver frisé. And such a pretty lining. An India sarsenet, if I'm not mistaken.' She stood back and gave the men a solemn look. 'Might I ask you gentlemen a personal question?'

All four nodded meekly.

'How much would you charge to make me a new mantua?'

Still giggling at their discovery, the Countess and Alpiew made their way to Virginia's chamber.

The girl was sitting by the open window with a self-satisfied smirk playing on her lips.

'I presume your boyfriend is back in harness,' said the Countess, pulling up a chair beside her. 'For today I see the fair-weather features are come out of their box and sitting upon your face again.'

'I saw him this afternoon, yes. And he promised that tomorrow he will take me away from here.'

'What of Denise?'

'I was being silly, I think. He laughed at me when I talked of her.' She lowered her eyelids and blushed. 'I believe youth and beauty have got the better of wrinkled old age, and my noble lord has finally come to his senses.' She wafted her hand around, and the Countess caught sight of a huge ring sparkling on her engagement finger.

'So congratulations are in order?'

Virginia gave a coy smile.

Alpiew suppressed a yawn.

'And I presume you will be attending tonight's masquerade?'

'John will be there, so yes, of course.'

'Have you a costume and a mask?'

'My father made sure the servants packed everything necessary for a successful stay here at St Germain.' Virginia smirked. 'I have the very latest: a shepherdess costume, complete with moulded mask.'

'Then we had better get a move on,' said the Countess, already on her way to the door. 'Or Alpiew and I will have to go as Adam and Eve with only a pair of leaves to cover our modesty.'

Lucy Whippingham had polished off the wine and gone from Alpiew's room by the time they returned, so the Countess and Alpiew munched the remains of the bread, while Alpiew glued the pieces of band-box and fabric with some gum they had bought at the scrivener's shop, and the Countess arranged them and stuck them down.

'I am serious, you know, Alpiew.' The Countess hastily smeared the front of her mask. 'We don't have much time.'

'To solve these mysteries, madam? We have till the day after tomorrow. Friday.'

'Actually, I was talking about making ourselves ready for the masquerade tonight.' The Countess laid the fabric down on the gummed pasteboard and pressed it down. 'So we know that tonight we must keep our eyes upon . . .'

'Everyone.'

'Everyone?'

Alpiew ran through the possibilities again, wondering if there was a single person they could exonerate. 'Yes, everyone.'

'Lady Prude has warned us of the *puella pulchra*. So we must watch mademoiselles Bontemps and Smith . . .'

'And Virginia.'

'Not to mention the ghost of Aurelia Brown. What was that, Alpiew? A bad dream of Mademoiselle Smith?'

'I saw the handkerchief. Perhaps her friend Mademoiselle Bontemps donned a blonde wig. In the dark of night, who could distinguish her features?'

'Then there are the gentleman embroiderers and their lady instructor.' The Countess laid her mask down and started on Alpiew's. 'The Duc to get rid of a love rival, the Duchesse or Mademoiselle Smith because . . . well, Mr Congreve put it so well in that play last year:

> "Heaven has no rage, like love to hatred turned,
> Nor Hell a fury, like a woman scorned."'

'No need to continue with the list, milady. No one can be overlooked. We must simply keep alert all the time.'

'Repeat the riddle-list thing to me.'

'It went thus –' Alpiew bit her lower lip – 'L.S.; Resurrection; Friday Night; Epiphany; Apocalypse: Death of the exalted whore."'

'It's all in the wrong order, isn't it? It's all New Testament except L.S. But in the wrong order.'

'The death of the exalted whore?' said Alpiew, sticking a row of beads round the eyeholes of her mask.

'That's from the Apocalypse.' The Countess rested her elbow on the paste brush and Alpiew hastily moved it. 'It should go: Epiphany; Friday Night – Jesus died on a Friday, after all; Resurrection . . . Then the Apocalypse, including the death of the exalted whore.' She was staring at Alpiew, hoping for inspiration. ''Tis a pity we don't have anything for a costume. Everyone will well know who we are.' The Countess screwed up her eyes and inspected Alpiew's clothes. 'Perhaps we could swap mantuas?'

'That would certainly cause a stir.' Alpiew laid down her glue brush and glared at the Countess. 'Your dress would stop at my knees, and mine would leave you with a great gap in the bodice area.'

'I'm hardly flat-chested myself, miss.' The Countess looked at Alpiew's cleavage then at her own. 'Though I do see . . .'

Alpiew ran a hand round her bodice and plumped herself up.

'Oh no!' shrieked the Countess, pulling her mask from the table. 'I have glued the two cards to my mask.' She tugged at the jack, ripping it in half. 'Lady Whippingham used their French names: pique dame and carreau valet.'

'Valet, you say? So Roger stays firmly on the list. Valet of diamonds. It makes sense. He works for the Duc, after all.'

'And of all the dames across the road, which among them could not be described as being affected with a pique? How's that?' The Countess held the first mask up to her face, and tied it round the back of her head with a calico tape. 'There are all these white feathers left over. You said that Lady Prude told Wackland she was chasing after Isabel that night?'

'I myself saw her coming down the stairs.' Alpiew fiddled with them, knotting a thread around their shafts. 'She did look frantic.'

'She would have looked frantic if she had just come from killing Isabel.' The Countess pushed her mask up. 'Look what we know now. It makes sense. I think Lady Prude did go up. She looked in Isabel's room, but no one was there, because Isabel was already lying dead in my room. In case we were sitting up chattering, she knocked at my door and got no reply, and so made her way down to see whether Isabel was with the Duchesse – she was clearly very disapproving of all that business.'

'And the Duchesse, worried and flustered by Prude's behaviour, came up to look for herself.' Alpiew bit the end off the thread and inspected her new headdress. The Countess pulled her mask down again. 'Poor little thing.'

Alpiew placed the headdress on her head.

'You look like a supernumerary in a bad production of *The Indian Queen*,' said the Countess from behind her green moiré mask, spangled with turquoise and purple.

Without either of them noticing, the Man in Black had opened the door and now stood silently on the threshold.

Behind him loomed two burly men sporting very fancy silk jackets, fluffy lace cravats, bulbous brocade breeches and huge, brown, bucket-topped boots.

'*Monsieur Jacques et Monsieur Gilles, Mousquetaires du Roi*,' he announced, while the two men performed a balletic ritual involving whipping off their ostrich-plumed hats, twirling them violently in the air and bowing so low that their luscious ringlets brushed the ground.

'Ooh,' said the Countess, lifting her mask and wearing it like a visor.

'La, la!' said Alpiew, feather headdress wobbling.

Everyone stood still for a moment, the two men posing in swaggering stance, the Countess and Alpiew gaping open-mouthed, until, smiling sweetly, the Countess asked, 'What are we to do with them, sir?'

'*Pour vous!*' murmured the Man in Black with an expansive gesture. '*Un cadeau. Pour le masquerade.*'

'Alpiew! Did you understand what he said?' The Countess had still not moved and spoke through her teeth. 'They're a present for us! To accompany us tonight.'

'Guttered gun!' said Alpiew.

'Indeed,' said the Countess.

The Countess and Alpiew and their two escorts entered the Great Hall early. They had been hustled rather hurriedly out of Alpiew's room by the two men, but didn't have enough French to explain that they didn't want to be the first to arrive at the masquerade.

So they were.

At one end of the redbrick room the musicians sat, still tuning up.

The wooden chandeliers were lowered and two boys clambered up step-ladders to light the candles with a pair of tapers. Along one of the side walls servants were still carrying in covered trenchers and platters of food.

The Countess, Alpiew and their two escorts stood nervously by the huge chimney admiring the ornate chimney board which covered the fire opening for summer.

'They're not such a good idea as at first they seemed, are they – Jacques and Gilles?' Alpiew looked the musketeers up and down. They were certainly ornamental, standing staring straight ahead, one hand resting on their hip the other hanging at their side, one knee slightly bent to show off the line of their gorgeous boots. 'What a pair of self-regarding coves they are. I should think they would never be happier than standing opposite a mirror. Mind you, for all their finery they may have the faces of pigs. Who would know under those masks?' Alpiew sighed. 'How on earth do we make polite conversation with them?' She shook her head. Her mask was itching. 'They don't speak English; we don't speak French.'

'To be frank, I suspect that speech is not their language, Alpiew. *Très bon. Délicieux,*' said the Countess elaborately, indicating the huge buffet. '*Miem! Miem!*' She smacked her lips. 'It looks like the Last Supper, all laid out like that. All you need are a few men sprawled over the table in long dresses.'

'The Last Supper!' said Alpiew. 'L.S.!'

The musketeers nodded grimly to each other and in unison shifted their weight from one foot to the other, simultaneously changing over which gloved hand rested on which hip.

'Good lord, Alpiew. So how does the order go now?'

'Let's recap.' Alpiew's mind was racing. 'L.S. – Last Supper; Resurrection; Epiphany; Friday Night; Apocalypse: Death of the exalted whore.'

'Oh dear.' The Countess visibly slumped with disappointment. 'Even with Last Supper, it's still balderdash.'

The two musketeers were facing each other, nodding.

'Do you think they're faking it, and can understand every word we're saying?' Alpiew was suddenly worried.

'One way to find out,' said the Countess. She imbued her voice with a flirtatious tone and turned coyly to the two men. 'Pish! Pox on you for a pair of worm-eaten, odious, fornicating, verminous blockheads!'

The two men gave a bashful bow. Through the eyehole of his mask one of them winked, the other blew a kiss.

'No. They don't understand a word.' The Countess glanced towards the food table. 'Look at those chargers, Alpiew. I can't wait to get at 'em.'

'Do you think you should eat here tonight, Countess? Last supper, remember. It might not mean that Aurelia had her last supper. Perhaps tonight will be the last supper for someone else.'

A short, portly man in a tinsel satin suit and matching mask bolted in, flinging his arms up, and crying: *Jamais! Jamais! Jamais!*

The Marquis de Béchamel made his way to inspect the food. The running shepherdess at his heels had to be Leonora Smith.

'Our Virginia won't be happy to discover she's not the only shepherdess in the room.'

'Identical mask too! She was so proud of having the latest costume. Little did she know how they are two a penny over here!'

'Perhaps it wasn't Virginia's daddy who did the shopping at all.' Alpiew laughed. 'Perhaps her stepmama packed the case.'

The musicians started playing. A lyrical chaconne filled the room.

A tall slim man in a Commedia dell'Arte mask came in next. He was wearing a beautifully embroidered jacket. The Countess recognised it instantly as the one created by the engineering club. The man surveyed the room, then strode over to the Countess.

'*Bonjour, mesdames,*' he said, and immediately started chattering with the musketeers in furiously fast French. Alpiew and the Countess recognised his voice. It was Baron Lunéville.

Béchamel meanwhile was pulling the lids off all his dishes and breathing in the aroma.

A group of masqueraders came in laughing, the music struck up a jig and the atmosphere no longer felt so stiff.

'I suppose having them here –' Alpiew nodded her head in the direction of the two musketeers – 'means we'll be sure of getting a dance.' She yawned.

'Countess, hello,' said Mademoiselle Smith, approaching from the top of the table. Up close, her mask was a strangely lifelike one, painted in flesh tones. It created a quite startling effect when she spoke through the rigid little mouth-hole. 'I gather there is to be a special guest here tonight. Strictly an informal visit, but still the Marquis is in a state of some excitement.'

'Might the guest be royal and French?' The Countess giggled with anticipation.

The musketeers took a step forward and looked from side to side, their hands on their sword handles, ready for action.

'I couldn't comment, I'm afraid,' said Mademoiselle Smith, inclining her head towards the musketeers. 'As nothing is official. It's a great pity His Majesty King James is not feeling well this evening. He will be unable to attend. And the Queen of course is occupied tending him.'

'It's nothing serious, I hope?' The Countess wasn't sure whether she was disappointed or relieved not to meet King James after all these years.

'A chin-cough, I hear. Anyway, it means the Marquis won't have a parade of royalty, but he hopes enough to get him the coveted Ordre du Saint-Esprit.'

Near the table Béchamel started jumping up and down and gesticulating wildly at one of the serving boys. Mademoiselle Smith ran off to placate him.

The room was filling.

Then, with a flurry of swords, hats and sashes, a parcel of masked musketeers entered the room, looking from side to side. Behind them came a tall gentleman in a flame-red velvet suit and red satin full-mask. His long, full, black wig had two peaks.

'It's him.' Alpiew elbowed the Countess. 'That's the cove that was giggling behind the screen at Versailles. Look at those two black horns of hair.'

The Countess fell into a full curtsey, but the two musketeers pulled her upright again, one of them holding his finger to the lips of his mask.

'I understand. Com pron,' she said, nodding. 'He's incog., of course, Alpiew. We have to pretend he's an ordinary mortal.'

'He *is* an ordinary mortal,' said Alpiew, looking up at the chimneypiece. 'I say, look at that –' She indicated a huge stone carving of flames, with a lizard in the middle. 'Is that a phoenix?'

'No, Alpiew, it's a salamander. The phoenix, being dead, rises anew from the fire. The salamander lives and thrives in fire.' She looked back at the roomful of people. 'Look, HM is heading for the food.'

'HM?'

'His Majesty.'

'Majesty?' A man with long white hair spilling out from his satyr's mask nudged the Countess. ''Ooo is zat person?' he asked, pointing towards the red guest. 'Do you know?'

The Countess whispered in his ear, so as not to worry the musketeers again.

'*D'accord!*' The white-haired man threw his hands in the air. 'So I must do my duty!'

The Countess wondered if he wasn't slightly cracked.

'He is very tall and slim, isn't he?' The Countess was admiring the back view of the man in red. 'Essential in a monarch.'

The little satyr moved off and stood near the buffet.

The royal guest was ladling spoonfuls of different varieties of pea dishes on to his plate.

'Come along, Alpiew. Let's eat.'

'I'm glad to say His Majesty is filling his plate.' Smith, the shepherdess, was again at their side. 'By the end of tonight we're hoping the Marquis will be sporting the blue sash. Do you like peas, Countess?'

The Countess gazed at the enormous table covered in platters, each full of green peas in various sauces or in different styles – pea tarts, pea fritters, creamed peas, pea salad, peas cooked with mint and spring onions – and paused. 'In moderation,' she replied.

'*Non! Non! Non! Où suis-je?*' Beside her, Baron Lunéville surveyed the table and emitted a low groan. '*C'est le purgatoire! Je suis en enfer!*'

Ahead of them the white-haired satyr in a half-mask was tasting small samples of all the dishes as he moved along the table behind the King. He whispered to a musketeer, who trotted along to the other musketeers, one of whom whispered into the King's ear.

'Look, Alpiew, he must be the official royal taster,' said the Countess. 'We need to watch whether he falls down dead of poison before we can eat.'

The King crooked his finger at Béchamel. A rapid exchange of dialogue followed after which Béchamel ran to Mademoiselle Smith and exclaimed violently.

'Help me, madam.' Mademoiselle Smith rounded on the Countess. 'The Marquis tells me that His Majesty says the sauce on the crowning dish is not the same as the one which he cooked up in the kitchens here last night and which was presented to His Majesty for supper at Versailles.'

The Marquis was sputtering like a damp firework again.

'Apparently His Majesty says there were no cocks' combs in last night's sauce. It was plain, white and perfect, according to the King. You were there while we prepared it. You watched Pipe prepare the cocks' combs. What can have gone wrong?

What can have happened in between the pot of sauce leaving the kitchen and turning up on the royal table?'

'Oh lawks!' A shudder went up Alpiew's spine. 'Where exactly was the Marquis's pot?'

'Hanging over the fire,' said Smith. 'I left Monsieur Béchamel's pot over the fire, ready for the coachman to pick up and drive over to Versailles.'

'It wasn't standing on a trivet at the side of the fire?'

'No. That was the Countess's glue.' Smith's hands flew up to her masked mouth. 'Oh no. Oh lord, save us. Don't tell me His Majesty was served glue on his peas!'

'Whatever,' said the Countess. 'He seemed to like it.' She was grateful for the mask to hide behind; her cheeks were on fire.

'Can you remember how you made it, Countess?'

'I . . . er . . . um . . .' the Countess stammered.

'Come along –' Mademoiselle Smith grabbed the Countess's hand – 'we must recreate that dish, or the Marquis is a ruined man.'

The kitchen was full of people pointing at one another and laughing. There was a fox, a dog, an eagle; amongst them stood a giggling gaggle of shepherdesses, all in identical masks and dresses.

The Countess and Mademoiselle Smith both had their masks perched on top of their heads when they blustered into the kitchen. A magpie pushed back her mask to greet them. It was Pipe.

'Quickly, Pipe! A pot and some flour.'

Pipe ran to fetch the flour, while the Countess pulled a pot from under the bench.

'What's going on?' A dog-man, sitting on the side bench pushing cloves into an onion, pushed his mask up too. It was Roger. He took one look at the Countess and pulled his mask back down, frightened she might mention what she'd seen earlier that afternoon. 'My ball,' he said, holding up the onion, which was tied with a white calico ribbon. 'Whoever heard of a dog without a ball? I would have had a bone, but the thought of carrying a horrid bloody thing round all night didn't seem such fun as a nice smelly clove ball.'

Pipe poured some flour into the pot.

'Wait!' shrieked the Countess. 'There was melted butter at the bottom of the pot, remember.'

'Water next?' cried Mademoiselle Smith.

'No!' cried the Countess. 'Milk.'

'Then?'

'To the fire,' said the Countess, struggling to lift the cast-iron pot.

'Let me.' Roger sprang forward, gripping his onion-ball between his teeth, and grabbed the pot handle. He stepped forward and his mask fell over his eyes. He tripped along for a few steps, and exclaimed, dropping his half-studded onion into the pan. He turned, saw no one had noticed, and sloped off up the spiral stairs to join the party.

Alpiew gave another sigh. Masquerades were her idea of hell, especially when you were followed around by a swashbuckling brace of buffle-headed muscle-men with not a word of English between them.

A shepherdess came towards her. She was expecting it to be Mademoiselle Smith back from the kitchen, but instead Virginia's voice emanated from the hole in the mask.

'I don't believe it, Alpiew,' she sobbed.

Alpiew braced herself for a tirade about the multiplicity of shepherdesses at the party.

'You see! Look about you, Alpiew. John is not here.'

'But he . . .' Alpiew bit her tongue. She wasn't going to tell Virginia about her meeting this afternoon. 'Don't worry, I'm sure he will be here.'

Out of the corner of her eye Alpiew saw the Duc de Charme in a Venetian mask wobbling through the door. Some disguise, thought Alpiew, suddenly realising that, as she too was wearing her everyday clothes, plus a home-made crimson mask and a headdress of white feathers, her own wasn't anything to shout about.

Another two shepherdesses wandered in behind the Duc.

'Did they all pool together to get a job lot of those costumes?' asked Alpiew.

'What?' cried Virginia.

'Every female here is a shepherdess. Look!'

One of the larger shepherdesses strolled up to Virginia. 'Like to dance?' she said in a husky voice.

'Certainly not! I am not one of *those*.' Virginia flounced away. 'I'll have you know, miss, that I am awaiting my fiancé. I am engaged to be married.'

The husky shepherdess lolloped away in another direction, but not before Alpiew could have sworn one of the eyes behind the mask winked at her.

'She's a temperamental young filly, that Virginia,' said a diminutive highwayman at her side. He looked at Alpiew in her white feather headgear, and ran his eyes up and down her dress. 'Well, I know the Countess promised me a shuttlecock, but this is beyond my wildest dreams. Mind you, you'd have done better to come as a bowl of melons.'

'Kiss my cooler, mister!' said Alpiew, raising a fist. But her instinct to lash out was curbed when she realised that from his size this tiny footpad could only be the Prince of Wales. 'Perhaps you had done better to come as a cheeky mischief-making monkey.'

Alpiew noticed that the two musketeers at her side bristled and grabbed the handles of their swords again.

'Stick 'em up!' cried the Prince, holding out his toy pistol.

Alpiew put her hands in the air.

'Yes, you see, that position enhances the bulge on both breasts.'

Alpiew thrust her hands down again. 'If you weren't who you are . . .'

'You'd take me into the next room and ravish me, I know.'
The boy put his gun back in its holster and sighed. 'Not much
of a party, is it?'

'Not unless you like peas, shepherdesses or musketeers.'

'Those two merry-andrews with you?' The Prince gave a
nod towards the musketeers. 'What a pair of self-regarding
prick-me-dainties.'

'I'm afraid so.' Alpiew noticed a man dressed as a dog lope
in and grab one of the shepherdesses for a lively jig.

The Duc de Charme was now dancing with another. He
seemed more wobbly on his feet than ever. One brimmer
too many, thought Alpiew. The Duc was here gallivanting,
but where was his wife? Unless she too was a shepherdess.
A mask was certainly one way to disguise a huge snorter.

'Your Royal Highness,' puffed the Countess, returning to
Alpiew's side and bobbing down into a curtsey before the
Prince.

'Ashby!' The Prince stamped his boot on the wooden floor.
'If you are not going to address me as my footpad name,
which is Jack Cutpurse, please remember you and I go on
nickname terms.'

'Are you a good Robin Hood-style robber?' asked the Countess. 'Or a violent villain, Jack?'

'Robin Hood! Don't compare me to that pea-green ninny,'
snapped the Prince. 'I wouldn't be seen dead in an apple-green
smock and stockings. I have style. However, as far as being a
bung-nipper –' he plunged his leather-gloved hand into his
pocket and pulled out a pink pearly bracelet – 'look what I
prigged this afternoon!'

The Countess took a look. It was no St Audrey bauble but
an expensive piece of jewellery. The Prince snatched it back
and dropped it into his pocket.

'Ladies and gentlemen,' announced the chief musician, 'the
next dance will be Jack Pudding.'

A flurry of musketeers suddenly surrounded them, looking
from right to left and back again. Emerging from the heart of

the huddle of musketeers, the scarlet royal figure held a gloved hand out to the Countess. *'Dansons, madame!'*

The Countess hesitated. Alpiew shoved her forward.

As the couple stepped out to lead the dance, Alpiew looked to the Prince.

'Who d'you cloy with, Jack Cutpurse? You the foist or the bragger?'

The Prince wiggled about on the spot. 'You two –' the Prince turned to the musketeers – 'please fetch some food for me and Mistress Alpiew.'

'They don't speak English.'

The Prince repeated his instruction in French and the two musketeers sashayed off.

'I'm no sneaking mort,' said Alpiew, 'but I reckon that you're part of a bulk and file. Am I right, Jack?'

'I, er . . .' The Prince bent forward and whispered in Alpiew's ear: 'My cant ain't so good, missus. What's all that stuff in plain English?'

'Well, me lad –' Alpiew looked stagily from side to side – 'my guess is how you're part of a gang. Am I right?'

The boy gave a solemn nod.

'And so who gets the snappings?' She bent in to whisper: 'The take. In other words, who gets the money?'

'Oh, I see!' The boy brightened up. 'The poor.'

Alpiew thought the boy must certainly have misunderstood what she was asking him. She leant in again. 'You prig the jewellery, am I right? Then you fence it, using courtiers, and servants – your bulk and file – and then the money – the snappings – comes back, but once you've got the snappings, then what happens?'

'It's my mother's stuff.' The boy stood on his tiptoes to get his mouth really close to Alpiew's ear. 'I am the bung-nipper, then I pass the stuff to Pipe, and she passes it on and on until it gets sold, by a real Frenchman from Versailles so it gets the best price and doesn't get linked back to us. Then the money – sorry, the snappings – comes back along the chain and I give it to my mother.'

'Your mother knows about this?'

'Oh yes,' said the Prince. 'She uses it to try and alleviate the lives of the poor people. If anyone notices, she passes it off as a small lottery win.'

'Which poor people?'

'You can't imagine how desperately hard it is for some of the people living in the forest and the villages near here.' The Prince looked around him to make sure they were not being overheard. 'My mother sends them food parcels and money. But ssshhh. No one must know. Especially the King of France. She's been in trouble with him before.'

Alpiew was reeling at her discovery. The whole jewellery-theft business was a secret form of royal philanthropy.

'What if they caught someone for it? Wouldn't they be hanged?'

'Should that ever happen, my mother would have to own up to the game. She wouldn't let someone hang, I'm sure of it. She keeps an eye on the local gaol and makes sure no one suffers on her behalf.'

'Why cannot your mother simply sell the jewellery her-self?'

'Because the world would soon know about it if she tried. And therefore they would know how much she disapproves of the poverty that surrounds us. And the French authorities would probably put an end to the enterprise. And it would be taken as criticism of our generous host, Louis. And do you know something else, Mistress Alpiew?'

Alpiew shook her head.

'From this position I can see right down the crack of your bosoms.'

'You cheeky whipper-snapper.' Alpiew jumped to an upright position and smoothed her dress down. 'But don't worry, Jack. Your secret's safe with me.'

'You dance so well, Ashby.'

The Countess positively wilted at the compliment. She took

a sprightly step forward then swung her leg round rather too enthusiastically, setting herself a-wobble, but the man in scarlet's grip was strong and she did not fall.

The Countess was utterly stumped for conversation, not knowing how to make small talk with the most mighty monarch in the world, especially when he was supposed to be incognito.

So she determined to concentrate on her dancing and thrust an enthusiastic foot forward.

'How did you enjoy your stay in ze Bastille?' said the man in scarlet.

Oh lord, thought the Countess. What a conundrum. 'It was . . .' she decided to play safe '. . . not quite as I had expected.'

The man laughed. His laugh was surprisingly rasping and high. But then Frenchmen were a different species.

'And apparently you left zat old friend of yours splashing around in ze moat!'

'Oh! Pigalle!' The Countess felt a terrible pang of guilt. 'I did tell someone, sire. Poor, dear Olympe. I hope she was all right. Do you know what happened to her?'

'Of course I do.' The man swivelled round and lunged forward into a complicated step of the dance. 'Let us say she survived.'

Alpiew took a seat next to the old satyr with long white hair. She noticed that the musketeers had formed a gaggle at the corner of the dance-floor.

The Countess was tripping it nimbly in the centre of the ballroom.

'Well, there's a turn up,' said Alpiew. 'Fancy my mistress cutting a caper with the King of France.'

Without looking up, the old boy went on munching his plate of peas.

'You must like your job. Don't you get frightened one day you'll have the bad fortune to taste an unlucky dish and get what's meant for the fellow in red?' she asked. As the man seemed to ignore her and just went on shovelling peas into his mouth, she continued: 'Do you live at Versailles?'

The man nodded.

Alpiew thought his supercilious little mouth, peeking out under his half-mask, gave him the air of an elderly lapdog.

'Splendid over there, ain't it? Criminy, what a place! Gold roof! And all those mirrors! I reckon as how the King likes to frighten people with it.'

'Really?' The man ladled another spoonful of peas on to his plate. 'How is zat?'

'It fills you with a kind of awe to be there. It's so big and so pretty, and everything there inspires you with wonder. Being master of something like that would make the King feel more like a king, in my opinion.' Alpiew picked a pea from the man's plate and popped it into her mouth. 'Mind you, I think it's a pretty terrible king that prances around in such extravagance while his people starve to death only furlongs away.'

The old man nodded and ate another spoonful of peas.

'And then there's that weird old prison of his.'

'Ze Bastille?'

'Mmmm. What a farce that place is. Everyone outside thinks it's a great dripping dungeon, a hundred times worse than Newgate, but it's not, you know. It makes prison seem quite the place to be. And what a brilliant idea of his, keeping that scary prisoner in there, the one they all talk about, you know, in the mask. And no one knows what the poor cove did, but they all know whatever it was it upset the King so badly he'll be kept there forever with no friends and no identity and no trial! Poor old fellow. Just to think of it makes your hair curl.'

'Does it?' The man stirred the peas about and took another spoonful.

'Let's say it would certainly make me think twice before upsetting the King . . .' Alpiew paused and gave her white-haired friend an up-and-down look. 'You wouldn't go and tell on me, would you?'

'You don't like peas?' said the old boy, turning round to recharge his platter.

'I do.' Alpiew watched the man ladle a spoonful of peas cooked with shallot and lettuce, and then some of the peas in white sauce on to a separate plate for her.

'*Alors* – tell me which dish you prefer,' he said, handing her the plate. 'Ze *pois à la Français* or ze ones with ze sauce Béchamel?'

Alpiew tasted as she gazed out at the dancers. The Countess seemed to be doing very well with the King. Shepherdesses were scattered throughout the room. The black dog was still whirling about with one of them, the Marquis dancing with another, the Duc de Charme teetering perilously with a third. Elsewhere on the floor two shepherdesses were clearly dancing with each other. Alpiew wondered if they were the demoiselles Smith and Bontemps.

'Well?' said the man. 'Which? Béchamel or *à la Français*?'

'Both dishes are delicious,' said Alpiew as a further shepherdess flopped down beside her. 'But I am surprised to find the white sauce strangely delicious.'

'We had it last night,' said the satyr. 'But tonight it is even nicer. I like ze slight onion taste.'

'That's done it,' said Virginia, interrupting without any concern for Alpiew's companion. 'John's not coming, is he? He's nothing but a liar and a scoundrel.'

'Did he tell you what costume he would be wearing?' said Alpiew. 'Perhaps he is here and you don't recognise him.'

'Don't be stupid,' snapped Virginia. 'If he was here, he would be dancing with me now, wouldn't he?'

The Duc swooped near, putting out a hand to steady himself as he almost tumbled on to the bench. His emerald ring caught the light as it flashed past Alpiew's face.

'He's off with that Denise again,' wailed Virginia. 'I know it. The swine.'

Alpiew felt that there was something increasingly strange about the Duc this evening. She knew that he was usually unsteady on those heels, but tonight she wondered whether he was very drunk, for he needed support to walk the smallest distance, and was leaning heavily on his dancing partner, a shepherdess.

'Perhaps John' has come dressed as the Duc,' she said. 'Perhaps he mistakes that shepherdess for you.'

'John is a man, through and through.' Virginia tutted. 'He would never do anything so ridiculous as to primp himself up as a French popinjay.'

Another shepherdess flopped down at the end of the bench, flapping her fan and panting. 'Still not want to dance?' she said to Virginia.

Without a word, Virginia flounced up and away.

The Countess had exhausted her attempts at small talk. The weather, the ballroom, the costumes, the superfluity of shepherdesses had all had a thorough airing, now she was hoping the music would stop, so that she could get a taste of the lovely food before it was devoured by everyone else.

'You know who I am, don't you, Ashby?' said the man in scarlet.

'It is a masquerade, my lord.' The Countess didn't want to look a fool or get herself into trouble. 'You know we do not generally reveal ourselves until the last dance.'

'Zat is true.' The man in scarlet did a pirouette and, as the final chords were played, took a bow. The Countess curtseyed in return.

'One more dance, Countess,' said the man in scarlet, keeping hold of the Countess's hand. 'For old times' sake.'

The leader of the musicians announced the next dance. 'Ladies and gentlemen, the next dance will be Friday Night.'

The Countess and the Man in Scarlet joined hands and faced each other, ready to start the dance.

Alpiew smiled to herself as she watched her mistress give a coy kick to her skirt.

'Take your partners, please, for Friday Night!'

Something was making Alpiew feel uneasy. Friday Night? *Friday Night!* It was a dance, not a deadline. Whatever was going to happen – the Armageddon, the Epiphany – it was going to start now.

She jumped up and peered out at the dance-floor.

The Duc took a step backwards, and flapped his jacket open. It was at that moment that she noticed the bulge in his breeches. From where she stood it was easy to see that, jammed into his belt, he had a pistol, ready charged and cocked.

As the musicians put their bows to their instruments to strike the first chord, the Duc seized his gun.

Alpiew dived out on to the dance-floor and pushed the Countess and the Man in Scarlet to the floor just as the shot rang out.

Dancing couples dived for cover, and the musketeers stormed on to the floor, pulling Alpiew up and holding her at sword-point, while they hauled the man in scarlet out of the room. The Duc ran.

A man in Moorish dress and a burly shepherdess gave chase. The floor was littered with screaming shepherdesses.

'What did you do that for, Alpiew?' wailed the Countess from the floor. 'We were just getting to know one another. And now they've hauled him away.'

'Did you not hear the shot? The Duc had a gun, madam. Are you sure you are not hit?' cried Alpiew, wriggling free of the two musketeers' grasp. 'He was aiming at you. It's not me you want to apprehend,' she shrieked to a sword-wielding musketeer who held his blade to her throat. 'It's the Duc. He fired the shot. You saw it all, didn't you?' Alpiew turned to get another eyewitness account from the white-haired satyr, but he too had disappeared. 'Where did that man go? He saw what happened.' She shouted across the room. 'Virginia! You must have seen. The Duc was aiming a pistol at the Countess and her dancing partner.'

'I only know that my heart is broken,' she sobbed. 'And now

the party is quite ruined, and John is not coming.'

The Countess clambered from the floor to the bench as the musketeers tied Alpiew's hands behind her back. 'You don't want to be taking Alpiew, you know,' she puffed. 'We're both on your side.' She tugged at the sleeve of a musketeer as they hauled Alpiew away. 'We're under orders from His Majesty.'

At the door the gang of musketeers barred the way to the Countess. But before Alpiew was hauled off she managed to hiss to the Countess, 'Trust no one. That wasn't the Duc.'

The Countess stood and gazed after her until they slammed and locked the door. 'One minute she says it's the Duc, then next she says it isn't.' The Countess sighed. 'What is one to make of the girl?'

'Are you all right, Countess?' Mademoiselle Bontemps, her shepherdess mask pulled up, loomed behind the Countess. 'I see you have a little cut on your hand. Wait on the bench while I fetch the Doctor.'

'I barely felt it.' The Countess looked down at the blood dripping from her finger. She wrapped a piece of table linen round her hand. 'Is my dancing companion all right? The Ki—, the man in scarlet. Was he hurt?'

'Play on!' called one of the musketeers from the floor. And the musicians climbed back upon their chairs and struck up a gay tune.

'May I?' A few feet from where the Countess sat, the black dog, alias the valet Roger, held out his hand to Virginia. The Countess caught her by the elbow. This would not be a good move for the child. 'He is only a valet!' she warned.

Virginia leapt to her feet. 'Countess, you may remember that last time I picked a groom and wound up with a lord. Who knows what this chap might turn out to be.' She skipped on to the dance-floor.

At the table beside the Countess, sparkling in his tinsel suit, Béchamel fell to the floor sobbing and gibbering in French. Mademoiselle Smith and Pipe stooped over him, patting his back.

'His Majesty loved it all,' said Pipe. 'You saw, Miss Smith. Tell him. I saw him. He loved it.'

Béchamel squawked a string of invective in French.

'He says the King barely took a mouthful, before going off to dance with . . .' The girl glanced at the Countess and decided not to translate the Marquis's words. 'Now that His Majesty has been whirled off, he says, it is all ruined. He thinks the King will forever associate Sauce Béchamel with being shot at by an effeminate madman on stilts.'

'I suppose the fellow is so hysterical he doesn't yet realise that his precious sauce is my home-made glue?'

'And nor will he.' Mademoiselle Smith bent down to whisper in the Countess's ear: 'I will convince him he invented it himself.'

'Where is my fucking husband?'

The Countess turned to face Lucy Whippingham, as ever the worse for drink. She wore no costume nor mask and swayed from side to side, gripping the neck of a half-finished wine bottle.

'And where is my lover, and it come to that?' She lurched across to Virginia and Roger as they danced by. 'Men are bastards, you know. All of them.' She leant in to the Countess to imply an intimate remark but still spoke at the top of her voice. 'And men are bad enough as they are without being women as well. Look at them! Half the women here are men, have you noticed? Look at that butch shepherdess eyeing up your ward. That's no woman. Look at the hairy forearms! And if it is a woman, God help us, I'd keep well clear. But then I prefer men to be men and women to be women.' She hiccupped and swayed off on to the dance-floor.

The Countess turned to the food table and picked up a spoon, ready to serve herself a generous portion of everything on show. But just as she dipped the spoon into the serving dish Mademoiselle Bontemps returned.

'The Doctor is in a room along the way. I'll take you there.'

'I'm all right really. It's just a scratch.' She looked down and saw that the cloth had a spreading red patch. Reluctantly she put her plate down and followed the shepherdess.

'I saw the man reach for his gun. It was obvious that he was aiming at either my mistress or the cove she was dancing with. Anyone would have done what I did.'

The man who had interviewed them at Versailles sat opposite Alpiew in a candle-lit chamber near the ballroom.

'And Friday night, by the way, I now know would be too late. It is the name of a dance. As the dance started, the Duc – or should I say, whoever is pretending to be the Duc – took aim. He didn't hit him, did he?'

'Hit whom?'

'The man in scarlet clothing who was dancing with my mistress?'

'The jewellery thefts – have you got any nearer to solving those?'

'I do know what happened, sir. It was a simple theft instigated by persons unknown. I believe they were temporary visitors to the chateau. Lady Prude dismissed them.'

The man gave Alpiew a sideways glance.

'And took the blame upon herself? That sounds rather unlikely.'

'She follows a certain type of religion, sir, which depends on self-mortification.'

The man made a note.

'Now I really need to get back to my mistress, sir, if you don't mind.'

'We have the Duc de Charme in custody. He made no fight when we picked him up. We found him sitting in his room, as cool as you like. He was dressed for the masquerade, sitting with his wife, the Duchesse. She howled like an animal as we took him.'

'I told you, it wasn't him. It was not the Duc. It was someone pretending to be him, wearing his clothes. What was the Duc wearing? I know he is not the man who fired the shot.'

'The pistol was lying in the corridor outside his room. It was practically still smoking.'

'I warn you,' said Alpiew, 'this night is not over. And if you have picked up the Duc, you will find out soon enough that he is innocent. From your list we have had L.S. – Aurelia's Last Supper; then the Epiphany – the assembly of three kings, or two kings and a king-in-waiting, but one of them was ill and did not make it to the party; then Friday Night – the dance; we still have an Apocalypse and a Resurrection to come. There is more mischief afoot, believe me.'

The Countess entered the dark room. A single candle guttered and wavered on the windowsill.

Dr Stickworth sat behind a desk next to the window, scratching out a letter.

'Thank you, Miss Bontemps.' He laid down his pen, and rose. 'Let's see the damage.' He looked up towards Bontemps. 'You get back to the masquerade. I can manage.'

The Countess unwrapped the bloodstained linen and the Doctor inspected her hand.

'We will need water,' he said, handing her the candle. 'Come along, I will take you elsewhere and we can get you sorted out in no time.'

He opened the door and led her through a number of strange rooms, and down a stone spiral staircase, then along a long narrow corridor and down again.

'These are storerooms, Countess. I keep my chest of medicines down here.'

The dank stone corridor had a chill of disuse.

'I hope the King was not hurt.' The Countess held up her bleeding hand to guard the flame. 'Did you need to tend to him?'

The Doctor made a strange sound as he took out a great rusty key, unlocked the door and stood back to let the Countess in first. As she passed him, the last thing she noticed before he blew out the flame and slammed the door shut was the twinkle of his emerald ring.

When Alpiew came back into the ballroom everything was restored to normal, except that all the musketeers had gone.

The Moorish man was at the buffet and the highwayman Prince was leading Pipe in a stately courant.

There was a dearth of shepherdesses. Alpiew wondered whether they hadn't all gone to find a flock of sheep to fight over.

One lonely shepherdess was dancing in a somewhat lascivious manner with Roger.

'I suppose you haven't seen my stinking husband?' Lucy Whippingham flopped down on to the bench at Alpiew's side. 'I expect he's off tumbling one of the wenches, if she can put up with the stink of snuff tobacco.'

'Have you seen my mistress?'

'She cut her hand.' Lady Whippingham grabbed hold of Alpiew's elbow and roared with laughter. 'That ward of yours is practically copulating with the Charmes' valet, have you seen?'

Their writhing movements were certainly nearer something that you'd see in a Covent Garden bagnio rather than the courant everyone else was at.

A slim man in a fox's mask pulled Alpiew roughly on to the floor.

'Where is your mistress?' Alpiew immediately recognised Wackland's voice. 'She is in grave danger.' He gripped Alpiew's hand and hauled her along. 'Keep up the pretence of dancing, for God's sake. There is a shepherdess here . . .'

'There are scores of shepherdesses here, Lord Wackland. Have you not seen 'em?'

'One in particular. My own flesh and blood, but I . . .' He broke off. Alpiew was sure that beneath his mask he was crying. 'She is full of evil. And she is directing it towards the wrong people. She killed Isabel, and Aurelia, and is in pursuit of your mistress. But it was another . . .'

'Lady Prude,' said Alpiew. 'I know. But why my lady?'

'I had a daughter, way back, fifteen years ago, when I was a pot-boy in London. I left my employment and went to work for Lady Prude's family. She was high born. I was the lowest of the low . . .'

They turned with the dance and, still holding hands, walked a few steps before pointing their toes out to the side.

'My wife died giving birth to that child. So for about four years I brought her up alone. Then her ladyship cast her eye upon me and we eloped, and married. The so-called Glorious Revolution took place at the same time, and thousands of English Catholics ran to France, so we pretended to adhere to that faith, and were well hidden in the crowd. I brought the child with me. Lady Prude said we could never have a hope of starting our lives anew with a child round our necks, particularly as the child was dark-skinned. So we put her into . . .'

'The Convent of the Order of the Filles de la Vierge.'

'Yes. And when, a few years later, Lady Prude left me to marry Lord Prude, I realised what I had done was all wrong.'

'But you were married, Lord Wackland – how could she marry another? Particularly if you were here in Catholic France?'

'I am neither Wackland nor a lord. I am plain Mr Smith from the Tower Hamlets. By marrying me, Lady Prude lost her own title and became plain Mrs Smith.' Wackland gave a scornful laugh. 'It couldn't last. After a few years she left me to return to the Society she had lost by marrying me. I went back to fetch my child away from the convent, but the nuns said she was dead.' Wackland sobbed. 'She was a pretty little thing. She looked like my mother, but with this warm brown skin of her mother's, like a gypsy child.'

'And she was really still alive, no?'

'But I did not know that. If I had, I'd have . . .' Wackland nodded, the smile on his fox mask belying his discourse as they

317

danced on. 'I wandered around France, and turned up here at St Germain, where all exiles wind up at some time. Lady Prude, now a widow herself, recognised me at once. She renamed me, and gave me a false title and a position in exchange for my silence over her bigamy.'

'And your daughter?'

'She tracked me down, with her threats to kill the woman who had helped me . . .'

'Dispose of her?'

'Those were the words she used. I never have knowingly had a conversation with her since I left her at the convent. But a few weeks ago I received a letter, saying she knew who I was and had come to give me back my title – plain Mr Smith – and to bring justice to the woman who had her put away. I thought she might be Aurelia, as the letter arrived a day before she did, but now I wonder. It could be any young woman here . . . Leonora Smith, perhaps. She bears my name, after all.'

'Lady Prude left a note for this mystery girl in the confession box in the parish church, am I right?' Alpiew spoke quickly. She needed more information to stop whatever catastrophe was about to be unleashed. 'She told your daughter that her offending stepmother was a writer, then had Lady Murdo-McTavish, the Countess and myself sent to the Bastille for our own protection?'

'That was the plan, yes.'

'Then, after Lady Murdo-McTavish met her ghastly end, Lady Prude panicked and realised it was all spun out of control, and had herself arrested?'

'I let her know she had got the wrong women in Aurelia and Isabel.' Wackland, behind his fox face, sobbed. 'Then I left another note for her in the confessional, telling her the truth, but she never came to pick it up.'

'So the girl still thinks the Countess might be her step-mother?'

As they turned, on the point-step, Dr Stickworth came into

the ballroom. Lucy Whippingham lurched towards him; he span on his heels.

'Come back, Sticky!' screeched Lucy, lunging towards him. 'You bastard!' She stood in the doorway and flung her empty glass after him. 'Just because your mother called you Hector doesn't mean you have to shaft everything in sight, you swaggering bastard.'

Hector!

The French name for the knave of diamonds.

Alpiew pulled away from Wackland and, gathering her skirts, ran after the Doctor.

THIRTEEN

Gallimawfry — a kind of hash

The Countess tried to accustom herself to the dark. All around her she could hear the slow damp dripping sound of the disused dungeon. The walls were wet and slimy to the touch. She imagined the cell she was in must be adjacent to the moat.

She felt her way with her fingers to the door. It was a heavy oak door with a small rusty iron grille. She peered out, but could see nothing but more dark dank walls.

The cut on her hand was beginning to throb.

Why didn't she follow Alpiew's example, and carry a tinder-box forever in her pocket, then at least she could light the candle?

She felt along the wall for a stone bench. Old dungeon cells usually had somewhere to sit. She edged along inch by inch. As her knee struck the jutting stone, her hands came upon something soft. Clothing. She pulled it up. It was damp but not wet through. She held it up and felt around its edges. It was a woman's mantua. It had clearly been here only a few hours. The fabric was a thin muslin. But why was it down here at all? She flung it back on to the bench.

Amid the cacophony of dripping she could hear something else. It was only the slightest sound. Footsteps. Light, tripping footsteps, more like satin slippers than men's heavy boots, and they were padding nearer and nearer.

The Countess stood behind the door.

A key turned slowly in the lock.

She held her breath and waited. Once the door opened she would try to make a run for it.

The door opened a mere crack.

The Countess poised herself before it, ready to run.

She peered out into the passageway.

She could make out the dark shadow of a woman's skirt. What little light there was fell upon the dull glint of a blade.

'Stepmama!' said a light female voice. 'Are you there?'

The Countess pressed herself back against the cell wall and crouched.

'You disposed of me, stepmother, dearest, and now I am come back to dispose of you.'

What was this about? The Countess had never had a step-child. The nearest she had ever come to that had been adopting Alpiew when her parents had died in the Great Plague.

The Countess pitched forward to push the girl out of the way, but as she moved she felt the knife pass through her skirt and stab her leg.

She wrestled the girl away. Then she picked up her skirts to run, as a frenzy of blows showered down in her direction.

Grabbing out at the girl's ankles, the Countess managed to unbalance her and, staggering blindly in the dark, she ran away along the black dripping passageway.

Alpiew had lost sight of the Doctor.

She stamped her foot and looked in every direction. The chateau was a maze of doors and rooms and stairways, and Stickworth knew his way around infinitely better than she did.

A tall shepherdess slipped out of a doorway and stood behind Alpiew. 'There is more to it, isn't there?' The shepherdess pushed back her mask. It was John. 'The assassination attempt wasn't the end of things.'

'They have taken the Countess.'

'Who is "they"? I'll help you, but you must tell me what you know.'

'Those idiotic bodyguards have arrested the Duc. But it wasn't him. It was Dr Stickworth.'

'I'll get my boys.' Pulling his mask back down, he loped off towards the ballroom.

Alpiew continued until she reached the top of a spiral staircase, where she found a clue to the Countess's whereabouts. In the centre of the grey stone step was a tiny splash of fresh red blood.

Lady Whippingham had said that the Countess had cut her hand.

She yelled back to John that she had picked up the trail and, following the intermittent drips, Alpiew dived down the steps, taking them two by two, until she stopped at the bottom and inspected the floor. The trail went left. She ran through a number of dark empty rooms before reaching another landing. There was a speck of blood on the steps leading down again. At the bottom she searched the floor. There were maroon Turkey rugs scattered about the place and it took her some time to decide to turn right. Again she ran on through dark rooms and passageways. Then she emerged at the entrance to another spiral staircase.

The path down was dark. It obviously descended into the disused cellars.

She had no candle or light. She considered going back for a moment to snatch a candle from a sconce in one of the rooms she had passed through, but decided time was more important than light.

Vivid memories of Isabel Murdo-McTavish's corpse splashed through her mind as she leapt down the dank steps.

The slippery stone floor twisted about and led her to an even wetter corridor.

Heavy oak doors went off either side of her. She tried them all, pushing them open fiercely in case anyone was lying in wait within.

She stopped and listened.

Somewhere nearby she could hear the tiniest of sounds, a

sniffling quiet weeping. On tiptoe she crept forward until she stood outside the door whence the sound came.

Pressing herself hard into the slimy wall, she shoved the door open.

Her eyes were becoming slightly more accustomed to the dark and she could vaguely make out the figure of a woman sitting on a bench at the far side of the dungeon. She knew it was not the Countess.

The woman rose and stepped forward.

She was wearing a shepherdess costume and mask.

'They have taken them both away from me,' she murmured. 'My lover and my husband. I'm all alone in the world now.' She reached out and grabbed Alpiew's dress. 'Please help me. My husband is taken to be locked up. Is he here in the dungeon? I am looking for them. Where are they gone with him?'

'You must help me, madam,' said Alpiew, grasping the Duchesse's cold hand. 'We must find my mistress, the Countess. She is in danger from the person who killed Isabel.'

'The Countess?' The Duchesse glanced about her, as she tagged along behind. 'She didn't run off with Isabel, did she?'

'No.' Alpiew marched on, slamming the cell doors open. 'But she liked her a lot.'

They reached a turn in the passageway. Alpiew stopped and held her finger up to her mouth. She craned her head forward to peer around the corner.

'Come on,' she whispered. 'Quietly.'

She took a few tentative steps. She could not be sure, but there seemed to be something filling the corridor ahead.

As they stepped softly along Alpiew could see the figure of a woman, swaying slightly. Was she coming towards them or slowly backing away? Whichever, the woman had seen them, for she suddenly started breathing very loudly.

Alpiew took a step forward.

With a panting sound the woman took a step back.

Alpiew plunged her hand into her pocket to find her tinderbox. She was wary about sparking it in this small corridor, as it would only give the advantage to the person standing in the dark.

The woman suddenly turned about and ran.

'Follow me,' Alpiew hissed to the Duchesse. 'Come along.'

She ran after the mystery woman, catching up with her and grabbing on to her arm within a few yards. She spun her round. Another shepherdess.

'Where is she?' shouted Alpiew. 'Where have you put the Countess?'

'What?' The woman lifted her mask. 'Is that you, Mistress Alpiew? This is Mademoiselle Bontemps. I am looking for Mademoiselle Smith – a footman passed on a message from her asking me to meet her down here.'

'Down here?' Alpiew exclaimed. 'Pish, what strange places you have for meetings.' She passed the Duchesse's hand to Mademoiselle Bontemps. 'Hold on to the poor Duchesse. She is a little bewildered.' She slammed the tinder-box into Bontemps' hand. 'And strike us some sparks while we walk so we can better see our way.'

Alpiew marched ahead, continuing flinging the cell doors open. 'Shine the light into the cells as we pass, in case she is inside somewhere, lying injured.' Alpiew kept the thought 'or worse' to herself.

The eerie scratching sound of flint against steel, and splashes of sparky light gave an even more sinister feel to the dungeons.

The Duchesse started to whimper.

Alpiew moved on.

'Hold,' cried Bontemps. 'Look!'

Alpiew peered into the cell. The sparks illuminated a pile of clothing, lying in a puddle on the flagstone floor, soaked through. She moved on.

They turned another corner and started on another row of cells.

As the tinder-box struck on the third cell, Bontemps let out a gasp.

Standing on the stone bench ahead of them was a woman. Another shepherdess.

As the spark died, with a blood-curdling scream the shepherdess leapt down upon them, her arms outspread, in each fist a dagger.

The Countess crawled along on all fours. By some miracle she had escaped from the mad shepherdess.

A sudden strange flickering light had distracted the girl, who had turned to listen. The Countess hauled herself to her feet and tiptoed away. She skipped into another cell, praying that the madwoman would pass her by, so she could run for it in the opposite direction.

She slid under the stone bench and lay in the puddle beneath, holding her breath and wishing the pounding of her heart would die down so she could listen out.

As she began to calm, she heard footsteps approaching and at the same time, a sudden caterwauling.

The dungeon door opened and the Countess could make out a pair of satin slippers a few feet from her face.

The shepherdess sat down on the bench above her.

The pale skirt billowed out and tickled her face. She tilted her neck away. Should she lie still and hope that the girl got bored and moved on, or surprise her by pulling her ankles from beneath her and hope to make a getaway while the girl regained her equilibrium?

She decided to keep still.

She could hear the shepherdess breathing, and wondered whether she was playing a cat-and-mouse game. Perhaps the girl could hear her breathing just as clearly, and was waiting for her moment.

She expected any moment that the girl would bend down and lash at her, trapped as she was, lying squeezed up against a stone wall. If that happened, the Countess realised, she was finished. There would be no chance.

The girl stood up.

The Countess took a deep breath and prepared for the worst.

The girl turned and faced the bench.

If it would not have entailed moving her arms, the Countess would have crossed herself.

Then the girl stepped up on to the bench above her.

She heard a muffled scream and sounds of a scuffle in the distance.

The girl spun round and jumped down. She seemed to be giggling as she moved over to the door and peeped out into the passageway.

The Countess wished she could see more than just a shadowy outline.

She lay still. A drip landed on her eyelid and she blinked, trying to disperse it. This only made things worse. The drip rolled down the side of her nose and lingered on her upper lip, tickling her and tempting her to sneeze.

The shepherdess moved again. She stepped into the doorway and, pulling her mask down she stepped out into the passageway.

The apparition flew down and landed on Mademoiselle Bontemps, knocking her to the floor with a yelp. The knife caught the edge of the tinder-box, sending it skittering across the floor.

Alpiew knew that, even if she retrieved it, the contact with water would have made it practically useless.

'Leonora?' said Bontemps, writhing under the flailing shepherdess. Alpiew tugged at the back of the shepherdess's muslin dress. The Duchesse put her hands to her head and screamed.

Bontemps rolled to one side, grabbing one of the girl's wrists, while Alpiew tried to snatch the knife from her other hand.

But instead of grabbing her wrist, Alpiew's hand wrapped around the blade. Yelping, she drew back. She flexed her hand a few times. It was bleeding, but no tendons had been severed.

She fumbled forward, grabbing out as someone brushed past

her, their footsteps tripping along the passageway into the distance.

'She got away,' said Bontemps, hauling herself up. 'Who was that? Is she quite mad? She could have hurt someone.'

Still with her hands to her face, the Duchesse was wailing. 'Isabel? Isabel? My lord Duc?'

'It's all been too much for her.' Alpiew turned to Bontemps. 'Get the poor lady upstairs, and in God's name fetch help.' Shielding her aching hand, she pulled open the door. 'Rouse some of those preening musketeers. And make sure they bring light.'

Alpiew ran into the passageway and followed the retreating sound of the madwoman's footsteps.

'Where are you got to? Don't hide from me any longer.'

The Countess recognised Leonora Smith's voice at once.

The Countess dragged herself out from under the bench and hobbled towards the open door. She was not going to be able to run, that was certain. The cut in her leg was bleeding, she could feel the hot blood dribbling down her calf. Her stockings must be torn too, she thought, peering out of the door.

She could not make up her mind whether to try to head back the way she had come, towards Leonora, or to try the other direction, leaving the possibility that it would be a dead end and that she would be trapped.

There was no question. Holding her thigh firmly with one hand she limped along the way she had come, even though by so doing she risked a further encounter with Mademoiselle Smith.

She stood at the next corner and waited. She slowly edged her head around to take a look.

Another face was staring back at her.

She cried out, but a hand covered her mouth.

'It's me – Alpiew.'

The Countess grabbed her arm. 'Thank God,' she whispered. 'Are you all right?'

'Cut hands. You?'

'She stabbed my leg.'

Holding on to one another they fumbled along in the dark, moving as fast as they dared along the slimy flagstoned floor.

'Why is she doing this?' hissed the Countess.

'Ssh!' Alpiew stopped. 'What is that?'

Behind them they could hear muffled footsteps, tentatively coming in their direction.

'She's behind us. Quickly! Let me take the weight.' Alpiew put her arm round the Countess's waist. 'Now run for it.'

They both limped along, Alpiew once losing her footing and sliding, but regaining her equilibrium fast enough not to take a tumble.

As they approached the next corner they slowed down.

Alpiew knelt and peered ahead into the dark.

Whoosh.

The knife slashed down.

The Countess leapt back.

'I am the Epiphany. I am the Alpha and Omega, the First and the Last, who was dead, and is alive.'

The masked shepherdess lunged forward with the knife. From her position on the floor Alpiew noted that she had lost one knife since their last encounter.

'You disposed of me, and I will be avenged.'

'Believe me, child, I do not understand you.' The Countess trembled, but tried to keep her voice calm. 'Tell me, please, what I have done. Then, when I know, take your revenge.'

The knife whished past her face.

Alpiew took a few crawling steps closer to the demented girl.

'You killed Lady Murdo-McTavish for the same reason, did you not?' The Countess spoke quietly. 'Surely we cannot both have been guilty?'

'It is someone here. I have letters to prove it. And I have seen my father too. That weak and faithless creature who stood by and let me be thrown away with the rubbish.'

Playing for time, Alpiew decided to try a tactic. 'Dr Stickworth is your father, isn't he?'

'That fool?' The girl laughed. 'I used him. He has his own obsession. All plots to kill the King of France for recognising William as the rightful King of England. It's all Jacobite this and Jacobite that with him, as though politics matters! He thought I was doing it to help him. I told him Isabel was a Huguenot spy, sent to catch him. So he helped me.' The girl reached into her pocket and pulled out a handkerchief. 'Once I knew his new name I had my 'kerchief embroidered with my new initials –' she waved the handkerchief – 'A.W. Daughter of a lord now! The seamstress said, "Alpha and Omega. The first and the last."' The girl gave a wild laugh. 'And that is what I am. The apocalyptical avenging angel. "The abominable and murderers and whoremongers and sorcerers and idolaters and all liars, they shall have their portion in the pool burning with fire and brimstone, which is the second death."'

Alpiew was very near the shepherdess's feet, and prepared to lunge.

'Calm yourself, child.' The Countess held her hands out before her and walked towards the girl. 'We will help you.'

'It must be you. You stole my father from me, and forced him to dump me, did you not?' The girl slashed the knife again, narrowly missing. 'If not you, who else?'

'Daughter?' A male voice echoed along the corridor behind them, and the flickering light of his candle threw dancing shadows on the glistening walls. 'We have come to get what we deserve.'

The Countess took a quick look back.

Wackland, his ghostly face illuminated from below, walked steadily towards them. Behind him, drawn and white, came Lady Prude.

Alpiew threw herself forward to unbalance the girl, but her hand slid along the slippery floor and she fell flat on her front.

In an instant the girl was down sitting astride her, the knife held aloft.

'Come any nearer,' she shrieked, 'and I will kill this woman.'

'I am your father. I loved your mother. And I loved you.'

'Not enough.' The shepherdess stood, feet astride Alpiew, and slashed the knife again. 'You didn't keep me long, did you, for all that love? You didn't even recognise me when I came to find you. Though I recognised you, Mr Smith.'

The girl tore off her shepherdess mask and flung it to the floor.

Aurelia stood before them.

'Oh God save us,' cried Lady Prude, crossing herself. 'She has risen from the grave.'

'I believed the nuns would take care of you,' said Wackland, edging closer. 'I did come back. They told me you were dead. I thought . . .'

The girl stepped away from Alpiew and grabbed at the Countess. She held the blade against her throat.

'You thought! *You* thought! You didn't think at all, did you? You let the buttered bun do that for you. The bitch you ran off with.' She shook the Countess hard.

'Leave her . . . It was not her . . . Let your wrath fall upon me, your father.'

'You came too late! Too late. And sent no money for my upkeep.' The girl spoke in a sing-song, childish voice. 'I was seven years old when the nuns sent me out to fend for myself. Hold up your flame, Father.'

Wackland lifted the candle.

'You threw me away for *this*?' The girl inspected the Countess's face. 'At least that Scotswoman was your own age.'

'It was me,' sobbed Lady Prude. 'I was the stepmother who didn't want another's child.'

Aurelia stared ahead. 'You? The nasty woman who looked down her nose and shouted at me when I came to the kitchen the other night without all my make-up and finery. "Take those plates in now," you screamed. So I did. Laced with powdered toadstools from the forest.'

'May God forgive me for what I have done to you.'

'It's not God who needs to forgive you,' said Aurelia, advancing upon Lady Prude. 'It's me. The little girl they called La Pucelle.'

La Pucelle! thought the Countess. The queen of spades – Joan of Arc.

Flambeaux and running feet came from both directions, and in a moment the corridor was filled with light as John and the musketeers, swords drawn, advanced on the scene. One of the musketeers had his arm round Leonora Smith, who seemed in a daze. She caught sight of Aurelia and buried her face in his ruffled shirt, crying, 'The ghost is back to haunt me!'

'I wasn't good enough for *you*, you pious, hypocritical hag! Did you dislike my dirty black face, Stepmother? I learned to paint and patch with the best of them. Look at me – I am beautiful, but underneath the Venetian ceruse, I am not white.' She tugged at the ribbon to her bodice, exposing the dark brown skin beneath the make-up line. 'Did you not want the world to know that your gallant husband, the sometime pot-boy, had besmirched himself making love to a black servant wench?'

'I'm sorry.' Wackland was sobbing. 'I'm sorry.'

The Countess and Alpiew pressed themselves back against the wall to let three musketeers pass.

'But you died, Aurelia . . .'

'Doctors can be ever so useful, Stepmama.' Aurelia advanced on Lady Prude. 'They have tricks and potions, and can vanish you away to a new life with a mere certificate and a line in a parish register.' She threw back her head and laughed. 'You were everywhere watching me. I knew disappearing was the only way I could do what had to be done. And how better to disappear than to die in a most expected manner in front of everyone?'

'Please, child, I know I did wrong . . .'

'No more excuses!' Aurelia jumped forward and plunged the knife into Lady Prude's stomach.

The musketeers seized Aurelia, who slumped, letting herself be taken.

The Countess and Alpiew supported Lady Prude as she staggered backwards.

'Oh God!' wailed Wackland, running forward to help her. 'Someone fetch the royal physician from upstairs at Court.'

'It's all I deserved,' cried Lady Prude as Wackland and John helped carry her up the stairs. 'I hope the child has killed me.'

FOURTEEN

Desert – a banquet of sweetmeats

'There must be something you can do with potatoes apart from boiling them to a pulp.' Pipe sat near the fire with a sharp knife, paring the skin from a small pile of potatoes. 'Back in Ireland we make bread from them too.'

Mademoiselle Smith sighed and turned back to the Marquis de Béchamel, who stood, in a sulk, near the courtyard door.

John, still in his shepherdess costume but without the mask, carried the Countess into the kitchen. 'Can you tend her wound, Mademoiselle Smith?' He laid the Countess down on a bench as Alpiew, cradling her bloody hand, pulled up a stool nearby. 'Now, is there anything else I should take care of?' He wiped his hands down the front of his smock.

'There is one thing.' The Countess flashed him a smile.

'What's that?' said John.

'Roger the valet.'

'I'd really rather not, Countess.'

'No, you buffoon!' The Countess shoved him on the shoulder. 'The Charmes' valet, Roger – he is under the main staircase having a very heavy kissing session with Virginia. I caught a glimpse as you whisked me past. You had better deal with him.'

John rolled up his frilly sleeves, pushed back his golden-locked wig and strode out, flexing his fingers and making a fist.

'She's only doing it to get your attention, you know,' she called, but he was out of earshot.

'L'Ordre de Deux Croissants!' The Marquis de Béchamel threw his arms into the air. *'Jamais! Jamais! Jamais! Deux Croissants! C'est un affront!'* He fingered the medallion hanging from a green sash round his neck, before spitting on to the flagged floor and flouncing out of the kitchen.

'He is upset,' said Mademoiselle Smith as she applied damp cloths to the Countess's wounds. 'He wanted to get the Order of the Holy Ghost and instead the King chose to award him the Order of the Two Crosses.'

'Nice to get a medal at all, I'd have thought,' said the Countess, thinking of her glue and how it would now be known all over France as Sauce Béchamel.

'However, I do see His Majesty's point. L'Ordre du Saint-Esprit is a very special decoration. The Blue Sash – you must have seen it. The Duc de Charme wears one. But that man has been a hero in so many battles. He is an exceptionally modest man. I hardly think it would be fitting, do you, Countess, for a mere *chef* to wear the Cordon Bleu?'

'How is the poor Duc?' Alpiew held up her hand while Mademoiselle Bontemps bandaged it.

'It's his wife I feel sorry for.' Mademoiselle Smith sighed. 'Such a nervous little woman. But I know the Duc will take care of her. He is a very kind person. People take him for an effeminate dupe, but he just likes all that glitter. And why not?'

'How dreadful for her to find the corpse of her love like that,' said the Countess. 'The Duc told me that, just before she was killed, Isabel had come down to say she was collecting stories with me and that we might both go out into the woods. She told him just in case anything happened to us out there in the dark. The Duc was going to check we both came back safely. So when Prude came bustling in looking for Isabel only a short while afterwards, naturally the Duchesse came to my room to check we had not left, and found poor Isabel . . .'

'Poor lady,' said Bontemps. 'What a terrible thing to discover. What made Prude suddenly go on the alert like that?'

'Lady Prude had received a warning note in the confessional, saying the stepdaughter would strike that night. She felt confident that Isabel was locked up, so imagine her horror when she saw her.'

'Aurelia was here in the chateau,' said Leonora. 'And had the confidence to walk around quite freely.'

'Oh good lord,' exclaimed Pipe. 'The Moorish girl in the kitchen! Wisht! With no blonde wig or make-up, no one would have known she was not another servant from the second floor.' She put her hands to her mouth.

'After the supper it seems she went upstairs to search out Isabel,' said Alpiew. 'She thought she was going to taunt her as she watched her die of the poison she had sprinkled over Isabel's plate.'

'But at that moment Isabel was fine,' the Countess said quietly, piecing it all together. 'She was going into my room just as the girl arrived on the landing.'

There was a silence as they all contemplated the horrible thing that had happened next.

'Afterwards the girl went straight down to Wackland's room and left a blood-smeared note, then knocked and ran away,' said Alpiew. 'But Lady Prude was in there with him. She saw the note and knew something terrible had happened, and went looking for Isabel.'

'And what has happened to Stickworth?' asked Bontemps.

'He was carted off to the prison of La Force. Aside from his part in aiding Aurelia, making an attempt on the King's life will not be treated kindly.'

'What was he thinking of?'

'He got himself involved in some extreme Jacobite group. They meet near the Cathedral at St Denis. Ever since Louis officially recognised King William as the King of England, the Jacobites have got very restless. I suppose he thought that by killing Louis . . .'

'I am starving!' said a figure in scarlet satin entering the kitchen and pulling off a long black wig to reveal spiky orange hair. 'Where is ze proper food? I could eat an ox. Raw. Complete with ze horns.' The Duchesse de Pigalle flopped down on the seat next to the Countess. 'Well, Ashby darlink, zat is the nearest I have ever been to making love to you!'

'But!' The Countess gasped. 'Olympe?'

'In order to get myself free from zat grim Bastille, I agreed to act as decoy tonight.'

'You mean . . . ?'

'Ze King was not here tonight. It was me. He knew it would happen if zey thought he came here. All ze spies knew there was something planned.' Pigalle grabbed a hunk of bread and spread it with gooey cheese. 'But what an ordeal! Having to eat all zose peas. Merde! Ze man is insane.'

'You mean to say, Olympe, that you chose me to dance with, even though you knew we were going to be shot at?'

'Well? You left me floundering about in the moat.'

'Ah. So we may cry quittance?'

'*Oui*, Ashby darling, we are equal snacks now.'

'Did you hear what happened to the wretched Aurelia?' Alpiew asked. 'And Lord Wackland?'

'*Lord* Wackland! Wackland Smith? Since when was he ze lord?' squawked Pigalle. 'He was once my pot-boy, before going to work for some frightful family of snobs in ze City.'

'Lady Prude!' Alpiew flexed her hand within its bandage. 'Sad, foolish woman. What is become of her? Did the King's physician give a prognostication?'

'Ze miserable old stick will survive.' Pigalle was slopping slices of cold meat on to a hunk of bread. 'Zey have carted her off to zat hospital run by nuns. I believe when she recovers she is going to take the veil. Under a little pressure from ze King. I saw zat man who is always dressed ready for a funeral preparing ze *lettre de cachet*.'

'Poor self-deluding woman,' said the Countess with a sigh. 'What a catastrophe.'

'For ze girl, Aurelia, you mean . . . It *will* be a catastrophe for her, I am sure. A catastrophe of zis variety.' Pigalle stood up, joined her hands behind her back and shook about, blowing down at her feet.

'Olympe, darling, I know you have always wanted to be a mime in a dumb-show, but what is *that* supposed to represent?'

'Joan of Arc, darlink! I would imagine Aurelia will be burned at ze stake. You cannot allow mad murderers to wander ze streets of France, even if they had lived the life of a piece of shit. It would not do.'

'So, Alpiew, dear,' said the Countess. 'Are we any clearer about that mysterious Biblical shopping list?'

'"L.S." Last Supper – for Aurelia, I presume; "Resurrection" – that is certainly clear now; "Epiphany" the proposed meeting of three kings – well, one king, one ex-king and a future king; "Friday Night" – the dance which was the cue for the assassination attempt . . .'

'I am very grateful to you, Alpiew,' said Pigalle through a mouthful of bread and cheese. 'Those musketeers were as much use as a eunuch in a nunnery.'

'"Apocalypse: death of the exalted whore" – was her planned murder of her stepmother, I presume.'

'Or it could simply be the ravings of a demented girl.' Pigalle grabbed another slab of meat and tore at it with her long teeth. 'Anyhow, none of it is of any import now.'

'I didn't recognise her,' said Mademoiselle Smith. 'At school she was a funny little creature.'

'I thought my make-up was good,' said Mademoiselle Bontemps. 'But hers is a masterpiece. And of course the blonde wig. Who would ever have thought . . . ?'

'Well, I feel sorry for the poor child.' The Countess sighed. 'To live your life thinking you are rejected like that . . .'

Roger the valet limped in. He was holding a wet handkerchief to his eye.

'Countess, you and Alpiew are sent for.'

337

'We're busy.' Alpiew looked back and saw, behind Roger, the Man in Black. He lingered on the threshold, cocking his finger. In his other hand was a sealed letter. 'Countess!' she hissed, nodding in his direction. 'Look!'

'Oh no,' wailed the Countess. 'God help us.'

'You'd better go.' Mademoiselle Smith tied a knot at the end of the bandage round the Countess's thigh. 'There!'

'Come along, child.' The Countess took Alpiew by the hand. 'Whatever he is going to do to us, it cannot be as bad as the last hour. And we survived that.'

'The last hour!' exclaimed Alpiew. 'You mean the last ten days.'

The Man in Black led them to the front door of the chateau.

'Oh no.' Alpiew looked at the big black coach waiting in the forecourt and her heart pounded. 'Not another . . .'

'*Lettre de cachet* . . .' the Man in Black lifted the letter and tapped them both upon the shoulder '. . . *du Roi, Louis XIV.*'

'Please, no!' the Countess howled. '*Not* the Bastille.'

The Man in Black shook his head.

'Oh God, no! Please God, not . . . not a *convent*!' Aghast, Alpiew gripped hold of the Countess. 'Please God, *anything* rather than that.'

'*Ordre de déportation.*' The Man in Black handed the Countess the letter. '*Exile en Angleterre.*'

'What does that mean?' Alpiew furrowed her brow and peered down at the *lettre de cachet*. 'Quickly, Countess, what does it say?'

'*Votre voiture!*'

'Deportation, Alpiew!' The Countess beamed from ear to ear. 'We are being forcibly sent into exile as enemies of the Jacobite court. We are going home, and this lovely, comfortable vehicle is to be our transportation.'

The wind was blustery as the packet boat pulled out of Calais.

The Countess and Alpiew sat together in the captain's cabin, sharing a hot mug of rum toddy.

They had left Pigalle outside on deck, flirting wildly with a gnarled old sailor in a grizzled wig. Privately the Countess suspected she was really only after his parrot.

In the far corners of the cabin, opposite one another but not speaking, sat John and Virginia.

'Oh dear,' whispered the Countess. 'Look at the space between them.'

Halfway between John and Virginia hung a painting of a man in a black wig. He wore a huge ermine cloak, casually tossed back to expose elegantly turned stockinged legs, and one outstretched hand balanced on a fine wooden cane.

In unison Alpiew and the Countess rose to their feet, each pointing at the picture with a bandaged hand.

'Alpiew!'

'Milady!'

'The legs!'

'The mouth!'

They turned to one another just as Pigalle hauled the door open against the wind, and came in, her hair sticking straight up, the sailor's parrot sitting happily on her forearm.

She followed their gaze and looked at the portrait of Louis XIV. 'Zat *charognard!*' she said, flopping down and pouring herself a tot of rum. 'May his *noisettes* be forever kibbled.'

'I was going to say, it's the white-haired old man in the satyr mask, the taster, from the party last night,' said Alpiew. 'That mouth. I'd recognise it anywhere. Like a sulky lapdog. But I thought you said the King was tall?'

''Ave you seen his shoes!' exclaimed Pigalle. 'Zey add six inches at least, zen ze wig puts on another six. In life he is a positive dwarf. I should know. I slept with him years ago, when I was a girl and he was good-looking.'

With an enigmatic smile the Countess sank down on to the seat.

'Well, well! He is a little joker, is he not?' she said, gulping down a mouthful of hot rum. 'And what a clever game to play with us all.'

She leant forward and whispered into Alpiew's ear.

'No!' said Alpiew, leaning back. 'You cannot be serious?'

'Oh yes, Alpiew.' The Countess raised her eyebrows and gave a sagacious nod. 'I think we have solved a mystery. It's a pity that no one in England will care about the solution, and that everyone in France will have forgotten all about the silly old Man in the Iron Mask before we ever return.'

'*Quel foutoir!*' Pigalle peered at the painting and squawked. 'Ze *roi des cons!* King of arseholes. You are right, Ashby. It *is* him. Ze *charognard* dresses up as a prisoner to hear what ze other prisoners say about him! I told you ze man was mad.'

'It would certainly explain why no one ever sees him in the Bastille. He's hardly ever there.'

'And he told us to put zat muck on our faces and jump into ze moat.' Pigalle was lurching about in a fury, the parrot flapping on her arm. 'When I next get hold of him I will have his balls to feed to Lancelot.'

'Who on earth is Lancelot?' said the Countess.

'Ze parrot, of course.'

'I don't know why you're being like this, Virginia,' snapped John. 'I was a hero.'

'You were with some old woman.' Virginia huffed and swivelled to face further away. 'I heard you boasting about it to the Duc.'

John rolled his eyes to heaven. 'How many times do I have to tell you? You are the only woman I need.'

'What about Denise?' said Virginia with a sob. 'North of Paris – I heard you saying you'd gone there with her.'

'St Denis, you mean?'

'Oh, she's a saint now, is she? Only a few days ago she was a basilisk.'

'Not basilisk, you fool!' John whipped his hat off and threw it into the air with frustration. '*Basilica*. Do you hear me? The Basilica of *St Denis*. It's a cathedral. It's where Stickworth and his cronies met up to hatch their plots.'

Pigalle flopped down on to the bench between the Countess and Alpiew, and the parrot let out a screech.

'What do you mean?' Blinking with the effort of the slow dawning of reason, Virginia turned her tear-stained face towards her ex-groom. 'There really was no other woman?'

'Of course not.' John opened his arms, and slid along the seat until he was close enough to touch her. 'How could there be, when I have you?' With a mutual sigh the couple dissolved into a passionate embrace.

'Ah, well.' The Countess pursed her lips and winked at Alpiew. 'I'd say it bears all the augurs of a long and happy marriage. Well, every marriage I've witnessed, anyhow.'

'So what are we going to do?' Alpiew held up her bandaged hand to point at the Countess's equally injured writing hand. 'If we cannot write, how will we earn a crust?'

'We can dictate to Godfrey.'

'Ah yes, dctut to gdfry. That *will* be fun.'

'And I see no reason, Alpiew, why tomorrow, when we reach London, we can't go straight round and claim our reward.'

'Reward? From whom?'

'Look! See for yourself.' The Countess glanced at John and Virginia, who were getting a little too amorous for the confines of a small shared cabin. 'In my opinion, the child has found a husband suitable to please even the most ambitious stepmother.'